Rowan Coleman lives with her husband and five [...] in Hertfordshire. She juggles writing novels wi[...] includes a very lively set of toddler twins whose [...] [...] she gets the chance, Rowan enjoy[...] and loves watching films; she is also attempting to learn how to bake.

Rowan would like to live every day as if she were starring in a musical, although her daughter no longer allows her to sing in public. Despite being dyslexic, Rowan loves writing, and *We Are All Made of Stars* is her twelfth novel. Others include her *Sunday Times* bestseller, *The Memory Book*, which was part of the Richard and Judy Autumn Book Club, and the award-winning *Runaway Wife*.

www.rowancoleman.co.uk
Facebook/Twitter: @rowancoleman

Praise for Rowan Coleman:

'I immediately read *The Memory Book* and it's WONDERFUL . . . I'm so happy because she's written other books and it's so lovely to find a writer you love who has a backlist' Marian Keyes

'Oh, what a gorgeous book this is – it gripped me and wouldn't let me go. So engaging, so beautifully written – I loved every single thing about it' Jill Mansell

'What a lovely, utterly life affirming, heart-breaking book *We Are All Made of Stars* by Rowan Coleman is' Jenny Colgan

'Painfully real and utterly heartbreaking . . . wonderfully uplifting' Lisa Jewell

'Like *Me Before You* by Jojo Moyes, I couldn't put it down. A tender testament to maternal love' Katie Fforde

ROWAN COLEMAN

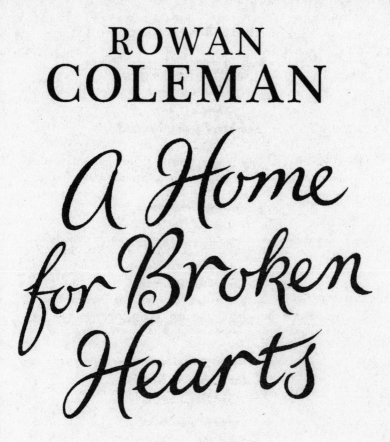

A Home for Broken Hearts

EBURY
PRESS

1 3 5 7 9 10 8 6 4 2

Ebury Press, an imprint of Ebury Publishing
20 Vauxhall Bridge Road,
London SW1V 2SA

Penguin
Random House
UK

Ebury Press is part of the Penguin Random House group of companies
whose addresses can be found at global.penguinrandomhouse.com

First published in 2010 as *The Happy Home for Broken
Hearts* by Arrow Books
This edition published in 2015 by Ebury Press

www.eburypublishing.co.uk

A CIP catalogue record for this book is available from the British Library

ISBN 9780091956837

Printed ⬚⬚⬚⬚⬚⬚⬚⬚⬚⬚⬚⬚⬚⬚⬚⬚⬚⬚⬚⬚⬚⬚⬚⬚⬚⬚⬚⬚⬚⬚ 4YY

Penguin R⬚⬚⬚   or our
business, ⬚⬚⬚   Forest

For Freddie, born 22nd August 2009

Almost One Year Ago

Ellen braced herself against the unforgiving expanse of faultless blue sky that stretched endlessly above her head, and wondered if such a perfect day was quite seemly on an occasion like this. Not a breath of wind stirred the leaves of the oak trees that surrounded them and the warmth of the sun prickled through her cotton shirt and suit jacket, causing a trickle of sweat to wend between her shoulder blades. The sheer weight of the heat seemed to compress her, squeezing her ribs together, imprisoning her heart. Struggling to catch each breath, Ellen had to fight the urge to simply run away, to find some small, quiet dark place where she could breathe again and close her eyes and pretend that none of this was happening. If her younger sister hadn't been there, gripping her arm so tightly that she would have bruises in the morning, then perhaps she would have fled. But Hannah was there, supporting her, restraining her, helping her – *forcing* her – to get through. It was Hannah who had told her to wear something lightweight and comfortable, a dress or a skirt, but Ellen had stuck to her guns and stuck to a suit. It was fitting, respectable, suitable for such an important occasion.

Funny, Ellen thought without a trace of amusement, focusing with determination on a single blade of bright green grass that lay against the toe of her shoe, it had rained on her wedding day. A cold drenching downpour had sheeted from a steely spring sky in a relentless onslaught.

They had laughed, Ellen and her brand-new husband when they had looked at their wedding photos, the pair of them standing outside the church, teeth gritted in rigor mortis grins against the cold. Ellen hadn't minded the weather on that day, the chill that raised goosebumps on her bare arms or the needles of fine rain that consistently assaulted her face, teasing her heavily applied mascara loose from her lashes. On that day all she needed to fight off the elements was the knowledge that the man who was now her husband, the man who she still could not believe had chosen her above anyone else, was standing by her side, his hand in hers, and that from that day on, he always would be. That sodden, foggy, miserable day had been her friend.

This day, this perfect July day that wheeled so recklessly around her was her sworn enemy, a predator waiting for her to break cover and bolt for safety, poised to pounce and rip her to shreds, because this was the day of her husband's funeral and a world without him in it became her enemy, determined to assault her with every weapon in its armoury. As the business of burying Nick went on around her, Ellen thought of home, of the cool clean stone tiles of her kitchen floor, the shelter of her shadowy bedroom, curtains still drawn as they had been since the day he died. At home it was easier to believe that he had not gone, at home she still felt safe.

Finding every single further second that required her to stand at her husband's graveside intolerable, Ellen gasped for breath, drenched from the inside out by the suffocating heat, flinching as she felt her son prise open her clenched fist and slide his fingers in between hers. Ellen looked down at ten-year-old Charlie and mustered a smile for him; he squeezed her fingers in return. He was supporting her, Ellen realised, ashamed. He was coping when she was not; fearless, bearing the unbearable with the kind of valour that her husband would have shown. Ellen took heart from Charlie, determined not to let him see how frightened she was, how lost, panicked and confused, hurt and bereft she felt. She wouldn't let him see that at that precise moment, standing under the blazing sun next to Nick's grave, she had no idea how to live from one minute to the next, let alone another day, another week or another year without her husband.

All she knew was that she longed to be at home.

Chapter One

Slowly the tip of his sword slid between the laces of her bodice, each breath from her heaving bosom forcing the opening a little further apart, revealing ever more of the milky white flesh concealed beneath . . .

'Mum.'

'Please, Captain, if you are any kind of gentleman don't – oh, please . . .' Eliza begged, her heart fluttering with both fear and undiscovered longing as the captain's dark gaze roamed over her tender form.

'Mum?'

'You are mine now,' he rasped, his voice husky with desire. 'Just as this house is mine now, just as this sword always has been!' Eliza gasped, her eyes widening as she perceived the captain's burgeoning weapon. 'Reconcile yourself to the knowledge that you are mine and I will have you at my will, first body then soul . . .'

'Mu-uuuuuum!'

Ellen's head snapped up as finally the voice of her son dragged her out of the darkened seventeenth-century chamber with a locked door where a young Puritan maid was about to be ravished by her rakish Royalist captor, and back to her kitchen table in Hammersmith. Discovering Charlie at her side, she slipped a folder on top of the latest Allegra Howard manuscript that she had been sent to copy-edit by the publishing

4

company she freelanced for, and fixed her gaze on him.

'Yes love?' she asked him mildly.

'What does burgeoning mean?' Charlie asked her with wide-eyed curiosity. Ellen squirmed – how long had her eleven-year-old been standing there reading over her shoulder?

'Burgeoning? It means . . . um . . . to . . . um . . . grow rapidly or sprout – like . . . um like buds in the springtime.'

'How can a weapon like a sword burgeon, then?' Charlie asked her, his level blue eyes searching out her gaze and holding it. 'Because it's made of steel, isn't it? Hard steel. Steel doesn't burgeon.'

'Obviously it doesn't!' Ellen agreed. 'I'll be correcting that! I don't know – these writers, they haven't got a clue about metaphor. I swear I could do it better myself. Now, what would you like for tea?' She asked even though she knew the answer, because it was the same every day.

'It might be a metaphor,' Charlie said casually, loosening his school tie. 'Maybe the writer is using his burgeoning sword as a metaphor for the man's erection, for example.'

'Charlie!' Ellen exclaimed, folding her arms across the offending manuscript as if she might somehow stop any further indiscretions escaping from it.

'What?' Charlie said. 'I'm only discussing literature with you, Mum.'

'Yes but . . . Charlie, you're only eleven – you shouldn't be discussing . . .'

'Erections,' Charlie repeated. 'I shouldn't be discussing erections with my mother? Who should I discuss them with?'

Ellen's mouth open and closed as she fought for an answer. For the millionth time, at least, in the last eleven months the

5

thought 'if only Nick were here' flashed across her mind. But Nick wasn't here, and Ellen had to try to learn again how to manage without him, something she felt she had had to learn and relearn a multitude of times.

'Well, because you're only eleven and I'm not sure it's appropriate for a boy of your age . . .'

'I'm nearly twelve,' Charlie reminded her.

'Your birthday's not for two months. Don't wish your life away, Charlie . . .'

The pair held each other's eyes for a second, the same unspoken thought passing between them.

'James Ingram's mother talks to him about sex all the time,' Charlie challenged her, papering over the gulf that stretched between them with practised ease. 'James Ingram's mother told him he could ask her anything he liked, and she's an *accountant*. She doesn't read porn for a living, like you.'

'P——! Charlie, you know full well that I don't read anything of the sort. I copy-edit romantic fiction for Cherished Desires, you know that. And if . . . if you have any questions about anything you can always come to me, of course you can.' Ellen felt the heat inflame her cheeks. 'Is…is there anything you'd like to talk to me about? Sex-wise?'

Charlie stared at her for a long time, and finally Ellen detected the spark of mischief in his deadpan eyes: he was teasing her in that way he had. Deadly serious, edged in equal measure with humour and what she often thought might be anger. Or perhaps frustration that he was changing so rapidly and she was failing to keep up with him.

'Er – no – that would be too weird!' Charlie grinned. 'I think James Ingram is a freak anyway.'

6

How Nick would laugh, Ellen thought. He'd come in from work sometime between nine and ten and they'd stand in the kitchen, him leaning against the counter while she cooked for him, telling him every last thing that Charlie had said or done, and he would laugh and say something like 'that's my boy'. With some effort Ellen held back the threat of tears and smiled at Charlie.

'So how was school today?'

'Same as ever, only I have to get my permission slip in, you know for the skiing trip – so can I go or not?' he asked, and Ellen realised that she would have preferred the most explicit question about sex that he could think of, compared to that one.

'Well Charlie – the thing is . . .'

Ellen sat back in her chair and wondered how to tell him what she herself didn't yet fully understand. She and Charlie were broke.

Nick's accountant, Hitesh, had visited her just before lunchtime. He'd been a regular visitor over the last few months, taking on the financial mess that Nick had unwittingly left her with and battling on Ellen's behalf to try and get it sorted out, which she was eternally grateful for, especially when neither of them knew how or if she would be able to pay him for all the time he'd given her. He'd told her on the phone before he came that now at least her affairs could be finalised, and that she should disclose any investments or savings that she might have had tucked away. Ellen had been unable to think of any. Nick dealt with all the money stuff, Nick dealt with everything.

When Hitesh had gone she had made herself a cheese sandwich and a cup of tea and sat at the table for a long time, staring unseeingly at the pile of washed saucepans gleaming like long-lost treasure on the draining board.

There had been two options open to her: to deal with the situation head on as Hitesh had advised, to look at her incomings and outgoings to see exactly how bad her position was, or to finish reading the first section of the latest Allegra Howard novel, *The Sword Erect*.

Ellen had had to put the book down midway through a chapter when Hitesh arrived. She been forced to tear herself away just as the feisty, yet innocent, yet unknowingly desirable heroine, young Eliza Sinclair, niece of a Parliamentarian supporter, had been locked away in her own home by the ferocious, yet wildly handsome, yet brutal, yet vulnerable Captain Rupert Parker, when he and his Royalist troops had commandeered her uncle's house for the King, taking all of its occupants prisoner. The captain, bewitched by beautiful dark-haired, blue-eyed Eliza from the moment he set eyes on her, admired her physical perfection, particularly her comely and generous bosom, even through her modest Puritan dress. Unable to control the depths of desire he felt, he had decided to have his way with his female prisoner, despite her protests and vain attempts to escape his clutches. Ellen had been forced to leave the action just as the oak stairs were moaning and creaking under his approaching footsteps while Eliza waited, trapped behind a locked door, helpless and alone, fraught with appre-hension. It had nearly killed Ellen to leave the next few pages unread.

So once Hitesh had left the choice had been an easy one, and within a few seconds Ellen had found herself lost once again in the heat of that locked room, struggling along with Eliza to fight her barely understood desires for a man she ought to hate, yet yearned to have.

Then Charlie had talked about erection metaphors and asked her about the school skiing trip and Ellen was firmly back in the last place she wanted to be, the real world.

'There is no money,' Hitesh had told her, sitting at her kitchen table. He spoke kindly, slowly, as if he wanted to be sure that she was really understanding him.

'None?' Ellen questioned. 'But the insurance, the appeal – you said . . .'

'I said I'd try, and I have – you know that I've been on the case since they first refused to pay out, months ago, fighting with them for the best part of a year,' Hitesh reminded her, sipping the glass of cold lemonade she had poured him, loosening the top button of his shirt. 'Nick was insured up to the hilt, if he'd got cancer or been run over by a bus you'd be fine, sorted for life. But it was death by dangerous driving, Ellen, *his* dangerous driving. Look, I know you don't need to hear all this again – but the skid marks on the tarmac, the distance from the road they found the car, the state of the wreck. The level of blood alcohol. It showed he took that bend at around a hundred and twenty miles an hour and he was just above the legal limit for drinking. I've come to the end of the line, there is no other appeal process or arbitration board I can go to. The insurance company doesn't care about you, Ellen, or your mortgage, or the years of premiums Nick paid. It doesn't pay out on death caused by reckless behaviour. You won't be getting any money from them. I'm sorry, but we need to face that and work out what to do next.'

9

Ellen twisted her wedding ring around and around her finger. She could hear Hitesh, but nothing he said seemed real. For the last year she had just carried on as normal, financially at least. She and Nick had had almost twenty thousand pounds in a savings account which Hitesh had helped her transfer into her household account to tide her over until the insurance money came through. It was meant to be a temporary measure, but month after month had passed and still there was no payout. Everything, the mortgage, the electricity, gas and whatever else there was had all been paid by direct debit from the household account. Ellen hadn't even thought to check the dwindling balance, confident that everything would be resolved. But now Hitesh was telling her that that money was running out. And then what?

'Hitesh, the money transferred from our savings account – it's nearly all gone? Won't there be anything left from the business?' Nick had run a small but successful advertising agency, or at least he'd always told everyone, including Ellen, how well it was doing. When the recession hit he'd pointed to their five-bedroom Victorian villa and his Mercedes on the drive and told Ellen not to worry.

'Advertising is recession-proof,' he'd assured her, planting a kiss on her forehead. It had fallen to Hitesh, not only Nick's accountant but also the executor of his will, to spend the best part of the last year winding up his business affairs, a complicated, murky affair that Ellen did not even want to attempt to understand.

'Wages, rent, bills – Nick was behind on all of them and he was late paying his taxes. I'd got him some wriggling time with the Revenue to sort out his cash flow, but he . . . didn't manage it. Most of what little capital there was in the business has gone to them, you're lucky that you're not left *owing* anyone any money.'

'It's just . . . I don't see how – is it really that bad?' Ellen was disbelieving. 'Nick never mentioned anything to me, he never gave the impression that things were tough, that we should economise.'

'You know Nick, he was a traditional man. He never wanted to worry you, and if he hadn't had the accident you probably would have never known. He'd have got all of this sorted out and everything back on track.' Hitesh smiled fondly. 'I don't know how, but he always did.'

'Do you mean we've been in this sort of mess before?' Ellen asked him edgily, uncertain if she wanted to know that the tranquillity and certainty of her married life had been compromised earlier.

'Now,' Hitesh avoided answering, 'I've had a look at your expenses. The interest-only mortgage you took out on this place is sizeable, if you tried to borrow that much these days no bank would give you the time of day. And you're tied into a fixed rate for another three years which is a shame because interest rates have plummeted, you'd be paying a fraction of what you are now if Nick had gone for a tracker. Should you try and sell and repay the loan, the redemption fee runs into the thousands, so . . .'

'*What?* What can I do?' Ellen asked him. For the first time, the reality of her situation was nudging its way into her consciousness. All she had concentrated on in the months since Nick's death was living from minute to minute without him, and that had been more than enough for her to deal with, it still was. And now time had run out, now she would have to do something for herself, she would have to find a way to cope with this situation – and she had no idea how to. Ellen twisted her fingers into a tight knot in her lap, feeling panic gripping her chest.

Hitesh paused, and Ellen wasn't sure if it was the warm day that made him so uncomfortable, or what he knew he had to tell her.

'Right – well let's look at the facts. This house is a good size, well located – you and Charlie could move out and rent it out, enough to cover the mortgage until you can sell up and pay it off without charges. You'd still need to find a way to support yourself and Charlie, of course, but rent on a two-bedroom place will be a fraction of your current costs and . . .'

'Rent out our home to another family? Move out, you mean?' Ellen swallowed, her mouth suddenly parched.

'Well no, you won't get the same revenue from renting it whole as if you rent it room by room to young professionals or perhaps students. What you're looking for is to maximise your assets. Now, it's a bit hooky renting without converting the mortgage to a buy-to-let, but I know a letting agent who'd deal with it on the q.t. . . .'

'But this is *home*.' Ellen barely heard her own voice as she whispered the words. 'It's Charlie's home, his safe place. You know how he's been since the accident. But at least he has his home, his room, his things around him. I can't take that away from him too. I can't.'

Hitesh had sighed, pinching the top of his nose between his thumb and forefinger, closing his eyes briefly. When he opened them he held Ellen's gaze, making her look him in the eye.

'Ellen, you know Nick was a friend of mine. Shamilla and I

consider you and Charlie like family. I don't want to see you in this position, if there was anything else I could do I would do it, I promise you – but there isn't. Nick thought he was invincible, he never thought he was made of flesh and blood like the rest of us. He knew that everything was riding on him coming up with the goods, pulling off a miracle like he always did – it was that kind of risk he thrived on. But this time he couldn't make everything all right. And even though he didn't mean to, he's left you in a mess. Now, if you want to stay in that house without it being repossessed then you either need to come up with two and half thousand pounds a month pronto just to survive, or you need to think again. And when I say pronto, I mean it – you don't have enough money in your account to pay next month's mortgage payment.' Hitesh leaned forward, his voice softening. 'I'm sorry to be harsh, but there it is. I have to make you see. Is there anyone else who could help you – I know Nick's parents are dead but perhaps yours . . . ?'

'They don't have any money,' Ellen told him, thinking of her mum and dad in their chilly bungalow in Hove, surviving on the state pension and very little else.

'Then you need another plan.' Hitesh paused. 'Look, take today to think about your options. Talk it over with someone. If you find another way then great, if not come back to me and I'll put you in touch with that letting agent.'

And Ellen had taken some time. But she had chosen not to think. How could she? How could she think about something that was as incomprehensible and irreversible as Nick's death?

If only Nick were here. The thought escaped her before she could do anything to stop it.

*

'Well?' Charlie asked her. 'Can I?'

'I don't know yet,' Ellen hedged. 'I need to think about it. It's a long way away and you've never been skiing before. I'm not sure if I want you so far away, it sounds dangerous to me . . .'

'Climbing the stairs sounds dangerous to you,' Charlie complained, frustrated. 'Mum, if you don't let me go everyone will think I'm a gay mummy's boy. They'll think I'm on free school dinners or a chav! You have to stop treating me like a kid. I'm not going to die you know, I'm not Dad.'

Ellen dipped her head, feeling the warmth of the manuscript beneath her fingers, as if the heat between Eliza and Captain Parker was escaping between the lines. Just a few flimsy pages away, another world – without debt, or dead husbands or angry boys who didn't know what they were saying or why – was waiting for her. A world where intensely passionate men stole you from your problems and ravished you into delirious submission, conquering you with their love. A world where you didn't have to do anything except be irresistible. How could she explain to Charlie that even though she knew he wasn't his dad, even though she knew it was highly unlikely that she would lose him as suddenly and as violently as she had lost Nick, she couldn't convince her heart to feel the same way.

'So, what would you like for tea tonight?' Ellen asked him, weary from the constant onslaught of emotional battles that raged on in her head.

Since Nick had died Charlie had only eaten the same thing that he had on the last day he saw his father alive: fish fingers, white bread, tomato ketchup and Frosties with semi-skimmed milk. She'd seen in turn a doctor, a child psychologist and a dietitian and all of them had said that the best thing was to let him get on with it as long as his health wasn't being compromised, but every time she fed him something from that all-too-short list, it was Ellen who felt like a failure. A mother who couldn't even nourish her own son, either with the kind of food he should be eating or the love and security he needed to feel in order to eat it. It was proof that no matter how much she tried to fight it Charlie had been steadily drifting away from her since they had lost Nick, each day edging a little further out of her reach. It wasn't just the money that made it difficult for her to say yes to this skiing trip. It was the thought of him travelling so far away from her that she couldn't stand. Ellen didn't think that Charlie blamed her for his father's death exactly. It was more that he seemed disappointed with his remaining parent. From being a quiet loving little boy he was now striving more and more each day to be entirely independent from his mother, and Ellen was sure that the skiing trip was part of that too, another thing he could do without her. The more he struggled to be free of her, the more she wanted to bind him to her, to keep him that same adoring little boy who held her hand at Nick's funeral.

Charlie dipped his head, his shoulders heaving in a sigh, and then after a second or two he put his arms around Ellen's neck and hugged her, leaning his body into hers. She tensed, taken off guard by the gesture of affection that had become so unfamiliar to her, missing the opportunity to return the embrace before Charlie withdrew.

'I'm sorry, Mum,' he told her, through lowered lashes. 'I'm sorry I'm a pain sometimes. I don't know why I say the stuff I do. I'm an idiot.'

'No you are not.' Tentatively, gently, Ellen put her hands on Charlie's shoulders and looked into his eyes. 'Charlie, this last

15

year – we've had a lot to deal with, you and I. And you, you have been anything but an idiot. You've been an amazing, strong, brave little boy . . .' She winced inwardly at her choice of words. 'Learning to get on without Dad. It's hard for us both and sometimes we do and we say things we don't mean to. None of it matters if we love each other and stick together.'

Charlie held her gaze for a second as if he wanted to say something more, something important. But instead he shrugged and stepped out of her embrace.

'Anyway, I don't care if the boys at school think I'm a gay, pikey, chav,' he told her bullishly, that relic of sweet boyishness passing as quickly as it had arrived. 'It doesn't really matter if I don't go skiing, I suppose. Emily Greenhurst isn't going and she plays the electric guitar.'

'The electric guitar. Really?' Charlie nodded. 'Charlie, I'll be honest. I don't know about the holiday. It's a lot of money and we're still sorting out our finances,' Ellen hedged. There was one person she could ask for help to pay for the holiday, even if the thought of letting Charlie go horrified her. These school holidays were always supersafe, Ellen told herself, despite her instinctive misgivings. The schools had to make sure they were these days . . . although hadn't there been that case on the news a few weeks back about a boy drowning in a canoeing accident? Ellen stifled her anxiety, she didn't want him to be the only one of his friends who missed out, even if this mysterious Emily Greenhurst wasn't going. Ellen knew that her younger sister Hannah would give her the money if she was prepared to ask for it, she just wasn't sure that she was, not even for Charlie. Hannah, the bright, beautiful, successful one had made it her business to be around for Ellen a lot since Nick died, she offered time and time again to help Ellen out with the bills, or take her and Charlie out for a treat – and Ellen knew that she should have been touched and grateful by her younger sister's concern, but she struggled to be. Hannah had always glided through life so effortlessly, the world falling into place around her. For most of her existence Ellen had felt as if she were trailing along behind her little sister, plodding through life while Hannah blazed a trail, like a bright shooting star. And then Ellen had met Nick and for the first time in her life she had something that Hannah didn't. A loving relationship, a husband and a son, a proper family home. And as foolish and shallow as it was, while she had those things Ellen had felt like her sister's equal, her superior even, ensconced as she was in the 'real' business of raising a family while Hannah flitted through city life, a dedicated career woman with plenty of money and loads of stuff but no one who really loved her and no one she really loved back. But now all but one of Ellen's treasures had either gone or were on the brink of being lost, and it would cost her a lot to turn to Hannah for help. Even for Charlie.

'I'll try my best, OK? And in the meantime please don't call people chavs or pikeys. Or gay, not if you're using it as an insult.'

'But it's OK if you're using it as a compliment?' Charlie quizzed her. 'Like, oh Simon Harper, you are so wonderfully gay!'

'Charlie,' Ellen repressed a smile. 'You are nearly twelve years old. You know what's wrong and what's right – try and stick to it, OK?'

'OK,' Charlie grinned. 'I actually think Simon Harper is gay though.'

'So fish fingers?' Ellen smiled, ever hopeful that one day he'd change his answer.

'Yes please, Mummy.'

Ellen didn't know what broke her heart more, the scars left by his father's death or the fact that sometimes, just for a fleeting moment her little boy forgot to be all grown up.

Chapter Two

'Well, I would have thought it was obvious,' Hannah said, stirring her third spoonful of sugar in her black coffee. Ellen's sister, younger than her by some nine years, lived on coffee, cigarettes and sugar and looked annoyingly good on it. 'Slender as a willow tree and just as bendy' was how she'd been known to introduce herself to potential lovers, which was pretty much any male within a five-mile radius. 'You have to do what that accountant says. You have to consolidate, let the place out and get somewhere small for you and Charles. I mean, Ellie, it's only a pile of bricks. It's not even as if you and Nick lived here all your married life, as if he carried you over the threshold on your wedding day. You've only lived there a few years and I never did get why you bought such a huge place when there was only ever going to be the three of you . . .' Hannah faltered, realising that she had put her foot in her mouth yet again, and stirred her beverage furiously, unable to meet Ellen's eye for a moment. Both of them knew that when Ellen and Nick had bought the house they planned to fill it with children, a real family home for a real family. But circumstances had changed and that had become an impossibility long before Nick died. Ellen smarted inwardly. It was just like her sister to hit on a phrase that could wound her the most, calling her home a pile of bricks. It was so much more than that: it was symbolic, of what her life used to be – of what it should have been.

'Anyway – it's just a place,' Hannah stumbled on. 'A reminder of everything that you've . . . lost. A fresh start – that's exactly what you need. If anything that house is a burden and it's one you need to be shot of.'

Ellen said nothing for a moment. Despite Hitesh's constant reminders that she needed to make a decision, it had taken her two days since his visit to bring herself to call her sister, and of course she hadn't really invited Hannah over for coffee to listen to her opinion or advice. The two women were so different in every respect that before Nick had died they barely saw or spoke to each other apart from required occasions; birthdays, Christmas – that sort of thing. After his death, though, Hannah had been around much more, which Ellen supposed that she ought to be touched by, her kid sister making an effort to be there for her when neither of them really liked or understood the other. But Ellen didn't get that feeling from Hannah: for some reason it felt like Hannah wanted to be around her and Charlie for her own sake, as if she needed distracting from Nick's death. Not long after the funeral, when Ellen had been at her lowest point, Hannah had found her lying in her room, her head buried beneath the pillow, and had carefully sat on the edge of the bed.

'Mum's made egg and cress,' she'd said. 'Do you want one?'

Ellen had not replied.

'Look.' Hannah had reached out and laid a hand on her shoulder. 'Look, I know how awful this is, how horrific – but you have to think that at least you had him, for a while. At least he belonged to you and everyone knew it. And now he always will.'

Unable to face her, Ellen had simply pulled another pillow over her head and cried herself to sleep. But later, when Hannah started making her regular visits, she thought about what she had said on that morning and wondered if her sister, who was so fond of personal dramas and life complications, was a little jealous of her. If Hannah somehow found grief, and the attention it garnered, glamorous.

It seemed impossible to Ellen, they were so different in every respect.

Ellen often speculated if it was because of the age difference. She had been born at the beginning of the seventies, when the world was still an optimistic and gentle place. Hannah, however, a surprise baby if ever there was one, had entered this world on the cusp of the eighties, kicking and screaming for more, seeming to embody the decade she grew up in, a brash and confident high achiever and always hungry for more success, more possessions.

Now almost thirty-eight, Ellen was dark, olive-skinned, with green eyes that Nick had loved and what Allegra Howard would describe as a comely figure, comfortably curvy, not that she gave much thought to her shape which she covered with supermarket-bought jeans and an assortment of T-shirts and shirts, most of which had been Nick's. Ellen had never been one to care about what she looked like. Nick often told her that was one reason why he loved her so much, his pocket Venus he'd called her in the bedroom, his goddess alone for him to adore, her hidden charms a veiled mystery to all but him.

Ellen inhabited the world that Nick had created for her and

rarely strayed from it. She existed in her home, in her books and for her husband and son. It had been a comfortable, comforting cocoon of a world, one that she struggled to find the energy to emerge from now, and one that she simply did not want to leave. Ellen did not want the world outside, she didn't need it. Her life was small, detailed and rich in the minutiae that only she cared about, and that was exactly how she wanted it, especially now.

Hannah, on the other hand, thrived on being noticed. Tall, taller than anyone else in the family including her father, and unfeasibly leggy. She had long ago perfected her glamorous look, boosting her naturally reddish hair with a monthly shot of chemical auburn, so that it fell in luscious and glossy waves to the middle of her back, and she was one of the lucky few for whom slim hips and a flat stomach did not rule out enough natural cleavage to put on a reasonable display for her many admirers. At just thirty she was one of the few women fund managers at T Jenkins Waterford Asset Management. She had ridden out the financial storm of the last few months better than many of her colleagues, whom she'd left by the roadside without so much as a backward glance. Ellen knew that Hannah earned well in excess of six figures and that she probably had enough money in various accounts to buy her house outright if she wanted to. But if it wasn't for Charlie's skiing trip, Ellen would no more have dreamed of asking Hannah to help her out financially than she would hammer nails into her eyes. The real reason that Ellen found it so hard was because she knew that her sister would want to help her and Charlie, she knew that it would give Hannah pleasure, and Ellen baulked at that. It wasn't an impulse that she was proud of, particularly when it meant that Charlie missed out, and she didn't really understand her motivations herself. Maybe if Hannah was jealous of her, she was jealous of Hannah too – life had always been so easy for her. Even when she got things wrong or made mistakes, it always seemed that the universe rearranged itself around her to smooth things over and make things better. Ellen had given herself a good talking-to before Hannah had arrived, telling herself that this request was not about her, it was about her son – but still she hesitated, unable to bring it up.

'The house is not just a pile of bricks – it's Charlie's home,' she stated quietly instead, sipping her frothy cappuccino that she had made with the elaborate and expensive coffee machine that Nick had bought her for her last birthday, even though she mostly drank tea. 'And when Nick and I bought that house it meant something special to us, it was the house we always dreamed of. The place – the place we planned to get old in together. Nick was going to do up a vintage motorbike in the garage and I was going to take up writing stories, you know, just for fun, and read them to him in the evening. And when . . . when we realised there would be no more children we'd decided that when Charlie was old enough we were going to convert the attic rooms into a little flat for him so he could have his privacy and we were going to get a dog, two dogs – a Labrador and a red setter. Nick always wanted a red setter.'

Ellen glanced up at Hannah whose features had tightened as she listened to her sister, as if the very idea of such a mundane and domestic existence offended her. Ellen could tell that Hannah understood so little of what she was saying that she might as well have been talking in a foreign language.

'Yes, but Ellie – none of that is going to happen now,' Hannah said impatiently. 'Don't you get it? Nick is dead.'

Hannah paused for a second, disbelieving, as if she too were hearing the news for the first time. She swallowed and took a breath. 'Your life has changed, it's not going to be like you thought it was. You need to wake up and deal with it.'

Ellen sucked in a sharp breath. 'I think you should go,' she said, pushing her chair back and handing Hannah her bag.

'Ellie – please – don't.' Hannah leant across the table and rested her hands on Ellen's forearm. 'Don't throw me out, I'm only trying to help.'

Ellen shook her head. 'No, Hannah – you're not trying to help. You're trying to march in here and tell me how pointless and pathetic my life is and how I should just sweep it all away, sweep everything that I have left of Nick away and go and live in a poky little flat somewhere because that's the sensible thing to do. Well, since when have you ever done the sensible thing? Just because none of what matters to me matters to you, it doesn't mean you have the right to trample all over it.'

Hannah stared at her for a second. 'All of the things that matter to you matter to me. I want the best for you and Charles. Look, you know me, Ellen – tact isn't my strong point. Haven't you heard of tough love? I know I sound like a heartless cow – but it's not just me that thinks this, there's your accountant, Mum and Dad – we're all worried about you, Ellen. You just can't go on sticking your head in book after book thinking that everything will turn out all right in the end. There aren't those kind of happy endings in real life – there is no tall dark and handsome stranger waiting to rescue you . . .' Hannah hesitated, and Ellen wondered if she heard a catch in her voice. 'Or any of us. And I know it's hard. I know Nick did every single thing for you and Charles – you're not used to coping. But now you have

24

to. You have to, otherwise the mess you're in is just going to get worse and worse until there's no way out and what about Charles then, when your house is repossessed and you don't even have that?'

Ellen sank back down into her chair. Hitesh, Hannah, her dad on the phone last night – they were all right. She had to do something, but it wasn't just that she had no idea what to do, she had no idea how to do anything. She closed her eyes briefly, fighting the urge to tell Hannah to get out. Hannah was right, she had to do something, and if anyone could think of what to do it would be Hannah, clever, resourceful Hannah. Her personal life might lurch from one catastrophe to the next, but when it came to problem-solving and lateral thinking Hannah was the expert.

'OK,' Ellen said. 'OK, I know you're right. But it's Charlie that I'm thinking about. He's lost so much – I don't want him to lose his home too. There has to be another way, doesn't there?'

'Well, you could earn more, for a start,' Hannah said, chewing her bottom lip, the way she always had from girlhood. 'I mean that job you do for that publishers, Naked Desires, or whatever it's called – how many books do you copy-edit for them?'

'It depends – Simon knows which writers I enjoy so he waits until he's got a new work from one of them. Somewhere between one and two every couple of months.'

'Well, that's crazy for starters.' Hannah spoke at speed, words tumbling out of her mouth at a million miles an hour as if there were never going to be enough hours in the day for her to say everything she had to. 'Especially when you only get – what – fifteen quid an hour? You need to stop treating the manuscripts like a hobby and start thinking of them as cash-making opportunities. They publish hundreds of those books, don't they? The horny old ladies can't get enough of them, right? If you stopped actually reading them and just concentrated on crossing the t's and dotting the i's then you could probably do one or even two a week. As for that Simon – he is the one that's gay, right?'

'We don't know that he's gay, just that he's a bachelor,' Ellen interjected, although she had to admit that the chances of a man as well dressed and as attractive as Simon Merry still being single in his mid-forties were unlikely unless his preferences did not include commitment-hungry females, and even then he seemed to have a distinct lack of men in his life too. Ellen suspected that he simply liked to keep his private life private and she respected him for that.

'Yeah, single, forty-something, never been married and runs a raunchy potboiling publishers – um, hello? If he's not gay then I'm not a ravishing redhead, and I obviously am. Anyway – talk to him. Maybe he could do more than just farm out bits and pieces to you. Maybe he could bring you in-house – or maybe he knows someone who knows someone. You have skills, Ellen, not to mention a First Class history degree that you've never used since you met Nick. You need to maximise your earning potential. How much do you earn per month right now?'

Ellen pursed her lips. Hannah's conversational style could be somewhat relentless but she could sense her sister working towards forming some idea, so she went with it. 'Not enough to pay the mortgage, the bills and keep Charlie in fish fingers. Not even if I read a book a day, which I don't want to do. I don't want to go through them like they're cannon fodder. They're *books*, Hannah. Wonderful books that someone has laboured over for months and months and put all their care and attention into. I want to treat them with the respect that they deserve.'

'We're talking about shag-a-minute bodice rippers here, Ellie, not Booker Prize nominees. Everyone knows the writers churn them out to a formula. I read in the *Guardian* that if the heroine isn't being ravished every ten pages then the so-called writer's not doing their job.'

'Well – that's just ignorance and prejudice,' Ellen said crossly, privately thinking that she had never actually calculated the average ravish count per book, but that Hannah probably wasn't that far off the mark. In fact in this new Allegra Howard it looked like Eliza was in for well-above-average ravishings.

'OK – so if you worked a bit harder you could make up maybe half of what you need to pay the mortgage. Let's think laterally – how can you make money with you and Charles still living in the house . . . well, even with you two still *in situ* that leaves three good-sized bedrooms . . . *that's it!*' Hannah clapped her hands together, her eyes bright, clearly pleased with herself.

'That's what?' Ellen was alarmed.

'You become a landlady. You take in lodgers! You said it yourself – those attic rooms are practically a self-contained flat already, what with the loo and shower that's up there – that's worth seven hundred a month. Six hundred for the other double with the en suite, and I know you, you won't move Charles out of his room but even that third bedroom is worth about five hundred. That will more than cover the mortgage and what you earn from copy-editing you can use to live on. Ellen, I've solved all of your problems, you may thank me now!'

Hannah beamed at her, her eyes burning brightly, and Ellen longed to be able to get up and walk out, only this was her kitchen. Hannah had done exactly what Ellen knew she would, she'd come up with an idea that no one else had, that could work for Ellen if she had some time to think about it, but her first instinct at being presented with the idea of filling her house with strangers was to run away. As Hannah waited for her reaction Ellen fidgeted in her seat, getting the feeling that she had somewhere else she really had to be. And then she realised that somewhere else was the book she was working on. A make-believe world that felt safer and more familiar than the one she actually existed in was her only escape route now. Ellen sighed. She was desperate to find out exactly how Eliza planned to escape the evil clutches of her nefarious uncle who had snatched her back from the captain after he'd been called away on secret business for Charles I. But various financial problems would not be solved in Civil War-torn England.

Ellen looked up at Hannah, who was studying her intently.

'But lodgers?' Ellen said. 'Two, maybe three strangers in the house? I'm not sure that would be good for Charlie – and besides I haven't the first idea how to be a landlady. I mean how would I split the bills? Would I have to make them breakfast? Where would they sit?'

'Where would they . . . ? Ellen, it would be like a house share. They'd cook for themselves, you could add on an amount to the rent to cover bills – you'd need to get a tenancy agreement drawn up, but I'm sure there's probably a boilerplate of one we could print off the Internet. You'd get a deposit in advance, have a few house rules – like no nudity in the living room for example – and Bob's your uncle. You'd probably hardly know they were there, I mean this is London. We're not exactly all for hanging around making friends with each other, are we? And just think, you get to stay in your precious house, for ever and ever if you want to.'

Ellen wasn't sure which of the words that Hannah had just sprayed her with hit home, but suddenly, she knew her sister was right. She was the only one who'd come up with an idea that could enable her and Charlie to stay in their home and survive. Yes, it meant opening up her home, the haven that Nick had promised her, where she could always close the door on the world and feel safe, to complete strangers, but as far as Ellen could see there was no alternative. Nick had done his best to look after her and protect her. He'd sheltered her from the world, made himself a cushion between her and its hard edges. But he was unable to continue to do that in death, no matter how carefully he'd planned to. Hannah had come up with a solution, imperfect as it was, and despite herself Ellen was grateful that she had a sister like Hannah, a sister who could always see a way round things.

'OK,' Ellen said cautiously. 'So, explain it to me from the beginning – what would I have to do?'

Chapter Three

Eliza felt the edge of her uncle's desk biting into the small of her back as he advanced towards her, his enormous weight suddenly bearing down on her, his foul wine-sodden breath hot and damp on her neck.

'No!' Eliza fought him, kicking and struggling against him, but her small frame was no match for his cumbersome bulk.

'I say yes, dearest niece,' he snarled, drooling, as his thick fingers pawed the twin moons of her bosom. 'All these years I have watched you grow into a most tempting fruit under my very roof, a ripe, forbidden fruit that I could not pluck for myself. I believed that my dear late wife raised you to be a virgin, a modest maid – and yet the first chance you get you sully yourself on a Royalist dog! Well now I have the measure of you, my dear, you are nothing more than a common whore, and while your captain is away I will use you as I please. Niece or no – I will pluck you!'

A thin piercing trill cut through the air. Ellen sighed, pushing the manuscript back across the table. The doorbell had sounded, ripping through the morning with its sharp invasive ring. Phones could always be ignored. Doorbells could often be ignored, but not this time. This time Ellen had to answer it – her first lodger had arrived, exactly on time.

Sabine Neumann was on a secondment from the Berlin office

of T Jenkins Waterford. She was to be posted in the London office for three months and needed a place to stay. As soon as Ellen had deferred to her sister's money-making idea, Hannah had pounced on her BlackBerry, remembering an email requesting temporary accommodation that had been sent out the previous day.

'This is perfect,' Hannah chirped, pleased with herself. 'She wants a recommendation and you don't want just any old weirdo turning up on your doorstep. I'll sort this out now, I'll tell her that it's the room with the en suite that's available. Let's hold back on the attic rooms, we want to get as much as possible for that, put in the room rate and presto – it's sent.'

'Whoa – wait a minute – how do we know that she's not a weirdo?' Ellen asked, panic rising, as her ever-decisive sister took action on her idea within seconds of having it.

'She works for my company,' Hannah shrugged.

'Ted Bundy had a job, you know,' Ellen told her.

'We do all that Neural Linguistic Programming business at interview stage, so they'd definitely spot a psycho. Then again they gave me a job, so who knows!' Ellen did not laugh. 'Anyway she's German, so she's bound to be tidy, efficient, quiet and well mannered.'

'If you choose to conform to a racial stereotype, that is,' Ellen had muttered.

Hannah's BlackBerry pinged. 'See? What did I tell you, efficient. She's replied already and . . . she wants the room! She's arriving in a week. Right, now – what should I tell her about bedding, towels, etc – do you want her to bring her own or do you have enough? I'll tell her she has to supply her own, after all you don't want to be lumbered with a load of laundry, do you.'

Hannah beamed at Ellen, in her element, and briefly Ellen was reminded of her sister as a little girl, mastering riding a bike without stabilisers. It had taken Ellen a whole summer to teach Hannah how to ride a big girl's bike, and the look on her face as she had sailed past Ellen who'd been whooping and clapping was exactly the same as the one she wore now. Ellen found herself smiling.

'One down, two to go,' Hannah went on. 'You should ask around too, Ellie, but in the meantime I could draft an ad for *Time Out*?'

'I don't know, I'm not sure – that really would be a stranger,' Ellen said uncertainly, the fleeting memory of a summer morning fading rapidly.

'I'll put my email and number on it so you won't have to deal with it, and I promise I'll weed out all the weirdos, right after I've dated them. Let's see . . . "Rooms to let. Well-located shared house. Must be a non-smoker. No pets." Perfect. I'll just log on to their website and . . . there – that's that posted. I'll pay for it on my credit card – you can pay me back when the rent starts to roll in, along with the money for the skiing trip.'

Ellen blinked. 'Hannah! But I haven't asked you to lend me any money for Charlie's trip – wait – how do you even know about it?'

'Charlie called me a couple of days ago and asked me if I'd spot him the cash. Of course I said yes, after I'd talked it over with you, obviously. So when do you need it? I could write you a cheque now if you like.' Hannah smiled brightly, clearly feeling she was on a roll in her new position as Lady Bountiful. 'You don't mind, do you, Ellie? After the year he's had a change of scenery, a chance to spread his wings a bit will do him the world of good, won't it? And it's not as if I'm giving you the money, just lending it – that's all.'

Ellen felt outmanoeuvred. Since Nick, Hannah had gone out of her way to form a special relationship with her nephew. She had always been mildly fond of him but now he had become the official apple of her eye, and Charlie loved it, he loved the outings, shopping trips and visits to the cinema. He loved his cool aunt, and much as it rankled with Ellen that he was so comfortable with her sister, it had never occurred to her that he might take matters into his own hands and call Hannah and ask her for money himself. Ellen was so used to knowing every aspect of her little boy's life, it came as a shock to realise that he had a world outside hers. Furthermore, she had unconsciously been glad to have a reason not to let him go so far away with the school, a reason other than the one that really unsettled her, the idea of him out there, vulnerable and unprotected.

'I'm not sure if he's ready to be so far from home . . .' Ellen began.

'It must be a worry for you, to let him go,' Hannah said. 'But you need to, Ellie. Now is exactly the time when he should be spreading his wings, finding out more about the world. We'd hate what happened to change him, wouldn't we? To take away his joy of life.'

'Are you saying that's what I do? Take the joy away?' Ellen was offended.

'No, no! I'm saying that you are still grieving, it's not been a year yet. It wouldn't hurt to let Charlie have a break from that – it's not until next February anyway, is it, this trip – so let's just agree that I'll lend you the money, you'll pay me back and see how you feel about it nearer the time. How's that?'

33

Ellen had nodded, mute.

'So anyway you'd better get that room sorted out. Today's . . . Wednesday and Sabine is arriving Friday – so that gives you two days to get ready.'

'She's coming already? Hannah, that's too soon. I haven't had time to think about it, to even discuss with Charlie what he thinks about strangers living in the house. Not all of us live our lives at high speed, you know.'

'You can say that again.' Hannah pursed her lips as she studied Ellen's face for a moment, her expression opaque. 'Ellie, time has run out for you – there aren't any more opportunities for faffing. If I know one thing it's when to take action, and now is that time. Besides, what is there to discuss? You're out of options. Charles will understand that, he's a bright boy. I could talk to him if you like?'

'No, no – I'll talk to him about it when he gets back from school.'

'OK, well, you do that – and with a bit of luck we'll have all your spare rooms occupied before you know it.'

'Good morning, I'm Sabine Neumann.' Ellen looked somewhat taken aback at the perfectly manicured hand that was extended towards her. Sabine Neumann was not at all what she had pictured. To her shame she had expected the German business-woman to be rather mannish, with short hair and a very firm manner, somewhere in her fifties. First impressions could not have been more different.

Sabine was about Ellen's age, with long blonde hair spiralling over her shoulders in a natural corkscrew curl. She had a bright smile and blue eyes that seemed literally to sparkle. Instead of the dour business suit that Ellen had expected she was wearing a white shirt over faded jeans, finished off with a pair of red Converse shoes. It was an outfit that Ellen could never picture herself in, not outlandish or over the top but confident, stylish.

'Welcome, Sabine,' Ellen said, feeling suddenly dowdy and mannish herself. 'Please come in. I hope that everything here is to your liking. I've never had lodgers before, this is quite new to me. I don't really know the etiquette but I hope if there is something that I'm not getting right you will tell me.'

'OK, I will,' Sabine agreed, with barely a trace of an accent, looking around the sunlit hallway. 'Your house is lovely, it's very Victorian – just how I pictured it.'

'Thank you,' Ellen said, casting an eye over the restored oak boards that glowed a deep gold in the morning sun, and the pale green and cream paint that Nick had chosen for this space, which made it such a warm and inviting entrance. They had spent an age touring reclamation yards to find the perfect lighting, settling eventually on a modest little crystal chandelier. Ellen noticed it needed dusting as she glanced up at it, picturing Nick on his stepladder, swearing as he wrangled with it, the beams of sunlight captured by its glass drops dancing on the floor and walls.

'And this is your family?' Sabine had wandered over to where a photograph of Ellen, Nick and Charlie hung on the wall. It had been taken a few months before Nick's accident, and had been Nick's idea. He had come home one day and told Ellen they should make a record of their family, something permanent they would be able to look back on, so that whatever might change in the future they'd always remember how things had been. Ellen remembered feeling rather puzzled, and she'd asked him if there was anything wrong, anything he was worried about. But he'd just laughed and ruffled her hair in that way he'd taken to doing and told her not to be so foolish, that real life was nothing like those books she was so obsessed with, stuffed with tragedy and intrigue. He'd found a photographer he'd liked and she came to the house, decking out their seldom-used living room with white sheets and throw cushions. Ellen remembered how Nick and Charlie had had to make her laugh to get her to loosen up after the photographer had shown them the first digital images on her laptop. Nick had joked that it was like having his photo taken with a maiden aunt. They had told her stupid jokes until finally Ellen had forgotten the camera was there at all, and now there they were, the three of them. That single moment captured them lounging back on the sofa, arms around necks, legs intertwined, laughing.

'You are very lucky to have such a wonderful family,' Sabine observed.

'I, well – yes, I was – I am.' Ellen fought that familiar prick of tears behind her eyes. 'Nick, my husband, died last year in a traffic accident. It's just me and Charlie now – hence the lodgers.'

Sabine nodded.

'I'm sorry. My husband is not dead,' she informed Ellen, her pretty mouth forming a thin line. 'My husband is in Berlin, I've left him. I couldn't stand looking at him for another second more, the lying, whoring piece of shit. It's not fair, is it? If my husband was dead I wouldn't mind but you – you loved yours and now you've lost him. Life isn't fair.' Sabine shrugged as if she'd just missed a bus she wasn't especially bothered about catching, and put one foot on the bottom stair. 'So now, perhaps I might see the room?'

The phone was ringing as Ellen left Sabine unpacking her bags, and she prayed it was not Hannah with news of another enforced lodger.

She was still trying to adjust to having one stranger moving into her house and into her life, passing comment on her photos, telling Ellen about her own private life. Hannah, Hitesh, her mother – everyone kept on telling her that she had to get used to the fact that her life had changed now, but Ellen found it hard. It was painful for her to accept that it had to change quite as much as it had.

Sabine was right, it wasn't fair. If Nick hadn't decided on a whim to borrow his friend's Lotus and take it for a spin down some quiet country roads after a late pub lunch, if he'd hadn't exceeded the speed limit by nearly double, if he'd *thought* just for one second about . . . Ellen halted that train of thought before it could develop any further, consumed with guilt that she could allow herself to even begin to feel angry with her husband. Nick would never have left her and Charlie in this kind of mess on purpose. He didn't set out on that summer day to kill himself purely to inconvenience her. He loved her like no man ever had or ever would again. And Nick had been an adventurer, an explorer – the kind of man to seize the day and wring every ounce of life out of it, reluctant to waste any precious seconds on sleep. That was what Ellen had loved about him first, his drive, his passion. That, and the fact that when she was around him, for the first time in her life she felt vibrant, a three-dimensional being of flesh and blood finally present in the world that Nick embraced so readily – she felt alive. It was a feeling that she hadn't been able to recreate since the moment she had discovered Nick was dead.

Biting her lip, Ellen quietened the same circle of thoughts that constantly rotated around her head and picked up the phone.

'Ellen, good, you're in.' Her boss Simon's voice sounded on the other end of the line, deep and melodious. Ellen breathed a sigh of relief. Simon was one of the few people who would not be demanding she took some kind of action, who would not persist in telling her where she was going wrong. If anything, with a little bit of luck he'd have something nice for her to work on – preferably the next instalment of *The Sword Erect*, as she'd almost finished the pages she already had.

'Hello, Simon.' Ellen's voice was warm. 'I'm in and I've just greeted my first lodger.'

'Ah yes, you told me about your new career as a landlady in your last email. In fact in a roundabout way it's sort of my reason for ringing today.'

'Really?' Ellen was puzzled. 'Why, do you need a room?'

'No, no, my dear – I'll get to that in a minute. First off tell me all about your first lodger.' Simon had evidently decided to put whatever request he had for her on hold for the minute. That was the other thing Ellen liked about him: while Hannah seemed to feel that it was her duty to talk at her and boss her around, Simon, a man she rarely spoke to and saw even less, actually seemed interested in her and how she was coping. He was one of the few people who ever asked her how she was. Sometimes Ellen didn't want to answer. Sometimes she hated the fact that he asked, but at the same time she appreciated it too.

'She's nice, I think.' Ellen pondered the ten or so minutes that she had spent so far in Sabine's company. 'She seems it, anyway, and she is happy with the room as far as I can tell. It's just strange, you know – different.'

'I know, Ellen, it must be hard for you,' Simon said, his voice softening. 'I'd hate to share my flat with anyone but Tibalt.' Simon referred to his ancient and grizzled cocker spaniel, who accompanied him every day to the Cherished Desires offices on Fulham Palace Road and lay all day under his desk emitting foul smells and loud snores. Simon was more devoted to him than any human, at least that Ellen knew of.

'Oh well, no – not that hard. And it's money, isn't it, money to keep this house going and disrupt Charlie as little as possible – talking of which, do you have any more of the new Allegra Howard for me? It's not like you to give me a book in dribs and drabs.'

'Not quite, I have something a little better.' Simon sounded hesitant. 'Ellen, I have Allegra Howard herself for you, if you will have her, that is.'

'I beg your pardon?' Ellen asked him, glancing up at the ceiling at the sound of furniture being dragged across the floor.

'Allegra – she's in a pickle, and she needs a fair maid to come to her rescue. I immediately thought of you, the fairest maid I know.'

'Me – but how could *I* ever help Allegra Howard?'

'Well, you know those dreadful spring floods they had a while back in Gloucestershire?'

'Oh yes, they were awful,' Ellen said, thinking of the pictures on the TV news of houses half filled with water, a teddy bear floating down what once had been a quiet avenue. Practically the whole of Tewkesbury was under water.

'Well, Allegra's seventeenth-century manor house took the brunt of it. It's going to take months to restore it just to a fit enough state for her to live in at all, and apparently her insurance company aren't keen to keep putting her up in the five-star hotels she been staying in. Allegra point-blank refuses to go anywhere near anything as unsavoury as a caravan or a strange rented house so I was thinking about what you said – how you mentioned that you were looking for tenants. I wondered if you'd have Allegra as one.'

'Me, have Allegra Howard staying here? Simon, I can't possibly.' Ellen pressed the palm of her hand to her chest, feeling her heart rate accelerate beneath her fingertips. It was a curious sensation. She'd read so many of Allegra's books over the years that she felt as if she knew the woman, and oddly as if Allegra knew her too, more intimately than perhaps anyone else. She could hardly believe she'd heard Simon correctly.

'Please, Ellen, she really needs somewhere nice and homely to stay while she tries to finish *The Sword Erect*. All of the drama has rather blocked her creative flow, she's lost her confidence a little and she needs someone to boost her up. I can't think of anyone better to take her in than you, the very person who loves and understands her books so well.'

'Allegra Howard in my third bedroom, Simon! You've been here – she needs to stay somewhere much better than a shabby old house in Hammersmith – besides, you said she wouldn't touch a rental!'

'That's where you're wrong, my angel. And your home is anything but a strange and unwelcoming rented house. Your shabby, old, beautiful, much-loved home is *exactly* what she does need, the poor old duck. And you wouldn't just be her landlady.

As you know, the latest book is set in the English Civil War and Allegra needs a bit of extra help – a research assistant if you like. To find contemporary local maps, brush up on the history – that sort of thing. Allegra's never been one to let facts get in the way of a good story, but our readers do like things to be at least a little accurate. Her last PA left because of . . . artistic differences, so the position is happily vacant. Besides, Allegra will only write in pen – lilac-inked fountain pen to be precise. One of your jobs would be to type up her work into electronic format. Just imagine – you'd be the first person in creation to read the new Allegra Howard! And she'd pay you – it wouldn't be a huge amount but it would double your rental income from her and I could top it up by a few quid – it would be worth it, you'd be saving my life.'

Ellen felt her heart pounding in her chest. In truth there was nothing she could imagine enjoying more than helping the great Allegra Howard with her latest work of genius. But could she do it, could she really?

She was certainly capable of helping research the background of the novel, after all, she had a First in English History – even if the only thing she'd used it for in the last ten years was to subtly point out some of the more glaring historical errors in Allegra's books. She was a competent typist and her job as a freelance copy-editor (might as well be 'free' lance, Hannah persisted in teasing her) meant she was well versed in punctuation and grammar – something else that Allegra seemed to find rather tiresome.

But this would be *the* Allegra Howard – the woman who had supplied Ellen with the alternative universe that she had so happily inhabited for the last few years, even before Nick had left her so suddenly. Allegra who created the heroines that Ellen loved to transform into for the few precious hours she spent immersed in those sheets of paper. Allegra who fashioned the kinds of manly, magnetic heroes that Ellen was ashamed to admit she frequently imagined making love to her with the same fiery passion that they lavished upon the shapely young maidens who populated Allegra's books. Quite often, on a quiet afternoon when Charlie was at school and Nick was safely at work, Ellen would find herself quite caught up in the moment as one of Allegra's rakes urgently pinned some feisty young woman to perhaps a ship's mast, or tree trunk, or, in one of Ellen's favourite books, *The Stallion Rampant*, a horse's back, and unable to contain his desire for her lovely body a second longer, would rip her clothes from her. Whipped into a frenzy by the exquisite sight of her naked breasts he would take her, his manhood searching deep within her, finding that sweet sacred spot, so at last she would come to know the true delight of physical love and be prepared to fall in love with him, if not at that exact moment then at least three or four ravishes later. After reading a scene like that, sometimes *while* reading a scene like that, Ellen would feel compelled to find her own sweet sacred spot and imagine that it was her full pert breasts that the hero's lips were so firmly latched on to and her slender yet shapely hips that he gripped with his powerful hands as he entered her again. And again. And again.

The physical side of her life with Nick had been lovely, but it had been tender and sweet rather than satisfying – he was always so gentle with her, as if she were made of cut glass and might shatter in his arms. Over the last year she had spent many a night muffling her tears in her pillow as she grieved over the loss of the intimacy that they had shared. But the orgasms that Ellen had had with Allegra Howard's heroes were more passionate and intense than any she had known, even with Nick. And Ellen was not at all sure she could look in the eye the woman who had fuelled her fantasy sex life for so long. The idea seemed impossible, almost like meeting God and letting him know what you thought of Creation.

'Look, Ellen.' Simon's voice startled her out of her reverie. 'I know that the idea of a lot of people you don't know in your home tortures you. No one understands that better than me. God knows, if I didn't have bills to pay I'd live as a recluse doing up my wreck of a cottage in Suffolk and never talk to anyone again, except you and Tibalt. You'd be doing me a huge favour if you took Allegra in. To be honest, her name is one of the few on the list that is guaranteed to turn a profit for the company. Allegra's sales carry a lot of our less established authors, not to mention paying my mortgage and hers. In this climate I need her to finish this latest book sooner rather than later. Her readers are used to three books a year and *The Sword Erect* is long overdue already. You love her work, you know exactly what her readers want from her books, I've long thought that you've got great potential to develop your career beyond merely copy-editing, and I know you'll look after her like a seventy-three-year-old woman needs to be looked after . . .'

'She's seventy-three!' Ellen interrupted. 'I would have said she looks at least twenty years younger in her author photo.'

'That's because she *is* twenty years younger in her author photo,' Simon told her. 'Anyway, I can't think of anyone better to help her through this dry patch.'

'So you're saying you want me to get her back into a wet patch,' Ellen joked quite uncharacteristically.

Simon chuckled on the other end of the phone. 'Ellen! Have you been drinking during the day?'

'I don't know, it must be *The Sword Erect* – this one is especially racy, Simon. I'll just have to hope that working on it won't corrupt me totally.'

'So are you saying you'll do it?' Simon pressed her. Ellen could hear the anxiety in his voice. Clearly she was his plan A and he didn't have a plan B. The idea of helping Simon out of a spot gave her unexpected pleasure.

'OK, OK – I'll do it!' She exclaimed, feeling giddy with the rush of the unknown. It was a sensation she hadn't experienced in the longest time. Meeting Allegra would be fine. As Simon said, she was a homeless old lady, not some soothsayer with psychic powers to see inside a person's brain.

'Ellen Woods – you are a magnificent woman,' Simon told her warmly.

'Oh well . . .' Ellen found herself flushing with pleasure as she stood alone in her hallway. It was rare for anyone to compliment her these days.

'There's just one more thing, Allegra will need a ground-floor room near a loo – is that a problem? She's not too great with stairs, not that she will tell you that and nor should you mention it.'

'Well there's the dining room, we don't really use it and it's got French doors that open out on to the garden. And we've got a downstairs loo and shower room. I could get Charlie and some of his pals to put the table in the garage. But what about a bed?'

'Oh, I'll buy you a new one, Allegra is quite fussy about only sleeping on virgin mattresses, as she calls them,' Simon told her. 'Also if you paint the room lilac, preferably with odourless paint, and get in some lilac furnishings so that it's all ready for her grand entrance around a week from now, then we're all set.'

'Lilac?' Ellen questioned him, pinning her whirl of confusion on that one word.

'Yes and a chaise longue, she needs a chaise longue to recline on while she's thinking up ideas. There's this website that delivers them in any colour you like. I'll order it and pick up the bill and get it delivered to you, shall I? Plus I'll have to ship in her desk – it was one of the few things that survived the flood, she's very attached to it. Don't worry about the expense, just send all the receipts to me and I'll settle them straight away. Anyway, my dearest love, I must dash. I've got Bernadette Darcy due in for an editorial meeting, apparently she's having problems with her country-house orgy. Can't think of enough positions for each chapter.'

Ellen set down the phone and looked at it for a moment, wondering if that conversation had really happened or if she had imagined it.

Allegra Howard in *her* house in a week's time. Ellen wondered where she could get lilac paint delivered from, pronto.

Chapter Four

Charlie eyed Sabine across the kitchen table, where she sat eating a bacon sandwich that she had made herself. Sabine had asked Ellen when she might be allowed access to the kitchen and realising that she hadn't given catering or kitchen arrangements a moment's thought, Ellen had told her whenever she liked. Sabine had gone out for an hour, returned with several Sainsbury's bags and then politely asked Ellen if she might have a shelf in the fridge, one near the top would be preferable.

'It will save on labelling,' she explained, although Ellen had no idea what she meant.

'Useful to have a big supermarket so close,' Sabine remarked as she munched her sandwich.

'I suppose it is,' Ellen smiled. 'Although I must admit I get all my groceries delivered once a week. I read that it's greener, because the delivery van has less of a carbon footprint or something. Besides I don't drive.'

'You never learnt to drive?' Sabine questioned her.

'Oh I learnt, it's just that living in London you don't really need to and since Charlie was born I sort of lost my confidence. I prefer not to drive, that's what I meant.'

'You still keep Dad's car taxed and insured though,' Charlie said, arriving home from school, his hair tousled, his uniform Friday dirty. Normally all that would greet him would be his mum sitting at the kitchen table, up to her elbows in some book or other; now he was met by a German blonde sitting in his usual chair. He had known that the first lodger was coming today. Ellen had discussed, or at least attempted to discuss with him what he thought about the idea on the same day that Hannah had suggested it, but Charlie had simply shrugged.

'Yeah, OK then.' Ellen had been nonplussed.

'Well hang on a minute, Charlie – let's think about this. It would mean a really big change, a house full of people – not just us here any more.'

'I know.' Charlie nodded.

'And you don't mind that?' Ellen asked him, wondering if she should feel put out that he was quite so relaxed about the end of their quiet little family.

Charlie had tipped his head on to one side. 'Mum, you really don't want to leave this house, do you?'

'Well, no – but you don't either . . . do you?'

Charlie looked thoughtful. 'The point is you don't want to leave, you can't leave. You need to be here and I know you think I don't know anything that's going on, but I know that money is tight, I know we need to make some. So we get in lodgers, it's fine.'

'But are you happy about it?' Ellen pressed him.

'I'm happy!' Charlie had exclaimed, grabbing a piece of bread and stuffing it into his mouth. 'Besides, Aunt Hannah says it's a good idea.'

'You mean she's told you about it already?'

'Yes, and if she thinks it's cool, then it's cool. Aunt Hannah knows about these things – she told me.'

'Oh, she did, did she? Well, that makes it all OK then.' Ellen had never voiced out loud how irritating she found the private joke that Charlie and Hannah had shared, ever since he was three years old, of only ever addressing each other formally. Nor had she ever admitted that it drove her mad that Charlie was so interested in every word Hannah said, that he respected her lifestyle and her career and the travel and material prizes that her work brought her, while he increasingly treated Ellen like she was the one that needed looking after. Before, Nick's word had been law, if he said something was good, bad or indifferent then Charlie agreed with him. Now it was Hannah's opinion he trusted. Ellen wondered if it would ever be her word again that meant most to her son.

'She said we needed the money,' Charlie told her. 'Yeah it will be a bit whack – but mainly I'm cool with it, seriously.'

Ellen decided now was not the time to remind Charlie that he was an English middle-class schoolboy and not a New York gangster rapper.

'Well, just so long as you know you don't have to worry about anything, OK?'

'I'm not worried,' Charlie had insisted, chewing the corner of his thumb as he spoke.

Ellen watched her son closely for signs of distress as he watched Sabine. There were three mismatched chairs at the kitchen table. When they had moved into the house Nick had taken them to a local junk shop where he had spotted a large ancient and battered pine table that he thought would be perfect for their new kitchen. Ellen had complained that it didn't have matching chairs, and Nick had laughed, waving his arm around him at the collection of disowned chairs of all shapes and sizes.

'I know,' he'd said, winking at an enchanted Charlie. 'Let's choose a different chair each. One that will suit us and be our chair whenever we sit at the table.'

Ellen had chosen a chair that she thought was most in keeping with the table, a humble pine affair with a simple back and straight legs. Nick had managed to find a dark wood carver that looked like it had once belonged in much grander surroundings and had ideas far above its station, with its turned arms and sturdy squat bowed legs. Charlie, much younger, still a baby really, had found a brightly painted chair that must have once belonged to an amateur artist. Every leg was painted a different primary colour and the backrest was an acidic green decorated with a painted eye. Ever since that day the three of them had always sat in their special chairs, until Nick died and then his remained stubbornly vacant, even Hannah knew better than to sit in it. Today Sabine was sitting in Charlie's chair and he took up residence in his mother's. Ellen leaned against the kitchen counter and watched, fretting about how to break the news to her lodgers that one of her kitchen chairs was off limits.

'This is a delicious sandwich,' Sabine told Charlie after she had finished chewing. 'Do you like bacon, Charlie? I love Danish bacon.'

'I don't eat bacon,' Charlie told her. 'I eat fish fingers, white bread, tomato ketchup and Frosties.' He issued the declaration like it was a challenge.

'Ah – you're a fussy eater.' Sabine nodded, as if nothing Charlie had said was out of the ordinary. 'When I was a girl I would only drink milk and I wouldn't touch any vegetables.'

'Even when you were nearly twelve?' Charlie quizzed her, making Ellen tense, wondering if he was as worried about his eating habits as she was or if some of the kids at school had said something.

'Oh yes, until I was much older than twelve. I didn't like vegetables until I was in my twenties, after several years of smoking and drinking. Your taste buds are young and tender, unsullied by alcohol or nicotine – it's normal for a young boy to only like a few things.'

'That's what I thought.' Charlie grinned at her, his shoulders relaxing, happily forgetting the ravenous appetite he'd had for nearly anything edible before his father died.

'So, Charlie,' Ellen said from her observation point. 'We got our second guest today. She's a writer, my favourite writer actually and she's arriving on Tuesday – so you and I have our work cut out turning the dining room into a bedroom and painting it lilac this weekend.'

'Lilac! Gross!' Charlie and Sabine looked at each other and wrinkled their noses, striking up an easy camaraderie that Ellen could not help but envy. It hadn't been that easy between her and Charlie for a long time, he always seemed so disappointed in her.

'I know, but the best bit is I'm going to be her research assistant which means more money – which means I can pay Aunt Hannah back for your skiing trip!' Ellen told him proudly. Whether or not she actually wanted him to go was immaterial for now, it was the fact that she no longer needed Hannah's money that was paramount.

'But Aunt Hannah's already paid for it.'

'I know, but it was just a loan – now I can pay it back.'

'Yes but Hannah's loaded and you're skint, so why don't you . . .'

'I'm paying for it, Charlie, end of discussion. I want to pay for it.' Ellen felt stung to the quick that Charlie had rejected her announcement so roundly.

'Yes but it doesn't make sense, what about the bills, the mortgage . . . ?'

'Charlie . . .' Ellen heard her tone rising against her will.

'May I help you paint this weekend?' Sabine asked mildly, taking a packet of cigarettes out of her shirt pocket, looking at them rather wistfully and then putting them back again. 'I don't have any friends here or a social life as yet. I would welcome the chance to get to know you better, plus I am an excellent painter. I do very straight edges. It's because I'm German, you know – we're very precise.'

Sabine winked at Charlie, who chuckled, and it took Ellen a second to realise that her guest was joking.

'Well, Sabine, if you're sure, that would be wonderful,' Ellen smiled. It seemed that for now anyway, having a lodger wasn't nearly as dreadful as she had feared.

The doorbell suddenly rang, and she tensed.

'Well, I will just go outside for a cigarette.' Sabine nodded at the kitchen door. 'Out there OK?'

'Oh yes, fine,' Ellen said, bracing herself to answer the bell, even though she knew who it was – Hannah.

'Charles.' Hannah nodded at her nephew as she entered the kitchen.

'Aunt Hannah,' Charlie replied with a small bow. 'A delight to see you as ever.'

'Charmed, I'm sure,' Hannah replied regally.

'Hannah.' Ellen watched as her sister sprawled in Sabine's now vacant chair. 'It's very nice of you to drop by, again, but you didn't say you were coming over tonight and it's just I've got a lot to do, a lot of sorting out for the next lodger.'

Ellen wanted Charlie to see that she could manage some things for herself.

'Oh God, please say it's not the second-floor suite you've let out?' Hannah exclaimed.

'If you mean the attic rooms, then no – I'm converting the dining room into a room for an elderly lady. Actually she's . . .' Ellen was keen to share her bit of news, but Hannah rushed on before she could.

'Oh good, that's a relief. I came for two reasons. I thought I'd say hi to Sabine, and offer to take her out for lunch on Monday and show her the lie of the land.' Hannah looked around. 'Where is Sabine anyway, have you confined her to her quarters? I'm dying to see what she looks like.'

'She's really fit,' Charlie assured Hannah, making his aunt and mother look at him. 'She's outside, smoking, and she's a total fox.'

'Oh Charles, you are growing up!' Hannah burst out laughing, Ellen did not.

Ellen privately smarted. Here was Hannah marching in, making everything about her as usual, disregarding any fledgling friendship that Ellen might have been forming with Sabine. Throughout Ellen's life, once anyone she knew met her sister, Hannah's burning sun eclipsed Ellen's quieter personality almost immediately. Nick was the only person Ellen had ever known who seemed quite uninterested in Hannah, and it was one of the reasons that Ellen had loved him so fiercely.

'Oh well, the other reason I came is because I had a response from the *Time Out* ad,' Hannah went on seamlessly. 'Clever and beautiful Aunt Hannah has found you another lodger!'

'Please say it's not a little old lady who only likes lilac,' Charlie begged, slumping in his chair to rest his chin on the tabletop as he watched his aunt with bright eyes, as if she were a particularly entertaining TV show.

'No, much better than that – he's a man! His name is Matt Bolton, he's twenty-six, a non-smoker and he's just moving down from Manchester to take up a job as a staff writer for *Bang It!*'

'Wicked!' Charlie's eyes widened.

'What on earth is *Bang It!*?' Ellen asked, her expression preset to disapprove.

'It's a lads' mag – you know the sort of thing, photos of busty babes, articles about computer games, how to get a six-pack in six weeks, that sort of nonsense. Anyway Matt had a column about being a single man in the *Manchester Evening Post*, apparently it caused a bit of an uproar amongst Manchester's feminist community and he was on the verge of losing his job when he got spotted by the editor of *Bang It!* and offered a job continuing the column down here. The offices are in Hammersmith, so this place is perfect for him. He was especially stoked about the idea of having his own loo and shower.'

'So you've already told him he's got the room.' Ellen's heart sank. 'Without checking with me first like you said you would, remember?'

'I said I'd screen the applicants and weed out any weirdos, and Matt's not a weirdo, he seems really nice on the phone. Besides he's got the money, he works down the road, I expect he'll be out most of the time, a young single man in London – you'll hardly know he's here.'

'No, sorry – I'm putting my foot down,' Ellen said firmly, feeling dizzy from how quickly her life was spinning out of control. 'You'll have to tell him he's not coming.'

'Oh Mum!' Charlie exclaimed, disappointed. 'I'd be the coolest boy in the school if one of our lodgers worked on *Bang It!* It'd make up for the old lady!'

'Yes. Hang on a minute, Ellie,' Hannah countered. 'Let's think about this a bit more. Why do you object to Matt?'

'Because my other tenants are females, and one of them is an older lady, a writer with sensitive needs. The last thing Allegra Howard wants is some man crashing around the place, swearing and talking about . . . God knows what. This is a house of women, we don't want any men.'

'Oh thanks very much,' Charlie scowled.

'Allegra Howard – isn't that the woman whose books you love so much?' Hannah asked, deflecting Ellen's tirade and making her foot-putting-down seem rather less effective.

'Yes, it is – she needs a place to stay while her flood-damaged home is being restored *and* she needs a research assistant and PA – and that's me. I've got the job. I'm getting paid and everything.' Ellen nodded emphatically on the final word.

'Really – Ellie, that's fab news – well done you. See what you can do when you set your mind to it?'

Ellen nodded, caught off guard by Hannah's enthusiasm and praise. After all, she hadn't really done anything yet – except answer the phone. Still, Hannah didn't know that.

'But I honestly don't see why that means you can't have Matt as a tenant. Like I said he'll be out most of the time, and when he is here he and Allegra will be separated by a whole floor! Besides, if the cover of her books are anything to go by she likes a strapping young man with his top off and it wouldn't do Charles any harm to have a man about the place . . .' Hannah stopped herself, probably from saying 'since Nick died'. Her face was still and dark for the briefest moment. 'You know, to watch footie with and talk about girls to.'

'Please Mum,' Charlie implored her. 'I would get total respect at school.' Ellen looked at him, puzzled. Was he really keen to have another man in the house or did he just want to please Hannah?

'You're really begging me to let a male lodger stay?' Ellen asked him.

'Like Aunt Hannah says it will be cool to have a bloke around, otherwise it will just be me and a load of old women. And Sabine.'

'Hey you, Sabine's not much younger than me,' Ellen protested, self-consciously tucking a strand of her dark hair behind her ear.

'Oh go on, Ellie – at least give Matt a try. I'll tell him he's on a one-month trial and if you don't like him you can kick him out after that. Just think, if you take Matt on then no more lodgers to look for, you can get stuck into your job and Charles will be settled with the new arrangements before you know it.'

'I will,' Charlie agreed.

Ellen felt her shoulders slump. It seemed that she was the victim of a fait accompli.

'OK, I'll give him a trial but if he smells or swears or is in any way a bad influence then he's out.'

'Great, he's getting an early train down from Manchester Monday morning, he's going to move his stuff in after his first day.'

'Hello.' Sabine appeared from the garden where she had been smoking amongst the ragged rose bushes that Ellen hadn't touched since last summer.

'Oh hello, you must be Sabine, I'm Hannah – we spoke on the phone?'

'Ah Hannah, hello, it's nice to meet you in person.'

'Well, I thought you might like to meet for lunch tomorrow and get some of the inside goss,' Hannah beamed. 'Seriously if I don't know it, then it's not worth knowing.'

'That would be very nice,' Sabine smiled. 'I find that no matter how old or how well travelled I am, beginning work in a new place is still just like starting school. A friendly face makes things so much easier.'

'That's what I thought,' Hannah said, making Ellen feel bad for resenting her sister's visit. Hannah was only trying to help her, she told herself. Hannah was being a good sister. Whatever it was, whatever dark little nagging resentment that kept on nibbling away at Ellen, whether it was left over from their childhood or if it was something new that had sprung up in the wake of everything else, she had to shake it off. She had to remember that she was lucky to have Hannah, and put all these irrational niggles aside.

'While I was smoking in your beautiful garden I was thinking that it is such a pleasant evening. I noticed a rather nice-looking pub down the road on my earlier shopping trip. Ellen, I wondered if you might take me for my first British drink?'

'Oh can we?' Charlie looked at Ellen hopefully, his eyes bright with expectation. This was the first time that anything, well, anything different or interesting had happened at home for him in a long time, Ellen realised, glimpsing an insight into what his life had been like for the last year. This change, this shake-up that she had dreaded was exactly what he needed. Perhaps it was what she needed too.

Ellen checked the wall clock. It was only just gone seven, it was the weekend tomorrow and she supposed an hour wouldn't hurt. It would be nice to be the one giving Charlie a treat for once, and Sabine's newness and friendliness would surely defuse the tension that always built between Ellen and her sister.

Ellen thought of the pub at the end of the road. Right now it would be busy with commuters on the way home, enjoying a cold drink standing in the evening sunshine. There'd be laughter in the air, a cacophony of voices, the scent of smoke mingling with the summer foliage. It would be crammed to the brim with happy relaxed people. But she had so much to do for Allegra Howard and so little time to do it. Really she had to start right away.

'You three go,' Ellen decided. 'I've got to get on the Internet, see if I can find someone who'll deliver paint tomorrow, and start on sorting out the dining room. I want you back in an hour, though – OK?'

'Marvellous, what fun to take my nephew for his first illegal drink.'

'Hannah!' Ellen reacted just as her sister knew she would.

'I'm only joking, Ellie,' Hannah giggled, winking at Charlie, who grinned delightedly at her in return.

'Aunt Hannah,' Ellen heard Charlie ask as they walked out of the door, the June sunshine still gilding the street with its warmth. 'Can I have a cider?'

'In your dreams, sunshine,' Hannah laughed. 'Don't want to give your mum any more reasons to be cross with me, do we?'

Once they had gone Ellen listened to the silence left in their wake for a second and then walked into the now seldom-used living room, hoping to catch a glimpse of them walking by the hedge that was desperately in need of trimming back, as a neighbour, whom she had never met or spoken to, had politely reminded her in the form of a note posted through the front door a month or so ago.

Ellen paused to look at the border she had planted so lovingly in front of the window, packed full of tall blue and violet delphiniums, yellow spiky star-like goldstrum, a multitude of multicoloured pinks and mauve coneflowers. She hadn't weeded or tended to the plants since last summer – in fact she had a feeling that her gardening gloves were probably still where she had left them, wrung together and cast down, mouldering in the depths of the border that she had been working on when the news came. And yet still, despite being half choked to death with weeds and rogue grass, the flowers had fought their way through to bloom again.

For a moment Ellen pressed her palm against the glass, remembering the smell, the feel of the soil between her fingers, the pleasure in seeing her planting design mature and take shape. And for a moment, she missed being out there, passing a polite word here and there with passers-by, feeling the heat of the sun scorching the nape of her neck. Ellen watched as a fat bumblebee tracked its way first up and then down the pollen-heavy head of a delphinium, ensuring its bloom would soon be gone. She wasn't ready for that yet, she wasn't ready to see her plants blossom and die, another summer over. She wasn't ready for it to be almost a whole year since she had last worked on that border, since the two very kind police officers had walked up the garden path and asked her if she would come inside so they could talk.

Ellen turned her back on the golden evening outside, pulled by the weight of the empty room that used to be so full of her and Nick, sitting together on the sofa any evening he wasn't working late. Holding hands, drinking tea and sharing chocolate, talking about Charlie and where they would go or what they would do next. Without having to look, Ellen knew that over the hedge the street was drenched with sun, and she could imagine the day's worth of heat absorbed by the pavement that would have radiated through the thin soles of her summer shoes, if she had gone with them to the pub. Perhaps she should have gone, she thought, running her hand along the cool painted windowsill, but somehow it didn't feel right. Even when Nick was alive they hadn't really gone out together, always content to stay at home curled up on the sofa that Ellen was trying not to look at. Home was Nick's refuge, his break from real life he sometimes called it.

Things were difficult now, they were painful and harsh, she thought, turning her face away from the glare of the outside to cool her cheeks in the shadowy room. But at least they *were* changing. At least here was some let-up to the unrelenting grief that had characterised every single minute of her life since Nick left her. Was it wrong to feel optimistic and even excited about the recent turn of events? Perhaps it was too soon to be attempting to get on with things, perhaps if she started to pull herself together now that would mean that she hadn't loved Nick enough. Queen Victoria had mourned the untimely death of her husband for over fifty years. Never again had she worn anything but black. She made the rest of her life a mausoleum to her husband. Should that be how any grieving widow carried on, an empty shell, existing only because she had to?

No, Nick would want her to get on with things, he'd want her to be OK. He'd be so surprised that she'd made it this far without him; he always joked that she wasn't safe to be let out on her own. Besides, being OK, having something to look forward to, something to do, didn't mean that she wasn't still carrying a burning hole in her chest where her heart used to beat.

Life could still be liveable, Ellen slowly allowed herself to realise as her eyes roamed the empty sofa, its cushions still dented with the weight of Nick's body. Even without her husband, her existence could still be bearable, even perhaps happy again, in a way. It was a previously unimaginable idea that when it dawned came as an enormous relief to her. The thought that the burden of grief she had become so used to carrying could, *would* one day at least be lightened, made Ellen feel a little giddy, and she experienced the first stirrings of something that had lain dormant in her for more years than she could remember. The pleasure of finding her own independence.

The outside world blazing at her back, Ellen realised she was smiling to herself. If two new people in her life could improve things for her so much, then a third could, at the very least, do her no harm. As Hannah said, Ellen would probably have hardly anything to do with Matt Bolton.

It wasn't too late to catch up with them, she could still go to the pub if she wanted to. Feel the last heat of the day's sun burning the nape of her neck.

Ellen thought for a moment, and then drawing the curtains on the living room she went next door to the dining room and started to clear out the sideboard instead.

Chapter Five

Matt Bolton blinked and pinched himself. He couldn't actually believe his eyes. Here he was on his first day on the job at *Bang It!*, watching a photo shoot. A photo shoot with two glamour models, who were getting much better acquainted with each other's assets than they had been when they'd turned up a few minutes ago.

'Life's good, right?' Pete Grossman asked Matt. He was the features editor on the magazine, and would be Matt's immediate boss and mentor. Standing a good four inches shorter than Matt, Pete, in his mid-forties, was nevertheless what many women would consider an attractive and well-built man. Matt could see that Pete would have been considered handsome once, and was probably something of a pin-up in his youth. A life of drinking and smoking and at least two expensive ex-wives had taken its toll on him, however, his skin thickened and ruddy and his possibly dyed black hair thinning around the temples. Once he'd been a cutting-edge young investigative journalist who battled on gamely in the midst of whatever war zone was most readily available. When he had bagged the job of the youngest-ever editor in chief of Britain's best-selling tabloid in his thirties, his future had looked golden. Something had happened to change all that, though. Matt had heard dark rumours that there had been some incident between him and a lesser member of the royal family that had seen him compelled to resign from his job and grateful for whatever work he could find since. He had been a feature writer at *Bang It!* for the last two years.

Pete had invited Matt along to the photo shoot almost as soon as he walked in through the office door that morning. He'd barely had time to park his suitcases under his desk before Pete had whisked him back out of the office.

'Mag rules,' Pete had explained on their way to the shoot. 'We always get the rookies along to one of these as quick as possible, stops them wasting time they could spend working wondering exactly what goes on here. Truth is it gets a bit dull after a while, you've seen one pair you've seen them all – know what I mean?' Pete tossed his head back as he laughed. 'No of course you don't, it's the best job in the world! Play your cards right and I'll get you in on the next casting, that's when the models come in and we get them to strip off in the office for us. Sometimes, if it's a bloke's birthday or somebody's stag night, we hold a casting for them when there isn't even going to be a photo shoot. Brilliant, all these girls taking their clothes off for free, doing whatever we tell them without a clue that we're just having a laugh and there is no job at the end of it. Brilliant. When's your birthday?'

'Tomorrow?' Matt joked. This was it. This was his dream job: London, women, national-magazine journalism. This was what he had been working for, a room full of topless girls and a minibar in the corner. Some people might think that Matt was a little shallow – and he was one of them – but he didn't care. Maybe this wasn't the kind of reporting that he'd had in mind when he set out on his writing career, maybe he had envisioned himself writing hard news from the centre of the Gaza Strip, but life, his life, had brought him to the closed set of a photo shoot for *Bang It!* magazine, and as far as he could see there was no way a red-blooded man could complain about that.

Matt *had* been a little worried, as he entered the closed set in a photography studio in Ladbroke Grove, that he'd let himself down, that he'd drool, leer, lose the power of speech – or worse still get an unwelcome hard-on that would mean he'd have to cross his legs and stay seated until it abated, like that time when he was fifteen and Miss Clements had worn a particularly low top to school. He'd been forced to stay behind after the bell rang and string out a conversation with her about history, even though every time she smiled or moved it only made the situation worse.

As soon as he was on the set, though, Matt realised that if he had done any of those things, he would have been the only one to care. The girls walked about in nothing but G-strings, laughing and talking as if they were fully dressed, the photographer only took an interest in them when they were in front of the camera, and the make-up and hair girl, a pretty redhead called Carla, dusted their breasts with glitter with all the erotic tension of someone basting a turkey. Even Pete seemed more interested in checking his emails on his mobile than watching what was going on.

The real test came when during a break Lindsey, a twenty-one-year-old from Doncaster, came over to talk to him.

'You're from up north too, right?' she asked him with a pretty smile. Matt tried very hard not to look at her breasts, which was difficult, because they were big and naked. And breasts.

'Yeah, Manchester – just got off the train this morning actually. You been down here long?' He attempted nonchalance.

'Since I started uni last September.' Lindsey's voice was sweet and light, it didn't seem to fit with her impressive physique, which Matt knew had to be natural because *Bang It!* didn't do fake, it was magazine policy. 'It's all right once you get used to it – a lot like home really, only everyone's got a funny accent.' Lindsey laughed and her natural bosom jiggled in Matt's peripheral vision. He prayed to all the gods he could think of that he would not blush. When he was younger all the women he was really attracted to made him go red from the tips of his ears to the ends of his toes. He'd literally boil with embarrassment, finding it impossible to make conversation with a girl he liked, unable to believe that any woman would take him seriously, even as a candidate to buy her a drink, never mind as a prospective sexual partner. Matt was well into his twenties before he realised that actually women liked him, and he didn't even have to try that hard to make them. They thought he was funny, his girlfriends told him, charming and best of all good-looking. They went on about his thick dark hair and his intense blue eyes. Apparently he also had the kind of backside that a lot of women liked and one girl had told him he had the sexiest hands that she had ever seen, although Matt failed to see how hands could be sexy.

Gradually Matt's confidence had grown and with it, his success with the opposite sex. He liked testing his luck, seeing how far he could get with girls that should, by rights, be well out of his league – and finding that most women were accessible after all. All you had to do was make them laugh, look them in the eye and really listen to them. Or at least appear as if you were really listening to them. He'd started writing a column about his dating exploits for the paper he was working for as a music critic. It had started as a filler on the music-review pages one week when they didn't have quite enough column inches and advertising was down. It was meant to be a one-off, but loads of people emailed in, said they'd liked it, that it had made them laugh. Before he knew it, it was a regular thing. Friday and Saturday he'd be out on the pull with his mates, Monday he'd be writing it up for the paper. He never used the girls' real names, of course. Some of the things that happened, it was enough to make a grown man blush – only not him. Not any more – not since the day he realised that a woman hadn't made him blush in months and he believed that he was cured. But rarely were the girls he met already mostly naked, and he wasn't sure if gently jiggling all-natural 34 Gs might not set him off again.

'Just look at 'em,' Lindsey laughed, clearly amused by his dilemma.

'I beg your pardon?' Matt asked her.

'My tits – you know you want to – just go on and ogle 'em. You've been looking at them all morning anyway – get a good look now and we can carry on talking without you looking like you're fit to burst. Give 'em a grope if you like!' Lindsey's shoulders shook when she laughed and so did everything else.

Matt cringed and shook his head.

'Really, I don't want to . . .' Lindsey put the flat of her palms either side of his face and jerked his head downwards with enough force to pull a muscle in the back of his neck.

'It makes no difference to me, love,' she said, keeping Matt's head in position for a few seconds more, where he could not help but take in the impressive view. 'You fellers go all gaga over them, but to me they're just lumps of flesh – no more sexy than my elbows. They're paying my way through uni so that I don't end up thousands in debt and that's it.'

'Wha . . . what are you studying?' Matt was surprised to feel relieved at being allowed to look her in the eye again.

'Quantum Physics, I want to invent time travel one day,' Lindsey told him. 'So far I'm on track for a First, so not just a pretty pair, hey? Do you want to give 'em a feel?'

Matt could not have been more relieved when they were interrupted.

'Back on set please girls, we need to get your school ties on,' the photographer bellowed.

'God, I hate it when they make me wear a costume,' Lindsey joked, rolling her eyes. 'Nice to meet you, Matt, and just between you and me, you should ask Carla out for a drink – she's been eyeing you up since you got here.'

Matt watched as Lindsey strode back over to the set, slipped a tie over her head and then handled her fellow model as if she was assessing the ripeness of a pair of melons.

'So are you cured?' Pete asked him.

'Cured of what?' Matt said.

'Glamour models.' Pete nodded at the girls, who frolicked with each other with a most professional elan. 'They're usually better equipped than a lot of girls, but they're still just girls. They're not going to be ripping your clothes off and inviting you for threesomes in the back of limos – not these two. Lindsey's got a fiancé and the other girl, Donna – she'll take her clothes off but she won't shag you unless you take her out for dinner more than once! Sometimes it's like being thirsty in the middle of water, up to our elbows in tits all day long, but can't get your hands on a pair.'

Matt thought of Lindsey's offer and smiled to himself. 'Right,' Pete went on, 'today was your treat – your story to tell your mates back home – but your job is to be an average bloke and write about things average blokes want to know about, cars, footie, bands, gadgets and how to get girls, and on a weekly like *Bang It!* that means you've got to get cracking today. There's a features meeting now, don't go in without any ideas or your new god our editor Dan'll rip you to shreds. You'll need to have uploaded all your copy, which means your column and two features, to the features folder by Wednesday. We put the magazine to bed on a Thursday, we get bladdered on Thursday night and on Friday we start all over again. So remember, even though your job is to be Average Bloke, you're not. Average blokes don't spend all day around naked women, they spend all day thinking about them – which is why our magazine is the field leader in the weeklies and the boss liked your column so much. So you know where you stand until your probation is up? Work like a bastard or get dropped, there is no in-between.'

'Yeah – of course I'm up to it,' Matt said with a bravado that he didn't quite feel. 'I'm stoked that I've got a chance to write for a national magazine. I'm going to give it my all, Pete – I swear.'

'Good, let's get back to the office then and get you on some real work. I'll be five minutes while I just talk over the secretary brief with the talent. Nothing like a half-naked girl sucking on a biro, I always say.'

While he waited Matt noticed Carla leaning against a window-sill, powder brush in hand, the midday light igniting a fiery halo around her hair. She was about his age, maybe a couple of years younger, slender, with a nice figure under her shirtdress. OK, it was only his first day here and he had to move into his digs later, but apart from the other articles he had to write the first instalment of his column had to be ready in two days – he needed some material. He could recycle something old, or make something up, but Pete had just made it perfectly clear that he needed to impress from the start, and what could be more impressive than bagging his first London date on the day he arrived? Perhaps hitting on a girl through work was a bit of cheat, but Matt's motto was always to strike while the iron was hot. Never pass up an opportunity, he'd lectured his regular readers.

'Hiya.' He approached her, his smile warm and friendly – open and casual.

'Oh, hi.' Carla looked him briefly in the eye before studying her chipped fingernails.

'This is all a bit mad, isn't it?' Matt nodded at the models. 'You'd think it'd be a turn-on but to be honest I'm more interested in a touch of mystery, someone who's not so obvious.' He noticed a smattering of freckles scattered across the bridge of Carla's nose. She had painted her fair lashes black but he could just see their natural pale gold right at the very roots, where they met the near-translucent skin of her eyelids. It was these small vulnerabilities that really drew him to a woman, not how she was built, or how she looked. It wasn't the tricks a girl used to make herself look better that Matt went for, it was the frailties she failed to hide that really touched him. They all had them, even Lindsey from Doncaster, for as much as she'd caught him off guard with her easy bravado it had been the white patches behind her ears where she'd failed to fake-tan that Matt had especially liked about her.

'You don't really think that.' Carla looked sceptical, her light grey eyes narrowing. Matt tried to imagine her in the morning, her face clean of make-up. It was surprising how different some women could look in natural sunlight and without any cosmetic aids. Despite her profession Carla was wearing hardly any, and Matt liked that about her.

'Listen, it's my first night in town tonight. I'm moving into my new place later – but could I take you for a drink first? It'd be great to have someone show me around a bit.'

'Really? I mean yeah, OK, why not? A drink, yeah that would be good. Great – I mean fine, whatever.' A range of expressions from surprise to delight to studied nonchalance flitted over Carla's face within a fraction of a second.

Seeing her mobile peeping out of the top pocket of her dress, Matt fished it out, careful not to touch her. He punched his number into it and saved it under his name.

'Text me, yeah? Let me know where to meet you.' He slipped the phone back into the pocket, feeling more heat between the two of them in that second than he had for the whole time he'd been talking to Lindsey.

'Bye then.' Carla swept the bristles of her brush over the tips of her fingers, leaving them dusted with glitter.

'See you later,' Matt told her. 'Look forward to it.'

Matt followed Pete down the concrete stairs of the studio and out on to the bright street crammed with office workers, clamouring for lunch and a little midday sun before they chained themselves back to their desks.

'So you've got your eye on Carla, then?' Pete nodded in approval. 'Nice little arse on that one and not a bad pair for someone so skinny.'

'It's just a drink,' Matt laughed as he followed him into the back of a black cab.

'A likely story! You and I know the score, Matt, and let me tell you, you might not spend your afternoons rolling around with naked models but you mention to any pretty little blonde you meet in the pub who you work for, and chances are most of them will be all too happy to show you what they've got in the hopes that you'll get 'em on the next cover.'

'Pete – you don't decide that!' Matt grinned.

'I know that, you know that – but they don't.' Pete chuckled. 'Best job in the world, mate. Best bloody job in the world.'

Matt glanced at his watch and sat up. It was almost eight p.m. He'd told the woman on the phone that he'd be at his new lodgings by seven at the latest. It was time to go. Carefully he eased himself off the bed, hoping not to wake Carla.

'Where you going?' she murmured, rolling over and exposing one delicate pink-tipped breast.

'I'm moving into my new place tonight, remember I told you?' Matt smiled, bending over and kissing her freckled shoulder. 'We were going to have a couple of drinks and then they turned into doubles and we came back to yours for coffee to sober up and . . .'

'Well, we did sober up.' Carla leant up on her elbows, her tangle of auburn hair nestling on her shoulders, her black mascara spread under her eyes intensifying their pale blue hue. She stretched out two slender arms to him, cocking her head to one side and curling her mouth into the sweetest smile in her armoury. 'Do you really have to go?'

'I do,' Matt told her. 'I need to move in, I'm already late.'

71

'Well, I'll come with you then,' Carla offered, already pushing back the bedclothes and reaching for her discarded bra. 'Help you get moved.'

'I've only got a couple of cases,' Matt said, nodding at his luggage that he'd left in the hallway. There were two reasons he didn't want Carla to come with him. He didn't really want anyone to know that he was going to live with a widow and her kid. It wasn't exactly cool, it wasn't exactly the *Bang It!* lad lifestyle that Pete told him he had to embody. But it was the only place he had found close to work that he could afford and that wouldn't mean spending a fortune in travel costs. It would do for now, at least while he was still on six weeks' probation. Once the job was permanent and he knew he wasn't going to have to go back up north with his tail between his legs he'd look for somewhere more . . . bachelor-like.

The second reason was he didn't want Carla thinking that what had just happened meant anything, that the sex they had had would lead to a greater intimacy. Matt had broken his own rules. He hadn't told Carla upfront that he wasn't looking for a relationship, and that he wasn't ready to commit to one woman. He hadn't told her that he wasn't looking for a girlfriend, his usual firm disclaimer when he approached any woman. In theory his blunt honesty should have put girls off, but so far that had rarely happened. Women heard what he said, they shrugged their shoulders as if they didn't care – but almost all of them seemed to think secretly that he would change. That they would be the girl that would change him, one night with them and he'd be desperate to settle down, get a couple of kids and a dog. Almost without fail they were deeply upset when they realised that Matt never stuck around for more than a couple of weeks at the most.

72

When he'd remind them about his disclaimer they'd look bewildered and hurt, as if they really believed that a few nights of sex, a few days of laughing and kissing automatically meant the beginning of a grand romance. Sometimes Matt felt bad about letting them down, but at least he always had his declaration to hide behind – proof that he had not led them on. But in the heat of a moment saturated with vodka, he had forgotten to make his intentions clear to Carla.

'You should stay right there, relax,' he instructed her.

Carla flopped back on to the bed, stretching her arms above her head.

'If you insist,' she smiled happily. 'Today certainly turned out a lot better than I expected. Not that I do this sort of thing all time – never, actually. There was just something about you that seemed . . . right.'

'For me too,' Matt pulled his jacket on and sat briefly on the edge of the bed. 'You are a fantastic girl, Carla.'

He meant it. Carla was funny, beautiful, and warm and engaging in bed. She deserved someone a lot better than him.

'And life's for living, isn't it? I mean how boring would it be if no one ever took a chance . . .' Matt didn't reply, even though he knew Carla was looking for some sort of reassurance. Obviously going to bed with a man she had met only a few hours earlier wasn't normally her style, she wanted him to tell her that she hadn't made a terrible mistake.

'So when do you want to meet up again?' Carla went on after a moment's silence. 'I'm supposed to be hanging out with my girlfriends tomorrow, but I could cancel if you want?'

Don't do that, Matt thought. Don't just decide to change all your plans for me.

'I've got to work,' he told her, glancing at his watch. 'New boy – lot to prove. Need to deliver a kick-ass column.'

'Oh OK, no worries – well just call me when you're free then,' Carla said, a tiny frown line insinuating its way between her eyebrows.

'Sure. See you.' Matt got up and picking up his cases left hurriedly. He knew she'd be flopping back on the bed, her fingers in her hair, wondering what she'd done.

'Hello.' A boy opened the front door and greeted Matt without the faintest flicker of a smile. He was a good-looking boy, with bright eyes and oddly a smudge of lilac paint across the bridge of his nose. 'Are you Matt Bolton because if you are, you're late.'

'I know, I'm sorry,' Matt said, taken aback by the boy, suddenly very glad that the last remnants of the vodka he'd indulged in with Carla had receded to no more than a slight fuzziness around his temples. Somehow he got the feeling he was going to need all his wits about him. 'I got held up at work, you know.'

'What were you doing?' The boy questioned him closely, with slightly narrowed eyes. 'Were you interviewing Chloe Brand, voted Britain's sexiest babe – was she wearing a bra?'

'Wha . . . what?' Matt spluttered, glancing around him as if this was a trap set to catch him out. 'How do you know about Chloe?'

'This kid Harvey, from school, nicks his dad's copies of *Bang It!* out of the recycling and brings them to school. He charges us a quid a look. It's worth it though.'

'Christ!' Matt laughed. 'Does your mum know?'

'No, and she'd kill me if she did, she still thinks I'm a little boy. So anyway – were you?'

'No, I was not.' Matt shook his head. 'I don't do that sort of thing – no one really does. They take those photos somewhere else far away from the office and then a staff writer makes up the interview.'

'Really?' The boy looked disappointed. 'You mean Chloe isn't really a huge Arsenal fan, and she doesn't really love to watch a match wearing only the team strip and a pair of stilettos?'

'How old are you?' Matt asked him, peering through the crack in the door to take in what looked like an ordinary hallway of an ordinary home.

'Twelve, nearly,' the kid replied. Matt could tell that the nearly part was very important to him.

'Makes sense. I guess I was interested in the same things at your age. Guess I have been ever since.' Matt lowered his voice. 'Look, if you want to pay a pound a pop to look at your mate's mags that's your business, but all I do is write stuff, all the words that you and your friends probably never look twice at. My job's boring, mate, I promise you.'

'Oh.' Charlie looked disappointed, then perking up slightly he asked, 'Do you have a PS3?'

'Not on me,' Matt told him. 'I shared one with my old flatmate but I had to leave it behind when I moved. I've got a PSP though, and a DS – is that enough for you to let me in?' He nodded at the doorway.

'Spose,' the kid shrugged and stepped aside, yelling, 'Mum, he's here!'

A woman hurried out of a back room, wearing an oversized man's shirt and a pair of baggy jeans, her dark hair tied in a knot on her head. Like the boy she was spattered with lilac paint. She had the most remarkable pair of green eyes, like a summer meadow.

'Oh you must be Matt,' she greeted him, holding out a paint-covered hand. 'We were worried that you'd been mugged or got lost, it's a jungle out there. I'm Ellen and this is Charlie.' She placed a hand on Charlie's shoulder, who reflexively shrugged it off.

'No, no – nothing so interesting . . .' Matt thought briefly of Carla's closed eyes as he had kissed her, the setting sun turning her skin a shade of pale gold. 'Just caught up with work, first day and all that. Sorry, your sister Hannah, is it? She gave me your number, I should have called and let you know I'd be late.'

'Oh, of course not – I don't want you to think you have to keep me apprised of all your movements. I'm not that kind of landlady. To tell you the truth I have no idea what being a landlady is all about yet. I'm sort of making it up as I go along.'

She began to walk up the stairs, talking as she went, and Matt assumed that he was to follow her. 'I'm not sure what Hannah told you. You know what the rent is and that it includes bills. You'll get a key, of course, and a shelf in the fridge in the kitchen if you want one – it saves on labelling apparently – but there is room for a fridge in your room and a microwave if you like. Otherwise just come and go as you please.'

Slightly breathless as they reached the top of the stairs, Ellen pushed open the attic door and stood back, allowing Matt into the room first.

'There's a large bedroom, a loo and shower room. My husband and I always thought that . . .' She trailed off for a second to a moment in time that Matt couldn't fathom before

76

snapping back into the present. 'Anyway, I hope you like it.'

Matt walked into the room and looked around. It was large, almost the whole footprint of the sizeable house, with dormer windows on one side that looked out over the street and Velux windows on the other, letting in plenty of light. It was furnished with a somewhat elderly-looking double bed, a rather worn red sofa, a dark wood wardrobe and a desk. Through a door to the right Matt could see the shower and loo. It was basic, it was perfect.

'It's great,' he said, turning to Ellen and letting loose his smile.

'Oh, well – good.' Ellen dropped her eyes from his, tentatively touching her hair as if she had only just remembered that she had screwed it up into a careless knot sometime earlier. Matt noticed the pierced holes in her earlobes, redundant without earrings.

'Um, Matt . . .' He watched as Ellen's mouth undulated with uncertainty.

'Yep?' he asked her, offering an encouraging smile. She was probably somewhere in her thirties, pleasant-looking – rather the sort of woman who after getting married and having kids gives up on trying to attract men, because she just doesn't need to any more. Matt had to admit that he was relieved. After talking to the openly flirtatious sister he'd been a little concerned that his new landlady would be something of a temptation, the kind of temptation that it was usually a very bad idea to give in to and of course he invariably did. But as sweet as she seemed, there was nothing about this woman to tempt him. She was a widow and a mum: as far as Matt could see those two things defined her. There was no danger of entanglement here.

'Ellen, I'm hard to offend – tell me what you're worried about.'

'Well, it's just that you've met Charlie.' Ellen finally found the courage to look up at him again. 'He's at an impressionable age and well, it's only been a year since his dad died. I don't think he's even begun to work that out yet.'

'Must be tough.' Matt nodded. His own father had walked out on him and his mother when he had been a little younger than Charlie. The fact that his dad was still alive somewhere didn't ease the sense of bereavement that Matt had felt for a very long time.

'You won't . . . I mean you wouldn't . . .' Elle struggled to form a sentence. 'It's just Hannah told me a bit about your work and . . .'

'You want to know if I'll be parading topless models through the house and leading Charlie astray?' Matt asked her, thinking of her son's questioning of him a few minutes earlier.

'Well, yes, frankly.' Ellen's smile was bashful and Matt noticed the very fine crinkles that blossomed prettily around the corners of her eyes.

'No, I won't. I promise.'

'Of course you're a young man,' Ellen said, as if the twelve years between them were really a hundred and twelve. 'You'll want to bring friends back. A girl sometimes, maybe even girls.' She stressed the last letter of the sentence with a raised brow.

Matt could not help but grin as the colour rose in her cheeks.

'All I'm asking is that you be discreet – you know, in the shared parts of the house.'

'Of course,' Matt assured her. 'Look, Ellen, this is your home. I know that. Your sister told me what had happened and why you're taking in lodgers. I don't want to make things any more difficult for you. You'll hardly know I'm here, I swear.'

'Thank you,' Ellen said. 'I'm sorry. I don't mean to be rude or put you off or anything like that.'

'Don't be silly.' Matt picked up one case and dumped it on the bed, where it bounced once. 'You're a mum, looking out for your kid. I wouldn't expect any different.'

'Right, well if you want to come down and make yourself something to eat or drink then feel free. I've got to finish painting the dining room for my third lodger, I think Hannah told you about her. She's due in a few days.'

'Old lady who writes sex books, right?' Matt asked her as he unzipped his case and opened the wardrobe to find a selection of mismatched hangers.

'Well it's more like historical fiction, but anyway Charlie and I – and Sabine, that's our German guest – will be in there if you need us.'

Matt glanced at his watch. It had just gone nine.

'She's arriving in a few days, you say?'

'Yes, I know.' Ellen looked stricken. 'I'll be lucky if the paint's even dry. I had no idea it would take so long. Trouble was the patterned wallpaper kept on showing through. We're on our fourth coat now and it needs at least one more and apparently the room absolutely mustn't smell of paint by the time she arrives. Come to think of it, Simon hasn't even told me when her chaise longue is to be delivered yet . . .'

Ellen frowned, and the tiny crease between her brows deepened.

Matt pulled his work shirt off over his head, discarding it in a tangled heap on the bed. He fished a faded T-shirt out of his case.

'Sounds to me like you need a hand.' He grinned briefly at

Ellen before pulling the top over his naked torso. 'It's the room at the back, right?'

'Only if you're sure.' Her smile was uncertain.

'Sure I'm sure.' Matt trotted down the stairs and Ellen waited for a moment before following.

For some reason she felt more out of breath on her descent than she had on the way up.

Chapter Six

It was a moonless night and the road was pitch black, forcing Eliza to walk slowly, feeling for ruts and stones with her feet as she went. She'd been walking for near on an hour now, yet still she was barely more than a mile from the house.

Over and over again she pictured her uncle lying on the floor of his bedroom, his blood seeping outward in a great pool, running in rivulets down the gaps in the polished floorboards.

'You've killed him!' Eliza had gasped, her bosom heaving as she stared wide-eyed.

'I had to.' The captain sheathed his sword. 'I was protecting your honour, my love.'

'You!' Eliza spat the word at him, all too aware of her state of undress made worse by his roving eyes. She desperately tried to cover herself with the ripped shreds of her gown and her bare hands. 'You who took me and sullied me first now seek to protect my honour. Ha! You are like all Cavaliers, a hypocrite and a liar!'

The captain took a step towards her as she backed away from him, looking around for something to cover her modesty and halt the desire-fuelled touch of his gaze.

'Eliza – I know that I sinned against you and against God. I swear when I first set eyes on you I felt more passion in my blood and body than I

ever thought possible. I had a campaign to wage, a war to fight and yet I could think of naught else but your sweet temptation. You consumed me and I tried, I swear on my life I tried to resist you – but I failed. I know that I will burn in hell for the way I have mistreated, you but Eliza – I am not sorry. I would endure eternal torture for even a few more moments of you.'

'I am glad sir, because I will kill myself before I let you touch me again!' Eliza cried.

'Is that really so, my love?' the captain asked her, his voice low and dark. 'When I had you in my arms I'm certain I saw desire and passion in your eyes too. Yes, I wronged you, but you are a woman, Eliza – and you have a woman's needs.'

Eliza gasped in horror. Never, never would she admit to the feelings that had stirred so unexpectedly within her loins as the captain had taken his pleasure of her. To her disgust she had begun to look forward to the captain's visits. Until her uncle had come to 'rescue' her, that was.

'That is not true,' Eliza whispered unhappily, suddenly exhausted and confused by feelings she could not understand.

The captain looked disappointed.

'Well, your uncle attacked a captain of the King's army – the penalty for which is death. He is gone and you have no more to fear from him, nor his cruel wife. This house is mine now and I am its master and yours, whether you wish it or no. I have wronged you, Eliza, but now I intend to make things right. I swear I will not touch you again until you and I are married before God. Go to your room, dress yourself modestly. I will make you my wife in the morning.'

Eliza twisted out of his grasp and fled to the door.

'Marry you!' Her eyes burned. 'Never!'

'You will,' the captain told her. 'You have no choice, don't you see that?'

As soon as the house was quiet she had crept out of her bedroom window, climbing down the wisteria just as she used to when she was a carefree girl.

No matter what the captain said or how desperate things got Eliza would always have a choice, even if it was her own death. For now at least, though, she was on the road to freedom, and her heart pounded with the heady joy of it. Eliza had no idea what she would do, a lone young woman with no money or protection in a time of war, but she swore that anything would be better than being made to marry the man who had ruined her, a man whom she hated.

'Hold there!' Eliza jumped, shrieking, as she was stopped in her tracks. Out of the shadows a man on a huge black stallion appeared.

'What's a young lady such as yourself doing tramping the roads at night?' he asked her, his voice low and rough. 'If you're looking for trade then you're in luck, there's a tavern nearby and I'm in the mood for a good rutting.'

'No!' Eliza gasped. 'I am not a . . . I'm just a traveller.'

'Alone and unprotected?' the rider asked her with interest. 'How very foolish. Still, now at least I've no need to pay you for what I desire, have I?'

Ellen jumped when the alarm clock sounded, and the pages she had been reading slipped to the floor, skimming one over the other as they fluttered gracefully downwards. Her alarm was set for 6.30 a.m., but sleeping much beyond five in the morning was something that she had been a stranger to since she lost her husband. She'd stay up late, as late as she could, fighting the drag of her heavy lids to the very last second in the hope that she would eventually wear herself out enough to sleep through until morning. But no matter how hard she tried Ellen's nights had evolved into an exhausting routine. She'd drift off over a book somewhere around two, sleep for a few fitful restless hours and just before five her mind would jerk her awake with the panicked sensation that she had forgotten something. Her heart would be pounding in her ears, her eyes wide open as they adjusted to the dark, her weary mind seeking, against her will, to remember the terrible truth. Then it would all come back to her, and in those first seconds it would tear through her just as vividly and as painfully as it had when the poor young policewoman had first had to break the news. Nick was dead, she'd remember. Nick was gone, he was not asleep in bed beside her and he never would be again. She would never hear his voice, never feel his touch, never again listen to the sound of his breathing. And as that reality washed over her yet again with the cold indifference of a wave breaking over a rock Ellen would have to spend several moments gasping for air, fighting both for and against life, until her heartbeat slowed and she thought of Charlie, asleep in his bed. He would be wanting breakfast in a couple of hours and she would have a reason, her only reason, to get up.

It was then that she would turn to her latest book, losing herself with relief amongst its pages until her alarm clock sounded the official break of day.

Leaning over the edge of the bed, Ellen collected up the pages of the manuscript of Allegra Howard's latest work and carefully reordered them. She remembered with a shock that it was Thursday. Today was the day that Allegra was due to arrive at eleven, which meant midday, Simon promised her, as Allegra made it her business always to be an hour late for everything. Ellen was happy about that, though, it meant that hopefully the paint smells would all be gone and the chaise longue would be just about in situ. Against the odds she had got everything ready for her VIP guest, and even if it had taken the help of virtual strangers to do it, she was proud of herself.

The timing of Allegra's arrival could not have been better, as Ellen had just finished the last of the manuscript pages that

Simon had sent her. She smoothed the sheets of papers out against her thighs and wondered about the book. Ellen couldn't deny that she was enjoying it, every second that she had been immersed in Eliza's story she had been there with her, relishing the guilty pleasure of imagining herself as the fulsome young woman with an exquisite body and beauty to match. Yet in *The Sword Erect* the heroine had endured more ravishing than Ellen could remember in any other Allegra Howard novel, or indeed any book that she had worked on in the Cherished Desires list. She had only read up to page thirty-three, yet poor Eliza had had her body manhandled by three different men already in the space of barely a week!

Hannah had only been half wrong when she joked that books such as these were written to a formula of a sexual encounter every ten pages. Sexual passion and erotic fantasy were what the readers wanted, it was what Ellen wanted – but all the other things that she loved so much about Allegra Howard's books were missing so far. Ellen wanted the adventure, the danger, the sights, smells and sounds of a world and time gone by that Allegra conjured up so brilliantly and that made her novels more than just run-of-the-mill bodice rippers. Simon had said that Allegra was having trouble with this book, and he wanted Ellen to help her get it back on track. The problem was, how did you tell a person you admired so very much that you thought she was getting it wrong? Particularly when all that qualified you to comment was that you enjoyed reading the author's work.

Ellen sighed as she leaned back against her pillow. Imagine having your person made free with three times in one week by different men, she thought, with a wistful edge that took her by surprise. All that interest in her bosom must be terribly gruelling for poor Eliza, but if Ellen knew Allegra at all then she could be fairly certain that her heroine would escape the clutches of this latest rake with little more than some unwanted kisses and fondling. Allegra put all her heroines in sexual danger but they only actually ever had sex with one man, and by the end of the book they'd be not only in love with him but married to him too, so that the usually inappropriate way that they first became physically acquainted (Allegra never used the word rape) would be happily absolved. Still, three men in one week driven to a frenzy of desire by your mere proximity – at least it meant that Eliza knew she was alive, that the world took notice of her when she passed by. The world went on outside Ellen's window and she had very little to do with it at all. Most of the time that was just the way she liked it, but every now and then she'd wonder how it would be to be more like Eliza – or even Hannah. To live life as if the world revolved around you and you had every right to expect that it danced to your tune. Now this house was her world, because it had been Nick's world too – and in many comforting ways it still was.

Ellen looked around her bedroom. It was exactly the same as it had been a year ago, stripped and varnished floorboards, covered here and there with faded rugs patterned with roses, an ornate oval Victorian mirror that Nick had bought her hanging over the solid pine dressing table he'd spent an age stripping down just after they had moved in. The wardrobe was still full of his clothes, the drawers still crammed with his things. There was still a dirty shirt in the laundry basket that Ellen could not bring herself to wash. And it wasn't just this room that was still so full of Nick, every room in the house was stamped with a presence that was still so strong it was almost tangible. Nick had laboured long and hard over this late-Victorian house, spending all his spare time stripping off layer after layer of inappropriate wallpaper, finding just the right light fixtures and ceiling roses to replace what had been ripped out when period detail wasn't so fashionable. It was Nick who'd dragged home the three small cast-iron grates that now sat comfortably in the fireplaces he'd exposed when ripping out plasterboard. He lavished the kind of attention on this house that he had on Ellen when they had first met, and she remembered for a time feeling a little jealous of the hours he spent lovingly blacking his newly acquired grates, his fingers caressing their organic curves as they had once caressed hers, but now she was glad that he had spent so many months making the house his own. It was as if he still existed here in every nook and cranny.

Ellen thought of the world outside her window, Thornfield Avenue, a quiet enough tree-lined street of Victorian houses just a stone's throw from Shepherds Bush Market and now Europe's largest shopping centre, Westfield – although she had never felt the urge to venture there despite Charlie's tales of the endless retail and junk-food opportunities that he and his friends had discovered. Nick had chosen this road as the location of their home not only because he'd fallen so in love with the dilapidated old house but because it had been residents' parking only, and a bus that went straight to a good school passed regularly at the bottom of the road. When they had first moved there Ellen had wheeled Charlie round the market in his buggy every day it was open, more just to see the colours, hear the noises and smell the smells than anything else. It had been a long time since they had done that together; now she was content to get everything she needed delivered to her door.

A sudden breeze wafted in through the crack in the sash window that she had left open through the night in concession to the stifling heat, carrying with it the scent of privet hedge and hot tarmac that brought her instantly back to that last morning with Nick.

He'd been sitting on the edge of his bed fussing about which underpants to put on.

'Does it matter?' Ellen remembered laughing, stroking his back. 'Who's going to see them but me?'

Nick had twisted to smile at her over his shoulder. 'I always promised my granny that if they ever had to scrape me up off a road I wouldn't bring shame on the family. Seriously, I've got this big meeting today – I think a man should be dressed to impress from the inside out.'

'Do you have to get up right now?' Ellen had asked him tentatively. Seduction was not one of her natural talents, and she had been unthinkingly brushed off by Nick enough times in the past to feel all the more hesitant about suggesting they share some intimate moments together.

'Yep,' Nick said, standing up, pulling the chosen pair of boxers over his buttocks. 'Lots to do today, love.' He'd bent and kissed her on the forehead before retreating to the bathroom to shave.

If only he'd taken the hint, Ellen thought wistfully. If only she'd been a little more brazen and bold and if when he'd turned to smile at her he'd been able to discern the look in her eye. If only he'd kissed her on the lips instead of the forehead, if only she'd wound her arms around his neck and kissed him back. Then at least she would have had one more memory of him, one more memory of what it felt like to have his arms around her, his lips on her neck, the sound of his breath in her ear. But none of that had happened, he'd walked out the door a few minutes later and had never come back.

Ellen lifted up the neck of her nightshirt and peered shyly down at her breasts. They were rather fulsome too, if not quite the perfectly pert twin moons that Allegra seemed to give all her heroines. They were still a nice shape though, still firmish and high due to a lifetime of sensible bras, and Ellen was secretly proud of them, although she did not feel the need to squeeze every inch of cleavage out of them and put it on display that her sister did. Nick had loved her breasts, he had loved all of her body, and when they were first married his adoration had made her glory in the swell of her bottom, the reach of her hips and the girth of her thighs. Ellen closed her eyes as she remembered the touch of her husband's fingertips dragging slowly over the rise and fall of her curves, his lips following in their wake. They had not made love nearly so frequently in what turned out to be the last few years of their marriage, but Ellen had accepted that, albeit regretfully, supposing that after ten years the passion and urgency that Nick had once felt for her was bound to wane somewhat, even if she still longed for him as much as she had the first time they had met. In fact, if she remembered correctly, which she knew she did, on the day that WPC Henderson and her colleague had walked up her garden path to break the bad news it had been almost six months since the last time. And now, now there would be no next time.

Slowly Ellen let her own fingertips travel upward over the thin cotton of her nightshirt. For a brief second, for the first time in a year, she allowed herself to imagine that it was Nick who was touching her, his fingers that gently massaged her body, his lips that teased her skin, his eyes that looked up at her . . .

Ellen sat up abruptly and snatched her hands away from herself, leaping out of bed as if she'd just discovered she'd been sharing it with something awful.

Flustered, she pulled one of Nick's shirts on over the same pair of jeans she had been wearing yesterday and, unable to locate her brush, ran her fingers roughly through her tangled hair. Coffee, she decided, what she needed was coffee, that would wake her up properly because what had just happened had been a sort of waking dream, not the thoughts of her conscious mind at all – not anything that she could have controlled. Ellen scowled as she headed barefoot downstairs, furious and embarrassed.

It hadn't been Nick's face she had seen, looking up at her, when she closed her eyes. It had been her latest lodger's – it had been Matt's.

Matt stared at his Mac screen and waited. This was his only his third full day in the office, and there was no time for special excursions today – it was press day. He had finished his piece on the exploits of a group of travelling England football fans, and written a review of the latest superhero flick that he hadn't exactly seen. But he still hadn't filed his column and the deadline was fast approaching. Apparently Dan the editor had said that the title Matt had used for his *Manchester Evening Post* column was not catchy enough and it didn't capture the spirit of *Bang It!*. Pete and Matt had kicked a few ideas around and then Pete had come up with an idea he loved so much that it was clear no further discussion was needed. Matt's new column in

Bang It! would be called 'Wham Bam! A Single Bloke's Guide to Sex in the City.'

Matt told himself this title had to be ironic, but in truth there wasn't that much about *Bang It!* that was ironic, except maybe the equal opportunities policy. Still, as Pete said, as long as there were girls who chose to take their kit off for money then he was all for equality.

The cursor hovered on Matt's empty Mac screen. He looked around: the office was quiet – for once everyone had their heads down struggling to make that deadline. Pete said it was always like this. On Monday everyone was casual, relaxed still. They'd often have that week's features meeting in the pub, or at the very least get the beers in and sit around talking about ideas with their feet up. The magazine staff would be messing about, looking up stuff on the Internet, inventing some new kind of office-based game – Matt had taken part in his first desk-to-chair Olympic 10-metre dash. Tuesday, things began to move. Wednesday everybody remembered they had a job and by Thursday there was no time for fooling around any more, serious work got done and in the run-up to deadline apparently the place went frantic.

'Don't be late with any of your copy if you want to make it past your probation period,' Pete had warned him. 'Dan doesn't put up with that.'

That was exactly what Matt was worried about. He'd been apprehensive about running into Carla since their encounter on Monday – but then he'd realised that she was freelance, not a staff member, and that if she ever worked for *Bang It!* again it would be on some photo shoot where hopefully he would not be. The chances of him bumping into her were slim. But what should he do about her? He should call her, he should at least explain to her that although he'd had a great time with her, and that she was a lovely girl, he wasn't ready for anything serious, especially not when he'd just arrived in London. The trouble was if he rang her up and told her that she'd probably say she was cool with it, she'd probably suggest they got together, no strings attached, and then after a week or two she'd want more. She'd want to plan stuff, make dates more than twenty-four hours in advance. She'd want to introduce him to her friends, expect him to be available every Saturday night and hang out with her every Sunday. And, if he reminded her that was not what they had agreed at all, she'd cry and get upset and tell him that she thought things had changed, that she meant something to him. Inevitably he'd end up hurting her. No, if he rang her, if he slipped into that mistake he'd be breaking his own rules, and leading her on. And before you knew it she'd be thinking she was in the dreaded 'r' word with you, no matter how clear you were that you weren't up for it.

He could visualise exactly what his first column should be, cocky Jack the Lad steps off the train and into a hot girl's bed. He should write about his technique, how he'd made the moves on Carla, how he'd let her think it was her plan to get drunk in the June sunshine and her idea to drag him back to her place. He'd lie about how voracious she had been in bed, transforming their brief encounter from one that had been sweet and hesitant to a passion-fuelled frenzy of lusty sex. He'd have to boost Carla's assets by a couple of cup sizes and make her a good deal more experienced in certain areas than she was, too.

Still it did seem a bit much, even for him, to write about a girl quite so soon after the event. Especially a girl like Carla, who wasn't out looking for casual sex, who'd been caught unawares in what Matt thought was probably an uncharacteristic bout of spontaneity.

His mind made up, he took his laptop out of his bag and opened up the file where he saved all his columns. He found one of his very first pieces and sent it to the desktop of his Mac. Rehashing an old piece was not how he wanted to begin his career at *Bang It!*. And he was well aware that if Pete or Dan found out then he could be ending it before it even began, but whether or not he wanted to see Carla again he had liked her. He liked her enough not to turn her into trash. Not just yet.

'So you nailed the little make-up girl on your first day then?' Pete arrived at his desk in a fug of sweat and cigarette smoke. 'Impressive.'

'A gentleman never talks.' Matt gave him a well-practised 'of course I did' smirk.

'No need to be coy about it, it's all over the place. She told Suze, Dan's PA, and Suze told everyone else.'

'Really?' Matt shifted in his seat. Carla wasn't as comfortably distant as he had hoped after all.

'She raved about you, mate – you never put "gentle and considerate lover" on your CV.' Pete chuckled to himself, catching the eye of Raffa, who grinned in reply.

'Bollocks!' Matt's reaction was instinctive. 'She was mad for it, mate, practically dragged me off the street. I didn't have a chance to be gentle or considerate, she had my kit off in less than a minute – and hers! That girl was ravenous!'

'Any good?' Pete asked him flatly. 'You'll have to tell Keith in production, he's been trying and failing to get in her knickers for weeks, poor sod. Reckons he *really likes her.*'

'Mate, top marks for enthusiasm.' Matt winked. 'Besides, we

93

all know there are some things that it's difficult to get wrong, know what I mean?'

Pete and the layout guy laughed.

'So, you going to see her again?'

'No, it was just for fun, she knows that.'

'You sure?' Pete asked him. 'Suze seems to think she thinks you're the next big thing in her life.'

Matt shrugged. 'I just got here, I'm not looking for anything serious, I told her that upfront.'

'Well, you've got an office full of people waiting to read your write-up. You know what? You should award her marks out of ten – that would be a laugh.'

'Great idea,' Matt said. 'Will do.'

He watched Pete walk away and after a moment closed the column he'd been about to rewrite. He had no choice now. He'd have to start from scratch.

Chapter Seven

'She's a freak,' Charlie hissed as he peered at Allegra Howard through the kitchen window. 'And she makes the house smell funny.'

'She is not a freak and don't use that word!' Ellen chided him. 'She's an old lady and she smells of lavender. Admittedly rather a lot of lavender.'

She crinkled her nose. Allegra's scent did rather more than linger in a room once she left it – it pulled up a chair and made itself at home.

'A freakish amount of lavender, one might say, hey Charles?' Hannah put in, digging Charlie in the ribs, the pair of them giggling like conspirators.

Ellen pursed her lips at her sister. Hannah had arrived just after five, at the same time as Sabine, suggesting she treated everyone to takeaway, which had caused Charlie to question her on who exactly she meant by everyone, was she including Matt and the old woman for example? And would it be OK if he still had fish fingers?

Hannah had extended her largesse to whoever might care to join them. Ellen knew the main reason her sister would leave work any earlier than nine p.m. was that she wanted to nose.

Hannah hadn't met Matt in person yet, and it often seemed to Ellen that her sister was determined to meet and greet in person every member of the male of the species on the planet. She would also be dying to see how Ellen would cope with the elderly whirlwind that was Allegra Howard. Ellen also suspected that because the lodgers idea was her own, Hannah felt that she had some ownership of it, some responsibility to make sure it went smoothly, so that her sister wasn't suddenly overburdened. Hannah seemed to pop up here every five minutes. If she came round any more Ellen would be tempted to charge *her* rent.

'She's old and set in her ways,' Ellen reiterated. 'And a very keen gardener by the looks of things. She's been out there ages now. Pruning.'

Ellen had been fraught with nerves when Allegra finally arrived with Simon at almost three in the afternoon.

'Ellen, darling.' Simon had greeted her with a huge hug, lightly kissing both her cheeks. 'Sorry we're late, Allegra had a little trouble deciding what to bring and what to leave in storage, we spent two hours deliberating over her Staffordshire china dogs.' He winked, stepping aside to reveal Ellen's new employer.

'May I introduce you to Miss Howard?'

Allegra Howard did not look at all as Ellen had expected. The publicity shot that graced all her book covers was dated and soft-focused in the extreme. It showed a smooth-skinned blonde woman of indeterminate middle age, tenderly holding a single rose against her cheek, while gazing into the distance with a faraway look in her eye, as if at that very second she was dreaming up her next best-seller.

Simon had already warned her that that photo had been taken

a long time ago, but still Ellen had expected Allegra to be dressed head to foot in some chiffon affair, her aged skin caked with too much make-up, her hair brittle with dye and lacquer. It was a cliché and an unfair one.

Allegra was a neat, stylish-looking woman, wearing a lilac suit and low beige heels, with her silver-blonde hair tied into a frail chignon on her neck. Apart from an ostentatious triple string of pearls around her neck, fastened with a ruby-set clasp, and three large diamond rings on her fingers, you might never have guessed that she was a best-selling author of lusty romantic fiction with the kind of commercial success that any writer would envy. Her genteel appearance had a rather aristocratic air.

'M . . . Miss Howard,' Ellen stammered. 'I'm so thrilled to meet you, I'm such a huge fan.'

'Nonsense, you are not a fan, writers do not have fans. You are a reader, a follower or an admirer. I do not approve of fans, such a garish word. And I insist you call me Allegra. Just because one is great, one does not expect special treatment. May I see my room now? I do hope it's south-facing, I did instruct Simon that it had to be south facing but he seemed to have forgotten.'

'Um, I *think* it is,' Ellen had said nervously as she led Allegra into the former dining room. 'It always seems to be sunny in here.'

Ellen held her breath as Allegra looked around the freshly painted room, terrified that the shade of lilac would be wrong, the chaise longue would not meet approval, or that despite her leaving the French doors open since seven that morning, the faintest smell of paint would be detectable to that elegant aquiline nose.

'I'd say south-westerly, wouldn't you Simon?' Allegra arched a pencilled brow, the corners of her mouth dropping minutely.

'Still it will do, it will do – which is more than I can say for those roses, what a disgrace!' Ellen had watched anxiously from the doorway, stricken as her new lodger stepped out on to the patio, its cracks filled with grass and weeds. Allegra shook her head at the unkempt and overburdened rose bushes that had once surrounded the windows so decorously, but now still endured the mouldering deadheads of a summer long gone.

'I must have beauty and order to work – all this chaos simply will not do. Bring me your secateurs, my dear, I must remedy this immediately. Fortunately I brought my own gardening gloves. You see, Simon dear, I was correct – one never knows when one might be required to handle foliage.'

Ellen had been frozen to the spot for a second, quite unable to remember if she even had secateurs, let alone where they were. Finally she realised that they would be hanging on a rusty nail in the shed at the bottom of the overgrown garden, its door probably jammed shut by inches-high grass and an invasion of convolvulus and its musty interior inhabited by various large and unchecked spiders. Ellen had not ventured down there in the longest time, the desire to prune her roses the very last thing on her mind. Feeling utterly inadequate, she remembered a pair of kitchen scissors that she thought might do the job and rushed to bring them to Allegra's newly gloved hands.

Allegra examined her offering with her neatly painted lips pressed into a thin line of disapproval and disappointment, but nevertheless she accepted them.

'If you'd bring me some tea, I'd be grateful,' she instructed Ellen. 'Oh and before you go you should know I'll take breakfast at seven thirty every morning in my room, a soft-boiled egg and wholemeal toast, no crusts, thinly spread unsalted butter. Before

ten I only drink English breakfast tea and whole milk, after ten
Earl Grey. I begin work at ten, break for a light lunch at one and
then recommence until five. I take dinner between six and seven
thirty and I retire by nine thirty every night. Simon will furnish
you with a copy of my eating plan, but you should know that I
do not eat red meat. We took the liberty of bringing the
ingredients of tonight's meal with us, but from now on I will
expect you to do all the marketing.' She looked at Ellen as if she
expected a response.

Ellen stared at her dumbfounded as Allegra's instructions
finally sank in.

'Oh, oh! You mean you want me to cook your meals too?'

'You have accepted the position of my personal assistant,
have you not?' Allegra enquired.

'Yes, but I thought . . .' Ellen floundered for a second,
realising that it was pointless debating with Allegra. Either she
was going to accept the old lady with all her needs and foibles or
she was going to have to ask her to leave, and the latter was
unthinkable.

Ellen glanced at Simon who shot her a rueful look, mutely
apologising for not telling her quite as much as he should have
done.

'Of course, whatever you say,' Ellen said hastily. 'It's just –
well I'll need some time in the week to work on the other
manuscripts that Simon gives me.'

'I beg your pardon?' Allegra looked horrified. 'You mean to
work on other writers' material while working on mine? Oh no,
no, no. I can't have that. Simon, this will not do at all.'

'Oh, no – Allegra, Ellen is mistaken and it's entirely my fault.
I don't think I explained to her that from now all the work she

does for Cherished Desires will be exclusively for Allegra Howard.' He smiled at Ellen. 'That's OK with you, isn't it, Ellen? You won't be losing out financially and of course you need to concentrate your mind entirely on Allegra's work in progress.'

'Yes, why deal with dross, my dear, when you can work with gold,' Allegra added.

'Not that Allegra is implying that my stable of writers aren't anything but wonderful,' Simon countered.

'Aren't I?' Allegra winked at Ellen, who was so taken aback by the gesture that she was momentarily at a loss. It seemed there was a sense of humour lurking somewhere underneath this grand facade.

'Well of course, I'd be delighted to just work on your books, they are after all my favourites.'

'Excellent.' Allegra smiled approvingly. 'Tea, then – while I marshal the nature that you have let rampage so wilfully.'

Simon followed Ellen into the kitchen, where he found her considering her PG Tips, wondering if they would do until she could stock up on Earl Grey.

'Don't look so alarmed,' he told her, gently resting his hands on her shoulders and turning her to face him. 'That woman, that's not the real Allegra. She's just old, and a bit lost and out of sorts. She's missing her home and her routine, poor old bird, she's just hiding it all behind that battleaxe out there. All this is as frightening for her as it is for you. I'm sure that once she settles in you and she will become great friends and she'll stop talking to you as if you're the help.'

Ellen relaxed as she looked into Simon's warm amber eyes. He had a knack of settling her down, washing calm over her with a few simple words. It was one of the reasons that she liked working for him so much. Nothing in life seemed to faze him and his confidence and optimism were somehow contagious, making you believe that the world was a much simpler place – at least while you were in his company.

It was a shame that Simon had yet to find anyone special in his life, Ellen mused. A tall, good-looking man like him, well dressed, all his hair still intact, financially secure, even in these difficult times, deserved the right person to love him. Perhaps Hannah was right, perhaps Simon didn't want that. Perhaps he chose a series of brief encounters rather than anything more, seeking out embraces in the dark, passionate kisses stolen under moonlight, names rarely exchanged, just a few moments of pleasure and then . . .

'Goodness me, Ellen Woods, what are you thinking?' Simon asked, cocking an amused brow.

'What, why?' Ellen pulled away from him, pressing the back of her hand to her cheek.

Simon studied her face closely. 'Just for a second there you looked like a smouldering, smoky-eyed siren planning your next seduction!'

'Me? Nonsense, I was thinking about cooking for Allegra, you idiot!' Ellen laughed nervously. 'Honestly Simon, you and I spend too much time reading romantic fiction. We must remember that real life is much more mundane.'

She turned to pour boiling water into the teapot that she had found languishing at the back of the crockery cupboard, hoping the rising steam would be reason enough to explain away the colour in her cheeks. Whatever had come over her? First that incident this morning and now this? What was happening to her? Months, years, if you counted her all-but-redundant sex life with Nick, of an essentially sexless existence, and now a rebellious streak was catching her unawares at every turn, mentally undressing more or less every man in sight, which amounted to only two, thankfully.

It was the upheaval, Ellen told herself. All the changes were upsetting her equilibrium, together with the particularly high ravish count in *The Sword Erect*. Once she had settled herself down to working with Allegra, her brain would be properly occupied and thoroughly distracted from all the sorrow and anguish that had dwelt there for so long. It might even become a quiet and peaceful place once again, concerned only with the small things. The details that so many other people missed but Ellen loved to pore over.

'So do you think Allegra would like special fried rice or noodles?' Hannah broke Ellen's train of thought.

'Neither, she is having . . .' Ellen picked up one of the recipes that Allegra had provided. 'A supreme of grilled chicken with steamed broccoli and new potatoes – and so are we. Simon brought enough to feed a small army, so I thought I might as well cook it for Charlie and me too.'

'Not me,' Charlie said. 'I'm having fish fingers.'

'Yes but I thought that tonight you might like a change?' Ellen suggested. 'You know, we're starting a new chapter in our lives and I thought you might feel like eating something new too, for a change.'

'I thought you said what I eat isn't a problem?'

'I did and it's not, it's just . . .'

'No, you know I don't like chicken or broccoli or any of that stuff. I'll have fish fingers. I can do it myself if you can't be bothered.'

'Of course I can be bothered, it's just I thought you might . . .'

'It's not that big a deal is it, sis?' Hannah asked her, slinging an arm around Charlie's shoulder.

'I just said it wasn't, didn't I?' Ellen snapped. She took a breath and forcibly lightened her tone. 'I'll do you some fish fingers now. Sabine, would you like to join us for dinner? There's plenty to go round.'

'Ooh yes please,' Hannah replied, before Sabine could answer. 'I'll get a couple of spare chairs from the shed.'

'Quick, she's coming in!' Charlie hissed, as if he expected them all to hide.

Allegra opened the back door and peeled off her gloves, glancing around the room.

'I've done my best but someone will need to clear up the debris,' she told Ellen. 'I don't do bending.'

'Thank you, Allegra, you didn't have to.'

'Ah, but I did,' Allegra told her reproachfully.

'Let me introduce you to my son, Charlie. And this is Sabine, she has the room above yours, and this is my sister Hannah.'

Allegra nodded stiffly at each in turn. 'I'll take dinner in my room. I like to listen to the radio in the evenings.'

Just as she was about to exit she collided with Matt who all but took the poor woman off her feet, only saving her from falling by catching her in his arms.

'Oh I am so sorry,' Matt told her as he released her. 'Are you all right?'

Ellen watched in disbelief as Allegra beamed at Matt, her face

103

lighting up with a smile that instantly peeled a good twenty years off her age.

'Please don't worry, it's not every day a woman of my age is swept off her feet,' she told him sweetly.

'What, thirty-five?' Matt's compliment was quite without guile. Allegra fluttered her lashes.

'So you are the young man Ellen told me about? Matthew Bolton?'

'I suppose I must be, unless it's young Charlie here you need to watch out for.'

'And you are a writer too?' Allegra asked him. 'You are, I can see the creative fire in your eyes.'

'That might be the two pints I had on the way home.' Matt grinned at her.

'How charmingly male,' Allegra said, placing the flat of her hand against his cheek. 'One quite misses the scent of testosterone in one's life. Ellen, I think we might model our hero on this dashing young man, I think he might be quite an inspiration.'

Ellen thought of Captain Parker, dark, moody and dashing, and looked at Matt, blonde, sexy and full of light, and couldn't see the comparison.

Allegra patted his cheek and then, coquettish as a girl, glanced over her shoulder and waved at him as she left the room.

'Top old lady.' Matt grinned round at the others.

'She liked you, that was for sure,' Hannah laughed, extending her hand. 'You are quite the charmer. I'm Hannah, Ellen's sister by the way, we spoke on the phone.'

'So now we are complete.' Sabine smiled approvingly.

Matt looked from Hannah to Sabine. A tall leggy redhead, sexily dressed, with the kind of look in her eye that if he'd met her in a pub or a bar he would have taken as a challenge, and a shorter curvier blonde, with what looked like a slamming body under her sensible work clothes. And both of them off limits, that was if he were to stick to his second rule, which he was determined to do this time. Never mess with girls you have to see on a regular basis. Not flatmates, not work colleagues (he didn't count Carla as one of those) and not friends' girlfriends. Especially not friends' girlfriends, he'd learned that from bitter experience. It was one of the reasons his PS3 was still in Manchester.

'You joining us for dinner, Matt?' Hannah asked him. 'There's plenty to go round.'

'Really? If you're sure, that would be great. I haven't had a chance to get to the supermarket yet.'

'That's OK isn't it, Ellie?'

Ellen pursed her lips. 'Well, not if you stay, Hannah – I might have exaggerated a bit about the small army. I've only got four portions.'

'You could have a fish-finger sandwich with me?' Charlie offered.

'Brilliant, if you're sure?' Matt looked at Ellen.

'Of course. I'll put the grill on.'

'Tell you what, I'll do the fish fingers in payment for the sarnies.' Matt beamed at her, taking the grill pan out of her hands and heading for the freezer.

Ellen watched him covertly as he rifled through the freezer drawers, and tried to imagine him in tight breeches and a white shirt open to the navel, with ruffled sleeves that fell over his knuckles. Turned out it wasn't quite as difficult as she had thought.

Chapter Eight

Ellen sat in her chair at the kitchen table, watching the clock ticking towards three a.m on Saturday morning, sipping camomile tea by the light under the units. She was wondering if she needed to do something practical in her new capacity as landlady, perhaps draw up a bathroom rota to make her look as if she were capable and in charge of this house that was newly brimming with strangers, but she realised such a rota would be pointless. Matt had his own shower room, she had her own en suite, Allegra's knees meant that she wouldn't be venturing upstairs and preferred to attend to her toilette in the downstairs loo. Nick had squeezed a shower in this little room for when he came back from his runs, and sometimes when he got in very late at night and didn't want to disturb Ellen. And as for the main bathroom, Charlie so seldom went near it voluntarily that Sabine might as well have called it her own. Still, Ellen felt there should be something that she should be doing rather than merely sitting back and letting these people simply be here. It was just that she couldn't think of anything, and perhaps that was a blessing, because she had the distinct feeling that working for Allegra Howard was going to take up an awful lot of her time. The old lady was rather . . . demanding.

Cupping her mug of warm tea in her hands, Ellen relived her first day of working for Allegra, and what had followed. It hadn't gone *quite* as she had expected . . .

She had brought Allegra breakfast right on schedule, and had found her already reclining on her chaise longue, neatly dressed in a pale lilac skirt and white blouse, open at the neck. Her fine hair had been expertly whipped into a chignon, her skin powdered and her lips coated with the kind of dry orangey-red lipstick that looked like it went out of production in the 1950s. Ellen could not imagine how long it would have taken Allegra to put together such a glamorous appearance. She had been up since six thirty herself, rousing Charlie for school and choosing something to wear that seemed appropriate for Allegra Howard's research assistant, deciding that supermarket jeans and a second-hand man's shirt simply wouldn't do. Finally she had settled on a faded khaki linen skirt that she had found languishing at the back of the wardrobe and a once-white T-shirt, now mainly grey, but at least designed for a woman to wear.

She'd felt self-conscious as she'd showered, aware of the other people in the house, the sound of Sabine's TV as she caught up with the markets around the world before she went into work and Charlie skulking about in his room, refusing to make an appearance until at least five minutes after he should have left, whereupon he would grab a piece of white toast from Ellen and munch it as he walked down the street. Most disconcertingly, she was aware, as she stood in the shower, letting the warm water run in rivulets over her shoulders and breasts, of the sound of Matt's shower draining away above her and the fact that he was standing naked over her head at that very second.

Ellen had switched the shower to cold and rubbed herself briskly dry, hoping to chafe off all her foolishness along with her dead skin cells. Something about having Matt in the house, together with reading Allegra's latest work, had combined to create these . . . very stupid, very foolish feelings. They weren't even feelings, they weren't even glimmers of feelings. It was just that Matt was a young attractive man, and she was a lovely woman who hadn't had any kind of meaningful male contact since long before Nick had died.

Her body had responded to his proximity, just as a flower opens its petals to the morning sun. These little flutters of desire that she felt when she looked at him, or thought about him, were physiological reactions, nothing more serious than sneezing when you get something up your nose. That was the reason behind all this foolishness. That, and that she had seen him with his top off.

In any case she would soon build up an immunity to him, just as she did to her mother's cat whenever she went home to visit and sneezed her head off for the first hour at least. The rush of blood to her cheeks whenever Matt looked at her, and the hazy half-remembered dreams, would fade away like a crop of hives.

Ellen considered her flushed face in the mirror, her cheeks still ruddy from the cold water, her eyes bright with the prospect of something to do. In the meantime she might as well enjoy these unfamiliar feelings. A harmless secret crush on a man a million miles out of her league wasn't hurting anyone, and while a part of her felt a little as if she were being unfaithful to Nick for even thinking about another man, another very tiny dark part of her that she was barely aware of was immensely relieved that she was still capable of feeling anything at all.

Allegra had examined her breakfast without comment, and dismissed Ellen with a single wave of her hand.

'Return at ten and we will begin,' she had instructed her.

Ellen had returned to the kitchen where she sat silently as Matt rushed around, pouring coffee down his throat in a single gulp and panicking about where he had left his mobile phone, until she noticed it on the windowsill. And just as Sabine popped her head around the door to say goodbye and before Charlie came crashing through to grab his daily bit of toast, Matt had bent his head and kissed her on the cheek, calling her a star.

Then all at once the kitchen was empty again, and Ellen was left alone with the sound of her heart pounding in her chest. She couldn't decide if it was the kiss on the cheek, the compliment or the fact that in a few minutes she was due to start her new job. Or perhaps it was the shock of having her peaceful house full of strangers and life, talking, eating, laughing out loud. No, shock wasn't the right word. What she felt was surprise, the surprise of finding that she rather liked it.

'So.' Allegra had repositioned herself on her chaise longue, her legs up, neatly crossed at the ankle. She motioned for Ellen to sit herself behind the burr walnut desk that Simon had arranged to be brought in. 'You've read the first few chapters of *The Sword Erect*. Your opinion?'

'Oh.' Ellen sat rather nervously on the amber-coloured leather of the heavily padded desk chair, thinking of the departure of the last PA over – what was it? – artistic differences? 'You want *my* opinion? On . . . on *your* book?'

'Well I certainly don't want it on the price of eggs.' Allegra scowled at her. 'Of course I want your opinion on my book.

Simon told me you have read all of my books – how does *The Sword Erect* compare?'

'Well . . .' Ellen hesitated, aware that she was anxiously knotting her fingers together like a schoolgirl caught out on a difficult maths question. She felt her tongue sticking to the roof of her suddenly dry mouth. No one had asked her opinion on anything in years, but for Allegra Howard to ask Ellen what she thought of her book was like Shakespeare dropping by and asking if she liked his rhyming couplets.

'Good God woman, it's a simple enough question,' Allegra snapped at her impatiently.

'I'm sorry . . . it's just um, well – you know. I feel a bit . . . self-conscious because after all what do I know, really?' Ellen chewed on her lip as the question hung awkwardly in the air.

'Let us hope you know something,' Allegra exclaimed. 'Simon told me you had an excellent eye and an instinct for fine-tuning a story. He promised me that if I came to stay here in this . . . *house* you would be useful to me. So – be useful. Tell me what you think of the book so far.'

Ellen took a deep breath, feeling the levels of anxiety that she had only experienced before when telling Nick she was pregnant with Charlie. It had been an accident, one of those things that happened despite the number of precautions used, and Charlie had arrived at least two years ahead of schedule in Nick's life plan. Before they had the house, the business and their lives together well established. Ellen had worried that Nick would not be happy, that he would blame her somehow, but after he'd had a few minutes to let the news sink in he couldn't have been more delighted. Her fears had been groundless then, and she was sure they would be again. People were not nearly as frightening as she often believed them to be, even artistic geniuses like Allegra.

'It's a real page-turner, that's for sure,' Ellen blurted. 'I couldn't put it down and when I ran out of pages I was very disappointed. I'm desperate to know what happens to Eliza at the hands of that dreadful man who accosted her . . .'

'But?' Allegra enquired down the length of her aristocratic nose.

'But? There is no but, I think it's brilliant in every respect.' Ellen beamed at Allegra, as if the intensity of her own smile might incite one in Allegra.

'Oh Ellen, please don't insult my intelligence. Of course there is a but. I know it, Simon knows it and you know it. It's just that Simon and I can't decide exactly what the but is. That buck, I'm afraid, has been passed to you. You must see the flaws with that keen eye of yours – what are they?'

Ellen swallowed and took a moment to frame her sentence. 'Well – I know it's only a first draft – and I usually only ever read your final draft for copy-editing purposes . . .'

'You don't. I only ever write one draft,' Allegra told her.

'Oh well, it's just that it seems that this book is a little lacking in . . .' Ellen lost her nerve.

'Lacking in . . . ? Spit it out, woman!'

'Substance.'

Ellen spoke the word quietly, as if she were revealing an unpleasant secret.

'Substance?' Allegra's tone was neutral, her expression implacable. Miserably Ellen realised that she was required to elaborate.

'Well, what lifts your books above the others,' she battled on, 'is the historical context, the attention to detail, the way that you bring alive the sights and sounds of another age. The characters, the plot are brilliant but – correct me if I'm wrong but I think *The Sword Erect* is the first book you have set in the English Civil War. It's such a rich and interesting time, yet you skirt around it almost as if it were incidental and . . .' Ellen faltered. For a second her passion and interest had swept her along but then she remembered she was standing in her former dining room telling one of the greatest historical-romance writers how to do her job. How could she, Ellen Woods, who had never done anything more than read books and correct grammatical errors, even presume to tell Allegra where she was going wrong?

'Of course that's just my opinion and my opinion is hardly worth knowing, in fact when I think about it I'm not altogether sure that it's right anyway.'

'And?' Allegra questioned her.

'And?' Ellen repeated the word as the faintest of echoes.

'You told me that I was treating the backdrop of the English Civil War as if it were incidental *and* then you were about to add something further. What?'

'It hardly matters.' Ellen squirmed, wishing the voluminous folds of the overstuffed leather chair would swallow her up and spit her back out in her world, the world where she existed in simple suspended animation and read and daydreamed and waited for her husband to come home and her real life to begin at the touch of his lips on her cheek.

'Ellen.' Allegra enunciated her name with such care that it sounded as if it should have a good deal many more syllables in it. 'If you and I are to work together then we must be straight with each other. I know that you are sitting there wondering how you could possibly have anything to say to me about writing, and

I understand why you would feel that way. But let me assure you one does not become as successful as I have without listening to criticism. I might hate it but I can take it and I am not in the habit of shooting the messenger, only torturing them a little. Yes, you are little more than a housewife with barely any experience of the creative arts but you are my reader, you are the person I write for, and now I have an opportunity to meet you face to face I want to know what you think. You need not be afraid.' Allegra's mouth hinted at a smile. 'Not very afraid anyway.'

Ellen braced herself.

'Your characters, especially your female characters usually have something else about them. Wit, intelligence – bravery. Something else apart from their beauty and perfect bodies that makes the reader wish they were them. I know that in the end everything will come right for Eliza, knowing that is sort half the fun of reading about the other things that happen to her, but at the moment I wonder if she is just a little bit too passive. Look at Helga in your Viking trilogy – despite being sold as a slave and ravished by her new master she always maintained her dignity until he had no choice but to fall in love with her. And Caroline in *The Pirate Lover*. Beaumont snatches her from the docks when she is lost and locks her in his cabin to have his wicked way with her for weeks, but she challenges him, constantly. She doesn't let her circumstances change who she is. Although Eliza puts up a bit of a fight and runs away she just seems to lurch from one ravishing to the next. I started to feel sorry for her and I've never felt that for your heroines before.'

Allegra nodded once and then was silent. Not for a few seconds or a few minutes but for almost half an hour. For almost half an hour Ellen sat in her chair and waited for Allegra to speak, unsure if she should stay or go – or even if she still had a job. Finally, her thighs cramping from being clenched for an extended period, she moved to stand up. But just then Allegra spoke, forcing her back into the chair.

'You're right,' she said simply. 'You are quite right. I've been relying on all the clichés, all the things that make a work of art, such as mine, no better than pulp fiction. Sex sells and I know that. I've become little better than a whoremonger.'

'Oh well, I wouldn't go that far . . .' Ellen began.

Slowly and with some difficulty Allegra stood up, straightening each vertebra one by one.

'Ellen, can I confide in you?'

Ellen gripped the arms of the chair, not absolutely sure she wanted the responsibility of being Allegra Howard's confidante. Still, unable to refuse, she nodded.

'Of course.'

'Ellen, I'm seventy-three. My home was destroyed by floods, nearly everything I've ever loved, all my memories, all my photos, my works of art – they were all swept away in a river of muck and sewage. I didn't think that it mattered, I always believed that mere objects weren't what made a person human – that it was their feelings, their experiences and memories that made a person exist. But when I was alone in my hotel room I realised that without my things, my photos to look at or my books to pick up, my memories were slipping away from me. And I'm slipping away with them, a little more each day. I'm vanishing.'

'No, no – you couldn't be more alert and sprightly,' Ellen assured her.

'Sprightly.' Allegra pursed her lips. 'It is always the curse of the elderly to be either frail or sprightly. I don't mean that I am suffering from dementia, I mean simply that I have reached a crossroads in my life. After seventy-three years of knowing who I am and what I want and what I *do*, suddenly I'm no longer sure, suddenly I'm afraid. With this last book I've been writing by numbers, papering over the cracks and hoping that no one will notice or care – but if you can see it, then so will everyone else and I'll be vilified as a fraud! They'll see that I don't feel like a writer any more. They'll see that I am not a writer any more. My creative fire was quite drowned in that flood along with everything else. Ellen, I am finished.'

Ellen looked into Allegra's pale blue eyes.

'No,' she said. 'No, you're not finished. You've taken a knock, you've had a setback and when you're . . . a more mature person then it's harder to move on from such things. When my husband died I couldn't imagine another day, another hour without him in the world. If it wasn't for my son I would have happily curled up and waited for my heart to stop beating. But I couldn't do that, I had to keep going and somehow I've got through my first year and then the lodgers happened and working for you, and for the first time I feel as if . . . there is a future.'

'There is a future for you.' Allegra looked down at her. 'You are young and beautiful. But for me? My future is behind me now and suddenly I find I don't have the energy to keep going. I don't have a husband or a son to keep going for. After all these years writing grand romances I forgot to find the time to have one myself. I just can't do it any more. I just don't want to.'

'But you do have someone to carry on for.' Ellen stood up, her legs on fire with pins and needles, and came around the desk, only just resisting the urge to touch the older woman.

'You have me and all the tens of thousands of people who have read your books. We need you, Allegra. We need the next Allegra Howard book and the one after that. You give us . . . hope. And even if what I said about *The Sword Erect* is true, that doesn't make it a bad book, I still couldn't put it down. I still couldn't wait to find out what happened to Eliza.' Ellen smiled. 'It still made me daydream about having my own Captain Parker crazy with lust for me. All it means is it isn't as good a book as it can be – yet.'

Allegra twisted her mouth into a knot of a smile.

'Let me help you fix those things,' Ellen went on. 'I know a little about history and what I don't know I can find out. I can establish the facts and the backdrop and you can weave them into the story and make Eliza a true Allegra Howard heroine. Fearless, defiant and undefeated by whatever life throws at her – just like you.'

Allegra looked into Ellen's eyes and slowly one feather-light hand floated upwards, its papery palm cupping her cheek.

'I believe that you might just be a very passionate person, Ellen Woods,' Allegra told her solemnly.

'Who, me? No, I'm just . . . normal.'

'A passionate person with a whole undiscovered universe locked away inside.'

'Really?' Ellen was sceptical.

'Really, and I hope that you and I will work very well together. The question is, where do we start?'

'Here,' Ellen said. 'Well, not here in my dining room. Here as in London during the Civil War. You see, it was a Parliamentarian stronghold throughout the war. With Eliza intent on escaping Captain Parker, it's natural that she would

116

head here, to a place where she would feel safe. Imagine the historical figures she could encounter, perhaps even Cromwell himself. She could become a sort of seventeenth-century poster girl for the cause. And I thought if the captain followed her into the enemy's lair in order to win her back, then—' Ellen stopped herself. 'I'm sorry, of course it's not up to me to think of the plot.'

'Nonsense. Keep talking,' Allegra told her, easing herself back on to her seat. 'Keep talking. I will see the pictures.'

And as the morning rolled into the afternoon they had talked over ideas, Allegra painting plotlines in the air with a sweep of her hand and Ellen suggesting historical figures and events that they could weave into the story.

Finally Allegra held up her hand.

'You must forgive me, Ellen, I'm not as invincible as I used to be. We missed lunch and I fear I must eat something soon or perish.'

'Oh no!' Ellen looked at her watch. It was just after three and before she knew it Charlie would be ambling through the front door. 'How awful!'

'Not at all, it has been rather wonderful actually.' Allegra's smile was warm. 'Let's finish now. Today we laid the foundations. Tomorrow we will write.'

As Ellen shut Allegra's door behind her and headed for the kitchen she realised that she hadn't felt so excited, so optimistic or such a part of something in a very long time. It was almost as if she had only just started to exist.

Charlie had bowled into the kitchen as Ellen was making a smoked-salmon salad for Allegra, one of the components of her eating plan that had been delivered by the supermarket earlier that day along with Earl Grey tea.

'That stinks,' he said, peering over Ellen's shoulder briefly.

'So what did you get up to at school today?' she asked him.

'You know, the usual,' Charlie said, ripping open the packaging of some new bread even though there was still a third of a loaf left in the breadbin.

'No, I don't know because you never tell me any more.' Ellen turned to face her son as he lathered with butter the slice of bread he cupped in the palm of his hand. 'When you were little I couldn't shut you up, you'd tell me about what you'd learnt, the games you'd played – you'd skip home holding my hand and talk and talk.' She smiled at him, seeing that tousled-headed little boy who'd once been her best friend. 'Now I can barely get two words out of you half the time. I know you're growing up and changing but – well, I'm still your mum. Come on, *something* must have happened today.'

Charlie crammed in a mouthful of bread and observed Ellen while he chewed.

'Not really,' he said on a swallow. 'Oh wait – James Parks asked Emily Greenhurst out and she said no.'

'James asked a girl out!' Ellen felt unsettled. 'Really, you are all asking each other out now are you, getting girlfriends and things?'

'No, not all of us.' Charlie looked gratifyingly horrified at the idea. 'Most of the girls at my school are right mingers – just James. He likes Emily because she's in this band and she's cool and she's not like the other girls, you know – she doesn't just giggle and talk about crap. She has opinions and she's funny, and she's got long hair sort of like the colour of honey right down to

118

her waist and . . . well anyway – James likes her but she knocked him back. It was funny.'

'*James* likes her,' Ellen smiled, reeling from the longest burst of conversation she had had out of her son in an age.

'Yes,' Charlie said. 'He was gutted. It was really funny.'

'So you gave him lots of friendly sympathy then?'

'No! We told him he was a gay for liking girls in the first place.'

'I think that's probably a contradiction in terms,' Ellen smiled.

'A what?' Charlie looked at her.

'Never mind – so you're not planning on asking any girls out just yet, then? Not this Emily, for example?'

'God no, Mum – *I'm not gay!*' Charlie exclaimed in horror, before scrambling up the stairs no doubt to find his DS, leaving Ellen alone with her salad, wondering exactly when and how gay had started meaning the opposite of . . . well, gay. And she wondered if she had been sticking her head in the sand, determined still to think of him as her little boy. Clearly he was becoming interested in girls, even if he wasn't ready to admit it. If Nick were here it would have been simple, Nick would have guided him along the rocky road of adolescence, helped him find his way from boyhood to manhood. But, as Ellen had to keep reminding herself on a daily basis, Nick was not here – she was all Charlie had in the way of guidance and she was only too aware of her inadequacies. She barely knew anything about being a woman, let alone how to be a man.

Later, when he had reappeared for fish fingers, his eyes still glued to his games console, Ellen had tried to talk to him.

'Charlie, you and I have never really talked about . . . well, about the things that you are beginning to be interested in.' She had slid the plate of fish fingers garnished with ketchup towards him. 'The thing is, you are learning to grow up and turn into a man and I'm learning too, learning how to be the mum of a young man. But you know, if you ever want to talk to me about those *things* then of course you can, and I will try and help as best I can.'

'Things?' Charlie looked up from his DS. 'Are you talking about sex again?'

'Yes, I suppose I am. When you talked about it the other day, I don't suppose I took you seriously enough. But you are growing up, there are things that you will want to know and, well – I'm just saying that you can ask me. I won't mind.'

Charlie had picked up his fork and stabbed it into a fish finger. He had looked at Nick's empty chair and said, 'I wish Dad was here.'

Before Ellen could respond Matt had arrived with a packet of fish and chips, and ruffling Charlie's hair promptly plonked himself down in the one vacant chair. In Nick's chair.

'Just gonna dash this down then I'm off out again, got a date,' Matt told an immobile Ellen as he unwrapped his takeaway. 'Girl from the chick magazine one floor below me, she lives round here so I'm meeting her down the road . . . What?'

Finally Matt realised that he was being stared at.

'It's just that . . .' Ellen started.

'You're sitting in my dad's chair!' Charlie bellowed at him.

'Am I?' Matt jumped up, spilling greasy chips, looking around as if he fully expected to find that he'd been sitting on a dead man's lap. 'I'm really sorry, mate, I didn't know.'

'You don't just come in here, move in and sit in my dad's chair,' Charlie shouted, sliding his plate off the table with a sweep of his hand and sending it crashing on to the tiled floor.

'I hate you!' he shouted and Ellen wasn't sure if it was her or Matt, or his absent father that he was addressing. In a second he was gone, thundering up the stairs, slamming the door behind him.

'Oh fuck, I put my foot in it didn't I?' Matt said, bending down and beginning to pick up the spilt food.

Frozen by Charlie's explosive reaction it took Ellen a second to respond.

'No, you weren't to know. I was going to mention it, but I didn't really know how . . . it's not something you just drop into conversation, after all.' Shaken, Ellen took a breath, fetched the dustpan and brush from under the sink and knelt down beside Matt, sweeping up the lumps of plate that had exploded on the tiles. 'It was my fault, I put him on edge, trying to talk to him about "becoming a man". I didn't know he'd be so sensitive about it, it only seems like yesterday that he was obsessed with Power Rangers and took his teddy to bed.' Ellen bent her head, letting her hair curtain her face as she struggled not to cry. 'And it's not as if he's got a dad to talk to or learn from any more.'

'Eleven, nearly twelve, it's a weird time for a boy,' Matt told her. 'Everything's changing, you know – your body, the way you feel – the way you speak, even. It's all up and down, and no one understands. I remember when I discovered . . .' He paused, sitting back on his heels and popping a chip he had just picked up off the tiles into his mouth.

'Discovered what? Girls?'

'In a manner of speaking.' Matt's smile was rueful. 'When I discovered – you know, the pleasure of my own body.'

'Oh I see.' Ellen put the dustpan and brush down, feeling

suddenly exhausted. 'But you were much older than twelve, weren't you?'

'Not so much,' Matt broke the news gently. 'Anyway, it's difficult for us men, you know. We've got to work out what it all means, how it all works, even how to walk down a road like we've got control of all our arms and legs, and we try our best to do it without anyone noticing, especially not our mums.' As they both sat on the kitchen floor he reached out and tucked the curtain of her hair behind her ear, chucking her under the chin as he might a small child. 'It's nothing personal, Ellen, it's not anything you are doing wrong. It's something he has to get through on his own, and for what it's worth by the time I was his age my dad was long gone and I turned out all right in the end.'

Whether it was his touch or the softness in his voice, Ellen didn't know, but the tears that she had been battling broke free and rolled down her cheeks.

'He must miss his dad so much.' Her voice was barely more than a whisper. 'And I'm not enough, I'm not nearly enough to make up for him.'

'He does miss his dad.' Matt spoke quietly, wiping away one of her tears with the ball of his thumb. He stretched a hand out to Ellen as he rose, helping her to her feet. 'And it hurts him like hell and he's angry and confused. And so are you. Look, I know I barely know you but for what it's worth it looks to me like you are doing an amazing job.' He dropped his chin and shrugged. 'My dad only left home and my mum spent the rest of her life in the bottom of a vodka bottle. You're keeping it together for Charlie and once all this settles down, once he sees the light at the end of the tunnel he'll realise that, I promise.' Matt ran his fingers through his hair and winced. 'What a fuckwit I am, crashing in here treading all over your feet. I'm sorry I sat in your husband's chair. But look, don't cry, yeah? Give us a smile. If you don't smile for me now it's going to be *nearly* impossible for me to enjoy my date with a leggy blonde subeditor.'

Despite herself Ellen complied. 'I am quite sure that a weepy middle-aged woman is not going to enter your head once,' she told him.

Matt shrugged again. 'First of all you're not middle-aged, and secondly contrary to popular belief I'm a sensitive guy. It'll ruin my night if you don't stop crying by the time I go out.'

Ellen wiped her eyes with the heels of her hands and smiled again. 'There, temporary relapse over with. Feel free not to give me a second thought. Truly, moving in here doesn't mean that comforting your landlady is part of the deal.'

'Well it wasn't specified in the *Time Out* ad . . .' Matt grinned. 'Look, I like Charlie, he's a good kid. Maybe next time I'm in I'll get him to link our DSs and play Mario Cart or something.' Ellen looked blank. 'What I'm saying is, maybe, if he likes, him and me can be mates. And maybe if there's any guy stuff he's worried about then he'll talk to me. I am, after all, an expert on guy stuff. I've got a column to prove it and everything.'

'Yes, your column – I'd like to read it sometime.'

'Er . . . I don't think you would.' Matt looked bashful. 'I mean, it's not exactly my finest work. And it's probably not exactly your cup of tea. But anyway, like I said. Me and Charlie, we can hang sometime.'

'You don't have to do that.' Ellen shook her head.

'I know,' Matt said simply. He looked down at his grease-stained trousers. 'But you know, I could have done with some-one to talk to when I was his age. Anyhow I'd better leap in the shower and get changed. Don't want the subeditor thinking I'm a takeaway-eating slob, I told her I'm into fine dining and that I love to cook.'

Ellen had waited until Matt had gone out before checking on Charlie who was watching TV in his room with his headphones plugged in, at first resolutely refusing to acknowledge her.

Ellen hovered for a minute, considering turning off the TV. Deciding that was too direct she sat down beside him on his bed in silence. After a minute or two he sighed and ripped off the headphones, flinging them on to the bed.

'Matt didn't know,' Ellen said. 'I should have told him, but I didn't exactly know how to . . .'

'Well put up a notice or something,' Charlie said. 'That's Dad's chair, Mum!'

'I know, I know . . . anyway he knows now. Look Charlie, how are you?' Ellen reached out and smoothed her thumb over his scowl as she used to when he was a little boy. To her relief he didn't flinch at her touch.

'I'm OK,' he said, looking up at her. 'How are you, Mum?'

'I'm OK,' Ellen said. 'I even think that I might be . . . good.'

'Do you think you're starting to feel better?' Charlie asked, watching her closely. 'Not so sad?'

Ellen hesitated, uncertain of how to answer.

'Because it's OK, I mean if you felt better, I'd like it,' he told her.

Ellen looked at him, pressing the tips of her fingers to her mouth. 'Oh you poor boy, have I been awful to live with these last months?' she said anxiously.

'No, not awful, just not you. It's almost like you're not really there.' Charlie struggled to explain. 'Like you're fading away. You get up, you feed me, you wait for me to come home, you feed me, I go to bed and the next day is the same. I like it that there are people here, that you have things to think about. I even like Matt. I just want you to be more like you again, like you used to be before Dad died. We used to do stuff . . . go places.'

'I know,' Ellen sighed. 'But I do think that I am feeling a bit better, just a little bit. I think it will be good to have people in the house and a new job. It's not that I don't miss your dad terribly, but it is good to have something else to think about.'

'Yeah it is,' Charlie said carefully. 'So maybe soon we might do stuff again, go places?'

'You really want to go places with me?' Ellen asked him, gently sceptical.

Charlie shrugged. 'As long as no one I know sees me.'

Ellen swiped him lightly, skimming the top of his head with the flat of her hand.

'Mum, do you remember when you, me and Dad went sailing in that really flat place – what was it called?'

'The Norfolk Broads.' Ellen smiled, Charlie was talking about a holiday that Nick had taken them on just over two years ago. He'd developed a brief but passionate interest in sailing and had even owned a share in a boat for a little while. That summer he'd taken them to see her, full of enthusiasm for the outdoor life, the fresh air and the wind in their hair.

Charlie chuckled. 'And Dad got really, really seasick and in the end you and me did all the sailing. He went actually green – do you remember?'

Ellen nodded, visualising that flat Norfolk horizon, the

endless expanse of sky that made her feel breathless just to think of it, all that space.

'We had a laugh then, didn't we? You and me?' Charlie asked.

Ellen nodded. 'We had the best time.'

'And we will do stuff like that again, won't we? We won't always just be here in this house missing Dad, because sometimes when I think like that and feel like that – that's when I worry. I worry that I won't ever be able to live like a normal person again. In case I shouldn't, in case it's wrong. Like it might not be allowed.'

Ellen felt the muscles in her gut clench. Had she done this to him? Had her own descent into grief dragged him down with her so deeply that he was afraid he might never resurface?

'Of course it's allowed, sweetheart – more than that, that's the way it should be. Especially for you, you've got your whole life ahead of you.'

'So have you, though,' Charlie reminded her.

'Yes, I suppose I have,' Ellen said thoughtfully. Until recently the concept had been an unbearable prospect, but now – now it wasn't *such* a terrifying idea.

'So then you have to start feeling better and maybe you and me could do something like go sailing. I think we'd have a laugh,' Charlie told her hopefully.

'And if I start to feel better do you think that you can too?' she asked him. Charlie's smile faded, his shoulders hunching, his body almost halving in size as he absorbed the question.

'Sometimes like at school or when I'm playing the DS or watching telly I feel all right, I feel normal and then something will make me remember and . . .' Charlie shook his head, unable to complete the sentence. 'Sometimes I feel a bit better.'

'I think that's what it's like,' Ellen said. 'I think sometimes you feel better and sometimes you don't and that as the days pass the times when you feel better get longer and the times when you don't get shorter. And I think that it is OK to feel better. Dad would want you to be happy, Charlie. He'd want that more than anything in the world.'

'He'd want you to be happy too,' Charlie told her.

'I know,' Ellen said simply. 'Well, let's give it a go for him then, yeah?'

'Yeah.' Charlie nodded. 'But you will tell everybody about the chair?'

'I will.' Charlie leaned into Ellen as she put her arms around him, resting his head on her shoulder for a second before pulling away and picking up his headphones.

'I know there's no school in the morning,' Ellen told him. 'But I still want this off by eleven.'

But Charlie's eyes were already fixed on the screen.

Exhausted, Ellen lay on her bed, closing her eyes and finally letting the tensions of a day that was almost complete drain out of her. Everything that had happened, her conversation with Charlie, the mess on the kitchen floor, gradually faded, and she found she was thinking of Matt and the sensation of his thumb tracing her cheek. Letting her weary mind drift anywhere it chose, Ellen imagined what it would have felt like if that thumb had journeyed further, running down her neck and brushing lazily over the tops of her breasts.

As she drifted off into her fantasy she saw herself as Eliza Sinclair, her body transforming into the impossibly perfect ideal that was Eliza's, and Matt as the captain unable to take his eyes off her, his desire for her tangible in the air that crackled between them as they stood alone in a . . . in a hay barn, Ellen decided.

'I love you,' Captain Matt whispered, taking a step closer to her so that she could feel his hot breath grazing her ear lobe. 'Oh Ellen, I love you.'

'And I you,' Ellen whispered back, allowing one lily-white hand to flutter to a rest on his manly chest and then boldly travel lower to where no maiden should ever venture.

'I long for you,' Matt groaned, clasping her hand and clutching it to him.

'Then take me, for I am yours, my love,' Ellen breathed, finding herself an expert seductress.

In seconds Ellen's thin white cotton gown had been ripped from her body, and her perfect breasts were crushed against Matt's firm chest as his hands and kisses consumed her in a burning sea of fire.

Hours had passed when Ellen woke to find herself still fully dressed, tangled in her bed sheets and suddenly wide awake. She looked at the bedside clock and sighed, pulling herself out of bed, peeling off her clothes and changing into a pair of Nick's pyjamas, bright red cotton with a green trim that she'd bought him one Christmas as a joke and which he had never worn. Still Ellen liked the feeling of them, hugging the outsize jacket around her body. It was guilt that had woken her, she realised. Fantasising about another man, worse still a real-life man , as if her husband had never existed, as if he hadn't been her lover, the love of her life. As if sordid fantasies could ever replace what she and Nick had once had.

Feeling the same sort of lurching horror as a drunk who'd woken up to remember exactly what had happened the night before, Ellen set off downstairs to drink tea and sort herself out.

She paused at Charlie's room, pushing open the door to find the TV still flickering, despite her command, tuned to some music channel that he seemed permanently glued to, and her son sprawled face down on the bed, his covers kicked on the floor. Treading carefully so as to avoid damaging any of the various possessions that he preferred to keep on the floor, Ellen swept up the duvet and laid it over Charlie's prone form.

'What the . . .?' he muttered sulkily in his sleep.

'It's just me, darling,' she whispered, and within seconds Charlie was lost again in the deep sleep that seemed to overwhelm him these days. She stood for a few seconds outside his room and listened. Faint music and the sound of hushed female laughter drifted down the stairwell. Matt must have brought his blonde subeditor home. While Ellen had been imagining him and her rolling about in a pile of hay, he'd been plying this girl with drinks and charming her with the same sweet smile that he'd comforted Ellen with earlier. And as this unknown woman had come back with him on their first date he must have done a pretty good job.

As she walked into the kitchen, Ellen shook her head, the tender soles of her feet jolted by the cool tiles. This day, a day of things happening, had gone to her head. For a moment she'd forgotten who she was and what she was for. She was Nick's widow and Charlie's mother and she was here to do the best that she could for her son. While that included the guilty pleasure of working for Allegra Howard it did not include wasting hours of her life dreaming about a man who'd never look at her in a million years. Her fantasies were far from harmless if they took her mind off the things that mattered.

She'd made herself a cup of camomile tea and sat at the

kitchen table staring at Nick's chair, wishing she could will him into existence just by thinking of him.

Ellen jumped when she heard footsteps on the stairs. Hoping it was Charlie coming down for a drink of water, she went to the kitchen door and opened it a crack. It was Matt and his subeditor. She had her coat on and he had . . . well, nothing but a towel wrapped around his waist. Ellen stifled a gasp, clasping her hand over her mouth.

'I can't believe you're kicking me out!' the girl giggled, swinging her arm around his neck to steady herself as she stumbled, clearly the worse for wear. 'Not after what we just did!'

'I know, and I don't want to,' Matt purred. 'It's just the landlady – she's old school, you know. A bit of a dragon. I'm risking getting evicted bringing you back here at all, but you're so gorgeous that I was powerless to resist.'

The girl giggled again and tightened her hold on him so that their lips met and she kissed him, swaying gently from side to side as they embraced, like a willow bending in the wind. As they kissed Matt's hand departed from her waist and headed for the front door latch. He opened the door a crack and manoeuvred the girl into the gap.

'Goodnight,' he whispered.

'You'll call me?' she asked.

'But of course,' Matt nodded.

'Promise?' The girl giggled but there was a hint of desperation in her voice.

'For sure,' Matt said as he shut the door on her. He stood there for a moment, his hand on the latch as if he suspected that she might come back. And then, horrified, Ellen watched him rub his hands through his hair and over his face and head straight for the kitchen.

Panicking, she shut the kitchen door, ran to the back door instinctively planning to escape into the garden, and then thinking better of it ran first to the pantry and then to the fridge, opening and shutting the door as if she might climb into it. She was still flapping about when Matt flicked on the unforgiving spotlights, illuminating the kitchen fully and catching Ellen red-handed and barefoot in her pyjamas.

'Oh shit,' Matt yelped. 'You scared the shit out of me!'

'I'm sorry, I was just up when I heard your . . . friend leaving. I didn't want you to think I was eavesdropping.'

'No worries,' Matt said cheerfully and then he frowned. '*Were* you eavesdropping?'

'No,' Ellen said. 'Well, a bit. OK, I heard everything.'

'Oh no,' Matt groaned. 'Listen, what I said about the landlady being a dragon, you know I was only saying that to get her to go, don't you? I don't think you're a dragon. All that stuff I said earlier – that's what I really think about you.'

'Honestly, it's none of my business,' Ellen said, pausing, confused and unsure exactly what she wanted to say or how. She had known that Matt worked for what was called a lads' mag, and that he wrote about women all the time, but the man she'd met and begun to get to know over the last few days hadn't seemed like the sort of man who'd date a girl he'd just met and bring her back to bed on the very same night. She'd foolishly forgotten that he was a virtual stranger, let her silly imagination run away with her and ended up feeling disappointed in him, even though she didn't have the right to be. Not in his choice of sexual partners, anyway. 'Actually Matt, it is my business a bit –

we talked about Charlie, remember? About him being at an impressionable age – and I know I said it's fine for you to bring people back, and it is. But will it always be like that – some girl that you've just picked up? Because if it is then you need to be a lot more discreet. What if Charlie had come down for a drink just then?'

'Shit, I'm an arsehole. I'm sorry,' Matt said. 'I just didn't think. I mean I seriously didn't think.' He shook his head, clutching his towel for dear life. 'Next time I'll go to her place.'

'So you liked her, then?' Ellen asked.

Matt looked confused. 'Oh no, not *her* place. I mean the next girl's place, whoever she might be. Next time I'll go there.'

Unsure of how to react, Ellen reached for her cup of tea. 'Well I'll leave you to it.'

'I suppose you want to know why I got her to go?' Matt stopped her with a question.

Ellen wavered. She'd never been around a man like him before, a bona fide Jack the Lad, and she did sort of want to know. But she did also have to get up in a few hours and she had just recently, only minutes ago in fact, banned herself from having anything to do with Matt that wasn't essential because the last time she had 'seen' him he had been standing naked in front of her with an erection that would rival any of Allegra's well-endowed heroes, on the brink of flinging her into a pile of straw and penetrating her very soul with his thunderous passion. Under those circumstances Ellen felt that standing alone in her kitchen with him – Matt wearing nothing more than a towel – at gone three in the morning did not qualify as essential. Particularly as he was clearly the sort of man who would not shy away from a casual sexual encounter.

132

Still, she wanted to know.

'Not especially, not unless you *want* to tell me?' Ellen waited, trying not to picture how old and silly she must look standing there in her pyjamas.

Matt took a pint of milk out of the fridge and drank directly from it, sitting down in her chair, the towel folding between his legs, just about maintaining his modesty.

'Too easy,' he said.

'What, she was?' Ellen asked him, leaning against the kitchen counter.

'All of it was. I met her in the lift at the office. I'm on the fifth floor and she's on the fourth. I asked her if she fancied a drink on the third and she'd agreed and made plans with me by the time she got out. That should have been a sign, you know. Girls who are too eager, you've got to watch them. But she's got great legs and a really nice set of . . . eyes. And men are shallow. I am shallow. So I turn up at the pub, a bit late, and she's there wearing this dress that's cut up to here and down to here.' Matt chopped the side of his hand first against the top of his thigh and then just below his nipples.

'I bet that really showed off her eyes,' Ellen said, smiling to see the surprise on his face at her joke.

'It did,' he nodded. 'All the blokes were looking at her and I liked being the one she was with. And she was a laugh. Then two gin and tonics down and she's all over me, hands everywhere, wants to come back to mine.'

'Sounds awful,' Ellen said drily. 'How on earth did you cope?'

'To be honest, that kind of girl who's so up for it is a turn-off. There's no challenge, no mystery.'

'Which is why you exercised your free will and said no thank you very much young lady,' Ellen observed, hating how much she sounded like his sensible maiden aunt.

'I know. I know that's what I should have done. But she's a woman, a hot woman and she wanted to go to bed with me. Like I said, I'm shallow.'

'Was it worth it, the sex?' Ellen found herself asking him, edging closer to the table and sitting down.

'It was fine,' Matt said. 'It was nice, but the second it was over I didn't want to talk to her any more. I wanted her to go. So I invented the whole dragon-landlady thing, sorry.'

'I don't think it's me you should be apologising to,' Ellen said, sounding much primmer and older than she intended. 'I mean, you must have made the poor girl feel as if you were really interested in her, you must have made her feel that it was OK to come back to bed with you.'

Matt scrutinised her long enough to make her dip her chin and break eye contact with him.

'Do you think I'm a shit?' he asked her.

Ellen shrugged, suddenly feeling overwhelmed with tiredness. She wasn't sure if she was expected to work with Allegra on a Saturday or not, but she would definitely have to get up to make her breakfast.

'I expect that when the poor girl wakes up in the morning she'll feel foolish and vulnerable and *she'll* think that you're a shit.' Ellen yawned. 'But at least you're honest. You don't dress up how you feel or think about things, you more sort of sling on a towel and lounge around half naked.'

'Oh shit.' Matt looked down at himself as if he'd only just remembered what he was not wearing. 'Shit. I've been here –

what, five days? And I've pissed off your son, called you a dragon and made an idiot of myself. Am I evicted?'

Ellen smiled at him, glad to see him like this, young, brash, half drunk, half naked and awkward. The real Matt, as disarming and as handsome as he might be, was nothing like the captain in her dreams. Perhaps avoiding him was the wrong thing to do after all; the better she got to know him the less he would embody that perfect hero in her head.

'Goodnight Matt,' she said. 'Get some sleep.'

'Night Ellen, and . . .' Matt paused, suddenly bashful. 'I'm glad you were up. It's not often you meet a woman you can talk to.'

'Unlike the ones you can have sex with,' Ellen replied. 'They're a dime a dozen.'

Chapter Nine

'Don't you reckon, heh?' Pete chuckled into his third lunchtime pint. A rising tide of red was creeping over his jowls and towards the tips of his ears with each swig of beer. 'Heh? Matt?'

Matt looked up from his own untouched beer and realised that he hadn't been listening to a word Pete had said since they'd sat down at the table. This was his third week at *Bang It!* and he was halfway through his probation. His first two columns had gone down well, with Dan and best of all with the readers. He'd had quite a lot of actual letters, which was rare in the *Bang It!* office. They usually got Suze to make them up in her lunch hour. Dan was pleased with him, but the more he worked for Pete the more he realised that half of his job consisted of babysitting his boss and keeping him at least vaguely on track. Nobody had said it out loud, of course, but the fact was Pete was an alcoholic, with a fondness for the odd line of mid-morning coke. Matt had no idea how Pete kept his job, but he did and he got the distinct feeling that as the rookie in the pack it was his duty to help Pete keep it. Still, the more he saw of his boss, who was permanently messed up – and even Dan, whose good looks and vigour were already being blurred by a lifestyle that would eventually erode them

– Matt secretly wondered if this was his dream job after all. Was this really what he'd been hoping for all those years back when he'd first tried his hand at journalism? He'd landed a job that meant he woke up every morning with a hangover, that was giving him a worrying laissez-faire attitude to naked breasts and that required of him, as a pinnacle of creativity, to think up ten different ways to write 'blow job'. He was sure he'd had other aspirations as a kid, when a report on *News at Ten* from a massacre in India had both brought him to tears and inspired him to want to do what that reporter had done, bring the really important news home to people in a way that made it seem personal, that made it matter. Somehow he had ended up here, an expert babe-hound, living the bachelor life surrounded by women. It had to be his dream job, how could it not be? Even if his drunken boss did somewhat take the edge off.

At just after twelve thirty Pete had arrived at Matt's desk looking hot and uncomfortable in a too-tight shirt and food-stained tie, beads of sweat decorating his brow despite the air-conditioned office, and once again commanded Matt to join him for a liquid lunch.

'Got to get out of this shit hole for an hour,' he'd sighed, pulling at his shirt collar as he glared around at the rest of the room. Everyone studiously avoided making eye contact with him. Matt got the distinct impression that his colleagues were smirking at him behind his back.

'I'd love to, but the thing is I still have to put this review to bed and I need to polish up my column a bit . . .' Matt began.

'What? No you don't, that draft you gave me was fine. I sent it to the features folder last night.'

'What? Pete!' Matt shook his head. 'I thought I told you, that was a first draft, I hadn't . . . refined it yet.'

'Refined it? Bollocks, this is *Bang It!*, mate, not *Woman & Home*. You're writing about shagging, not how to fluff up a muffin – although now I come to think of it that makes a pretty good euphemism.' Pete's chuckle was filthy. 'Take it from an expert, that column was perfect. Now get your coat, you've pulled.'

Reluctantly Matt had slid back his chair and followed Pete out into the midday glare of the street and to the Red Lion, the pub that was just around the corner from the office. That column *had* been perfect, perfect for Pete that was. Matt had written it based on his evening with the subeditor. Last week he'd rehashed a column from his Manchester days, but he didn't know London well enough to make it completely authentic. He had thought that one city would be very much like the next, but that wasn't true. While Manchester was big, vibrant and packed full of all kinds of life, compared to London it felt almost like a village. Of course he felt more at home in Manchester, it *was* his home – he'd grown up there. But it was more than that. London was so huge, both dirty and beautiful, sprawling and crawling with humanity, layer upon layer of life that he'd barely had a chance to scratch the surface of, that Matt wasn't sure he could begin to get his head around what made the place tick, or even the little bit of it he had seen so far.

He knew he had to work harder to capture the essence of his 'hunting ground' in his column, so he'd written his subeditor article with Pete in mind, and as a consequence it was dirty and graphic and treated its female focus in turn as an object of lust and then ridicule. If he was honest Matt had knocked it out in minutes, returning to the office one evening after a stint in the pub, feeling gung-ho and keen on impressing his new bosses. But since then he'd had second thoughts. Thoughts that involved the subeditor, who had been funny and generous, passionate and open. He'd called her easy, but easy wasn't really the right word. More that she was willing, willing to take a chance on him, willing to live life to the full – and after all that was pretty much his motto. The poor girl hadn't really done anything wrong other than trust him, and it seemed unfair that she should be pilloried for it. Even if he had invented a name for her and changed her job to that of editorial assistant she would know it was about her.

And now the piece was out there and there was nothing that Matt could do about it, unless he wanted to make himself look like an idiot. He'd probably hurt a perfectly nice girl, for no good reason. Matt struggled with this latest bout of guilt. Back home he'd written piece after piece about girls he'd met in passing and it had never seemed to matter then. But recently, maybe after everything that had happened just before he left, he had started to see, to feel, the consequences of his actions. It was a new awareness that was not a particularly useful attribute for a features writer on a lads' mag, and it was something he'd have to stamp out if he wanted to really fit in at *Bang It!*. Matt couldn't put his finger on when exactly these reservations had started to insinuate their way into his psyche, but he was fairly sure it was before he got on the train to London. He was certain that his landlady had had an awful lot to do with how his conscience was now pricking him, at precisely the wrong moment in his life.

Small-hours chats with Ellen in the kitchen had become almost a regular feature over the last couple of weeks, and Matt had begun to realise that he looked forward to finding her sitting cupping a steaming mug of tea between her palms, despite the summer's unremitting heat. He'd walk into the kitchen, pretend to be surprised to see her, she'd apologise, like she always did for nothing in particular. He'd claim he was just getting a drink of water and she'd say she'd take her cup of tea to bed. Yet invariably they'd sit and talk over the day, the day he'd had trying to make a feature out of lads' holiday sex, and the day she'd had inventing ever more treacherous situations for the heroine in this book Allegra was writing. Her dry comments and faux-matronly disapproval of his latest antics would always make him laugh – she was unexpectedly witty.

Once he'd given her a draft of his column to read and waited, breath bated, surprised at how anxious he was to find out what she thought of his writing.

'Wow,' she'd said after a moment. 'I'd hate to get on the wrong side of you.'

'You don't think it's funny?' Matt asked her. It had been a recycled piece about a beautician he'd met back home, who'd made the mistake of hurriedly waxing her bikini line into a Brazilian while Matt waited for her in the living room, believing her to simply be visiting the toilet. It had turned out that it was a job best not rushed, and the poor girl had emerged in pain and bleeding quite profusely from some rather delicate areas. She'd tried to cover it up but had eventually confessed, and Matt, ever the gentleman, had soothed the affected area with an ice pack. There were jokes about plucked chickens and stubble rash. Pete had loved it.

'It is funny, I suppose,' Ellen said uncertainly. 'But it's also kind of . . . mean. Does your column always have to be mean?' Matt had thought about it for a moment and concluded that for

Bang It! it probably did. He hadn't shown her any of his work again, but that didn't mean they didn't have plenty to talk about.

Although he would have never guessed it in a million years, he found her life fascinating, watching her feel her way through each day, tackling a world that was entirely new to her, reinventing each minute that passed, like a butterfly emerging from a cocoon. Matt recognised her valour, and admired it.

He couldn't exactly claim that he had made any friends since he arrived in London. He had mates, yes, through work, lads to have a laugh and a drink with, but he had underestimated how much it mattered to have someone you could really talk to, without needing to put on a front or an attitude. Matt had left his lifelong best friend behind in Manchester along with his PlayStation, and it was his fault that they didn't talk any more. Ellen had become the nearest thing to a friend that he had in this huge, sprawling, unforgiving city. No, that was wrong, she *was* a friend and theirs was a small-hours friendship, characterised by crumpled cotton pyjamas, tangled scooped-up hair and steaming cups of tea on sweltering summer nights.

As Matt had travelled into work that morning after their first small-hours talk, he'd found that he kept picturing her as they had both knelt on the kitchen floor, when Charlie had kicked off about his dad's chair, the tears standing in her eyes, displaying the raw vulnerability that she wasn't even strong enough to hide from him, a virtual stranger as he had been then. And he could not shake the image of her later, in the kitchen, in those stupid red pyjamas that hid whatever curves she might have, her face worn with worry. He had sat there, the body heat of the subeditor still cooling on his skin, and for those few minutes at least he was happier just talking to Ellen than frolicking with any willing blonde. And she had told him off, only a little and so mildly that he might not have noticed, but when he finally tumbled into the already rumpled sheets of his bed he realised that he felt regret about what had happened between him and the subeditor. It was not a sensation familiar to him. He decided that he would call her, not to ask her out again or to try and take the relationship further, but just because calling her seemed like the decent thing to do. After fifteen minutes in the company of Ellen, Matt found that he wanted to be decent. It was a feeling that intensified the more he got to know her. Nevertheless it was now two weeks since his night with the subeditor and he hadn't called her yet. It seemed like the desire to be decent was not strong enough to impel him to act.

What had begun to trouble Matt was just how often he thought about his landlady, and whether the kinds of things he was thinking or feeling were the kinds of things that invariably ended up trashing a friendship. Even now, as Pete went on about some women at the bar, Matt kept thinking about Ellen standing barefoot in those pyjamas. There could not be a less sexually stimulating image of a woman, and when he thought about her it wasn't sex that was at the forefront of his mind at all, but for some reason he was unable to shake that memory that seemed so firmly lodged in his brain. It would pop up at any given moment, quite taking him off guard.

'Bloody hell, mate – that brunette. Look at her, you can tell she likes sex. Look at them hips, they are not the hips of a girl who doesn't get flipped over, grabbed by the arse and properly shagged from behind.'

Dragging his thoughts back into the pub, Matt looked up. Sitting at the bar were two women enjoying a lunchtime drink,

142

both dressed in what seemed like the unofficial uniform of office workers round here of pencil skirts and white shirts, although the blonde's had a faint pink candy stripe. They both had long glossy straightened hair. The blonde was slightly skinnier, with small high breasts that offered no challenge to the buttons of her shirt, and the brunette was curvy, rounded in all the right places. They were both pretty, Matt thought, but he especially liked the way the zip at the back of the brunette's skirt strained against the girth of her hips. She was by no means fat, but like so many women she'd chosen to squeeze into a skirt one size too small for her, which personally Matt didn't mind at all. He imagined the red welts that her discarded garments would leave bitten into her skin when she undressed later that night, and absently thought how he'd like to trace a finger along those phantom seams and find out where they led.

'You take the blonde, I'm going for that hippy little minx.' Pete surged up out of his chair and finding his feet entirely out of touch with his legs, immediately blundered back down into it again. He scowled at his empty glass.

'Fuck, they've made the beer stronger in here.'

'Or you had a couple of vodkas on the quiet before we even went to lunch?' Matt suggested mildly. How on earth was he supposed to police a man who kept bottles of spirits concealed all around his office?

'I'll be all right in a second, I just need a few of these peanuts to line my gut,' Pete slurred. 'Here's the plan. You go over there, sweeten them up, keep your hands off the one with the big tits, she's mine. Tell 'em we work at the magazine, offer 'em a photo shoot, tell 'em you can make them rich and famous and then arrange to meet them in here later. I'll be your wingman.'

Matt looked up at the girls, who by now had noticed the attention they were getting. They looked neither impressed nor flattered and the blonde waved her credit card at the barman, clearly keen to settle up and get back to work.

'I don't think they're interested, mate,' Matt said. 'Tell you what, how about we get you back to the office and get a few coffees down you before the features meeting this afternoon? Maybe you could have a little kip.'

'No, no, no – they're interested,' Pete insisted, slamming the palm of his hand firmly on the tabletop, talking loudly enough for the whole bar to hear. 'That blonde's giving you the eye, go on mate, you go over, give 'em some of that charm you're so famous for, go on. Warm the frigid bitches up.'

The two women stood up, collected their bags and shooting Matt a contemptuous look, mouthed something under their breath that he strongly suspected was the word 'arseholes', and left with their noses in the air.

'They've gone, mate,' Matt said, relieved, glancing at his watch. 'Time we should be gone too.'

'Fucking hell!' Pete shouted, angrily gesturing with his hand so that Matt's nearly full pint shot across the table and rolled on to the floor, spreading a sea of lager across the polished boards. 'You fucking let them get away! I haven't had a decent shag in fucking weeks. Fucking hell, Matt, you . . .'

'Get him out of here now.' The barman had leapt across the bar and now stood with his hands on his hips, glaring at the sodden man. 'I can't have him in here intimidating the customers, swearing his head off. It's my job on the line if my boss hears of it. One more stunt like that and he's barred and so are the rest of you cocky bastards.'

He glared at Matt, genuinely angry.

'God, I'm sorry – we're going, I won't let it happen again . . .' Matt tried to imagine the fall-out from Dan and the lads finding out that they'd been banned from their favourite pub because the rookie had let Pete get out of hand. It shouldn't be a reason for him to fail his probation but he wouldn't be surprised if it was.

It took some minutes to drag an angry and resentful Pete to his feet and many more to push him, reeking of stale alcohol and something more that Matt didn't want to think about, to the door and out into an exhaust-filled and oppressive afternoon on the Fulham Palace Road. The hundred yards to the office entrance and the air-conditioned shelter it offered seemed very far away.

'Let's not go back,' Pete coaxed blearily in Matt's ear. 'Let's go over the road to that Irish pub. They'll serve any fucker . . .'

'Pete, we've got an editorial meeting in under an hour and you're totally fucked. You need to get back and sober up quick.' Matt was resolute.

'I'll be fine,' Pete said, lurching into Matt so that he in turn staggered into a passing woman, nearly knocking her off her feet and unleashing a tirade of curses from her in a language that he was very grateful not to understand.

'No you will not, we're going back.' Matt put one arm around Pete's back, supporting him under his hot and fetid armpit, and with gritted determination propelled him down the road and into their office building. With relief he saw the lift doors slide open and he bowled his charge into the cubicle before it could move.

It was only when he had Pete propped in a corner of the lift, pinned in place by Matt's steadying hand on his chest, and the doors had closed that Matt realised they were not alone. The blonde subeditor stood to one side, staring resolutely at the panel of illuminated numbers. His gut sinking, Matt really wished that he had found the time to make that call.

'Hello . . .' Matt trailed off. He'd called her the subeditor so repeatedly that her actual name had escaped him.

'You got home OK then?' he enquired belatedly, talking to her back. 'The other night?' Her shoulders rose and fell in an almost imperceptible sigh before she turned to face him, her pretty features set and tense.

'Yes thanks, luckily I found a taxi at the end of the road who didn't turn out to be a mugger or a rapist.' Unsurprisingly she was angry with him, but not as angry as she would be if she ever got sight of that column, though. He remembered Ellen in the kitchen, her quiet disapproval when he'd told her about his night with this woman, and he squirmed.

'Everything OK then . . . ?' Matt cursed himself mentally; her name simply would not come to mind. She barked a mirthless laugh.

'Lucy,' she said flatly. 'My name is Lucy and yes everything is fine, except that I'm the kind of idiot who wakes up with a fuck of a hangover after letting someone who is obviously an utter, utter twat take me home, get me into bed and then kick me out in the middle of the night without so much as even phoning me a taxi. And you don't even remember my name, you arsehole!' She rolled her eyes to the ceiling. 'God I hate myself. I make myself sick. I did everything the magazine I work for is constantly telling its readers not to do – and for *you* of all fuckwits. I mean sure you're pretty, but that's about it. You've got the conversational skills of an mentally impaired Rottweiler and your bedroom skills are frankly lacking in finesse.' She sighed as the lift stopped at her floor. 'When will women finally learn what cunts men are?'

'Hey hang on, that's not fair – Lucy!' Feeling compelled to go after her and to have his moment of decency albeit a couple of weeks late, Matt momentarily stepped away from Pete who immediately threatened to topple like a felled tree, forcing Matt to stay where he was and shore him up again. He called out of the lift just as the doors slid shut. 'I didn't turf you out, it was like I told you, my landlady . . . and anyway I was going to call you . . .' The lift doors closed before Matt could finish his explanation, which he realised belatedly wouldn't have done him any favours with Ellen.

Still, he felt unjustly slighted. How did Lucy know that he hadn't been about to call her and ask her out again, how did she know that he hadn't been telling the truth about his landlady being a dragon? Of course he would have called her a cab, only his mobile was dead and . . . and the landline had been cut off. Matt sighed as the lift hefted up one more floor, groaning as if it too could smell Pete's rancid fragrance. Lucy was right, he'd behaved like a total shit. She had him bang to rights, and weirdly he liked her more in that moment than he had in any other in their brief acquaintance. In all fairness to her, what he should do was find that column and pull it from the shared folder and replace it with something else. But Pete and Dan had seen it and liked it already; he'd look like some kind of half-arsed cowardly idiot if he tried to come up with a reason to change it now.

'You fucked her too? You bastard,' Pete slurred as Matt dragged him on to the magazine floor. After a moment's hesitation about what to do with his addled charge, Matt bundled him into the men's toilet and pushed him into a cubicle.

'Stay there, don't move, I'm going to get you coffee.'

'Bastard,' Pete murmured, resting his forehead against the cubicle wall, his eyes closing and his jaw slackening simultaneously.

Matt paused briefly to look at himself in the mirror, running his fingers under the cold tap and then through his hair before patting his damp palms against his hot cheeks. Then he headed out to find coffee.

'That for Pete?' Suze asked him coolly as he filled first one and then a second plastic cup at the coffee machine. Matt considered lying but as Dan's PA, Suze missed nothing, and it was fairly obvious that she did not like him, which was a bad thing. Suze seemed to wield a disproportionate amount of power in the office: she was the only woman whom none of the lads talked or joked or made smutty innuendoes about. Suze ran Dan like a military operation, making him look much more efficient and capable than he really was, and everybody knew that if you were on the wrong side of Suze it was only a matter of time before you were on the wrong side of Dan. Matt had been trying to warm her up to him since the first week he'd arrived, but no amount of flattery or charm could coax that perfect pout into a smile. Maybe by showing that he was taking care of Pete (if accompanying a known alcoholic to the pub could strictly be called taking care of) he would somehow impress her, show her that he was more than just another Jack the Lad.

'Yep,' Matt told her, grimly serious. 'I'm trying to sober him up again. He does this a lot, doesn't he? This is the worst I've seen him, but I bet it's not the first time.'

'Or the last,' Suze said primly. 'Dan puts up with it because

Pete helped him a lot when he was a rookie, got him some breaks that got him where he is today. That's why he's practically the only person in the industry that'll give Pete a job – but he won't be able to turn a blind eye for much longer. The old fool's getting out of hand.'

'What should I do?' Matt asked her miserably, hoping that appealing to her expertise would flatter and impress her.

'Get that down him, then get him into his office to sleep it off. Whatever you do don't let him come to the meeting. If he turns up drunk then Dan'll have no choice but to sack him, which would put Dan in a foul mood – bad news for the rest of us. The trick is to keep Pete on an even enough keel to make it OK to keep him on.'

'Right,' Matt said, staring at the two coffees and wondering if the watery grey concoctions would be nearly enough to perform the required miracle. 'But how do I stop him leaving his office if I'm at the meeting . . . ?'

Suze looked him up and down with an ill-disguised sneer that made Matt worry about what exactly he'd done to deserve it, and shrugged.

'You'll have to stay with him,' she instructed him. 'Don't worry, Dan loves your columns, especially the one about Carla, he laughed out loud when he read it. And the guys thought it was the funniest thing they'd heard in ages, you did a real hatchet job on her, didn't you? You don't need to be at the meeting to impress him.'

'You do realise that it wasn't really about Carla, don't you?' Matt winced, beginning to understand the chill in the air that had persisted ever since his first column had been printed.

Suze pursed her glossy lips and tipped her chin back.

'Let me see – how did it go? "Redheads are supposed to be fiery in the bedroom (and every other room) and this make-up-girl minx was no exception,"' she quoted verbatim. '"It was obvious from the first minute we met that it wouldn't take much to get her to take her clothes off, but what took me pleasantly by surprise was how quickly she ripped off mine! The second we got into her apartment she had me pinned up against the wall, powerless to resist as she rubbed her gorgeous body up against me . . ."' Suze broke off, shaking her head in disgust. 'I get it, I get that I work for a magazine that treats women like lumps of meat to be pawed at. But at least those girls in the pictures choose to take their clothes off and want a load of men they don't know to wank off over them. It's their choice. Carla didn't choose that.'

'She chose to come out with me, though,' Matt defended himself. 'And she chose to go to bed with me, even if it wasn't exactly like that. It's not as if I forced her. She chose to be with me.'

'Yes – the poor bloody bitch,' Suze said bitterly. 'And it's all my fault. *I've* been encouraging her to get out there again and meet men. *I've* been telling her that not all men are bastards like her ex and that she should take a chance.' She shook her head. 'Did you think for a second to find out anything about her apart from her cup size? For the last year she's been trying to break free from some tosser of a photographer who cheated on her, stole from her and beat her up. A few weeks ago she finally had the guts to get shot of him for good. Then you turn up and act all sweet and charming, act like you're interested in her, and she makes the mistake of taking you at face value and going too far too fast. That makes her naïve – but it doesn't give you the right to treat her like a joke and it doesn't give you the right to spread her all over the pages of a national magazine like one of those cheap sluts on the cover. She was just about getting her act back together and you've destroyed her all over again. But don't worry about it, Matt – Pete and Dan and all the arseholes out there on the floor think it's hilarious. So, good for you, Matt. Bravo. Enjoy babysitting Pete.'

Suze thundered out of the office, jogging Matt's elbow as she went so some of the coffee in the plastic cups slurped over the side and burnt the back of his hand, causing him to drop both of them on the floor.

'Fuck,' Matt muttered as he pulled out reams of paper towels from the dispenser bolted to the wall next to the coffee machine and trod them into the slowly spreading lake of coffee. 'Fuck, fuck, fuck.'

What was it about the women round here that made them want to break his balls today? It must be something in the water, he never got this grief back in Manchester. But then again he'd never messed about in his own back yard at home either, except on that one very, very ill-advised occasion. It probably wasn't that London women were more pissed off than northern ones, it was more that they knew where to find him.

And in his mind's eye there was still that image he couldn't get rid of, that made him feel all the more uncomfortable about what he had done since he arrived here.

Ellen in her red pyjamas, standing in her bare feet on those cold kitchen tiles.

Chapter Ten

'Well my pretty little Puritan maid, God must love me very much to bring me such a treasure on the road,' Eliza's abductor purred as he watched her in the candlelight.

Eliza spat at him, twisting against the ropes that bound her hands above her head to a beam in a room at the coaching inn. He had brought her here, paying the leering landlord handsomely not to come to the room, no matter what screams he might hear.

'And such a fiery maid too,' he continued, his eyes lazily travelling her length. 'What sport I will have with you, my love, in fact if you please me I may keep you with me permanently. I never expected you to be quite so beautiful.'

'I will die first!' Eliza hissed at him, fury mounting in her like a volcanic eruption. Was she an animal, a chattel that she could be passed so roughly from man to man with none honouring her as a human being? She pulled again at the ropes above her head and her attacker laughed, thinking she was struggling in vain. He had not glimpsed that with every rough rasp of the rope against the serrated edge of the beam another strand frayed and spun away. So far Eliza had struggled her way through about half of its thickness.

'Yes you will,' he told her, drawing a knife from its sheath and turning the blade so that it glinted in the candlelight. 'Be most assured, my love, if

you do not give me the pleasure I seek you will die, I have no time for a mewling wench who brings nothing but misery.'

In one swift cat-like move he brought the blade to her throat, and Eliza nearly choked on the stink of his fetid breath, his dark eyes burning a hair's breadth from hers.

'Hold still, vixen, 'twould be a shame to scar such a perfect hide.'

Eliza trembled more in fury than fear as the rogue traced the tip of his blade down the length of her neck and over the swell of her bosom, until it was inserted between the laces of her bodice.

'Let's see what treasure lies buried here, shall we?' he whispered, his voice thick with desire. In one swift motion he swept the blade downwards, severing the ribbons that were all that protected Eliza's much-abused modesty.

'You animal,' she hissed at him as he stood back to appraise his work, using the moment to drag and drag frantically on the rope once again.

'All men are animals,' he told her, quite unoffended. 'We have but basic needs, good food, good wine and as much rutting as a man can bear.'

His two hands clutched the opened edges of her bodice and ripped them asunder, shredding her thin cotton mantle. Eliza sobbed, outraged that once again her person was being so violated. She would not let it happen again. She would not let another man debase her so.

'Oh my sweet, my love,' the villain growled, his eyes burning with lust as he tore the rest of her gown from her. 'What perfection.'

Eliza screamed as his filthy hands enclosed her soft white flesh, squeezing and pawing her, his rotting teeth biting and nipping at the swell of her breasts.

'No!' she shouted, yanking once again on the thinning rope with strength that she barely knew she possessed. At last the rope broke. Both Eliza and her captor tumbled to the floor, he pinning her, her hands still bound at the wrist beneath his bulk.

'You cunning little bitch,' he said, with more admiration than anger. 'The game is on now.'

Eliza writhed and fought as he continued to maul her, forcing his knee between her thighs. Horror swept through her like ice when she realised that one foul hand had released her only to unlace his breeches. She sobbed in despair, certain that now there would be no escape. And then she saw the knife he had used to cut her clothes from her lying on the floor, almost within her reach. It lay just a few feet away, yet with her hands tied it was useless to her.

'Unbind me,' Eliza said suddenly, her calm voice belying the rage and fear that possessed her.

Stopped in his tracks for a moment, the monster looked at her, puzzled.

'I think not, my love. I do not fancy any scratches to take home to my wife and besides, I enjoy this more when the subject is, shall we say, confined.'

'You have won, you have conquered me.' Eliza forced herself to look into his bloodshot eyes. 'I am not such a fool that I would fight a lost cause. I am a woman alone and must find protection where I may. Unbind me and I swear that I will not scratch you, and my hands free will bring you more pleasure than tied. I bid you, my master, unbind me and I will do whatever you bid me.'

The vile beast sat up astride her, taking a moment to admire the sight of her, her flesh gleaming in the candlelight.

'Very well, I will. And on the morrow I will take you back home, where I will tell my wife she has a new maid and you will be at my beck and call whenever I require you. I shall become your protector, my love.'

'I am grateful, sir,' Eliza told him, though every word burnt through her tongue like acid. He bent over and loosed the rope that bound her wrists, making her retch as he lifted each bruised and chafed hand to his lips to kiss.

'And now my sweet, we seal our bargain.'

Eliza forced herself to wait passively as the brute buried his face in her neck, his hands once more pawing and grabbing at her while freeing himself from his own clothing. She gritted her teeth, her eyes fixed on the knife, determined that no man would ever again enter where he was not welcome. With a supreme effort she reached for the knife and without allowing herself a moment to think plunged it into the back of his neck with all her might.

Ellen paused, her fingers hovering over the keyboard. Allegra had stopped talking. She raised her head to look at the older woman, who was reclining on her chaise longue, her eyes closed. They had decided that morning that as Allegra was so late with the book it would be quicker for her to dictate it to Ellen, who would type it directly into electronic format. Ellen waited and still her boss did not move a muscle.

'Allegra?' Ellen's voice was low. Perhaps the old lady had drifted off, although Ellen could not believe that was possible after the breathless excitement of the passage that she had just typed up. More likely she was in the throes of some creative moment of enlightenment – having never spent much time around truly creative people before, Ellen wasn't sure what the throes of creative enlightenment would look like. Simon had said that Allegra was suffering something of a writer's block, or at least a problem with establishing the flow of the story, but Ellen couldn't see what he meant. When she attempted to write her own stories, something she hadn't been able to bring herself to do since Nick died, she'd sit in her chair at the kitchen table and chew the end of a biro until something came to her, usually some nonsense about a woman and her house and her husband and her son. She'd um and ah and huff and puff over a couple of paragraphs at the most.

Her attempts at authordom, as Nick referred to them, always made him chuckle. He used to come in, peer over her shoulder for a brief moment and then rub the back of her neck and say something along the lines of 'still no inspiration strike then, I see?' And perhaps he had been right, perhaps her laboured efforts and crossed-out scribbles had shown that she had never had a real feel for writing. Look at Allegra, she had just mentally downloaded at least a couple of thousand words in one go. Perhaps for real writers, real *artists* as Allegra surely was, the process was much more spiritual, like an emotional release. Afraid of disturbing her but uncertain of what to do now, Ellen whispered her name again.

'Allegra?'

'Ellen.' Allegra spoke her name with some resignation, as if she had just been woken from a rather wonderful dream.

'That was – that was utterly brilliant,' Ellen breathed, unable to contain herself. 'I was right in the moment, with Eliza. It's so exhilarating and liberating! What happens next? Will Captain Parker come and rescue her and take her back to the manor?'

Allegra's near-translucent lids fluttered open. She observed Ellen from across the room.

'No my dear, it's rather too soon in the story arc for a happy ending, we need to put Eliza in rather more peril first, I'd say.'

'Yes, of course,' Ellen agreed. 'If it was up to me there wouldn't be a story arc, all the characters would start out happy, be happy and then end up happy. But I suppose that would make for a rather dull read.'

'Have you ever worked on any of Melanie Love's titles, Ellen?'

'Yes, once or twice,' Ellen nodded, thinking of the sugary

faux-Regency romance novels where the nearest any of the characters got to peril was dropping a handkerchief.

'Well then you'll know dull is exactly what that kind of book is. Not to mention moronic, but still if there are people to read that kind of rubbish there will always be people to write it.' Allegra's smile was razor-sharp. 'Now it was you who got these rusty old cogs working again, and the words flowing. What do you think Eliza would do next?'

Ellen pondered Eliza standing over the corpse of her attacker. How would she feel? Frightened, exhilarated, confused? Allegra had agreed to move the action to London – now it was just a question of how to get a fugitive female murderer there.

'What if she dressed herself in his clothes, cut her hair, took his horse and made her way to London dressed as a man?' Ellen suggested tentatively.

'How very Shakespearean,' Allegra mused. 'It could work, though. How much of a fraud does it make me, I wonder, that my assistant is the one coming up with all the ideas?'

Ellen got up from her chair and walked around the desk, resisting the urge to sit on its polished walnut surface, as she was certain that Allegra would not approve. Instead she leaned against it, enjoying the slight breeze that wafted in through the open French doors, carrying with it a scent of roses in full bloom, mingled with the aroma of next door's freshly cut lawn. Less alluring was the stench of mouldering plant life, last summer's dead splendour, never cleared away and still rotting slowly into the earth. Beyond the unruly and unpruned cherry tree at the bottom of the garden, its fruit rotting amidst its roots, there would be the neat, trimmed and weeded borders of the garden that backed on to hers, and the garden that backed on to that one, going on and on for ever in a suburban patchwork of love and attention. Ellen imagined her own garden standing out, a single frayed unruly square besmirching the whole design. Perhaps, she thought, perhaps it *might* be time to venture into the garden again. She watched a pair of cabbage whites dance and flutter around the open door before lifting off in haphazard zigzags into the empty sky. Perhaps another day she'd go out there and assess what needed doing. She'd think about it, anyway.

'I might have had the idea, Allegra – but you put it into words,' Ellen told her, her eyes shining from the thrill of being involved in the process. 'You're the one who makes it so exciting and so real! I could never have done what you just did, I don't know how you do it – the words just streamed out of you. It's amazing – you're amazing. So just because you're a bit stuck on the plot it doesn't mean you are not a writer any more. You're more than that, you're a born storyteller. I feel so lucky that I get to see you in action.'

Allegra's smile was wan, but she sat up a little and smoothed her hair back from her face, seeming somewhat bolstered by Ellen's enthusiasm.

'So,' she said. 'We have our heroine, in disguise, speeding towards London where . . . she hopes to find sanctuary with her father's childhood friend.'

'Yes, yes!' Ellen nodded.

'And for once he will be a kind and fatherly figure who will want to look after her and protect her, and not rip her clothes off,' Allegra added. 'We always need at least one decent man per book, apart from our soon-to-be-reformed hero. It adds balance. Now, as you quite rightly mentioned, at the moment the plot is lacking a little historical context – where should we send Eliza running to that will add that aspect to the book?'

'Well, I was thinking – and this is just an idea, so say if you think it's rubbish – that she could go to the Tower of London. In the Civil War it was a Roundhead armoury with a permanent garrison posted there. They also used it to imprison a couple of dangerous Royalist supporters. I thought we could make her protector the garrison's general?'

'Perfect – he could be an honest and forthright man who believes in the true cause of the war and in a republic for the people.'

'Exactly – the people of London were so sick and tired of Charles and his blinkered belief in divine rule by that time,' Ellen told her. 'They really believed that England could be a republic, where all men and women were equal. It's quite revolutionary when you think about it, not that it would have ever worked, especially not with Cromwell in charge.'

'And,' Allegra said thoughtfully, 'perhaps while she is there Eliza can become involved in some secret mission, some way to help the Puritan cause? Now is the point in the arc when we want to start to show that her experiences have changed her.'

'That she isn't just a girl any more – but that she's becoming a strong independent woman,' Ellen added, seeing herself for a moment as if through a window. A woman on her own, earning her own money, paying her own bills. It gave her an unexpected jolt of exhilaration.

Allegra nodded. 'Yes, yes – it's perfect. Then our dear Royalist Captain Parker will have to stray right into the enemy's nest to track down the woman whom he does not yet know he loves . . .' Allegra paused. 'Let's say he's followed her trail, gathered that it must have been her who murdered our villain – a villain that we can make into someone important to the Royalist cause – and perhaps it is Captain Parker who is charged with discovering the murderer and then has to bring his own true love to the noose!' Allegra's eyes sparkled as she spoke.

'Brilliant!' Ellen clasped her hands together. 'You see? Now you are the one who's coming up with all the ideas. Soon you won't need me to do anything but type.'

'I'm not at all sure about that,' Allegra smiled. 'I've known you only a short time and yet I have a feeling that you are my amulet, my lucky charm. You get this old brain creaking again, Ellen.' The two women smiled at each other, Ellen feeling a rare moment of pure pleasure.

'I have a splendid idea,' Allegra went on. 'We've worked so hard these last two weeks, knocking this manuscript into shape, we haven't been out of the house! How about you and I go on a research trip to the Tower, you know, soak up the atmosphere, find out a little more about the history. Afterwards we can make Simon take us to lunch at that Conran restaurant – the one at the foot of Tower Bridge – what's it called? He's been promising me a good lunch for weeks now.'

'Pont de la Tour,' Ellen said slowly. 'And yes, that would be a good idea – but don't forget it's peak tourist season. We wouldn't be able to move for the crowds, we'd get no sense of atmosphere at all. And in this heat with all those people, I'm not sure you'd enjoy it, Allegra.'

Ellen thought of the throngs of people that were always pressing into every nook and cranny of London's tourist hot-spots, and her heart raced at the thought of being caught up in that great indifferent crowd of strangers. She swallowed and ook the image from her head, choosing instead to focus on a ladybird that was crawling up the glass of the open French door. Now that the inside of the door had been freshly painted, Ellen noticed that the outside was peeling and cracked. Vaguely she wondered if all the external woodwork was in need of similar repair.

'You have a point.' Allegra wrinkled her nose at the thought of a mass of the great unwashed. 'Although it rather irks me that I am getting too old for crowds. During my life I've found that almost all the best things happen in crowds, parties, orgies – that sort of thing. Still, how are we to know our locations if we do not visit them?'

'Easy!' Ellen smiled. 'Google Maps.' She opened the Web browser on her laptop and brought up the right page. After a few minutes she found the location and took it over to show Allegra. 'See, you don't actually need to go anywhere any more, you can walk down almost any street without ever leaving the house. It's brilliant!'

'Good Lord.' Allegra peered uncertainly at the screen. 'Soon no one will ever leave their homes, we will all be living virtual lives in a virtual reality.'

'Yes, but when you think about it that's sort of what a novel is, isn't it – a virtual reality,' Ellen said. 'I don't think it's all that bad, is it? There's nothing wrong with having a place to escape to. A place to feel safe in.'

'Perhaps.' Allegra watched her. 'But I tend to think that life is made up of the muck and grit, the dirt and danger of the real world. The world we are born into, kicking and screaming and gasping for air. To try and escape the daily fight is to excuse yourself from living, isn't it? And you want to be a writer, Ellen, to be a writer you need to live life. Not watch it go by your window.'

'I don't want to be a writer!' Ellen smiled. 'I don't have the talent for it. I just love reading and sometimes I've had a go at writing for fun, but I could never do what you do, Allegra. It's just not in me.'

'Well, that is arguable, but if it isn't in you then perhaps that's only because you are not in it.'

'I beg your pardon?' Ellen asked her, but Allegra merely shrugged.

'Very well, agreed we will not visit the Tower in person, but I am still determined to have my good lunch and I am determined that you will come with me. After all you are just as deserving as I am, if not more.'

'Well, um, thank you,' Ellen said, her smile wavering. 'Thank you. I'm sure that would be really nice and I'd love to come – if I can.'

'That's settled then, I shall telephone Simon about it this afternoon,' Allegra said. 'Now let's talk about Eliza and Captain Parker. She hates him, and with good reason, after all he took from her something that should have been hers alone to bestow. But now she's had those terrible experiences with her uncle and the man she's killed she might perhaps see a subtle difference. The captain did not hurt her and he made her feel the awakening of desire that she is unable to forget, so although she hates him she yearns for him too.'

'Mmmm,' Ellen said. 'The thing is, I've read all your books and I love them, but I've never quite been able to get my head around the fact that the man who forces himself on a woman at the beginning of a book can be the same man she falls in love with at the end. I mean while I'm reading it, swept along with all it, it makes sense, but afterwards, I wonder – would that really happen?'

'Of course not, but this is fantasy, dear – and whether we admit it or not many women fantasise about being overpowered by a man, being absolved of any responsibility for whatever sexual pleasure might be about to befall them,' Allegra told her. 'Don't forget most of my readers are married or older women, they are not practised seductresses – in real life they would never stray from the right path, so in their fantasies they often have no choice. Goodness knows, the debate about whether my sort of fiction glamorises rape has raged on for each of the thirty years I've been writing, but what I'm writing isn't real, it's a safe environment where a woman can indulge in certain thoughts. I haven't met a woman yet who wouldn't secretly like to be tied to the bedpost with a silk scarf or two and toyed with a little by her lover.'

'Haven't you?' Ellen exclaimed, genuinely shocked.

Allegra's smile was mischievous. 'Well, wouldn't you have liked it?'

'Me? Tied up and . . . no it was never like that with me and Nick.' Ellen found herself blushing, flashes of the last time she and Nick had made love materialising before her eyes for one painful moment, him moving above her, his eyes closed. Her watching him, willing him to look at her, just for one moment, to see her the way that only he ever could. It had been a quiet, sacred, special thing, the last time they had made love, and afterwards she had rested her head on Nick's chest and listened to his heartbeat as he slept.

'What a shame, so what was sex like?' Allegra asked her

baldly. Ellen hesitated. One thing she had never done was discuss her sex life with anyone other than her husband. Not even with him, to be honest. It simply wasn't something they had ever sat down and talked about.

When she had first met Nick she'd been working as a research assistant at the British Museum, cataloguing and dating the mass of artefacts that the museum owned but did not have the room to put on permanent display. And when she'd come into work glowing after a night out with him, her friends and colleagues would quiz her on every tiny detail of her date, even questioning her on Nick's prowess in bed. Ellen had told them nothing, partly because she was far too shy to talk about anything like that, and partly because there was hardly anything to tell. For the first few months of their relationship Nick had barely touched her, their physical contact hardly stretching beyond a goodnight kiss, his hand resting chastely on her waist. This would invariably leave Ellen on the wrong side of her front door wondering exactly what it was he saw in her, when he seemed to desire her so little. Once, after months of dating him, over dinner after a glass of wine too many she had asked him flat out if he fancied her. Nick had laughed out loud, making Ellen feel, she remembered, rather foolish.

'Do I fancy you?' He'd sounded amazed. 'Have you seen yourself, Ellen, with your black hair and green eyes and those curves . . . ? My God, I don't think there is a man alive who wouldn't want you.'

'But then why haven't we . . . I mean it's been nearly six months and we haven't even, you know.' Ellen had leaned across the table, feeling the excess of wine slosh around inside her skull. 'You haven't even tried to put your hand up my top.'

Nick had looked at her as if he were very slightly disappointed in her for even asking. It was a look that had set her back in her chair.

'Don't you get it, Ellen?' he'd asked her, seeming a little offended. 'You are the woman I am going to marry. The woman who is going to have my children and who I am going to spend the rest of my life with. What's six months in a lifetime? When we make love for the first time I want you to know that it's special, that it's for ever. When I make you mine, I want to make sure that you *are* mine. We have all the time in the world, Ellen. We have for ever, after all.'

Ellen remembered how breathless she'd felt when his finger-tips had reached across the table and touched the back of her hand, the electric shock that had shivered through her body at the merest suggestion of contact. She had been overwhelmed by the romance of the moment, consumed with happiness at her luck in finding a man who would cherish her so.

'Yes,' she'd whispered happily. 'Oh yes Nick, I will marry you.'

'Hang on, darling,' Nick had chuckled. 'I haven't asked you yet. All in good time, you'll find out when I'm ready – and for now let's just take our time, shall we?'

And after Nick had chosen his moment, proposing to her over a picnic held on the banks of the Seine, and they were married on the date that he chose, Ellen had decided to take his advice and give up working for the museum. Her friendships had gradually dropped away and by degrees Nick and then a little later Charlie had become her life, a life that she revelled in. It was funny, but in all those years, up until that very moment, Ellen had never once missed the tipsy nights out that she used to enjoy with the girls. Somehow, though, talking to Allegra brought back to her what it used to be like, how she never laughed in quite the same way or as hard with her husband as she had with her female friends. And yet now she wasn't at all certain that any of the numbers she had for them in her battered address book would still be relevant. She'd lost all those people who were once so important to her without even noticing, she'd been so caught up in her new life with Nick.

Hannah had asked her once with a raised eyebrow and a nipped lip what her sex life with Nick was like, and Ellen had told her to mind her own business. She never talked about that kind of thing with anyone, but especially not Hannah. Nick would have been appalled. And yet, somehow, it sort of felt OK to talk about it to Allegra. Allegra was impartial, like some Greek goddess reigning over a chessboard of mortals. Her interest in Ellen's sex life wasn't salacious or intrusive, it was impartial.

Ellen slid her bottom up on to the surface of the desk, forgetting what Allegra might think as she pondered her question.

'It was quiet – you know. Nick was always so gentle with me, so tender. I mean he made me feel unbelievably beautiful. He used to love it that he was the only man in the world who got to . . . well, look at me, you know – that way.'

'You are unbelievably beautiful, that's simply a fact,' Allegra told her. 'It's a rare beauty when even in those sacks you insist on wearing, with your hair all scraped up and having clearly been nowhere near make-up in several years, you still have that glow about you, that look of a woman, to paraphrase Margaret Mitchell, who needs to be kissed, and well, by someone who knows how.'

'I'm not sure about that.' Ellen's eyes widened, haunted

momentarily by her fantasy vision of Matt gripping her firmly in a hay barn.

'So your husband was gentle with you, was he passionate too?' Allegra persisted with her line of questioning.

'Oh yes, well I mean he didn't rip off my clothes or fling me about. That just wasn't Nick, but he was very passionate about our marriage, about the way it should be.' Ellen smiled fondly as she remembered. 'He was an old-fashioned boy, with old-fashioned ideas. He was the man who went out in the world, the breadwinner – and I was his sanctuary, his wife waiting for him at home. I know it seems outdated and archaic now, but the truth is, Allegra, that Nick was exactly the kind of man I needed. I'm not a go-getting career girl like my sister Hannah, I don't . . . didn't . . . function all that well on my own, I haven't got what it takes. Nick made me realise that I didn't want to be out in the world, fighting my corner. I wanted to be there for him and he wanted to make a safe place for me. When we bought this house he closed the front door behind us and told me that I was home now, and I never had to worry about the world outside again. I felt so . . . cherished.'

'And your husband was your only lover?' Allegra asked her. 'You were a virgin when you married him?'

'No, of course not! I was twenty-four when I married him. I'd had two other "proper" boyfriends but it was nothing special with them. With the first one I remember I was scared because I hadn't told him I was a virgin. I didn't want him to think I was inexperienced so I just lay there totally rigid with fear, until eventually he stopped and asked me what was going on. I had to tell him then and he was really sweet about it, turned out he was a virgin too, and we muddled through somehow. That was

Graham – we went out together for a year and then after him there was this man at the museum, my boss, I'm ashamed to say.'

'And did he throw you across his desk, rip a hole in your tights and take you?' Allegra sounded hopeful.

'Goodness no, he was a lot older than me and he had recurring back trouble. We never really clicked in *that* way. Anyway it only happened a couple of times before I met Nick and I realised for the first time in my life what it meant to really want someone.'

'What did Nick think of your lovers? Was he jealous?' Allegra enquired.

'No – Nick never asked me and I never told him. It was as if when we came together we started on a new page, as if nothing that had happened before mattered. It was us two against the world.'

'I see,' Allegra said thoughtfully, eyeing Ellen. Her assistant's tawny skin was a little flushed from the conversation, the slight breeze that found its way through the French doors lifting tendrils of her dark hair away from her skin. 'And now?'

'Now?' Ellen queried.

'Ellen, you are still a young woman, a young, attractive and clearly passionate woman. Now surely is the right time for a new chapter in your life. So – who will make love to you now?'

'Oh God – no one!' Ellen stuttered. 'No, no one. I was, I am Nick's wife. I always will be. I could never . . . not with anyone else. It would be a betrayal. And besides, what about Charlie? I have to think of him, the last thing he needs is me, you know, doing it.'

'Are you sure?' Allegra asked her. 'Perhaps a more fulfilled and satisfied mother is just what he needs – either way, it's clear to me, even if it isn't to you, that you are a very sexual person.'

'Me? Allegra, have you noticed that you think about sex a lot? You are obsessed!' Ellen laughed, but she didn't deny Allegra's assessment. 'The truth is I just can't ever imagine meeting someone who could replace Nick. There isn't anyone, it's as simple as that.'

'Well perhaps not as a life partner or a husband, those kinds of men are very hard to come by, which is the reason that I have never married. But lovers? Lovers are ten a penny. For example, what about your handsome lodger?' Allegra's smile was wicked, her eyes sparkling with mischief. 'I'm seventy-three, I haven't enjoyed "congress" for many months but I can still imagine that young man in a number of uncompromising positions.'

Ellen's mouth opened and closed as she tried to process all the information that Allegra had just given her. Deciding it was none of her business to ask, she concentrated on the salient bits. 'Matt? As if he would ever be interested in *me*!'

'He's a man, my dear, he's interested in anything with a pulse, more or less – but that wasn't the question I asked you. I asked you if you were interested in him.'

Ellen blushed, thinking again of her haybarn fantasy, her face betraying her without a thought of loyalty to its owner.

'Well he is very handsome,' she admitted. 'And quite, you know, masculine – he's got very nice arms. Oh look – yes, he's a man and he wanders about the house in a towel sometimes, and he's quite tactile, not in a sexual way. But any man touching you when it's been so long, it reminds your body what it's like and . . . I did enjoy that side of my marriage. It is hard to come to terms with the fact that all that is over for me. But Matt and I – I'm like his older sister, we're friends.' Ellen dropped her gaze to the floor, not wanting to reveal quite how much she enjoyed her kitchen chats with her lodger. 'I can't think about him in that way, it would just be wrong!'

'Rubbish,' Allegra told her stoutly. 'Matthew isn't the kind of man to turn down any sexual experience. Here he is, a virile, experienced young man in your house. It's almost as if the gods have brought him to you for your personal delight. He might open up a world of possibilities to you, and bearing that in mind you might want to consider taking him as your lover.'

'My – *what*?' Ellen all but shrieked. 'Allegra, don't be so ridiculous. As if I ever would and even if I would, even if I could, as if Matt would ever look twice at me, as if *he* would ever want *me*! He just wouldn't . . . would he?'

'Certainly I don't believe he would fall in love with you, propose to you or cherish you in quite the same way as your late husband seemed to,' Allegra said thoughtfully. 'And I'm sure that whatever interest he had in you would wane in due course. But I am also quite sure that, as long as you understood that and were determined not to fall in love with him, if you set your mind to it you could have him in your bed whenever you chose, at least for a while.'

Words failing her, Ellen emitted a kind of strangulated squeak, and glancing at her watch was glad to see that it had gone five in the afternoon. She had been so engrossed in her talk with Allegra that she hadn't heard Charlie come in.

'Well anyway – that's that for today,' she said, hurriedly saving that day's work. 'I'm going to see what Charlie wants for tea – would you like anything before dinner, Allegra?'

Allegra smiled, clearly satisfied with her meddling. 'I am quite replete, thank you,' she told Ellen. 'I think I might take a nap now and indulge in some daydreams of my own. Thank you for today, Ellen, you don't know how much it means to me to have found you to work with.'

Ellen was so touched that she forgot to be shocked, and she was glowing with the after-effects of the praise when she called up the stairs to Charlie.

'Darling? Do you want tea yet, or do you want to wait?'

There was no reply. He was probably plugged into some contraption or other, listening to music on the iPod that Hannah had bought him or playing his treasured DS. Wearily Ellen mounted the stairs and obligingly knocked on the door before opening it, as Charlie had made her promise to do. But the room was empty. He wasn't back from school yet, she realised, feeling a swell of panic balloon in her chest.

'Well that's OK,' she said out loud. 'I mean it's only just five and he is nearly twelve. He'll be in the park or with a friend. It's perfectly fine. Nothing to worry about.' Yet she crossed to the landing window that looked out over street after street of houses and towards the park that suddenly seemed so very far away. Ellen placed the flat of her palm against the glass, withdrawing it quickly as if she somehow might get sucked through it into free fall, like she had seen happen in a film once about a jetliner that had lost cabin pressure.

'He's just off somewhere and he's forgotten that he's supposed to phone me if he's staying out with friends,' Ellen reassured herself out loud, a tremor in her voice despite her calming words. Quickly she went back downstairs to the phone in the hall and dialled the number of Charlie's mobile. She had been furious with Hannah for giving this to Charlie soon after Nick had died, as if gifts could replace his father, but she was

171

now grateful that she could contact him. Or at least she would have been grateful if her call hadn't gone straight to answer-phone, which meant that the mobile was either turned off or didn't have a signal.

Ellen swallowed, staring at her redundant telephone as if it were some kind of mysterious cipher that held more answers than it chose to reveal. Why would Charlie's phone be turned off, and where might he have gone where there wasn't a signal? There wasn't anywhere around here that didn't have a signal. She knew that because there had been that campaign in the local paper about the phone masts that had been put on top of a block of council flats a few streets away. The residents had formed a protest group, anxious about brain cancer or something. They had lost in the end, proclaiming that people in private housing would never be subjected to such risks, which Ellen had felt bad about – but still the place virtually bristled with masts. Where around here could Charlie be that could be out of reach of a mast – or had he had gone somewhere very far away? Or what if his phone was turned off? Ellen felt freezing fear settle on her chest like a block of ice. Had someone turned off Charlie's phone to stop him asking for help?

Her hands trembling, she picked up the phone, pressed redial and left a message.

'Charlie, it's Mum, look darling it's nearly five thirty and you're not home. Be a love and give me a call when you get this, I know you think I'm a silly old thing, but I worry.' Ellen success-fully managed to brighten her voice, but the artifice dissolved the moment she put the phone down, and she stood uncertainly in the hallway looking at the front door, willing Charlie to come through it.

Perhaps he was just down the road, she thought. Perhaps if she went to the garden gate and looked down the road she'd see him coming, dragging his school bag along the pavement, his blazer tied around his waist by the arms, scuffing his shoes with every step.

Ellen went to the front door and put her hand on the latch and her heart leapt as she heard a key turn in the lock. Happily she flung the door open.

Sabine stood, her keys in her hand, surprised to find Ellen on the other side.

'What are you doing there?' she asked. 'You nearly gave me a heart attack!'

'Oh Sabine.' Ellen did not mask her disappointment, her eyes travelling over Sabine's shoulder to the heat-hazed road beyond. 'I was waiting for Charlie – he's late and I was worried – did you see him, coming up the road?'

Sabine glanced at her watch. 'Charlie is twelve nearly and it's a lovely summer's evening – he'll be playing football or something with his friends. There isn't anything to worried about, I'm certain.' She put her hand on Ellen's shoulder, seeing the concern etched in her face. 'Ellen, you are shaking – please don't be so afraid. I'm sure that Charlie is fine. I know you must worry about him more after what happened to your husband, but I promise you dreadful things like that hardly ever happen. Statistically the chances of a terrible accident befalling another member of your family are very slim. Come, let me make you a cup of tea.'

Not exactly comforted, Ellen nodded and let Sabine lead her into the kitchen. She knew that Sabine was probably right, that Charlie was probably fine and that he probably hadn't phoned her because as with everything he did right now he was determined to prove to her that he wasn't a baby any more, but still it was a struggle to master the cold sweep of panic at the thought of her son out there in some unknown place in the world.

As the kettle boiled Sabine smoothed four sheets of A4 paper out on the table in front of Ellen. Each side was filled with writing, divided into sections and colour-coded with a variety of highlighter pens.

'You are a professional with words, would you look at my list – tell me what you think?' Sabine asked her, taking two mugs from the draining board.

'What's this, something to do with work?' Ellen scanned the list, temporarily distracted. 'I'm not sure I'll know what to think, Hannah's the one you want to talk to.'

Sabine snorted as if Ellen had just said something utterly ridiculous, then seeing Ellen's raised eyebrows she shook her head.

'No, this is not work. This is *my* list. My disgusting treacherous husband and I talked and talked on the phone last night. He wants us to try again, he wants us to be together and have children and be a proper married couple like his awful parents. Well, I told him that I could not even consider it until he addressed all of the problems in our marriage. So he suggested we each write lists, lists of things that we don't like about each other. He believes it will start a discussion and perhaps enable us to reconcile, the vile whoring adulterer. So I said "Yes, OK, I will do it." After all we have been married two years now and I am not the sort of person who does not try her best, even though the scum-sucking arsehole does not deserve my best. He emailed me his list after we talked but I am still working on mine: Please, take a look, see what you think.'

As she spread the sheets out in front of her Ellen glanced at the kitchen clock as it ticked towards six. With Sabine here she did feel a little calmer, it hardly seemed anything out of the ordinary that Charlie wasn't home yet, Sabine was so sure he would be soon. If Sabine was unconcerned then she would do her best to be too, at least for the next twenty minutes. After all, life would be impossible if every time things went a little unexpectedly, she expected two police officers making their way up the front path. Ellen made a bargain with herself. If he had not appeared by six fifteen she would allow herself to be anxious and panic again, but until then she would not worry. She tore her eyes from the clock and looked at the list as Sabine, sitting in Charlie's chair, put a cup of steaming tea down beside her.

'Pages one and two,' Sabine explained, 'are highlighted in green and come under the category of irritants. Little things that annoy me but don't especially mean the end of a marriage. There are thirty-seven items in this section. Read it, I've written it in English so that I could ask your opinion.'

'Why my opinion?' Ellen was puzzled.

'Because you had the perfect marriage, you know what it takes to make a relationship work.'

'Do I?' Ellen wondered out loud as she traced her finger down the first side of the green list. Item one – failure to pick up own dirty socks from floor, item fourteen – refusal ever to see a film at the cinema that does not involve violence and scenes of a sexual nature, item twenty-six – mean when it comes to spending own money. And so on and so on right down to item thirty-seven – leaving unpleasant stains on the bed sheets without any attempt to share the laundry chores.

Ellen didn't care to know exactly what that meant.

'Well that *is* quite a lot of irritants,' she said.

'Exactly,' Sabine replied. 'Was your husband ever so annoying?'

Ellen thought. It used to annoy her that Nick never remembered to put the milk or the butter back in the fridge and that instead of loading the dishwasher he'd pile all the dirty plates in the sink, filling it with water that would soon grow greasy and cold – but then she'd remind herself that he was out at work all day and that it was her job to make sure the house ran smoothly, and she'd put the curdled butter back in the fridge and pull the lumps of sodden food out of the blocked sinkhole, and any irritation soon passed. And she would have happily have put away a thousand more cartons of milk and unblocked a thousand more stinking plugholes if it meant that he would be back in the house again.

'No, not really,' she told Sabine apologetically. 'And although those things are annoying, well – we are all human, aren't we? We all have little foibles. If you love someone, you put up with them.'

'I thought as much.' Sabine sounded resentful as she put the second sheet of paper in front of her.

'Here is the amber list, the things that really upset me a great deal but which if he agreed to change sufficiently might not rule out us getting back together. There are twenty-one items in this section.'

Item five – flirting with every single woman ever encountered, even my mother.

Item eleven – always mentally undressing other women, even unattractive ones – and being really obvious about it, even my mother.

176

Item sixteen – openly watching porn when my favourite TV shows are on.

Item twenty-one – spending more money on lap dances than on my birthday present.

'Oh my.' Ellen looked up at Sabine. 'He really does that?'

'Yes, he's a member of a gentlemen's club, the yearly subscription is hundreds of euros, never mind what he pays for lap dances while he is in there. And yet what did I get for my birthday? A juicer.' Sabine knitted her lips into a tight knot and crossed her arms. 'True, I asked for a juicer, but a little something more – something he chose himself would have meant a lot.'

'So it's the fact that the strippers cost more than your birthday present that upsets you, not the actual strippers themselves?' Ellen asked her.

Sabine shrugged. 'Men will be men. For my odious husband going to a strip club at the end of a night out is like an Englishman going for a curry.'

'Really?' Ellen wondered what heinous crime Sabine's husband could have committed for her to hate him quite so openly, if it wasn't going to strip clubs.

'So finally the red list.' Sabine's expression dropped, pain etched across her face. Ellen braced herself.

'There is only one thing on this list,' she said, pushing it over so that Ellen could read it.

Item one – writing love letters to another woman.

'Writing . . . you mean you found out he was having an affair?' Ellen gasped.

'Yes,' Sabine nodded sadly. 'Not a sexual one, a sexual one I could have understood, perhaps even forgiven. No it was much

177

worse than that. He has always stayed in touch with his childhood sweetheart, I knew that. But then a few months ago I found these letters from her, so passionate, so full of love and regret that they could never be together. So I looked on his laptop, he thought he'd hidden them, but he never was very good at keeping a secret. I found copies of all of his letters in his accounts folders. Telling her how he would always love her, how if things had been different, if they had taken a chance when they had the opportunity . . . He was so tender, so romantic – he is never like that with me.' Sabine pressed the palm of her hand to her chest. 'Honestly, Ellen, if I had come home to find him in bed with another woman it would have hurt less. Now I know that I am second choice, that he settled for me because he can't have her. How do I get over that?'

Ellen looked at the words printed meekly on the page before her. A simple collection of letters that when organised, in this one particular way, became so brutal.

She felt another tiny rent in her heart as she realised again just what she had lost. Nick had been her first choice and she had been his. Their marriage had been rare and fortunate indeed.

'Sabine, I honestly don't know. All I can say is that he does seem to be trying. If you mean so little to him why would he trying to save your marriage at all?'

'She is a Catholic. She will not divorce her husband,' Sabine said wanly. 'If she were free, would he still be trying to save our marriage or would he be running into her arms?'

Ellen didn't have an answer for that. 'What did he write on his list?' she asked instead.

Sabine's laugh was hollow. 'There are three items on his list in total. One of them is that I do not laugh enough. Laugh enough!

I would laugh if only he were ever funny. But there is nothing funny about this.'

'No, there isn't,' Ellen agreed. There was Allegra, encouraging her to go out in the world again, even to take a lover, as if such a thing might be possible – and yet here was Sabine, living proof that men like Ellen's lost husband were very rare indeed. She had been lucky to have had a man who respected and loved her as much as he did, perhaps luckier than she knew. No one would ever care about her like that again.

'He says that I should be more spontaneous, but I don't like to be spontaneous. Not without thinking about it first.' Ellen thought that Sabine was joking, but managed to stifle her laugh when she saw the other woman was deadly serious.

'And he says I care too much for appearances. Would he want me if I were fat, or grey, or never took any care with my hair or clothes?' Sabine unconsciously gestured at Ellen, who wouldn't allow herself to be offended, because after all she never thought twice about the way she looked.

'So what do you think? Do you think that these lists will help us reconcile?'

Ellen glanced at the clock; it was twelve minutes past six.

'I have to be honest, Sabine, I'm not really an expert on relationships, I've only had one important one. But if the lists of things you don't like about your husband are this long and if one of the things includes him being in love with another woman, I don't really see how you could ever get over that. I know I couldn't.'

Sabine's face crumpled and she buried her face in her hands as if she had just heard the bad news for the first time.

'But what do I know?' Ellen added hastily, putting a hand on

Sabine's shoulder. 'I am probably completely wrong – only you know what your marriage means to you and him.'

'You are right of course,' Sabine sobbed. 'Of course I can't take him back, what honour or pride would I have left if I did so knowing he was always thinking of another woman? It's just that I love him, Ellen. I love the evil, disgusting pig. I love him, I always have and he's ripped all that to shreds.' Ellen wrapped her arms around Sabine and let her sob into her neck, keeping her eye on the clock. In twenty seconds she would officially start panicking again.

Just then the front door slammed shut and Ellen heard voices in the hall. Charlie's voice and someone else's . . . Hannah's. For a few seconds she was flooded with relief, an emotion that soon turned to fear-fuelled anger.

Ellen withdrew her arm from Sabine, who stood up and went to the sink to splash water on her face, piling her lists back into her bag as she went, clearly keen not to be caught crying.

'Hi, Mum,' Charlie greeted her happily as he crashed open the door, adding to the dent in the plaster that he'd been working on for some months, even though Ellen repeatedly begged him to be more careful. 'You'll never guess what, it's really cool. Aunt Hannah's bought me a PlayStation 3 and a load of games!'

'Charlie – it's gone six – where have you been?' Ellen asked him her voice low and tight, the terror she had been fighting to repress suddenly forming a heavy lump in her chest.

'With me, Ellie,' Hannah informed her brightly. 'Thought to myself what a beautiful afternoon, too good to waste in an office, so I bunked off work a bit early, picked up Charles from school and we went to the West End for a bit of a spend-up.

After all, what's the point of having money if you don't use it? Don't mind, do you?'

'Don't mind?' Ellen found that she was shaking again, shocked to her core by exactly how frightened she had been at not knowing exactly where Charlie was, of thinking of him out there in the world alone. Her cheeks flared and her voice trembled. 'You take my son off for nearly three hours, buying him expensive presents without asking me, without even letting me know where he is! Hannah, I've been worried sick!'

Hannah blinked at her, rubbed the end of her nose and laughed. 'Ellie, don't be so ridiculous.'

It was a match to the touchpaper of her fury.

'I am not, I am not, I am NOT ridiculous!' Ellen shouted, advancing on her sister with each word, until they were just a few inches apart. Hannah stared at her, her confusion making her seem mildly amused by Ellen's outburst, which served to madden Ellen even further. 'Don't you get it, Hannah? You might be Charlie's aunt, but you don't get to just take him! You don't get take him places, buy him things he doesn't need without asking me first. I am his mother, not you!'

'But—' Hannah looked perplexed.

'I told her you'd said it was OK, all right?' Charlie shouted, stepping between his aunt and his mother, shielding Hannah from her older sister. 'I told her I'd phoned you and that you didn't mind because I *knew* that if she asked you you'd say no, because you just want me to be stuck here in the house all day like you are and to *never* go anywhere and to *never* have any fun at all. And I turned my phone off so that you couldn't spoil everything like you *always* do. And anyway *everyone* else has got a PlayStation except for me and if Aunt Hannah wants to buy me one then I don't know why she should have to ask *you* and at least she does take me out, at least she will go places with me, which is more than you ever do!'

'Charlie.' It was Sabine who spoke, her voice calm and level. 'You are unfair to speak to Ellen like that, she was only worried about you.'

'And you can shut up – it's none of your fucking business!' Charlie yelled at Sabine.

'Charlie Woods go to your room right now!' Ellen thundered furiously, startled by the volume of her own voice, which was seldom, if ever, raised. Needing no further prompting, Charlie picked up the bag his console was in and made to leave. 'And you can leave that there for a start,' she told him.

'What?' Charlie whirled round, his eyes burning. 'It's mine, I'm setting it up upstairs.'

'No, no you are not.' For those few seconds Ellen concentrated every ounce of her anger, panic and anxiety on him and discovered she was glad when she saw him shrink a little under her glare. 'You are leaving it in its bag with its receipt until I decide what to do with it.'

'Or what?' Charlie challenged her. 'Going to take it back to the shop, are you?' Ellen felt her brief moment of power dwindle away. 'No, didn't think so. Fine, do what you like with it. I don't give a toss.' He kicked the bag halfway across the floor, its journey stopped with a thud by one of the kitchen cupboards, and then slammed savagely up the stairs.

Ellen turned to look at Hannah, who stood fidgeting with the strap on her bag. Her eyes were bright, a nervous half-smile fixed on her lips as if she didn't quite understand what was going on. 'Don't you see at all what you've done?' Ellen asked her.

'Honestly, Ellen, Charles shouldn't have lied to me about calling you, but really what's the big deal if I buy him something every now and then? God knows, his life is so depressing, he deserves a treat or two. And I thought what with ... well, it being nearly a year since the accident it would be good for him to have something to take his mind off things. And you know how much he's wanted one of those, I really didn't think it would do any harm.'

Ellen shook her head, it was as if her sister lived in her own impervious little bubble, immune to the effect she had on the lives around her.

'Hannah, perhaps you should go.' Sabine spoke quietly, but if she was attempting to defuse the situation it was too late.

'How dare you,' Ellen growled at her sister. 'Charlie and I have been through hell together over the last year and we're not back yet. Don't you think I know how hard it's been on him, it's been hard on me too. But I'm his mother, and I'm the one doing my very best to keep things together for him. You know how difficult it is for me to make ends meet, and you swanning around playing the big "I am" doesn't help. It's almost as if you're trying to make him like you more than me!' Ellen's revelation escaped her lips before she could stop it. Was that why she was so angry? Was it purely jealousy, seeing Hannah spend the kind of time with Charlie that she didn't seem capable of herself?

'Well that wouldn't be hard,' Hannah mumbled, rolling her eyes like an insolent teen, which blotted out all Ellen's other thoughts.

'I've had enough of this, Hannah. I don't want you round here or Charlie for a while. Yes – yes it is the anniversary of Nick's death soon, it's going to be hard enough for Charlie and me without you trying to stir things up. So can you please just leave us alone to get through it? After all, *we're* the ones who loved him, *we're* the ones who lost him. You, you have nothing at all to do with what we are going through.'

'Oh you selfish self-centred bitch.' Hannah's laugh was shallow, rubbing disjointedly against the insult. 'You really do think the whole world revolves around you and this fucking house, don't you? You love to play the martyr, don't you? To have everyone beating a path to your door to tell you how marvellously you're managing, how terrible it is for *you*. Well what about me, Ellen?'

'*You?*' Ellen exclaimed. 'What about you, Hannah? I'm his widow, I was his wife. You . . . you were his sister-in-law who frankly he could hardly stand to be around. What the hell are you talking about?'

'What am I talking about . . . ?' Hannah paused, her tongue running nervously over her lips. 'I'm talking about you wanting to keep Charlie locked up here like some little doll that only you get to play with, about you not sharing him, not letting him have any kind of life because you don't want one. *That's* . . . that is what I'm talking about.' As she spoke Hannah's expression became ugly and vicious, her finger jabbing into Ellen's face.

'You have no idea what it's like to lose someone you love – you have no idea what it's like to love anyone apart from yourself,' Ellen spat at her.

'I have no idea? I have no idea – well that is a laugh. If you knew—'

'Hello all!' Matt appeared through the kitchen door, very glad to be home, immediately realising that he'd walked into the middle of something. He froze to the spot. 'All right?' he asked weakly.

'Hannah, come on.' Sabine stepped in, putting an arm on Hannah's and taking the opportunity to steer her towards the front door. 'Let's go down the road and have a drink, you and I. I have some work questions for you.'

'Yes, let's – let's go for a drink, let's have some fun like normal people,' Hannah shot over her shoulder as Sabine led her away.

Slowly Matt put his bag down on the table.

'Fuck – what was all that about?' he asked. 'You two looked like you were about to rip chunks out of each other.'

Ellen sank down into her chair and found that she was trembling. 'I don't really know,' she said, touching the back of her hand to her boiling cheek.

'Well look, don't tell me if you don't want to, but in my experience booze usually makes a bad situation a million times worse.'

'Booze . . .'

'Yeah, Hannah, she was tipsy wasn't she? I'm sure she didn't mean anything she said.'

'My sister hadn't been drinking,' Ellen told him. 'She wouldn't, not when she was looking after Charlie. She might be thoughtless, but she does love him.'

Ellen felt a pang of remorse: she had allowed herself to become so afraid that when Hannah and Charlie did arrive she'd simply attacked without thinking. None of what had happened had really been Hannah's fault, she had believed that Charlie had told Ellen where he was going – and could she really blame Charlie for wanting an afternoon out of the house, having some fun for a change? He had made it abundantly clear he didn't get that with her, and he was right. Ellen saw herself for a moment, trapped in her home like a fly in polished amber, but even if that was true, even if she was trapped she still could find the will of desire to escape. What was it about Hannah that made her so instantly furious? Privately she could concede that she was jealous of how easily Charlie and Hannah got on, but it was something more than that. Something that had happened since Nick died that she couldn't quite put her finger on, that meant that whenever Hannah was around Ellen felt disjointed and uncomfortable. Theirs had not been an easy relationship, not since they were children, but rarely had it been as strained as it was now. Perhaps it was because Hannah was making such an effort to be there for Ellen now.

'No? Well I'm wrong then.' Matt took her denial lightly. 'It's probably because I'm spending too much time around alcoholics. It was just her eyes – you know, a bit bleary and bloodshot. She looked like people do when they've had a lunchtime drink. But I'm probably wrong. It seems to be my speciality today.'

Still lost in her thoughts, Ellen looked down at the tabletop and re-ran everything that Hannah had said. There had been something, something that she hadn't said out loud but that had been there in the room between them, as real and as solid as this table. Hannah wouldn't have gone anywhere with Charlie if she'd been drinking, would she? Admittedly she was stupid and selfish and vain; if Ellen put all the things she found annoying about her down on paper the list would far exceed Sabine's in length. Hannah was about as irritating as a person could be, but she loved Charlie – she surely wouldn't have done that?

Ellen looked at Matt, who sat across the table from her

seeming at a loss as to what to do. Poor man, she thought. This is the last thing he needs after a hard day's work.

'Tell you what, you tell me what the fight was all about and I'll tell you how I officially became the shittiest man on earth today,' Matt suggested.

Settling back in her chair, Ellen described everything that had happened, looking up at Matt as she spoke. 'I let it all get out of hand, didn't I? I overreacted.'

'I dunno,' Matt told her. 'I'm not a parent but I imagine that in this day and age not knowing where your kid is can be pretty scary.'

'Nick often told me that I was prone to overreacting,' Ellen told him. 'He said that I questioned him too much and sometimes made him feel like he couldn't go anywhere or do anything without me knowing about it. He said that I was too emotional, my skin too thin – that I responded to every little thing with my heart instead of my head.' Ellen raised her chin as she remembered. 'He used to say, "Christ, Ellen, home is supposed to be a place I want to come back to, not somewhere I have to avoid. Try thinking once or twice before you open that mouth of yours." '

'Really?' Matt said, taken aback. 'Not sure I agree with him there. Whenever you open your mouth you usually have something pretty interesting or clever to say.'

Privately he thought that Ellen's late husband sounded like a bit of dick, but there was nothing in the way she talked about him to suggest that she thought anything of the sort.

'I should go and talk to Charlie, shouldn't I?' Ellen said. 'Perhaps I'll tell him he can keep the games console but he can't have it till his birthday in September, what do you think? I know

Hannah meant well, trying to distract him from the anniversary – but it's not gifts he needs, or even distraction.'

'Sounds like a good idea,' Matt nodded.

'I don't want to lose him, I don't want him to drift away from me. He's everything to me – I'm not trying to stifle him, or keep him prisoner. I just love him, I just really love him – he must see that.'

'I bet he does,' Matt said. 'I bet he's in his room right now realising he's been unfair to you. He's just kicking out, testing boundaries. He's trying to grow up and for him it's going to be harder than it is for a lot of kids. It'll be painful for you both.'

'I'll go and talk to him,' Ellen decided, half rising from her chair.

'You know what?' Matt rested his hand on her forearm. 'Give him a sec, yeah? Give him a chance to settle down.' He put on the table a filmy plastic bag that had been resting by his legs. 'I stopped off and bought some lagers on the way home. Want one?'

He cracked open a can of Stella and drank straight from it. After a moment's hesitation Ellen followed suit.

'So tell me about how you became the shittiest man on earth, again?' she asked him.

'You know what,' Matt said, stretching his legs out and smiling at her. 'It doesn't really seem that important any more.'

Chapter Eleven

Matt watched Ellen watching Charlie across the kitchen table. For once he had arrived downstairs and ready for school in time to have breakfast at home, which was interesting because as far as Matt could tell Charlie still wasn't talking to Ellen.

'Good morning darling,' Ellen had said, unable to disguise her surprise and pleasure at the prospect of getting fifteen minutes to make amends with Charlie before he went to school. 'Did you sleep OK? I came up to talk to you last night but you were flat out already . . .' Tentatively she reached over and touched the top of his head as if she were about to ruffle his hair, but then thought better of it a second too late to completely pull out of the manoeuvre. Charlie shrugged off her touch and picked up a piece of toast that she had put in front of him.

'Look.' Ellen sat down opposite him. 'I'm sorry I shouted and got so angry last night. It was because I was worried, Charlie, I got all worked up and, well, by the time you came home all the worry had turned into anger and I took it out on you. That was wrong.'

Charlie said nothing, keeping his eyes down as he munched.

Ellen sighed and sat back in her chair. 'But it was wrong of you to go off without telling me where you were going or who with. And it was wrong of you to lie to Hannah about telling me.' Still Charlie was unresponsive. 'So I've decided that I'm not going to take the games console back . . .'

Charlie's snort was sarcastic and derisory as he rolled his eyes to the ceiling and shook his head. Matt, as he ate his cornflakes leaning up against the fridge, observed this with interest.

'And,' Ellen continued, 'if you apologise to me and Hannah for lying then we can say that it's a birthday present and you can have it in September. What do you say?'

Charlie looked up at her, his blue eyes vivid in the morning sunshine as he appraised his mother with near-naked contempt. If Matt had been able to place a bet on what the boy was about to say just then, he would have put all his money on something bitter, reproachful and insightful, something cruel but true, because the cruellest things were often the most true. But Matt would have lost all his money because Charlie uttered only one word.

'Whatever,' he said.

Matt watched Ellen's shoulders tense, her whole body a battlefield where her anger and desire to be friends again with Charlie fought on.

'So what do you have to say?' Ellen asked him.

Charlie got up, scraping his chair across the tiles so that they screeched in agony.

'Take it back to the shop,' he told her levelly. 'I'm not apologising.'

He picked up his school bag in one hand and his remaining piece of toast in the other and walked out, slamming the front door behind him with such force that the mugs rattled on the draining board.

'I didn't handle that too well, did I?' Ellen said, more to herself than Matt. 'You know, this is my job, being a mother – it's what I've made my whole life about and now I can't even do that any more . . .'

Matt put his cereal bowl down on the table, briefly resting a consoling hand on her shoulder, before picking up his keys and laptop bag. He'd stayed in last night, watching TV in his room, aware that Ellen had gone to bed early and exhausted. As a consequence they hadn't had their post-midnight meeting and when he'd woken up that morning well rested and without a hangover, Matt realised that he had missed it.

'If he didn't care about you, or what you thought or what you said, then he'd have just gone straight to school,' Matt told her, grabbing his jacket. 'But he didn't, he got up and ready early so that he could come down here and ignore and insult you – see, it's not all that bad!'

He paused to look at Ellen, dressed in a man's shirt again, her long hair as yet unbrushed, tumbling over her shoulders in a rare moment of abandon before being twisted into its habitual knot at the nape of her neck. She looked like she'd been in bed with a lover, Matt realised with a tiny thrill, letting himself speculate for one more illicit moment, picturing Ellen in the seconds before she pulled that shirt on, imagining her lying semi-clad on her bed, her black hair spread out on the pillow, trickling between her breasts which were . . . It was hard to guess exactly what her body was like under the clothes she wore, which was partly the reason that wondering about her was so interesting. Unlike many women who seemed to make it their mission to obliterate mystery with low-cut tops and high-cut skirts, and, in the case of the models who graced the pages of *Bang It!*, far less than that,

Ellen kept everything hidden, covered. She locked her body away, which just at this moment and to Matt's great surprise made it seem even more intriguing. And he knew that even if, when he unbuttoned that shirt, the body underneath it was far from the airbrushed perfection that he was bombarded with daily, he would still feel that rush of discovering a new found land. He would still desire her, for all the physical frailties and scars that made her the woman she was, as vulnerable as a piece of glass, something that for that dangerous moment he wanted to hold in his hands.

There are places that you don't go mate, Matt reminded himself sternly as, feeling his gaze on her, Ellen looked up and then down quickly, heat flaring across her face as if she had guessed exactly what he had been thinking. *And your widowed landlady is one of them.*

Women were wrong about him. Carla and Lucy the subeditor, all the other angry bitter girls he'd left in Manchester, they thought he was a moral void, an incarnation of woman-hating evil. This was despite the fact that he had always, almost always, been upfront and honest with all the women that he'd met about his intentions, if not about the column that they were quite likely to appear in. But he had some standards, and Ellen was the line he would not cross. As much as she had started to fascinate him, there was something else going on – he liked her. He liked her too much to try and sleep with her, and more than that he wanted to help her, he wanted to do something to smooth the frown that dissected her brow so neatly in half.

'Better run,' Matt said. 'It's deadline day – the whole place goes crazy! But look, try not to worry, all right – this is just boy stuff, it'll pass.'

'I didn't handle that too well, did I?' Ellen said, more to herself than Matt. 'You know, this is my job, being a mother – it's what I've made my whole life about and now I can't even do that any more . . .'

Matt put his cereal bowl down on the table, briefly resting a consoling hand on her shoulder, before picking up his keys and laptop bag. He'd stayed in last night, watching TV in his room, aware that Ellen had gone to bed early and exhausted. As a consequence they hadn't had their post-midnight meeting and when he'd woken up that morning well rested and without a hangover, Matt realised that he had missed it.

'If he didn't care about you, or what you thought or what you said, then he'd have just gone straight to school,' Matt told her, grabbing his jacket. 'But he didn't, he got up and ready early so that he could come down here and ignore and insult you – see, it's not all that bad!'

He paused to look at Ellen, dressed in a man's shirt again, her long hair as yet unbrushed, tumbling over her shoulders in a rare moment of abandon before being twisted into its habitual knot at the nape of her neck. She looked like she'd been in bed with a lover, Matt realised with a tiny thrill, letting himself speculate for one more illicit moment, picturing Ellen in the seconds before she pulled that shirt on, imagining her lying semi-clad on her bed, her black hair spread out on the pillow, trickling between her breasts which were . . . It was hard to guess exactly what her body was like under the clothes she wore, which was partly the reason that wondering about her was so interesting. Unlike many women who seemed to make it their mission to obliterate mystery with low-cut tops and high-cut skirts, and, in the case of the models who graced the pages of *Bang It!*, far less than that,

191

doesn't like me going places. It's like if I'm not at school or at home she freaks out, even when I do phone her and say I'm going to the park or round a mate's house or whatever, she pretends she's cool about it but I know she isn't. I know she's sitting at home worrying, waiting for me to come back and that spoils everything. I can't have any fun when I know she's in the house, all anxious. So I thought I wouldn't tell her, I thought if I didn't tell her she wouldn't worry. I told Aunt Hannah we had to be back by five but she's always late, that's just what she's like – she doesn't worry about anything, you see. She has a laugh.' Charlie shifted his school bag from one shoulder to the other, slipping his blazer off his shoulders at the same time in one practised movement.

'OK, I sort of get why you didn't tell her,' Matt said. 'But you must have known she wouldn't be best pleased about you coming home with a great big expensive present.'

'Dad would have let me have it,' Charlie muttered, kicking at an empty Coke can with the toe of his shoe.

'Would he?' Matt asked tentatively. He wanted to know about Charlie's dad, Ellen's husband – but he didn't want to frighten the kid off by asking too many questions. 'Big on presents, was he, your dad?'

'He liked to surprise me.' Charlie's mouth evolved briefly into a smile. 'He used to go away a lot, on business trips and stuff, and he'd always bring me something really cool back and not just something you'd get at an airport. Once he brought me back a BMX, and I had an iPod before any of my mates and the last time, the last thing he brought me was my DS. It never used to matter if it was my birthday or not. Dad never needed a reason to give me a present.'

'He sounds like a pretty generous guy,' Matt observed, privately wondering if the gifts were to make up for a father's long absences.

'He was,' Charlie affirmed with a nod. '*And* he was funny. He was the funniest man *ever*, he really used to make me and Mum laugh. She used to laugh so hard that tears would come out of her eyes, seriously!' Charlie looked at Matt, determined to make sure that he believed him about his father's peerless talent for comedy.

'I bet,' Matt said, wondering what it would take to make Ellen laugh like that again. 'What else do you miss about him?'

'His smell,' Charlie said softly. 'He had this smell that was just Dad. When he'd get in from work he'd always come and see me, even if it was really late. Give me a kiss, because I was still a little kid then and I liked kisses. And he used to smell of aftershave and the cigarettes that Mummy used to pretend she didn't know he smoked and just . . . him. Even if I was properly asleep when he came to kiss me goodnight, I'd still know he was there. I'd smell him in my sleep. And I miss his hugs. And playing football with him in the garden on the Sundays when he was home and taking our bikes down the park or, last May he had a bit of time off work so he took me, just me and him on our own to Center Parcs for a long weekend and we did all these things, biking and climbing and swimming, just us. And we had dinner together and we talked and talked and talked, just us two. And he said that he'd always love me, no matter what happened. I should always remember that he loved me more than anything . . .'

Charlie trailed off and Matt didn't attempt to prompt him further, taken back fifteen years by those words. He'd heard that phrase before. 'No matter what happens, remember I love you,

195

son.' His dad had said that to him, one Saturday, over a McDonald's after he'd taken to him to see Man United at home. Matt remembered he'd blushed and told his dad not to be so soft, worried that someone might overhear. What he hadn't realised as he sat there on a hard plastic chair under the strip lighting was that that was the last Saturday, the last day that he would ever spend with his dad. By Sunday morning his dad had gone, God knows where, with this woman who, he'd told Matt's mother in a note written on the back of a takeaway menu for the local Indian, he could not live without. Matt had never seen him again and from that day on he had always considered his father a liar, and that a father's love meant little if he could live without his children.

Had Charlie's dad been preparing his son for some change or upheaval too? The anniversary of the accident was coming up, Matt wasn't sure exactly when but he knew it was sometime in July, because Hannah had warned him it might be a sensitive time when he took the room. Was it possible that Nick Woods had known exactly what he was doing when he crashed that car? Maybe things were so bad with his business that he'd seen his life insurance as the only way of providing for Ellen and Charlie, and he'd taken Charlie away for a final holiday to give the boy some memories. Then again, he hadn't exactly thought that through, Matt reflected. Causing your own death ruled out any payout, which was why Ellen was in such a financial bind now, and by the sounds of him Nick was quite a controlling guy, unlikely to make such a basic mistake.

Besides, suicide didn't ring true. From what little Matt knew about the man he didn't seem like the kind of guy to throw it all in, no matter how noble his motivation might have been. He was a huge man, metaphorically if not literally. He'd loomed large in his family's life. He wouldn't have ever given up, he'd have battled on to make sure that his wife and son always saw him that way, as their hero. So if Charlie's dad hadn't been preparing him for his death, what had he been preparing him for?

More likely, Matt thought, dropping a consoling hand on Charlie's shoulder, he was letting his own past colour what Charlie had just told him. More likely Charlie had had the kind of father who'd genuinely loved him, who'd searched out time to spend with him, who had simply wanted his son to know how important he was in his father's life. For Charlie's sake, and in some small way his own, Matt really wanted that to be true.

'Mate,' Matt said. 'This must be fucking awful for you.'

'It is.' Charlie stifled a sob, half turning away from Matt, coughing up words on each gulp of air. 'It is fucking awful because he's *dead* and he isn't coming back. I'm not going to get to go biking or swimming or do anything with him or . . . or smell him or hug him ever again . . . am I?' The question was so plaintive and desolately hopeful that Matt felt tears sting his own eyes. He guided Charlie over to a bench in a nearby bus shelter and sat him down, standing in front of him to shield him from the prying eyes of passers-by.

'Listen, if you want to cry, mate, you cry. It's good for a bloke to cry every now and again. I'll stand here and make sure no one sees.'

Matt felt a curious sensation in his chest, like a slow tear that ran from his sternum to his gut, as he stood there looking down at Charlie. The boy's head was buried in his hands, his shoulders shaking with silent sobs. Matt dug a hand into his pocket and pulled out, along with some change and half a packet of gum, a screwed-up tissue.

'Here.' He tucked it into one of Charlie's hands. 'You can mop up the snot with that.' Matt wasn't sure how long he stood there over Charlie as he cried, directing his threatening gaze towards anyone who threatened to intrude on what little privacy the bus shelter afforded, but he knew that it was long enough to make him late for work and Charlie late for school. He'd have to take Charlie into school now, even though this would make him still later at the office; he couldn't let him go the rest of the way alone.

After a busload of people had congregated at the stop and then lurched away on the next bus, Charlie screwed the heels of his hands into his eye sockets and blew his nose on the sodden tissue. He looked up at Matt.

'Do I look like I've been crying?' he asked him anxiously, the blue of his eyes made all the more intense by his red-rimmed lids.

'Yeah, a bit,' Matt said. 'But you can say it's hay fever. Hay fever makes you look all puffy and shit too.'

Charlie nodded, looked at his watch and leapt up. 'I'd better get to school, else they'll be calling Mum and she'll freak out again.'

'I'll come with you,' Matt offered. 'Tell them it was my fault you're late.'

'You don't have to do that,' Charlie said.

'I know, mate,' Matt said. 'But I want to, OK?'

They stood side by side, swaying in silence as the next bus that arrived took them the short distance to Charlie's school. After a while Charlie asked him a question.

'When was the last time you cried?'

Matt glanced down at the boy. The last time he had cried had been when his best mate from childhood, Gaz, had found him having sex with Gaz's girlfriend in the back of a nightclub last year. His friend had punched him in the face and told his sobbing girlfriend – the girl that Matt knew Gaz had been planning to propose to that night, because he'd shown Matt the ring and already recruited him as best man – that she was a whore and a slag and he never wanted to see her again. Matt remembered the way she'd looked at him, Angie, tears and snot streaming down her face, blaming him, begging him to sort it out, to tell Gaz that it was all his fault, that he'd started it. But he hadn't done that.

Gaz had not been able to forgive either him or Angie. Matt realised that he'd lost one of the few constant things in his life because he had been unable to resist the temptation of having that which was taboo. It didn't matter that Angie had been flirting with him for months, that whenever Gaz wasn't around she'd find reasons to touch him, brush against him, make sure he could see down her top or up her skirt at every available opportunity. It didn't matter that she'd been playing a game with him. He shouldn't have gone there. He shouldn't have crossed the line and when he'd realised that he'd broken Gaz's heart and his too, he had cried. He'd curled up on the mate's floor he'd been forced to crash on and he had cried his heart out.

'Last time I cried?' Matt glanced skyward. 'When Arsenal beat the mighty Man United – but that was ages ago, so I'm over it now.'

Charlie smiled. 'You've just been lucky is all, you wait, once our defence matures we'll be back on top again.'

'Yeah, back on top of the Championship,' Matt teased him.

'That defence has been maturing for about five years now – they'll all need a bus pass soon if they mature for much longer.'

'Ha, ha.' Charlie punched him lightly in the arm. 'At least we don't cheat.'

'What? It's a miracle any one of your lot can walk down the street without trying for a penalty, you dirty southern bastards.'

Matt was pleased to hear Charlie chuckle. A good swear word never failed to amuse boys of a certain age.

'Look, I like a kickabout – so you know, if you fancy it, you and me sometime? We can recreate some great matches where my lot whopped your lot's arses, there's about a million to choose from. That's if you fancy it.'

'Cool,' Charlie said, looking up at him. 'Thanks Matt, that'd be cool.'

The bus stopped and they got off.

'And I'm here, you know, if you want to talk about bloke stuff. Ask me. I'm a professional.'

Charlie smiled and nodded, slowing as they reached the school gates.

'Before we go in there, promise me something, yeah?' Matt asked Charlie as he pushed open one of the gates. 'Be nice to your mum when you get in. Remember that she loves you more than anyone in the world, too.'

'I know . . . I will.' Charlie looked concerned. 'I get angry with her, I get angry because she's stuck. She's broken and stuck and she doesn't want to get out. I can't even remember the last time she went out of the house, not for months though.'

'Well maybe it's a bit soon, mate,' Matt said, assuming Charlie was exaggerating. 'Cut her some slack – it's still not a year since your dad died. Maybe she needs a bit more time.'

'No, you don't understand.' Charlie was insistent. 'She's stuck and she wants me to be stuck with her and that makes me mad.'

'Well then, it's up to us to think of some ways to unstick her, isn't it?' Matt said, although he wasn't exactly sure what it was that Charlie meant.

'Us? Really?' Charlie asked him.

'Sure, it's official. You are my best mate in London. Besides, I like a challenge, although I think your mum is doing pretty well by herself right now. New job, new lodgers – that's not exactly stuck in the mud, is it? She's really trying.'

'Maybe.' Charlie looked uncertain.

'Right, so tell me – is your teacher a bloke or a bird?'

'A bird,' Charlie laughed.

'Then we're sorted.' Matt winked at him. 'Never been a woman yet I couldn't charm.'

Chapter Twelve

Eliza's hand trembled as it rested on the heavy steel door handle that felt cold beneath her heated palm.

On the other side of the door was the man who was her new protector, her father's dearest friend, General Robert Wright, Commander of the Garrison of the Tower of London, believed to be a Royalist spy in the very heart of the Parliamentarian camp. His name was James Malbeck, he'd arrived from the north with a letter of recommendation from Cromwell himself, and his credentials could not have been better. But ever since he'd been taken into the garrison, where all of London's arms and defences were stored and planned, the Royalists had seemed much better informed about their enemy. There had even been an attempt to fire the powder stocks, which if it had been successful would have seen the great White Tower burnt to the ground and London open to attack once again. Robert said that only someone with inside information could have known exactly where they kept the powder stocks, and how to break through the numerous iron doors and locks that stood between the Tower's most precious secrets and any intruder. The miscreant had been quick and expert, caught with match in hand purely by chance, when the hour was almost too late.

'It has to be Malbeck, Eliza,' Robert told her a few nights after she arrived. 'I know it's him but I cannot simply accuse him. I need proof and

I am not at all sure how to find it without him realising what's afoot and fleeing before justice can be served.'

Eliza had rested her head on the old man's knee as she sat at his feet and he stroked her hair. She was desperate to find a way to repay him for what he had given her, the greatest gifts that her young heart could imagine: fatherly kindness, a refuge for those who surely pursued her after what she had done, and most of all a good night's sleep. She was safe at last, no Royalist would ever dare follow her to the very heart of the Republican cause.

Eliza longed to be able to help Robert, to help the cause, to help the country and root out the evil that lurked within the thick walls of the Tower.

It had taken her days to persuade her guardian to allow her to question Malbeck herself.

'No Eliza, what sort of friend would I be to your father if I let you, an innocent child, put yourself in peril once again?'

'I am an innocent no longer, Robert. I am a woman of nearly nineteen now and I am greatly changed.' Her sooty lashes swept her cheeks as she lowered her lids. 'I know much more of men than I would wish – but it cannot be unknown. I know that James Malbeck cannot take his eyes off me whenever we are in the same room. I know that if I tempt him but a little he will tell me much. I can get your proof for you, dear friend, please let me. Let me help the cause that I love more than my own life, which is worth so very little now.'

Robert looked down at the young woman whose head should have been filled with no more than pretty ribbons and making lace collars and dreaming of the man who would one day be her husband. But all of that had gone for Eliza now, and he saw that the only way he could soothe the fire that burnt in her breast was to let her have her way, for he was certain that she spoke true – she was as strong and determined as any man in his garrison.

'Very well, daughter of England,' Robert had told her solemnly. 'You have your wish.'

Now, as Eliza pushed open the door, she felt as if her heart might beat its way out of her chest, but even as fear flowed through her veins like iced water she was absolutely focused on her intent.

'What the . . . ?' Malbeck did not complete his sentence as he saw who was interrupting him so late in his quarters.

'Madam? Is there something amiss, do you require assistance?' he asked her, his gaze roaming the length of her body as a wolf might appraise a lamb presenting itself for slaughter.

'Yes sir.' Eliza smiled temptingly as she locked and bolted the door behind her before leaning back against it, her hands folded behind her, her blade clutched within them, making sure that Malbeck would get the full benefit of the gown made for a meaner-figured woman that strained across the fullness of her bosom. 'The something amiss is that there is no soul in the whole of this great castle who can amuse or entertain me. I come to you to relieve me of my predicament.'

Malbeck's eyebrows soared and she could see him struggling with the realisation that the garrison commander's ward herself had come to his room alone, something a respectable Puritan girl would never do. Eliza knew the men of the garrison talked about her and about what had happened to her on her long journey here. She knew that, sullied and mishandled as she was, many of them thought of her as fair game, and that it was only Robert's protection that stopped them from trying their luck with her themselves. Now Malbeck looked as if he could not believe his good fortune.

'So tell me, my lady, how might I best entertain you?' He sauntered over to stand close to her, his gaze now openly seeking out the swell and valleys of her breasts.

'Sir, I am dog sick of all these Puritans,' Eliza breathed. 'I swear not a one of them knows how to be happy. I pray God that Cromwell is vanquished and that we might have gaiety and laughter in the land again.'

Malbeck stepped back, snapping his gaze up to meet her eyes, and for a moment Eliza wondered if she had gone too far too fast. But Malbeck seemed amused and intrigued by her boldness.

'Careful what you say, madam, by rights I ought to have you hung for what you have just uttered.'

'Sir.' Eliza watched him from beneath her lowered lashes. 'It seems that I am at your mercy. Do what you will with me.'

Malbeck came another step closer to her, so that his thighs pressed her back into the door, his hot breath beating down on her skin.

'Malbeck, if you value your life then I suggest you step away from the lady now.'

Eliza gasped as the figure of Captain Parker loomed out of the shadows. Instinctively she shied away from him, drawing her arms across her body and in doing so revealing what her hands had concealed.

'You . . . !' Malbeck stared at the blade, more shocked at the sight of the weapon than that of a man clearly familiar to him. 'You meant to kill me? Parker – have you saved my life? Surely such a beauty could not kill a man.'

'She's done it before, sir, and I am certain she would do it again if she found it necessary.'

'You!' Eliza spluttered the word, overwhelmed by the storm of emotions that broke across her heart. 'How? Why have you come here – do you intend to hound me to my grave?'

Captain Parker stepped forward, looking at her as a man might survey someone whom he had both missed with every waking moment and hoped never to see again.

'Malbeck,' he said, without taking his eyes from Eliza. 'You are discovered, you must leave with me tonight and return to Oxford at the King's command. Eliza my love, it breaks my heart to tell you this but yes, it is my mission to hound you to your grave. It is my duty to find the murderer of one Sir Edward Clancy, the King's favourite, and bring her to the gallows.'

'You? You who have ruined me, who have destroyed my life, come to drag me once again from safety and kindness,' Eliza sobbed, her eyes welling with tears. 'Why you? Why?'

'Because I would have no other man handle you roughly again, my love. I must do my duty to King and country, but I will see you are treated kindly and fairly. I will protect you.'

'Protect me as you drag me to my death?' Eliza cried.

'Though the pain of it will surely kill me, I must,' Captain Parker told her.

Suddenly there was a frantic hammering on the other side of the door.

'Help me!' Eliza screamed, flinging herself against the door that she herself had barred.

'And now,' Captain Parker said with grim determination, 'we must away.'

'Oh that's awful,' Ellen said, looking up at Allegra.

'Yes, I know – the description is far too sketchy and half-hearted, it won't do at all. We will have to go back and rewrite that section, otherwise the readers will feel cheated.'

'No, I didn't mean that – I meant Eliza being captured and dragged off by Captain Parker. Surely he won't see her hanged, not if he loves her. Surely he'd rather hang himself, wouldn't he?'

'Would he, though?' Allegra mused. 'We already know that he's a scoundrel. Handsome he might be, and a sensational lover to boot – but he forced himself on Eliza and now is racked with guilt. Perhaps he'd rather see her dead, and not have to think about her at all.'

'Really?' Ellen was dismayed. 'But I mean, doesn't he love her, wouldn't he do anything to save her? He is going to rescue her in the end, isn't he?'

'Who knows?' Allegra smiled. 'But I can tell you one thing, Ellen. It's best that we don't know, because if we don't know then neither does our reader.'

'Ohhhh.' Ellen sighed with relief. 'But in the end he'll save her.'

'Perhaps not. In life there isn't always a hero to save a damsel in distress. Perhaps it would be better if we made Eliza clever enough and brave enough to save herself. Women don't always need men to rescue them, you know.'

Allegra raised her eyebrows and looked pointedly at Ellen, but it was a·glance that went over the other woman's head as she turned in her chair to gaze out of the window to the bottom of her garden, where her thoughts so often seemed to be drawn these days. Ellen could see splashes of colour in the untamed greenery. The vivid blue of the irises that she had planted when they first moved in sang out against the lush green of the unkempt grass, and the hot orange of lilies burned brightly in the sun, brought on early by this unlikely June heatwave. Across the fence that was starting to rot and which sagged at one end since spring storms had battered it, Ellen could see her neighbour's washing drying on the line. She had a new dress, hanging limp and still in the dead heat of the morning. Red cotton, buttoned down the front and belted at the waist, the sort of dress that made other women look smart and sexy. Ellen would see her neighbour sometimes, walking down the road in one of her outfits. She always walked purposefully, as if she had somewhere really important to go. Ellen tried to remember the last time she had had somewhere important to go.

'Do you hope for a hero?' Allegra asked her out of the blue.

207

Ellen turned back to her. 'Me? A hero? Whatever makes you say that?'

'Well, your husband took care of you and your son for so long, and now you are all alone and putting up with strangers in your home in order to make ends meet. Don't you wish some handsome man would come and whisk you off, take you away from all this? To float through Venice in a gondola, perhaps, or take you by the hand and lead you along the Great Wall of China. Or even just to kick pebbles on the beach in Suffolk. Don't you wish for something to happen, something unexpected and wonderful to take you out of this house and away?'

A brief image of sea stretching into a boundless sky flashed into Ellen's mind's eye and she felt her heart contract.

'I don't suppose I've really thought about going anywhere,' she said mildly. 'I suppose that all I've thought about for the last year is how to stay here. So no, I don't long for a hero . . .' Ellen paused, thinking again about the way that Matt had looked at her this morning. He couldn't have been looking at her *that* way, she must have imagined it. Young sexy men didn't look at frumpy older women like *that*. It was simply impossible – she looked terrible and old and unkempt and he looked young and fresh and as if he could have any woman he wanted. And yet, just for that split second, their eyes had met and she had felt like her fantasy version of herself, standing in her white dress in a hay barn on the brink of ravishment.

'Just a lover then perhaps?' Allegra asked her.

'Oh Allegra – stop it!' Ellen exclaimed. 'I'm not at all sure it is seemly for a woman of your age to be constantly talking about sex.'

'A woman of my age! Pah!' Allegra was disdainful. 'Let me tell

208

you, my dear. The body might sag, decay and crumble all around but inside I still feel the same desires and impulses I felt when I was eighteen, which is why you should be making the most of what nature gave you while you still have it, instead of keeping it shrouded away like a museum piece. Besides, if anybody is allowed to be obsessed by sex, it is me – it is rather my stock-in-trade.'

'I don't keep myself shrouded away – I just like to be comfortable, and what's the point of dressing up when you work from home?'

'When you have a very desirable and probably willing young man cavorting around half naked in front of you, then I would say there is every point,' Allegra told her, stroking the tips of her fine fingers from underneath her chin to the top of her décolletage, as if she were remembering a lover's embrace. 'I had a younger lover once. I was sixty-three, he was forty-two. I recommend it, it was most exhilarating. Be assured I'd be setting my cap at young Matthew if it wasn't for the fact that your need is greater than mine.'

'I don't have any needs,' Ellen retorted, surprised to find herself giggling like a schoolgirl. She looked at the older woman, who regarded her with a knowing smile that Ellen found quite disconcerting. 'Besides, why would he ever be interested in me? He spends his whole day with a bunch of half-naked twenty-year-olds!'

'Tell me what the best part about Christmas is,' Allegra asked her.

'Pardon?' Ellen frowned.

'The best part about Christmas is the anticipation. It's looking at your presents, all so beautifully and temptingly wrapped, and wondering what might be concealed beneath. In most cases unwrapping the gifts is as good as it gets, usually there is something unutterably dull lurking beneath which requires you to look pleased and say thank you. But I think . . .' Allegra appraised Ellen for an uncomfortably long time. 'Young Matthew would find delights equal to if not more pleasing than anything he might see at work beneath your wrapping.'

'Allegra.' Ellen flushed, briefly picturing Matt's hands on the buttons of her shirt, slowly undoing . . . no – rapidly ripping them asunder before burying his face in her soft flesh. 'It is hot in here, isn't it?' she said, glancing at the open patio doors. 'I think I need to buy a fan if the weather's going to carry on like this. I can probably get it delivered with the next supermarket shop. Or maybe we could get one of those air-conditioning units . . .'

'Ellen.' Allegra spoke over her. 'Ellen. I'm sorry if I've made you uncomfortable. I can't help it, it's the prerogative of an old woman like me to meddle. Besides, I find that I like you, which is most unusual for me. I hardly ever like anyone. So if you find my meddling goes too far I give you permission to tell me.'

Ellen looked into Allegra's hooded eyes and tried to imagine ever talking to her mother the way that she talked to Allegra, and realised it would have been impossible. Whenever she spoke to her mother they discussed the weather, Charlie, Hannah's latest achievements, the height of her parents' neighbour's privet hedge and her father's back problems. They rarely talked about anything . . . internal. In fact now she came to think of it Ellen had never had that kind of friendship with anyone. At school she was bottom of the social heap, the shy, lumpy, awkward girl. At university she'd spent more time in the library than at the bar, and when Nick came along the friendships she had forged at the museum soon became redundant. This was what it was like to have a friend, Ellen realised. This wasn't uncomfortable, it was good. It was good to be rebuilding her life in her own modest fashion, finding her way in the world from within these four walls, forming friendships with people she hadn't known at all a few weeks ago. When she thought about it, a little bubble of pleasure rose in her chest. Nick had been so convinced that she would never be able to manage if left alone out in the big bad world that he had convinced her too, and yet here she was – not out in the big bad world exactly. But coping, no, more than coping . . . *living*. Nick would be so surprised, and, Ellen hoped, proud. She hoped he would be proud of her.

'Look, if I'm honest,' she said slowly, 'I do think Matt is, you know . . . attractive and I do sometimes wonder what it would be like . . . but even if he does want to unwrap me . . .' Ellen stalled as Allegra snorted laughter. 'Even if he did look at me like that this morning in the kitchen . . .'

'I knew it!' Allegra looked triumphant.

'Even so,' Ellen went on, 'it's not a year since Nick died, Allegra. The anniversary is in a few days days and to me it still feels like yesterday that the police turned up at the door and asked me to sit down in the front room. I love him. I love my husband. Thoughts and feeling and fantasies – they are OK, fun even. Like reading your books because they are safe, as you said. But I couldn't ever do anything for real, not ever.'

'Not ever?' Allegra asked her. 'Ever is a very long time, Ellen. People are quick to tell you that life is short, and you yourself have good reason to believe that. But I promise you, when you are alone life can seem very, very long.'

'When you love someone as much as I loved Nick, and when you know that he loved you every bit as much, that doesn't just go away, it doesn't just evaporate. I felt that way about Nick since the first moment I saw him. I don't think it's possible that I will ever feel differently. After all, that's what love is, isn't it? It's eternal.'

Allegra leaned her head back against her chaise longue.

'It would be nice if that were true,' she said. 'But love is like anything else, it's ephemeral, as fragile as a spider's web on a windy day.'

'But in your books love always conquers all,' Ellen said. 'You've written some of the most romantic work ever, your job title is romantic novelist!'

'Yes, I have always felt a bit guilty about peddling that myth, but as you said I write fantasies and women want to believe in romance.' Allegra shrugged. 'Like children want to believe in Father Christmas and Christians are desperate to believe in God.'

'But . . .' Before Ellen could go on the doorbell sounded, spreading a trickle of fear through her chest the way it always had since she heard it chime on 12 July, nearly a year ago.

'Well it can't be Hannah,' she said, looking in the direction of the front door as if she might be able to discern who the visitor was through a brick wall and two solid oak doors. 'I wonder who it is?'

'You could try the radical approach of answering the door and finding out,' Allegra said drily. The bell rang again.

'I'm not expecting anyone. I had the supermarket delivery already,' Ellen said doubtfully, remaining firmly seated.

'Oh for God's sake, woman – answer the bloody door

before you force an aged woman to get up and do it for you.'

Utterly reluctant to open her house to whatever might be waiting outside, Ellen forced herself out of her seat and went into the hall. Her heart pounding in her chest, she made herself place her hand on the latch. Taking a breath she opened the door, flinching against the invasive sunlight that flooded into the hallway.

'Ellen.' Simon beamed at her, his arms outstretched ready for an embrace. 'I was beginning to think you'd gone out!' He pulled her over the threshold and briefly into his arms before releasing her back inside. 'Look at you, you look radiant. I hope you don't mind me interrupting you, but I read the pages that you emailed me last night and they were so fantastic that I thought I'd come and take you and Allegra to lunch to celebrate. I've booked the River Café at one.'

'You've booked . . . but Simon, look at me.' Ellen retreated into the hallway, gesturing down at herself. 'I can't go anywhere dressed like this!'

'My love,' Simon smiled. 'A woman as beautiful as you could go anywhere in sackcloth and still outshine every other soul there, but it's fine. I've booked a cab and it's not coming for half an hour. Plenty of time for you to gild the lily while I tell Allegra what a literary genius she is.'

'And yet still no Booker nomination – where's the justice?' Allegra emerged from her room to greet Simon, having discreetly reapplied a little lipstick first. With a fresh spray of her favourite perfume lingering in the air, she kissed him lightly on either cheek, one hand resting against his chest with the practised grace of a woman who knew exactly how to behave around men. It was an impressive skill, Ellen thought, realising that she had only ever learnt to behave around one very particular man. 'I wondered when I might get the kind of attention that I deserve from you as the writer who single-handedly pays your bills. Did I hear you say River Café? Of course it's not as good as it used to be and it's not the Ivy, but it will do I suppose.'

'That's settled then.' Simon took Allegra's hand from his chest and kissed its palm, before turning to Ellen. 'Darling, before you go and improve on perfection do you have anything cold to drink? It's hotter than hell out there.'

Ellen looked from Allegra to Simon and back again, her feet firmly rooted to the floor.

'Simon, it's just – I don't have anything to wear. I really don't have any clothes, nothing nice at all. I haven't bought anything new since . . . well since Nick's funeral and I just . . . I'm all grungy and hot and I'd need a shower . . . Look, you two go without me. Allegra always looks so lovely, I'd just embarrass you.'

'Nonsense,' Simon protested, 'you could never do that – Ellen, I've already said, you look perfect just as you are. I mean that.'

'Besides, if Simon is pleased with the new chapters of our book then it's just as much down to you as it is to me. You are my muse, Ellen – and you have the best ideas. I insist that you come and take the credit that is due to you.' Allegra smiled encouragingly.

Ellen chewed the inside of her lip, knotting her fingers together as she led them both into the kitchen and poured Simon a glass of cold water from the fridge.

'It's just . . . if you'd called and I had known that you were coming I could have got ready. I can't drop everything. You and

Allegra go. Please. I'll stay here and . . . tidy up a bit.' Ellen gestured around the immaculate kitchen that sparkled like a new pin.

There were several seconds of discomfort while the three of them stood there, not quite certain how to proceed.

'Actually, Simon, dear.' Allegra spoke up, tucking her arm through Ellen's. 'Do you know I think she might have the right idea, it is terribly hot out there. Probably too hot for an old lady like me, we drop like flies in this weather you know. Too hot or too cold and the Grim Reaper has a field day. So as I'd rather finish this book before I shuffle off my mortal coil, perhaps it *would* be better if we had lunch here, if my gracious hostess wouldn't mind?'

Ellen felt Allegra's fingers tightening briefly around her arm and felt reassured.

'Oh, I've got loads – as you know, the supermarket delivered this morning.' Ellen went back to the fridge, letting the chilled air calm her hectic cheeks. 'There's smoked salmon, and Brie, grapes – oh and cold chicken from yesterday, fresh French bread, loads of salad and some wine. I'm sure I could rustle something up.' She turned back to look at Simon. 'If you don't mind, Simon. As Allegra would feel more comfortable here, that is.'

'Of course I don't mind,' Simon said, looking a little bewildered. 'Like Allegra said, the River Café is long past its best anyway. I'll just cancel the car and come and help you chop something.'

Simon wheeled in Allegra's desk chair and with Nick's chair tucked discreetly under the table, the three of them settled down for lunch, Ellen content to listen as Simon waxed lyrical about the latest chapters of *The Sword Erect*.

'Who would have thought a suburb like Shepherds Bush would suit you quite so well, Allegra?' Simon said, leaning back in Charlie's chair, sipping a glass of wine. 'I'm thinking of phoning the builders and telling them to delay the restoration of your house for as long as possible.'

'I must admit it is far more tolerable here than I expected.' Allegra smiled briefly at Ellen. 'I find Ellen rather refreshing, a vast improvement on that last dreadful stain on humanity that I was saddled with. Shame she wasn't washed away in the flood waters, the ungrateful wretch.'

'Lord, I'd hate to get on your bad side,' Ellen said. 'What did she do that was so terrible?'

'Breathed,' Allegra said, with such finality that Ellen considered the subject closed.

'And Eliza is really starting to live. Do you know, I think she is your best female character yet.' Simon deftly changed the subject.

'That's because in my mind's eye Eliza is Ellen,' Allegra told him. 'Or rather what Ellen could be if she would allow it.' Ellen expected Simon to laugh out loud, but instead he simply watched her over the rim of his wine glass, until she lowered her gaze.

'Yes,' he said, with just a trace of humour. 'Yes, I can see Ellen rampaging around the countryside, offing assailants and saving the day. Leaving a trail of lovelorn men in her wake.'

'Did you know that Ellen has a suitor?' Allegra said, that mischievous meddling glint returning to her eye.

'A suitor?' Simon sat up a little in his chair. 'Who, pray?'

'Her young lodger is quite taken with her. I am trying to persuade her to take him as a lover but she is most resistant. Don't you think she should grasp the nettle, so to speak?'

'God, I hardly know!' Simon said, tucking in his chin and blushing. 'But I would think that it would be something for dear Ellen to decide – not you or I. Really, Allegra, when will you consider it time to stop being such a bad influence? It's hardly seemly at—'

'If you say my age I will off you myself with this bread knife,' Allegra told him with some menace.

'Simon is right, though,' Ellen said. 'Next you'll be suggesting we put on miniskirts and go clubbing!'

'I wouldn't rule it out,' Allegra smiled. Simon shook his head.

'Don't take Allegra seriously, she's like Titania in *A Midsummer Night's Dream*, she can't help but stir things up.'

'I always thought that whole debacle was more Oberon's doing than his poor queen's,' Allegra said mildly. 'But there you are, that was ever the way of the world. Women get the blame for the actions of men.' She levelled her gaze on Ellen. 'Except for women who take action, that is,' she said.

'Is that the time?' Simon looked at his watch and sighed. 'Ellen, thank you for a lovely lunch. It kills me to have to leave you with this old harridan but I must get back to the office. We've got a launch meeting for our new series, we're trying something contemporary. Unbridled passion on the photo-copier, that sort of thing.'

'Sounds appalling,' Allegra muttered.

'Just make sure she finishes the book,' Simon told Ellen, cupping her face in his hand and kissing her briefly before looking sternly at Allegra.

'And as for you, remember you're a pensioner.'

He escaped before Allegra had time to brandish her knife.

After he had gone Allegra sat at the table while Ellen busied herself putting away the lunch things. It was almost three and she was hoping that Charlie would come straight back today, that there wouldn't be any tense minutes wondering what was happening to him and that maybe, just maybe when he came in he'd be smiling, perhaps even want to talk to her. She worried about the anniversary of Nick's death, which had started to loom large on the horizon, she worried about what Charlie was thinking and how she was handling it or if she were handling it at all.

'Do you know that with just a little effort you could be quite the siren?' Allegra said as Ellen stacked the dishwasher, a loose lock of hair trailing down her back. Ellen did not reply, caught up as she was in her own thoughts. 'Didn't think so,' Allegra said quietly to herself.

Chapter Thirteen

Occasionally, so occasionally that when it happens you find yourself pleasantly surprised, things work out the way you want them to, which was how Ellen felt when Charlie came home just before four, bounding up the stairs and even humming.

Released early from work by Allegra, who had said that she felt a little tired (which was Allegra for 'tipsy') and needed to rest her eyes (which was Allegra for 'nap'), Ellen had decided on impulse to go through her wardrobe. Spread on her bed were a selection of dresses and skirts, vapid remnants of a past life when she used to think about what she looked like. She picked up one of Nick's favourite dresses, a pale blue cotton affair printed with tiny chintzy flowers, with a square-cut neck, little cap sleeves and covered buttons down the front. She held it against her body as she looked in the mirror, smoothing it over her breasts and shaping it to her hips.

Odd how it didn't look like her dress any more, or even like anything she would choose to wear herself. The colour clashed with her olive skin and green eyes and the length, which fell just below the knee, made her look a good deal shorter than she was. And if Ellen remembered rightly the little covered buttons used to pull uncomfortably over her bust, so that she had feared making any sudden movements with her arms in case they pinged off one by one. She had hated wearing this dress, and yet she had worn it because Nick had chosen it.

Hearing laughter drifting in through the crack in her bedroom window, Ellen went to investigate, pulling back the thick cream lace curtain that she habitually kept drawn. Standing on the street beneath her was her neighbour, wearing the red dress that she had seen on the line, and she was talking to someone else, perhaps another neighbour. As she hovered behind the curtain, Ellen peered at the man, but she didn't recognise him. That didn't mean anything, though, she realised – the whole street could have changed ownership in the last year and she wouldn't have known a thing about it. She remembered that just after Nick's funeral many of her neighbours had visited, most dropping cards through the letter box, wanting to show support but not intrude, but some knocking on the door asking if there was anything they could do (as if there could be). Ellen's red-dressed neighbour, Laura something, if Ellen remembered correctly, had arrived with a casserole in a dish. It had been the first morning that Ellen had been on her own in the house and she wouldn't have opened the door if she had remembered that she didn't have to, but habit had moved her body before her brain could engage.

Laura had looked tired, drained, as she held out the dish.

'It's just chicken,' she said by way of a greeting. 'I remember that after my husband left me I didn't have the energy to eat anything. You've got a little boy haven't you, so I thought you might want this. It's nothing much, forty-five minutes in the oven at one eighty should do it.'

Uncertain of what to say Ellen had taken the casserole, a faint earthy scent of chicken and vegetables wafting upward, incongruous on that summer morning.

'Thank you,' Ellen had said, at a loss to know how to respond.

'You don't have to thank me,' Laura said. 'Just drop the dish back when you've finished.'

Now, as she stood in the window, Ellen realised she still had the earthenware dish sitting in the back of her kitchen cupboard. She hadn't spoken to Laura since.

Laura laughed again and pressing her hand on the man's chest, leant in and kissed him, not on the cheek or even the mouth but on his neck, just beneath his jawline. Shocked by the moment of unexpected intimacy, Ellen withdrew further behind the curtain, but she did not stop looking, It seemed much more had happened to her neighbour over the last year than losing a casserole dish and acquiring a dress. Ellen watched as the pair linked fingers in one last gesture of familiarity before parting ways, slowly, until their hands pulled apart, and one last over-the-shoulder smile was exchanged.

As Ellen watched Laura walking purposefully down the street in her red dress she wondered if her life would ever be something like that again, a world of possibilities, a view with a far horizon. Her heart quickened a little in her chest as she thought about feeling the sun on her hair, the touch of a man's pulse beneath her lips.

Flinging her blue dress on to the bed Ellen looked over her meagre collection of clothes, wondering, just for fun, if there was anything in there that she might wear if she were going to seduce Matt. The thought made her chuckle as she rifled through one sensible outfit after another. Even before Nick, her dress sense hadn't been desperately daring. She wondered

221

whether Matt had ever been seduced by a woman in a stitched-down pleated skirt and polo-neck sweater. Hannah always knew how to dress, Ellen thought, eyeing a pastel pink cardigan that she had no recollection of ever owning. If there wasn't this invisible, unquantifiable obstruction between the two of them, she would ask Hannah to give her some tips. Sometimes, Ellen thought as she sat down on the bed and raked her fingers through the clothes, she wondered how she and Hannah could possibly be related.

'There must be something in here worth wearing,' she muttered to herself. She had yet to find anything when Charlie came thundering into her room.

He stopped in his tracks when he saw her, as if he'd only just remembered that they'd been fighting.

'Hello,' he said.

'Hello,' Ellen said warmly, biting off the word 'darling' before it could escape her lips. 'Good day?'

'Yeah, not bad actually,' Charlie said, sounding surprised by the revelation.

'That's good.' Ellen gestured at the bed. 'Thought I'd sort some stuff out for charity.'

'Dad's stuff?' Charlie asked, glancing at the half of the Edwardian oak wardrobe that was still crammed with Nick's clothes.

'No, not Dad's things. Not yet. My old things.'

'You should get some new clothes,' Charlie said, fingering a folded piece of paper that he'd pulled from his trouser pocket. 'If you like I could come shopping with you on Saturday. We could go to Westfield, it's got millions of shops, there's bound to be something you like – you should see it, Mum, it's massive.'

'I know, with shiny floors and a cinema! You told me, sounds like it would be an easy place to get lost in.'

'I don't get lost when I go there with my mates, I know it like the back of my hand!' Charlie told her. 'I'd look after you.'

'Really?' Ellen smiled. 'You'd really go clothes shopping with your old mum?'

'If you like.'

'Well . . . shall we see, nearer the time?' Charlie's shoulders sank just a fraction of a millimetre and he handed her the piece of paper.

'What's this?' Ellen asked him, unfolding it.

'It's parents' evening, again. End-of-year things, you know – see how we've been doing,' Charlie told her as she read the letter. 'It's next week, you have to fill in the time you want to come and give me back the slip. Mrs Jenkins wrote you a note on the back.' Ellen turned the letter over. Sure enough, Charlie's teacher had written a message there in green biro, with the fat round handwriting that all teachers seemed intent on passing on to their pupils.

'Dear Mrs Woods – Sorry to have missed you last term – really hope to see you here this time, it would be great to discuss Charlie's progress with you. All the best, T. Jenkins.'

'Parents' evening, that's come round again quickly,' Ellen said. 'I didn't know they did another one at the end of the year.'

'You missed the last one,' Charlie reminded her. 'And the arts opening evening. You didn't go to that either.'

'I know, Charlie, I'm sorry.' Ellen looked at the letter. 'It's been a bit of a year.'

'But you can come to this one, can't you?' he asked her.

'Of course,' Ellen said.

'Really?' Charlie watched her closely.

'Yes really, of course really,' Ellen said. 'We'll go downstairs now and write it on the kitchen calendar.'

'I'm not allowed to come with you,' Charlie said as he followed her down the stairs. 'You know, so they can talk about me behind my back – but I was thinking if you didn't want to go on your own you could ask Matt.'

'Matt?' Ellen frowned. 'Why would I ask Matt to go to your parents' evening?'

'Because he wouldn't mind and if you didn't want to go, you know, on your own, he would go with you. Matt's cool.'

'Is he? Is Matt cool?' Ellen asked him, amused. 'When did you decide that?'

'He walked a bit of the way to school with me this morning.' Charlie shrugged. 'We talked a bit about stuff. He's a mate.'

'Really?' Ellen was touched. Whatever they had talked about, it had obviously helped Charlie in some way, he seemed much brighter. She just had to remember that all the effort that Matt was making for her and Charlie was because he was a decent young man, not because he had any ulterior motives.

'I'm glad, Charlie, but I don't really think I can ask him to come with me to parents' evening. I'm sure he's got better things to do.'

'I'll ask him then.' Charlie was insistent.

'But there's no need . . .'

'Mum, I really want you to go to parents' evening this time. I *really* want you to go,' Charlie said slowly and carefully, as if he were talking in a language that Ellen wasn't fluent in.

'I will go,' she said, pulling open a drawer and taking out a pen. 'Here, pass me the calendar.' Charlie took the calendar,

Seasonal Scenes of Sussex that her mother always gave her every Christmas when they visited, just as she always gave Ellen a tin of Cadbury's Roses every Easter visit, and passed it over to her. It was still folded open on January, showing a steel-skied blustery beachscape, snow dusting the wet sand. Ellen shivered when she looked at it before folding her way through an entirely empty half a year, each month's page almost indecently nude of any notes, dates or events. Finally she stopped on June and then, realising that this month too had almost expired, exposed July, illustrated with a park of flowers in full bloom, children in sun hats paddling in a toddler pool.

Ellen scrawled the words 'parents' evening' on 2 July. 'There. Now I won't forget.'

'And you have to fill in the form, say what time you want to go,' Charlie reminded her, spreading out on the kitchen table the letter that she had left on her bed. 'Do it now and I'll put it in my bag.'

'Fine,' Ellen said, wondering why she had begun to feel a little pressured by her son. After all this was what she wanted, time with him, talking to him. She filled in a time slot, folded the letter along the dotted line and tore off the response slip. 'I've said eight o'clock.'

'Cool, Matt will be home from work by then.'

'Charlie, for the last time I'm not asking Matt to come with me!' Ellen exclaimed.

'Aunt Hannah then?' Charlie pressed her.

'No! Why do you think I need a chaperone?'

'Come on, Mum, you know why,' he retorted, heat rising in his cheeks.

'Well? Are you worried I'll embarrass you or something?'

Ellen challenged him. 'Get drunk and try and pull the headmaster?' She had hoped to make Charlie laugh, but his expression didn't change.

'No, I'm worried that you won't go,' he said.

'But I've told you I will, I've written it here!' Ellen brandished the calendar at him as proof.

'You said you'd watch me try out for the school football team,' Charlie reminded her.

'Is that what this is about? You know I had a migraine that day, and anyway I thought that you'd rather not have your mother standing on the touchline embarrassing you.'

'And you promised we'd go down and visit Gran and Grandpa this half-term.'

'Yes, but Grandpa's back went and I thought it would be better not to trouble them. They are getting old, you know. Besides, they came up in the end . . .'

'We haven't had one day out this year. If Dad was here we'd have done something. Gone to Thorpe Park, maybe – something.'

'I know, I know, Charlie. I know I've been an awful mother this year, the truth is I just haven't been able to face things . . .'

'That's not the truth!' Charlie said furiously.

'What then?' Ellen asked him. 'Tell me, Charlie, what is the truth? Why are you always so angry with me?'

'The truth is you *never* go out. You *never* go anywhere. You never leave this house, and you haven't since Dad's funeral! That's the truth, isn't it? Admit it, Mum, just admit – you're too scared to go out any more. You've got that thing.'

'What thing?' Ellen asked him, feeling as if each word her son had spoken was a physical slap.

'I looked it up on the Internet, and it's you. It's exactly you.'

'What is?' she asked him with an exasperated laugh.

'Agoraphobic. You're agoraphobic, Mum.'

Before Ellen could react, Sabine walked into the kitchen, dumping her bag on the table, her face set in an uncompromising frown.

'Ellen, I'm sorry but I think Hannah is in trouble.'

It took a second for Ellen to register what Sabine was saying – she was still reeling from Charlie's bombshell. This was why he was so angry with her and so distant. He'd got it into his head that she had *agoraphobia*, of all things.

'What's wrong with Aunt Hannah?' Charlie asked Sabine, before Ellen could.

'I went to see her today, to ask her for lunch – she hadn't answered her extension or email and when I got to her floor she wasn't in her office, so I asked her assistant to leave her a message. He told me Hannah had left, that she had been summarily dismissed over a week ago. For that to happen without a verbal or written warning means that she must have done something . . . bad.'

Ellen sat down with a bump, struggling to process all of the words that had been hurled in her face. First Charlie and now this . . . She looked at Sabine.

'What – wait a minute. You're telling me that Hannah's lost her job, that when she took Charlie out yesterday she'd already lost it – but why? Why wouldn't she have told us and what could she have done that was so bad that she didn't even get a warning?'

Sabine shrugged, holding her fingers under the cold tap and then patting her face and neck. 'The assistant wouldn't say, but I asked around. There are rumours. They say she'd lost her focus, made some bad decisions that cost a lot of money and . . .' Sabine glanced at Charlie.

'What?' Ellen asked her.

'They say she was . . . turning up at work under the influence.'

Ellen stared at her hands that were pressed flat against the tabletop so firmly that the tips her fingernails blanched white.

'Under the influence of alcohol?' Charlie queried. Sabine looked uncomfortable but didn't reply.

'What *do* you mean?' Ellen asked.

'I heard . . . I heard she'd been caught drinking on the job, but like I say, they are only rumours. I don't know anything for sure.'

Ellen and Charlie looked at each other, equally disbelieving. Hannah liked to party, and she enjoyed a drink. And Ellen wasn't naïve enough to believe that her sister hadn't taken part in some of the other excesses that were prevalent in the city. But it was incomprehensible to her that Hannah would have let things get so bad that she was drinking at work. Her career, her professional reputation, the way she looked – all these things were paramount to her. Ellen could not imagine what could have happened to change that.

'That can't be right, that doesn't sound like Hannah at all. Her work has always been everything to her. Something really bad, really big must have happened to make her throw that away . . . maybe that's why?' Ellen thought of her sister's ever-increasing visits over the last few months, her sudden uncharacteristic desire to be around. Ellen had been so caught up in her own emotional maelstrom that she hadn't stopped to think that Hannah might have problems of her own. 'No, surely she would have told me if something really bad had happened?'

'No she wouldn't,' Charlie said. 'She knows you hate her.'

'Rubbish, we fight and fall out and she drives me mad, but we're sisters. Hannah knows that I'd always be there for her. I mean she's the strong one, she's the tough and together one.'

Sabine shook her head. 'All I can tell you for sure are the facts. She doesn't work for the bank any more. That's all I know. I'm sorry to be the bearer of bad news. I didn't know what to do about it.'

'I'll call her,' Ellen said, fetching the telephone from the hall.

But when she called Hannah's flat there was no answer, and her mobile went straight to answerphone.

'Perhaps it's because she knows it's you. I'll try her,' Charlie said, fishing his mobile out of his pocket and dialling his aunt. Hannah didn't pick up, again.

'Maybe Gran and Grandpa have spoken to her?' Charlie looked disappointed that his aunt didn't appear to want to speak to him either. 'Call them, Mum – see what they know.'

Ellen shook her head. 'No, I'd better not ring, not until I know something. I don't want to worry them, not with Mum's blood pressure. And Dad will probably want to come up here and look for her, like he did that summer she ran off with that busker. No, Hannah is still Hannah. She's still a grown-up. I mean, we only saw her yesterday and she was a bit off – but she was OK. We'll wait, she'll turn up or call. If she doesn't it'll be the first day in months that I haven't heard from her in one way or another.'

'But what if she's in trouble, what if she can't call or come round? We could go round to her place,' Charlie suggested. 'It's only a couple of Tube stops to Ladbroke Grove.'

'She's not there, Charlie, she's not answering the phone,'

Ellen told him edgily, irritated that her son was picking now to illustrate his preposterous point.

'That doesn't mean she's not there,' Charlie insisted. 'She might be lying on the floor choking on her own vomit or something. She might be dying and really, really need rescuing.' As he spoke his eyes filled with tears. Ellen pulled him to her and put an arm around him. 'I don't want Aunt Hannah to die.'

'Charlie, Hannah's better at looking after herself than anyone I know,' Ellen told him.

'So was Dad,' Charlie said quietly. 'Can't we just go and check?'

'Charlie.' Sabine spoke softly and calmly. 'I'm afraid I've panicked you. I'm sure that your aunt is fine. After all it's been a week since she lost her job, you saw her just yesterday and she seemed OK, didn't she? There is no reason why she wouldn't be just as OK today.'

'Yes, I suppose . . .' Charlie sniffed, brushing the back of his hand across his eyes. 'If anything, she seemed even happier than normal, really cheerful and energetic. I didn't say anything because . . . Well, because, you know, you were cross, but she was talking about taking me on holiday to New York or somewhere.' Sabine and Ellen exchanged a look.

'Then she is probably fine, maybe even happy about what's happened. I expect she wants some time alone to work out whatever is going on. She will tell you and your mum everything when she is ready. Your mum is right to want to wait.'

Charlie looked at Ellen. 'But if she rang you now and asked you to go round, you would?' he challenged her.

'Of course I would, Charlie,' Ellen told him levelly. 'Look, I'll try calling again in a little while. In the meantime let's get dinner on and see about your tea, and try not to worry, OK? You go and play your DS for a bit and I'll call you when things are sorted.' Charlie looked to Sabine, seeming to need her extra affirmation, and she nodded. He picked up his school bag and slouched out of the room.

'How serious were these rumours?' Ellen asked her, as soon as she heard Charlie's footsteps disappearing up the stairs.

'There was talk of some CCTV footage showing her drinking from a bottle of whisky in reception after hours. But I don't know, Ellen, it could just be gossip. It's a big office, a lot of people are very jealous of Hannah, they'd like nothing more than for her to have left in disgrace. Keep trying to call her. That's all you can do.'

'Perhaps Charlie is right, perhaps I should go round there.' Ellen pictured the street outside her front door, the yawning expanse of road that stretched towards the Tube station, with another four roads and an underpass to negotiate on top of that. She didn't want to go, that was true. She didn't want to tackle the heat and noise and throng of people that would be crowding the hot and stinking trains. She did prefer to stay at home, she did enjoy the quiet tranquillity of her house and, yes, the world that revolved around her here was enough for her. It always had been. But that didn't mean she wouldn't go to Hannah if Hannah needed her. That didn't mean she couldn't go, not if she had to.

God only knew where Charlie had got this idea that she was agoraphobic.

'Ellen, forgive me, I don't know you or Hannah very well. But I do know sisters, I have a big sister myself and there is nothing I hate more than her seeking me out to tell me how wrong I am and how right she is – you should have seen her crowing over what happened between Eric and me.' Sabine went to the fridge and took two bottles of beer from her shelf. 'If you want to be friends with Hannah then it is best to wait for her to come to you, after all if she wanted your advice now she would have told you everything already and she hasn't. Beer?'

Ellen nodded, and Sabine slid a bottle over to her. She hoped a drink might quell the niggling feeling of discomfort that had wormed its way into her gut, and the underlying sensation that something was very wrong with Hannah. That was just the way she was now, Ellen told herself, pressing her hand against the fold of her belly as if she could physically quiet her concern. Anything, anything at all that nudged her out of her daily routine set her heart racing as if she were balancing on a high wire. Something worse, something like Charlie arriving home late or Simon inviting her out to lunch made it pound and twitch, missing beats with reckless abandon, and for a fraction of a fearful second feel nothing but a hollow lifeless sensation in her chest until it thundered on, leaving her breathless and afraid. But that was her weakness, her legacy of losing her husband, not some prescient supernatural power. It couldn't be, because she hadn't sensed a single dark thing about the day that Nick had died. She'd been in the front garden, picking the deadheads off the roses, when the police car pulled up outside. There hadn't been a moment of discomfort or distress even then, even when they walked up the garden path, not quite able to look her in the eye. Not until she'd sat down on the sofa in the front room and looked into the policewoman's eyes had the truth had hit her like a sledgehammer. She'd felt short of breath, winded, ever since.

'So my husband received my list,' Sabine said, taking Charlie's chair.

'And?' Ellen asked. 'What did he make of it?'

'He thought it was a little long. He said if he'd known that we were going to nit-pick over every little thing then he could have made his list much longer. He could have included things like I let my bikini line grow out or that I stopped putting make-up on for him, which isn't true. I just don't like to slap it on like a prostitute, that's all.'

'So, what did you decide?' Ellen asked her, sipping her beer and wishing she'd added some for herself on to her supermarket delivery.

'I've told him to go to her,' Sabine said.

'To the woman he's been writing to?' Ellen gasped.

'I have to, Ellen, I thought about it and I realise I have no choice. After all as Sting says, if you love someone let them go. I've told him if he loves her, he must go to her, even if she is married, he must tell her how he feels, he must try and win her. How can I live with a man that I know is always dreaming of someone else, and be happy? I can't, so I told him to go to her.'

'And what did he say?' Ellen asked her. 'Is he going?'

'Yes.' Sabine nodded bleakly. 'He is going to take leave next week and go and see her in Austria. She is *Austrian*, Ellen,' she emphasised, as if that were adding insult to injury.

'And that's it, your marriage is over?' Ellen found it hard to believe.

'Not quite.' Sabine glanced at her watch. 'We have an appointment for a Skype chat in a little while,' she said. 'To talk about my decision.'

'So he's not rushing off to try and be with this woman then, even though you told him to go?' Ellen asked her, as curious as she was shocked. 'He still wants to talk? That's a good sign.'

'Is it?' Sabine sighed. 'Or is he just absolving himself? After all, if I've told him to go, given him my blessing, then he has no reason to feel guilty does he?'

'Goodness,' Ellen said. 'Are you sure you want to give him that freedom?'

'Not really. But what other choice is there? If I force him to stay I will always be wondering if he would rather be somewhere else.'

'And you wouldn't think of, oh I don't know, finding someone here to have a revenge fling with, or something?'

Sabine looked appalled at the idea.

'English men leave me very cold,' she told Ellen, adding as an afterthought, 'Well, Matt is very sexy, and you can tell by looking at him that he knows his way around a woman's body.'

'Do you think so?' Ellen asked her, leaning a little towards her, realising that the third of a bottle of wine she had drunk earlier combined with strong German beer had made her somewhat tipsy, almost tipsy enough to numb her body's physical tics. 'Do you think he'd be a passionate lover?'

'Do you?' Sabine asked her, amused. Ellen leaned her chin into the heel of her hand, missing her mark so that her head slipped and her neck jarred.

'Allegra thinks I should take him as my lover, as if I could just sort of lift him off the supermarket shelf and get him to satisfy my every whim. Stud-on-a-stick sort of thing.'

Sabine spluttered beer as she laughed. 'Allegra is probably right. Matt would go to bed with you, I'm sure you wouldn't have to go to much effort if that was what you wanted. But don't think it would be love, Ellen, or anything like it. For him it would be a sexual experience and nothing more. Don't go down that road unless you are prepared to accept that.'

'Oh God, I'm not going to go down that road at all,' Ellen laughed. 'Going down roads is the last thing I want to do, at least according to my son! No, I'm a widow and a mother. I'm thirty-eight, boring and old. Besides, I have a lot more things to worry about. A sister who's lost her job and a son who thinks I'm agoraphobic, can you imagine?'

'Agoraphobic?' Sabine repeated the word as a question. 'Interesting.'

'Yes, you know, someone who is afraid of going outside. He's got it into his head that that's me. That I'm scared to set foot outside my own front door. Just because I'm a homebody, and I don't like people or crowds or a lot of noise. But that's just me, I'm quiet, and shy. I am a very quiet and shy person, Sabine, I am not the sort of person to be having emotion-free sex with a much younger man.'

'Really? Are you sure?' Sabine looked amused and then thoughtful. 'Actually Ellen, I have lived here nearly a month now and I hope you don't mind me saying that I don't think I have seen you go out once, not even into the garden.'

Ellen shrugged. 'Well I'm not sure I have been out in the last month. But that's not that unusual for me. I mean I work from home, I have to be at home for Charlie when he gets in from school. My life is in this house, there isn't any need for me to go anywhere.'

'No need perhaps, but you don't even want to go for a walk to the park, sit on a bench and enjoy the sun on your face?'

'That would be all very well if I had time, but I don't. Time is not something I have,' Ellen insisted. 'I really don't think it's that big a deal.'

Sabine glanced at her watch again. 'I expect you are right,' she said. 'Now I must go and talk to my husband. I hope you manage to get in touch with Hannah. I'm sorry that I worried you and Charlie so much.'

'Don't be, I'm glad I know that something's going on with her, it sort of explains why she's been the way she has recently. It will be some big Hannah drama, some man at the bottom of it, no doubt. Sooner or later I'll find out what it is and it will all blow over. Good luck with Eric.'

'Thank you,' Sabine said very politely, leaving Ellen sitting alone in her kitchen. After a second she rose from her chair and preheated the grill for Charlie's fish fingers. Then she started to get out the ingredients she needed to make Allegra's risotto primavera.

As she stood at the kitchen sink filling a pan with water, she looked down the length of the back garden towards the gate that had long been obscured by undergrowth, at the line of rooftops that serrated the skyline beyond it, silhouetted against the stubbornly faultless blue sky.

When *was* the last time she went out, she wondered, as the water filled the pan and then began to run over its edges, numbing her reddening hands as she stood there motionless. Ellen thought of the empty calendar that lay open on the table behind her, devoid of both dates and memories. Her mind tracked back over month after month, struggling to recall anything particularly memorable in any of them. There had been Charlie, her books and the pain from the horrible gaping seeping open wound that losing Nick had carved into her, and that was all she could remember. Each day – which had seemed like an uncrossable desert that she had had to claw herself across from dawn till dusk – now seemed like one featureless globule of time, an existence that had been occupied by very little besides her treacherous body's continued insistence on staying alive, no matter how she felt about it.

The truth was that Ellen couldn't remember the last time she had ventured further than her front door. Dropping the pan in the sink and slopping freezing water everywhere, she turned and with numb damp fingers picked up the pristine calendar of Sussex views, gazing at each empty month, stretching her mind as far back as it would allow, to last Christmas.

It had been a dark, desolate affair, made all the more despairing by the effort that went on around her and Charlie to make it at least bearable. Her parents, confused and embarrassed by her grief, were driven up from Hove by Hannah, bringing Christmas lunch with them packed neatly in her mother's twenty-year-old Tupperware. After giving and receiving unwanted gifts the five of them had laboured over lunch, in what would have been silence if Ellen's mother hadn't insisted on filling them all in on the details of Mrs Hopkins' hysterectomy. Hannah had drunk herself slowly into oblivion, Charlie had bolted to his room at the first available opportunity and Ellen, paralysed by the memory of how Christmas used to be, of what it should have been like now and how it would never, never be the same again, had sat through the Queen's speech with her mother while her father snored in the corner.

With a shock, Ellen realised that she had no memory of going out of the house even then. What little shopping she had done had all been online, her family and a succession of well-meaning but unwanted visitors had come to her. Was it truly possible that she hadn't left the house in six months?

Feeling suddenly sober and washed with the same kind of dread that she got when she felt she had forgotten something important, but wasn't sure what it was, Ellen forced herself to scratch around in her memory for anything, any detail or incident in her life since Nick had died that would allow her to get a grip on some event or happening. As much as she racked her brain she could find nothing until just a few weeks ago, when Hannah told her that she had to take in lodgers.

She sat back in her chair and looked around at her kitchen, rigid with horror as she realised the truth.

She had not left this house since her husband's funeral. She had not been out in almost a year, and worst of all – she had not noticed.

Chapter Fourteen

'Your round, rookie,' Pete told Matt, his sweaty booze-saturated face looming far too close for comfort. 'Get 'em in, son.'

'Yeah, yeah, OK – when do I stop being a rookie?' Matt asked him, gathering up a selection of half-empty glasses and taking orders for the assembled staff of *Bang It!*. Thursday night and that week's issue had just been put to bed, after what he now realised was a customary routine that involved panic, shouting and a large amount of swearing blind that the whole thing was going to shit even though somehow it didn't. Naturally when they pulled off their weekly miracle of getting *Bang It!* to press, everyone went down the pub to celebrate by getting as many beers as possible straight down their necks in the shortest period of time, or in Pete's case the whisky that seemed to seep out of his open pores. It was an exhausting and strangely dissatisfying routine, and Matt still struggled to really feel a part of it. He'd expected to thrive on the adrenalin rush of putting a weekly magazine together in a matter of days, but when the first fresh copies rolled in, looking and reading almost exactly like those of the previous weeks, he found himself wondering what the point was. Then he'd remind himself that this was his dream job, and that soon enough he'd have killed so many brain cells through alcohol abuse that he wouldn't worry about it any more anyway.

'You stop being a rookie when I say so,' Pete told him, accompanying him to the bar where Matt waved a twenty at one of the bar staff, knowing full well he'd need at least another one of those to pay for everyone's drinks. 'You're still on probation, and so far you haven't exactly excelled yourself.'

'What?' Matt said. 'Bollocks.'

'I'm serious, mate, you're coasting it – you look lazy.'

'Lazy?' Matt protested. 'I've worked my arse off since I got here. Literally.'

'Look, the writing's good, funny and that – but so far you've pulled two girls who more or less dropped in your lap and rehashed a load of old stuff. We need more from you, more derring-do and adventure. Birds from the same office building are OK, but they're easy pickings. Our readers want you to be what they're not – the hunter, the master, the maestro – the man that can have any woman any time. The dark destroyer. You need some variety-shagging, mate. A policewoman maybe, or a nurse.'

'So you're saying I should base my column around your top ten all-time favourite stripper costumes?' Matt shook his head.

'It's not my worst idea.' Pete shrugged, taking as many of the assembled drinks as he could carry, including his own large single malt whisky, and teetering off towards the table where the waiting hordes greeted him with a cheer after he lost only one of the drinks. Downing his own shot in one, Matt ordered a replacement. They'd been in here for an hour and already he could feel his head swimming with the heat and the alcohol, not that he'd want any of them to know that. Being able to drink like a bastard and still turn up for work the next day was one of the job requirements, but for some reason Matt just hadn't been in the mood for it recently. The pub made him feel restless and uneasy, and he realised with something of a shock that at that moment he'd much rather have been at Ellen's house, sitting at the kitchen table while she pottered around, drinking cups of tea and seeing whether he could make her laugh. Steeling himself, Matt ordered another shot and downed that too. He was far too young to want to be in instead of out; he'd have to drown the impulse with booze before it took hold completely and he bought a pair of slippers and started planning his life around television. He went back to join his colleagues.

'I was just saying,' Pete belched at Dan as he lumbered back into his seat, 'I reckon we need more of a challenge for young Matt here. Give the readers something to be impressed by. I mean that Carla, anyone could have had her if they could be bothered with the stringy little thing.'

'Everyone has,' Raffa joked with a wink directed at Matt.

'Ha, ha,' Matt said drily.

'And that little blonde piece downstairs, from the tarts' magazine – she's always got her arse and tits hanging out, looks like a hooker. Pulling her took about as much effort as scoring a burger from a drive-through McDonald's.'

Matt chuckled as he gazed into his beer, but privately he was thinking of Lucy marching out of the lift, her eyes glittering with rage. He had the distinct feeling he'd underestimated her. Almost like he hadn't seen her, even when they'd been in bed together.

'Drive-through shags, there's an idea,' Dan said, stroking his chin. 'Look that up on the Internet, Raffa, do it now, son. If there isn't a drive-through brothel somewhere in Nevada, next round of drinks are on me. If there is, which there will be, then, Matt, I want a feature on that by Monday, cool? Interview some of the girls, the punters, get some pics – you should be able to do it all online and on the phone.'

'Sure,' Matt said, wondering how the hell he was going to pull that off, imagining himself making a call that went, 'Oh hello, are you the madam? Hello, I'm a journalist you've never heard of from England writing a piece for a magazine you've never heard of. Please can I interview your hookers on the joys of working in a drive-through brothel, and would you mind sending me some pictures? But only of the fit ones.'

The sad truth was that that was exactly how the conversation would go.

'I've got it!' Pete bellowed, making Matt wince. 'We pick his next victim. All of us tonight. We pick a girl from this pub and that's the bird he's got to bed for his next column and his challenge is to make it happen, no matter who we choose.'

'Right, well hang on a minute,' Matt started to protest, but he was shouted down.

'What, like pull-a-pig night?' Raffa chimed in. 'Like we pick a proper minger and he's got to do her no matter what?' The assembled men guffawed at the idea.

'Er, I don't think so,' Matt countered, feeling the alcohol fizzing in his fingertips, his head swimming as he was swept along on a tide of his colleagues' testosterone. If he was going to survive this he'd have to man up and go with it, they'd eat him alive if they knew that the last thing he wanted to do tonight was chat up some random girl and that really he'd like to go home and drink tea with Ellen. 'I'm the man, the master – the maestro.

Anyone can pick up an old dog grateful for a sniff of any bloke. If you're going to challenge me then find me something special, something that's going to take a bit more effort than batting my lashes and giving her a smile.'

'He's right, the punters want fantasy, not fact,' Dan said. 'We've got to pick a fittie. Tell you what, to make it more interesting we get to decide what your opening line is.'

'Yeah and you have to secretly record it on your phone so we know you've done it,' Greg grinned.

'And you have to get a picture of her tits on your phone too.' Raffa nodded. 'Close up, no face or nothing, just tits – then we can print them in the magazine and score them out of ten.'

'Oh my fuck, that's a genius idea.' Dan clapped Raffa on the shoulder.

'Whoa, OK,' Matt laughed to cover his discomfort. 'And if I pull this off?'

'Or if she pulls you off,' Raffa snickered.

'Your probation ends tomorrow,' Dan told him. 'You're on the team.'

'And if I don't?' Matt countered.

'Same deal, only you're off the team.' Dan raised an eyebrow. 'Got the balls to take that bet?'

'Don't need balls to take that bet. Fucking piss-easy,' Matt assured him with a beer-based bravado that he didn't enjoy.

'OK then.' Dan twisted in his seat, scanning the bar for a likely target. Matt felt uneasy as he watched him. What Dan was doing was no different from what he himself might do on a night out, looking for a girl to chat up – but when he did it it was random, chance, there was always a possibility that it wouldn't work out. Dan picking a girl out for him that he was definitely supposed to have sex with really did make it seem as if they were choosing a victim, and Matt never liked to think of any of the women he spent time with as that.

'Her.' Dan nodded in the direction of a pillar, where two women dressed in short, flowery summer dresses, were talking, bare tanned legs tapering down to high heels much in evidence, their heads close together as they sipped from straws in some lurid alcopop.

Matt was dimly aware of sniggering and elbow-digging as Dan made his selection. It had to be said they were the fittest women in the bar, and more than that, proper women. Well dressed and confident-looking, as if getting chatted up by a man was the very last thing on their minds. This really would be a challenge.

'Blonde or brunette?' Pete asked, with a death's head grin that Matt found unsettling.

'Brunette, brunettes always have the best nipples,' Dan declared, making Raffa's shoulders shake with uncharacteristically repressed laughter. 'Are we all agreed?' The group cheered their rowdy assent in unison, causing the unsuspecting woman to glance up briefly in their direction. Matt caught her eye and held it for a second until she lowered her lashes, turning back to her friend and whispering something that made the other woman laugh. If it was about him, Matt was fairly sure it wasn't complimentary. She looked about thirty, the high-maintenance type, who obviously lavished much attention on her skin and hair, and clearly worked out, judging by her lightly muscled thighs and arms. There wasn't a crease on her forehead or a line around her full-lipped mouth, she was perfect, and yet if Matt had been making his own decision she would have been the last woman that he would have chosen. There were no secrets there for him to discover, he was certain. She would have any hint of imperfection concealed.

'Yeah, I like her,' Dan said. 'She looks hot, like a right goer – might teach you a thing or two, Matt, my son. And she's got a great pair, so couldn't be more perfect. Off you go now.'

'Wait a minute, I can't just pile in there,' Matt said. 'I need to do a bit of groundwork first, fleeting eye contact, shy smiles, that sort of bollocks.'

'Er, no you don't, you big gay,' Dan told him. 'Get in there and set your phone to record. Your opening line is . . . "I've never seen skin as beautiful as yours, do you moisturise?" '

The table erupted into laughter.

'Are you trying to make me look like a fucking serial killer?' Matt shook his head.

'Yeah,' Dan nodded, taking Matt's phone off him to check it was recording. Satisfied, he handed it back and indicated the brunette. 'Go on.'

'Well, don't all look, OK?' Matt asked in vain. He downed his drink and headed for his target.

The woman spluttered into her drink when he delivered his line, glancing briefly over his shoulder at his assembled colleagues who were now all suspiciously silent.

'You on a dare or what?' she asked him, looking him up and down with barely concealed contempt. Matt pulled out his self-deprecating 'I know I'm a bumbling fool but look how cute I am' grin.

'That was a shocking line, wasn't it, but it is true – you have beautiful skin. Seriously, you look about sixteen.'

The woman smirked. 'So do you,' she told him. It wasn't a compliment.

245

'Yeah, I am youthful, but that's not a bad thing.' Matt tried his 'I know where a clitoris is' eyebrow-raise. 'It means I've got the stamina to give a woman what she wants.'

'What, a pair of Gucci shoes?' the woman retorted, quick as lightning.

Matt took a second to regroup, all too conscious of the baying pack of hounds at his back, ready to rip him to shreds at the first opportunity. He needed to try another tack.

'Did you know that you could be a model?' he asked her, cringing inwardly.

'Yes,' she said. 'I do know. I am a model. Model slash presenter actually.'

'Oh well, there you go. I was right then.' Struggling, Matt listened to line after line fall totally flat. He'd always thought he was a proper charmer – but maybe that was because the women he normally picked on were a lot more drunk and a lot more susceptible than this one, keen to lap up every hackneyed compliment as if it were gospel. Maybe he always sounded so shallow and shit like he got his lines from a Christmas-cracker joke, maybe he'd just never heard himself properly before. Matt wondered what his chances were of finding another job – maybe Lucy would put a word in for him at her magazine. But then again, maybe she wouldn't.

'Come on then,' the brunette pressed him. 'You're trying to pull me, aren't you? Don't give up now – God loves a trier and so do I.'

'OK, you're an intelligent, sophisticated woman, you don't want any of the flannel and the lines.' Matt took a breath, pinning his career on the next few words. 'The truth is I really want to make love to you, what do you say?'

The brunette exchanged a deadpan look with her friend.

'I say if that was your best shot you've blown it. Seriously, mate, you didn't ask me my name, or anything about me. Are you on the clock or something? Seems to me like you're just trying to pull any bird so you can write some sleazy magazine article about it.'

'I . . . but . . . OK, how do you know?' Matt said, his words almost lost in the cacophony of jeers that set off behind him. 'You've been in the magazine, haven't you? Look, I know that makes me look like a prick, and I have no idea how I haven't remembered a woman as beautiful as you, but I promise you that is not what this is about.'

The woman slowly looked him up and down as if she were appraising a stud horse.

'OK then,' she said with a nod.

'OK then what?' Matt asked her.

'OK then I'll shag you,' she told him, looking him directly in the eye. Matt suddenly felt quite nervous, certain that the parts of him that were basic requirements for such an endeavour had just shrunk away to nothing.

'Really?' he squeaked.

'Yeah, but on one condition.' She raised a flirty brow that made Matt think a million scary and exciting things.

'Name it,' he whispered.

'You'd better ask my husband first,' the woman told him. 'After all he is your boss.'

'He's . . . what?' He looked around to find the entire staff of *Bang It!* gasping with laughter, banging on the table while Dan held up his glass and winked at him.

'I said you should have asked me my name. It's Aimee, Mrs

Aimee Sutherland, and that moisturiser line, that was Dan's first line with me. It worked out a lot better for him.'

Leaving Matt speechless, Aimee sashayed past him in her Gucci heels, and bending over her husband, grabbed him by the collar. 'Right, now you really owe me dinner, come on – we're going.'

As Dan stood up and kissed his wife, he was literally crying with laughter. 'That is the funniest thing I've heard in years,' he said. 'Seriously, we should put that on the website. Babe, you were brilliant.'

'What do you mean, put it on the website?' Matt asked him miserably.

'I mean that when I checked your phone, I called my phone and put you on speaker. That was brilliant!'

'You bastard!' Matt proclaimed, picking up Pete's drink and downing it in one. 'That whole thing was a wind-up.' He looked miserably at Aimee. 'Oh God, I'm so embarrassed.'

'You should be, love,' Aimee laughed. 'Don't know how you got your reputation for being a ladies' man.'

She grinned at her friend who seated herself next to a suddenly silent Raffa.

Matt grinned too; he had no choice but to take it on the chin. It *was* pretty funny.

'So am I fired then?' he asked Dan.

'You should be, but I can't bring myself to do it, you're too entertaining.' Dan glanced at his wife. 'I'm too drunk to eat – how about a line and a club, yeah?'

Matt shook his head when everybody else was nodding theirs.

'You know what, I'm going to get back.'

'Back where, to where you left your self-respect?' Raffa laughed.

'No, I . . .' Matt stopped himself saying he wanted to have a shower and go to sleep in front of the telly. 'I've got a bit of a project going on.'

'A woman?' Pete asked him.

'Yeah, a real challenge, a little older – but, you know, really sexy.'

'You mean like a cougar?' Raffa suggested.

'Or a milf?' Greg put in.

'Yeah, no – she's a lady. You know, refined, quiet and shy.'

'And you reckon you can crack her?'

'I reckon under those frumpy clothes she's got a slamming body,' Matt said. 'It's only a matter of time.'

'Wait, are you talking about your landlady?' Pete slurred. 'The one who's taking in lodgers because her husband snuffed it?'

'Whoa, low blow – you're going for a woman on the rebound from death? Mate, that tops trying to pick up your boss's wife any day of the week.' Raffa sounded admiring.

'Firstly, I didn't know I was trying to pick up the boss's wife, and secondly, her husband's been dead nearly a year,' Matt said uncomfortably.

'You are a dark, dark bastard,' Dan said approvingly. 'Matt, the dark destroyer. Go for it, mate. There's a features idea, what depths would a bloke go to to get his end away, hey Raffa . . .'

Matt picked up his stuff and headed out into the mercifully cool air of the night, the last remnants of light only just fading even though it was getting on for eleven. As he headed back towards his much longed-for room, his stomach churned and his head spun. It wasn't just the mixture of beer and whisky; he felt disjointed and out of place. Like when he'd woken up after a big night and known that he'd done something to offend someone but he couldn't work out what; only this time he knew exactly what he'd done, exactly what he'd said, and he hated himself for it. He didn't think about Ellen that way at all. He did think of her sexually, that was inevitable, she was a beautiful woman, with a body that hinted at much more, and he was a man. Of course he thought about her like that, but he didn't think of her as a project, an easy target. That was the very last way he thought about her; if anything, he had this unfamiliar urge to look after her, to protect her.

As Matt walked down his road, his head hung low, he considered turning back, finding his colleagues and going out after all, but then a noise in the shadows stopped him in his tracks. He listened, uncertain of what he had heard.

'Matt?' A figure lurched out of the shadows and under the streetlight. It was a second before Matt took in what he was seeing.

'Hannah?' He stepped forward and caught the woman just as her knees buckled. Looking down at her, he saw her make-up smeared down her face, her eyes bloodshot and swollen, but there was more than that, a livid bruise was inflaming her left cheek just under her eye, her clothes were dirty and torn. 'Fuck, Hannah, what happened?'

'Will you take me to Ellen's?' Hannah asked him drowsily, clearly still under the influence of something. 'I need to go to Ellen's, I need to tell her something. I'm trying to get there but it seems so far and I'm . . . I'm hurting.'

Matt folded his arm around her waist and took her weight against his shoulder.

'Hannah, what the hell happened?' he asked her.

Hannah swung her head round to look at him, her bleary eyes unable to focus, her brows drawn together in a frown.

'I don't know,' she told him. 'I don't know what happened.'

Chapter Fifteen

In her dream Ellen was in a library, no, not a library – *the* library, the one at college, where the tall dusty shelves that stretched from floor to ceiling were closely crammed together, leaving only a narrow space to walk between them. It was hot and dark. She could feel sweat gathering at the nape of her neck, she was looking for something, she was looking for the way out.

Searching for a clue, she ran her finger along a shelf of books like none she had ever seen in the university library, each one a fat well-fingered paperback, with purple, pink and red spines cracked along their length as if each one had been avidly read. Ellen picked out one book and saw an illustration of a woman on the cover, the tops of her arms gripped and pulled back forcefully by a muscular topless man so that her breasts surged forward, straining against the laces of what appeared to be some kind of white nightdress. Ellen frowned, puzzled by what was so familiar about the image. She tried to make out the title, gold-embossed swirling letters, but they did not seem to make sense no matter how hard she looked at them. She stared and stared at the image of the woman on the cover, her expression caught somewhere between agony and ecstasy, the internal struggle between desire and propriety expertly caught by the brush of the artist. There was something familiar about the woman, her long dark hair tumbling over one shoulder, her full lips baring her teeth in what might have been either a growl or a groan of ecstasy. Then, with a flush of embarrassment, Ellen realised that she was looking at an illustration of herself in the throes of undeniable passion. And the man who was restraining her, his lips buried in her neck? She could not tell, he was fair and well built, but she could not see his face. Perhaps it was Nick, she wondered, trying to recall if Nick had ever grabbed her so purposefully. Ellen moaned, remembering the gentle pressure of his palm on her inner thigh, the first indication that he wanted to make love. His first move always, even before kissing her. Or perhaps it was Matt, Matt who was seducing her away from quiet respectability, his strong fingers gripping her so hard that they would surely leave their imprint on her flesh, branding her as his. At last she could make sense of the title. *Ellen's Escape.*

This was it, this would show her the way out of this maze she was trapped in, where every corridor, every room led her round and round in ever-decreasing circles back to where she began. The book had to have the answers.

Desperately Ellen flicked from page to page, anxious to see what secrets they would reveal, but each one was blank. Yellowing cream, slightly rough in texture and entirely empty.

'But what happens?' Her voice echoed between the shelves. 'What happens to me next?' Perhaps she had to fill in the answers, she found herself thinking. Perhaps to escape her story she had to write it.

'Ellen?' She spun round. Matt was standing behind her, shirtless just as the man on the cover of her book was, his muscled torso glistening with what might have been sweat but smelt like

253

rose oil, his well-developed pectoral muscles rising and falling as he took each heavy breath.

'You've come,' she whispered. 'You came. I've thought about it and I'm ready for sex, let's have lots of sex.'

'Ellen?' he said, softly, insistently. 'Ellen?'

'Yes, the answer is yes, yes I want you, I want you. As a strong independent woman I will let you take me now!' Ellen flung herself back, bracing her body against the bookshelf. 'Rip off my clothes, only be careful with the buttons on this top, it's my favourite.'

Matt took a step towards her and gently shook her shoulder.

'Ellen? Ellen, wake up. Wake up. Ellen, wake up.'

Groggily her eyes opened and she focused on Matt. She smiled, one hand lazily fluttering up to caress the side of his face. And then she realised she wasn't dreaming any more and Matt was actually leaning over her bed.

'Bloody hell!' Ellen tried to sit up, but found herself pinned down by a tangle of sheets. With some difficulty she unravelled herself with one hand while trying to maintain her modesty with the other. It would be tonight of all nights that she had finally surrendered to the sweltering heat and given up her pyjamas in favour of one of Nick's cotton shirts.

'What are you doing here?' she asked Matt breathlessly, dragging a sheet up over her chest. She could be mistaken, but the look on his face didn't exactly point to a seduction attempt.

'I'm sorry,' he whispered, careful not to look at her. He sat on the edge of the bed, his weight causing her leg to roll a little closer to his. 'I didn't know what to do, I thought I'd better wake you. You were having a pretty radical dream.'

'Have I slept in? Is it morning?' Ellen was confused, and then a flash of her dream came back to her. 'Oh God, was I talking in my sleep?'

'Nothing I could make out.' Whatever he had heard or seen Matt seemed utterly uninterested, which Ellen found simultaneously disappointing and a relief.

'Look, it's not morning,' he went on. 'It's about midnight, I think.' He paused, as if uncertain how to go on. 'Hannah's downstairs.'

Ellen felt her shoulders relax. She leant back against the headboard.

'Typical.' She ran her fingers through her hair. 'She worries us all to death and then turns up on the doorstep whenever she feels like it. Seriously, that woman thinks the world revolves around her. She has to learn, she can't just turn up here attention-seeking any hour of the day or night.' Unthinking, Ellen swung her bare legs out of bed, hastily pulling on Nick's dressing gown that still hung on the back of the bedroom door. 'I'm going to tell her she can bloody well go home and come back in the morning.'

Just as she reached the door Matt put a hand on her shoulder and stopped her. Ellen turned to look at him.

'Ellen, you don't understand.' In the half-light that fed through the open door Matt's expression was unreadable, but something about the shadows under his eyes and the incline of his head sent an ominous shiver through her. 'Look, I don't know what's happened, but Hannah's pretty messed up.'

'Drunk, you mean?' she asked him.

'Probably, she might have taken or been given something too.' Ellen's sigh was one of exasperation. 'But wait, it's not just

255

that. Something's happened to her, she's hurt and she can't remember how. You need to come and see her, Ellen.'

Matt took a step closer and finally she could see his expression. He was really worried.

'Oh my God, what's she done now?'

Ellen didn't know what she expected to see when she pushed the living-room door open, but it wasn't the sight that greeted her. Matt had left Hannah on the sofa, where she had curled herself up into a tight ball and appeared to be sleeping. Ellen flicked on a lamp to get a better look at her sister, who unconsciously screwed up her eyes against the invasion of light. The first thing Ellen noticed was the blood in Hannah's hair, dried now, a thick black lump matting the auburn strands into a clump. There was a bruise on her left cheek, and her lip was swollen and cut. The neck of her shirt was torn and there was mud streaked along her skirt, which had ripped up the seam revealing the tops of her legs. But the sight that sent ice through Ellen's veins was a smear of blood, dried and flaking, on the inside of one of her thighs.

Ellen pressed her hand over her mouth as she stared at her fitfully slumbering sister, forcing herself to stay silent. After a few seconds she peeled her fingers away from her lips.

'Where did you say you found her?' she asked Matt, her voice strained.

'At the end of the road, she just appeared out of nowhere, looking like that. She seemed really out of it, I think she'd been in someone's garden, maybe she passed out there. I don't know how long she'd been there, but I think she was trying to get to you. I didn't find her, she found me. If she hadn't seen me I'd have walked right past her.'

Hesitantly Ellen knelt on the carpet next to her sister, her hands hovering over her, uncertain of what to do, and then biting down on her bottom lip she gently touched her on the shoulder.

'Hannah, Hannah.' Ellen spoke softly, almost unwilling to bring her round, but knowing that she must. 'Hannah. Wake up, it's me, Ellen.'

Hannah opened one swollen eye with some difficulty and looked at Ellen through the tender slit of her lid.

'Ellen.' Her voice was cracked and dry. 'I hurt.'

'I know, I can see that,' Ellen told her gently. Instinctively she pressed the back of her palm against Hannah's forehead, as her mother used to do to each of them when she suspected a temperature. Hannah's skin was cool; she must have been outside for some time. Unsure, Ellen glanced up at Matt, who shook his head. He had no idea what to do either. Ellen had to try and find out more.

'OK, Hannah, Hans?' She waited for Hannah to open her eyes again. 'You need to sit up, OK? Let me get a good look at you.' Ellen was suddenly reminded of the last time she had nursed Hannah when they were both children, when Hannah had been her tiny little sister, utterly in awe of her, taking her lead in almost everything. Back when her mother's friends used to look at the two of them together and say, 'What a lovely little mother your Ellen makes.'

Hannah moaned. 'Don't want to, Ellie, want to stay here. I like it here. Want to sleep now, hold my hand . . .'

'I know, I know you want to sleep and you can soon. But first of all I need to see all your hurts. Let me look . . .'

Hannah grimaced in pain as Ellen awkwardly wrapped her

hands around her and heaved her bodily into a sitting position. Hannah's head lolled on her neck, but she smiled when she caught sight of Matt standing by the door.

'My hero,' she grinned, reopening the cut in her lip. 'Matt rescued me, Ellie, I was lost and he found me, he's so brave and handsome – like a hero in one of your books . . .'

Ellen knelt in front of Hannah, placing her hands either side of her head to enable her to look into her sister's eyes. One was now almost completely closed, the other heavy-lidded. Once long ago Ellen had been the designated first-aider in her department at the museum: she tried desperately to remember something about head injuries. Hannah could be drunk, or she could have taken a serious knock to the head. Gingerly Ellen felt over her sister's head for more cuts or bumps, but the only one she found was what looked like a fairly superficial cut on her forehead. Heads bleed a lot, Ellen remembered, but even so it was clear that someone or something had hit Hannah very hard.

'Hannah?' Ellen struggled to hold her sister's attention as her chin flopped on to her chest. 'Hannah! Were you in a fight? Who hurt you?' Ellen asked her, her eyes tracking the rest of all of her sister's visible injuries. Her knees were cut and dirty, fingerprint-sized bruises were blossoming on her forearms and there was dirt beneath her broken nails.

'Don't know,' Hannah said blearily, listing towards Ellen, who had to grab her shoulders to keep her upright. 'Want to sleep.'

'No, no you can't sleep. She can't sleep, can she, Matt? What if she isn't drunk, what if this is concussion? They always say that you mustn't go to sleep if you have a head injury.'

'Shall I make her a coffee?' Matt offered.

'Yes, good idea. Make her a strong one.' He looked relieved to have an excuse to leave the room, and Ellen didn't blame him.

'Look, Hannah, I know, OK, I know you've lost your job, that you've got into some kind of trouble at work. I know all that, you've got nothing to hide, OK – so just tell me what happened to you?'

Without warning Hannah flung her arms around Ellen's neck and dropped her head on to her shoulder, almost sending the pair of them tumbling back on to the carpet. 'I'm sorry, Ellie,' she sobbed tearlessly. 'I'm so, so sorry.'

With some difficulty Ellen eased her sister back against the sofa cushions.

'You don't have to be sorry,' she said, fighting the confusion and fear that made her want to run from the room. 'Whatever's happened, it's not your fault. Please, Hannah, I'm trying to work out what to do.'

'Will you promise to still love me, Ellie, promise me?' Hannah begged her plaintively. 'If you still love me then I'll be OK, I know I'll be OK.'

'Of course, silly,' Ellen told her, remembering with sudden clarity how Hannah used to climb into her bed when she was scared at night. She could have been no more than three and Ellen about eleven. Ellen remembered how she had loved the feeling of Hannah's small warm body curled up against her, and how protective she had felt of her little sister, wrapping her arms around her and promising that no harm would come to her. Promising her that she would always love her.

'Come on now, Hannah. Come on, try and remember.'

Hannah pulled her head up, her expression exactly the same as that of the little girl she had once been, caught with her hand in the biscuit tin. 'I was bored so I went out.' She frowned painfully. 'For a lunchtime drink. It was nice, really nice and hot and I sat outside and drank cider. I like drinking, Ellie, when I drink the pain stops for a bit . . .' Hannah drifted off again, her eyes fluttering shut.

Ellen wanted to ask her what pain, what pain could her bright, beautiful, successful sister possibly be trying so desperately to ward off? But she held her tongue. As difficult as it was she needed to keep Hannah awake, she needed to know what had happened to her.

'Hannah? Hannah, look at me?' Hannah reluctantly wrenched open her good eye. 'Have you been drinking all afternoon?' Ellen asked her. 'Did you fall over, did you get hit by a car?'

Hannah frowned. 'I don't think so. Did I?'

'OK.' Ellen struggled to know what to say. 'OK so you were at the pub, sitting in the sun and then what happened?'

'Oh! I met some people, really nice. Lots of fun.' Hannah nodded, smiling as she remembered. 'They bought me drinks, it must have been later on because they'd finished work for the day. City guys, you know. City guys are always the most fun. They bought me champagne and we . . .' Hannah hesitated as if unwilling to go on.

'What, what did you do?'

'I don't want to talk about this now, want to sleep, Ellie. Don't be cross with me any more.'

'I'm not cross,' Ellen told her. 'Please Hannah, I know this is difficult but I think it's important – did you take anything, or did anyone give you anything?'

'I danced.' Hannah frowned. 'I danced on the tables for them and then . . .' Her eyes closed for a second, her face clearing as she fell into a brief precious unconsciousness. Ellen felt guilty for shaking her out of it again.

'Hannah!' Ellen's voice was sharp, her chest heavy with dread. 'Then what happened?' Hannah's head snapped up again.

'We got thrown out for being rowdy. So me and the boys went somewhere else . . . where did we go?' She looked perplexed. 'I don't remember.'

'Boys, you mean the men you were with? How many, Hannah? What were their names?' Hannah brightened.

'One was called Nick! Nick, Ellen, can you imagine? I mean I know it's a common name, but it was nice. It was nice to have a reason to say it out loud again. Nick. Nick. Nick.'

Ellen shook her head, fighting her frustration. 'What happened with Nick, Hannah?' Instantly Hannah's face became a picture of unhappiness.

'Oh Ellen, I'm sorry. I'm so, so, sorry.'

'You don't have to be sorry, I've told you that. You don't have to be sorry about anything, OK? None of this is your fault. Did this Nick have sex with you?' Ellen pressed on, dreading the answer.

'Yes,' Hannah said, eliciting a sob from Ellen. 'Yes, and I'm sorry, Ellen. I'm so, so sorry. I didn't mean it to happen, it just did. I didn't realise what I was doing, or how it would change everything.'

'Hannah, was it against your will? Was it him that did this to you? Were you . . . were you raped, Hannah?'

'Raped? Don't be so silly, he would never hurt me.'

Ellen sank back on her heels, unable to put together any of the pieces. Hannah had got drunk, met some men, probably

261

taken something, and had sex. But none of that explained the way she looked, her injuries. Had something happened to her later?

'Then what happened to you, Hannah, how did you get hurt? What about the others, what about the other men that were with this Nick?'

Just then Matt reappeared with a mug of steaming coffee.

'I'm sorry I was so long, I thought I'd better make real coffee, thought it would be more effective than instant,' he mumbled, unable to look either woman in the eye. 'OK, I'll get out of your way, shall I?' he offered.

'Would you stay?' Ellen asked him, her green eyes large. 'Please.'

Unwilling to leave her to deal with this alone, as much as he might have wanted to, Matt nodded and sat down in the armchair opposite the sofa, folding his hands and dropping his head as if braced in prayer.

'Hannah, you need to try and remember what happened tonight. After you left the pub with Nick and the others, what did you do then?'

'We went for a walk!' Hannah seemed pleased with herself. 'The boys said I could do with some fresh air and we went for a walk, in the park. I suppose that must have been how I got so muddy.'

'And you had sex with this man?' Ellen asked her again.

'Oh no, no.' Hannah shook her head slowly, contradicting herself completely. 'No, they wanted to but I didn't. I said I was tired and I was going to get a cab and go home but then . . . I think I fell asleep, that's right, I was so, so tired. And when I woke up again I was alone.' Hannah sighed. 'I'm still so tired,

Can I go to sleep now, Ellie, can I? Will you hug me while I'm asleep?'

'No Hannah, listen, I need you to look at me and listen to me for a minute, OK?'

Hannah focused her gaze on Ellen.

'Hannah, I think . . . I think you've been attacked, beaten up and maybe even raped. I think we need to call the police and an ambulance, OK? I'm going to do that now.'

'No, no.' Hannah shook her head again. 'No. I just need to sleep, Ellie. I'm very tired now.'

'I know, but we need to get you looked at and we need to find out who hurt you like this.'

'Why?' Hannah blinked.

'So the police can arrest them!' Ellen told her.

'No. I'm OK, I'm fine. I don't mind the pain. I deserve the pain, the pain is nothing at all, because now you know. Now you understand and you've promised to still love me so everything is fine. So that makes all of this OK. Sleep now. Do you know, I feel like I haven't slept in almost a year. Not since . . .' Hannah drifted off.

'No, Hannah, this isn't OK. Hannah?' Hannah crumpled sideways, her head thudding against the cushioned arm of the sofa. 'Hannah? Wake up. I'm going to call an ambulance, OK, and the police.'

'No!' Hannah suddenly sprang awake at Ellen's words. 'No, no, no, no, Ellie, please, please don't. *Please*. I don't want the hospital, I don't want the police. I just want to sleep. I just want to stay here with you. I'm fine, Ellie, I'm fine, I'm fine, I'm fine.' For the first time that evening she looked anxious and scared. 'Please, Ellie. Please let me stay here with you, don't make me go to the hospital. I'm fine, I'm really fine. It's just like that time I fell out of the tree and you thought I was dead, I was fine then, wasn't I? I was fine.' A dry sob tore through Hannah's throat. 'I don't want to talk about it any more, Ellie. Don't make me.'

Resolute, Hannah inserted her thumb in her mouth and dragging a cushion across her belly, drew her legs up beneath her and closed her eyes.

Ellen looked at Matt. 'I don't know what to do,' she said bleakly. 'Look at her. Something clearly awful has happened. Someone's hurt her and I don't know who or how or why. Should we call an ambulance?'

Matt looked at the slumbering woman.

'Maybe we should wait, let her sleep. Wait for her to wake up and see if she can remember anything else. It's possible she drank far too much and fell over a few too many times on her way home. She looks bad but she was talking OK, and she didn't seem in too much pain, she didn't seem to have any trouble breathing.'

'But what if she's got internal bleeding, or a brain injury?' Ellen said anxiously. 'We should call an ambulance, they'll take her to hospital, X-ray her and things.' She realised that it would be a relief to pass her sister into someone else's capable hands.

Matt bit his lip, leaning forward, resting his wrists on his knees.

'If we take her to hospital now, they'll call in the police. When I was a cub reporter they sent me to cover this case of a young schoolgirl attacked by a load of teenagers. I talked to her parents. They said that what she went through after the attack was almost as bad as what those lads did to her. If we take Hannah in now, they'll be wanting to test her for all sorts, gather evidence. She'll have to talk to the police, give statements. Hand in her clothes, they won't let her wash or sleep. Sure, she's messed up, but we don't know that anything bad happened yet. Do you really want to put her through all that if she's just had too much to drink and a bit of a wild night out with some guy she picked up? And she really doesn't want to go, you saw that.'

Ellen gestured at Hannah. 'This was not a bit of a wild night out, Matt. You can see that.'

Matt looked again at Hannah, her head buried in her folded arms, her bruised and bloody legs drawn up and tucked under her.

'I don't know what to say, Ellen,' he said. Ellen's face was etched with worry and indecision. He had a sudden urge to go to her and put his arms around her, to tell her not to worry, to lean on him and he would look after her. 'Call your doctor, there'll be an on-call GP who will come to the house. At least then when they've had a look at her we'll have a better idea of what to do.'

A wash of relief swept over Ellen as she looked back at her slumbering sister. Of course, of course if she called an ambulance now she would be expected to go with Hannah to the hospital. She tried to imagine accompanying her sister into the clammy night, sitting beside her as the ambulance sped along, listing from one side to the other, the siren ringing in her ears. Ellen felt every muscle in her body contract in panic. She'd been in the back of an ambulance before, and that time it had been her strapped to the stretcher, frightened and alone as the paramedics talked over her head and she knew that whatever happened she had lost her baby at just twelve weeks. But that was years ago, Ellen told herself. Nearly seven years since the ectopic pregnancy had ruptured her Fallopian tube, since she had almost bled to death and her chances of conceiving again were slashed to nil when they discovered that her other tube was blocked. Seven years since she'd woken up in hospital alone, waiting terrified for Nick to arrive back from a business trip in France, frightened of telling him that their dream of a big family had been ended, frightened about disappointing him again.

Ellen had been out of the house many times since then, and she hadn't been scared of unfamiliar people or places, even if her excursions had gradually dwindled down. And even now, even though Charlie was right and she had spent the best part of a year indoors, that didn't mean she couldn't go out. She could if she wanted to, if she *had* to. But when she looked at her bruised and battered sister she realised how glad she was that she didn't have to test that theory. Not yet, anyway.

'I would feel happier if she would go to hospital,' the doctor told Ellen gravely as they stood in the hallway. It had taken over an hour for the emergency GP to arrive and that was only after Ellen had pleaded with the dispatch handler, who'd told her after she'd described Hannah's injuries that she had to take her to hospital. Eventually Ellen had got the help she wanted, but only after she'd threatened action if anything happened to Hannah due to lack of medical attention.

'But I can't make her go,' the doctor sighed. 'If she is competent and conscious, it's up to her. She's groggy, yes, but there is no sign of concussion or internal bleeding as far as I can tell. That doesn't mean it's not there, though.' She handed Ellen a prescription. 'There are no broken bones and these anti-inflammatories will help with the bruising and pain, but I don't want you to give her anything for at least another six hours, just in case there is anything I haven't spotted. If she becomes unconscious, or anything changes for the worse, you will have no choice but to call an ambulance. Even if she doesn't get worse, try and persuade her to go to hospital for more extensive checks once she's sobered up. That's my recommendation, there's nothing I can do about it if she won't follow it.'

Ellen nodded, acknowledging the disclaimer. She took the prescription and folded it first in half and then quarters. She was aware the exhausted and dishevelled young woman was desperate to leave, but there was one more question she had to ask her.

'Doctor, do you think that . . . do you think she's been raped?'

The doctor dropped her head. 'I'm only able to make a judgement on where your sister allowed me to examine her, so I can't comment. I would say that these injuries have been inflicted on her by another person. They aren't the kind sustained in a car crash or from falling over.'

'She wants to have a bath,' Ellen said. 'But if she does then there'll be no evidence, will there?'

The doctor regarded Ellen with bloodshot brown eyes. 'Look, my day job is a police GP down at the local nick. I deal with this sort of thing all the time and to be honest less than fifty per cent of rape victims report what's happened to the police, and of those that do less than ten per cent of cases result in a conviction. If there was any forensic evidence it would only prove that your sister had sex. *If* the police felt they had enough for a case, and *if* they tracked down who might be responsible, which is a big if, she'd be asked about her drinking, her drug consumption. About spending all day drinking with the people who might have attacked her, or might not have. Even now it's still her word against theirs, if that's what happened, and we don't know that it did. I'm not even sure she does.'

'So you're saying I should let her have a bath and do nothing?' Ellen asked her, incredulous. 'That whoever did this to her just gets to carry on with their life like nothing's happened?'

'I'm saying that one way or another your sister has had a hell of a day, and she still might be seriously injured. Let her do whatever makes her feel better and keep an eye on her for any signs of deterioration – if she starts vomiting or blacking out, has difficulty breathing or any belly pain, and make sure you look out for signs of her stomach becoming rigid or swollen.'

'Thank you for coming,' Ellen said politely as she watched the GP hurry up the path on her way to the next emergency. Bleakly she shut the door on the outside world and leant her back against it.

'Here.' Matt emerged from the living room and nodded at the folded paper in Ellen's hand. 'Is that a prescription?' Ellen nodded. 'There's that pharmacy at the twenty-four-hour Sainsbury's, isn't there. I'll go and get it.'

'Did you hear what she said? Do you think I shouldn't report it to the police?' Ellen asked him, handing over the prescription.

'I don't think it's up to you, I think it's up to Hannah – and for now all she wants is a bath,' Matt said. He picked up his jacket off the end of the stairs. 'I'll be ten minutes.'

'Matt?' He paused, his hand on the latch. 'Thank you, thank you for being here.'

'Not a problem,' Matt told her.

After he'd shut the door behind him Ellen stood looking at the spot where he had been standing for a moment, and then she went upstairs and ran Hannah a bath.

A little more alert since the doctor had looked at her, Hannah had insisted on bathing alone, while Ellen sat outside the door, asking her sister whispered questions every few minutes, afraid she would pass out again and slip beneath the water. Ellen was thankful that Charlie had got into the habit of sleeping with his iPod plugged into his ears. If she was lucky he wouldn't wake up, not yet. She didn't want to have to try and explain any of this to him.

Hannah had stayed in the bath for an hour, reluctant to come out even when, with numb buttocks and an aching back from sitting on the floor, Ellen had come in with fresh towels and a clean pair of men's cotton pyjamas. At her sister's demand she had turned her back while Hannah dried herself, gasping periodically in pain. The mirror clogged with steam, Ellen had found herself looking into the dirty bathwater, now pinkish in hue. When Hannah was dry and dressed Ellen had taken her hand and led her into her bedroom, pulling back the covers so her sister might lie down and tucking her in.

'How are you feeling?' Ellen asked Hannah, who rolled on to her side with her back to her.

'I'm starting to sober up, worse luck,' Hannah said, as if she had nothing more than a hangover after a big night out. 'And everything hurts.'

'Not much longer and you can take something for that,' Ellen said. 'Hannah, do you think that after you've rested a bit more you should go to the hospital . . . ?'

'No,' Hannah said. 'No. I'll be OK. I just want to stay here. I want to stay here and I never want to leave.'

Ellen nodded; that at least she could understand.

*

'This is so typical of Hannah,' Ellen said suddenly. Through the kitchen blinds the dawn was casting a greyish dreamlike light over everything.

'What? What's typical?' Matt jerked awake. It was now almost five. For the last few hours, since Hannah had drifted off to sleep again, the two of them had sat in the kitchen in silence, Matt's head nodding occasionally on to his chest. Unable to lie down next to her sister Ellen had not slept, but instead climbed the stairs periodically to check on her, watching the rise and fall of her chest, the expression on her battered face, watching for any signs that her condition might be worse than it looked. She had recalled the countless times she had watched over Hannah when she was tiny.

Ellen had not been pleased when her mother come home from the hospital with Hannah in her arms. She had not been pleased at all with her new little sister, a peaches-and-cream baby, perfect from the moment she arrived in the world, charming everyone she met even before she could talk, even before she could smile. At eight years old Ellen had felt like a gigantic and hulking changeling, the cuckoo in the nest, sticking out like a sore thumb in her newly remodelled family, with her dark skin and dark hair that she apparently got from some great-aunt she had never met. She was nothing like this stellar little creature who brought so much light into the house, who made everybody coo and smile. But still, despite herself, Ellen had loved Hannah, she had had no choice but to love her, and was completely devoted to her from the moment that she first picked her up. They had shared a room from the beginning, Hannah's cot jammed alongside Ellen's bed in their narrow bedroom. Terrified that something might happen to her little sister when she wasn't looking, Ellen would force herself to lie awake, gazing through the bars of Hannah's cot, watching the rise and fall of her chest, checking the expression on her faultless face for any signs of dark dreams or distress.

When Hannah was a little older, old enough to be afraid of the dark, she would hold Ellen's hand through the bars of the cot, her tiny chubby fingers curled around Ellen's long slender ones until she slept, and Ellen would never remove her hand from Hannah's. Even when her arm raged with pins and needles or she longed to be able to roll over, she would leave her hand in Hannah's for as long as her sister needed it there.

The last time she had gone to check on Hannah, who seemed immobile in what she hoped was oblivious sleep, Ellen wondered when that had stopped, that love and devotion between them. The worst that Hannah had done to her was to be more beautiful, more clever and more successful, and Ellen had long ago accepted that it was her role to be outshone by her sister whenever they were together. It wasn't jealousy exactly that she felt at the realisation – especially not after she met Nick and had Charlie. Whatever the reason, somehow they had grown apart, and she wished that Hannah would leave her alone like she used to, she always felt more her own person when Hannah wasn't there. It was as if Hannah's mere presence highlighted the shortcomings in her life that Ellen preferred not to think about.

'What's typical?' Matt repeated. He sat up straight, rubbing his palms over his face and blinking himself awake.

'When things went wrong, when she'd made a mistake, instead of admitting it or doing something to try and make it better, she'd always get herself into even more trouble, as if that would somehow blot out whatever the real problem was. Even when she was very little she'd take risks. When she was six she broke this china figurine that my mother loved, it was a dancing lady or something, and Hannah had been playing with it and dropped it. Instead of telling Mum she climbed the tallest tree she could find in the garden. She got up it OK, but on the way down she panicked and slipped, knocked herself out on one of the roots. I thought she was dead, I really did, she was so still and pale – I had to run and tell Mum and it was a huge drama, and of course no one minded about the figurine as long as Hannah was OK.'

'Don't really think this compares to climbing a tree,' Matt said, puzzled.

'Then when she was eight she wanted this doll from the toy shop. Well it wasn't her birthday or anything, so one day when we were in the town looking round the shop with our pocket money while Mum was in the supermarket she decided to just take it, slipped it under her skirt. And she got away with it, only she realised that she couldn't go home with it. So while I was at the till buying something she got on the bus that stopped just outside, no money for a ticket or anything. Just got on the bus and sat at the back and didn't get off.

'Mum and Dad were frantic, and I was blamed for not watching her. A policeman brought her home when she got off at the last stop in Brighton. They were so relieved to see her, no one but me noticed the doll at the bottom of her toybox. It's been the same ever since. Whenever she's done something stupid or wrong she pulls a stunt like this, gets herself into trouble, gets herself hurt so that everyone will forget what she's done and feel sorry for her.'

Ellen got up abruptly and put the kettle on again.

'You don't really think that's what she was doing this time, do you?' Matt asked her. 'Hannah wouldn't deliberately put herself in that kind of danger just so that no one would be cross with her.'

'No, no – I suppose not. I know this isn't the same – it's just . . . I feel guilty, I suppose. Something's been going on with her, something big and dark, and she's been spending all this time around me and Charlie, and I've minded. I haven't wanted her here. All she's been doing is trying to be a good sister, and all I've been doing is pushing her away, which is why I haven't noticed that she's been struggling with her own problems. I haven't seen anything outside those windows in a year.' Ellen nodded at the outside world as she poured boiling water on two fresh tea bags. 'And now this, this awful brutal thing. If I'd been paying attention, really looking at her . . . I always thought that we should be like two peas in a pod, me and Hannah. That sisters would have this . . . bond. But right now I feel I know her less than ever.'

'Maybe it's a kind of guilt,' Matt suggested. 'Maybe she's punishing herself.'

'What on earth could she have possibly done to make her think she deserved that?' Ellen asked, glancing at the ceiling. 'She drank too much, tried to drown out whatever it is that's been hurting her – but being attacked like that? That not Hannah's doing. Someone, some people saw how vulnerable she was and they deliberately hurt her when she wasn't strong enough to stop them – and it's killing me that I don't know what happened. The worst of it is, I don't think even she knows.'

'Maybe, for now, that is for the best. Maybe she just needs some time to figure it out.' Matt stood up and stretched. 'Look,

I need to get ready for work, take a shower – I'd stay home if I could, but I really can't.'

Without thinking Ellen went to him and put her arms around him, hugging him to her. It was not until he returned the gesture that she remembered she was only wearing a shirt under her dressing gown. She let a beat pass in his arms before she stepped back.

'Sorry,' she said awkwardly. 'I'm a bit overtired, it's making me inappropriate. What I meant to say was thank you. You didn't need to be any part of this, but you were. I really needed a friend last night and I'm grateful. So thank you.'

Matt didn't speak for a second. Her soft body so briefly moulded into his had aroused wonderful sensations, despite his exhaustion. He hadn't wanted her to break the embrace, but to stay exactly where she was. He'd wanted to hold her.

'It's not a problem,' he mumbled, glancing out of the window to avoid her eyes.

'Here, take this with you, I've put extra sugar in it.' Ellen handed him a cup of tea.

'You know what,' Matt said, pausing at the door. 'One thing is obvious about your sister.'

'Oh, and what's that?' Ellen asked him.

'She cares more about what you think of her than anything else,' he replied.

Chapter Sixteen

The last person Matt expected to see sitting, no, lounging at his desk, when he finally made it into work was Lucy, the subeditor from downstairs. He'd thought it was oddly quiet when he walked into the office, none of the usual banter or jokes going on. Raffa, Steve, even Pete were all sitting at their desks apparently concentrating on work. As the weekly deadline was past, this was unheard of, particularly when there was a leggy blonde in the vicinity, in this case leaning back in Matt's chair with her ankles crossed on his desktop.

'Er, hello?' Matt slowed down as he approached her. If he wasn't very much mistaken, the last time he'd seen her she'd called him the worst swear word he could think of, one which even he baulked at using. What did she want with him now?

'You always this late?' Lucy asked him archly.

'Had a bit of a heavy night,' Matt said warily.

'Lured some other poor victim into your lair?'

Matt thought of Hannah's bruised and battered body curled up on Ellen's sofa, and cringed inwardly. How much difference was there really between him cruising bars looking for tipsy women to talk into bed, and the men that Hannah had encountered? The thought hadn't escaped him and it had been haunting him ever since.

'Look, Lucy, it's been a tricky night . . .'

'Ah, *now* he can remember my name!' Lucy exclaimed. 'I thought you might think it was . . .' She picked up a copy of *Bang It!* folded open to reveal Matt's column. ' "Leggy blonde bombshell" or maybe "insatiable curvy babe"?'

'So you've seen the column then,' Matt said wearily, wondering why on earth he'd thought it was a good idea to date a woman who worked one floor down, and why on earth he had decided to write about her. What had he been thinking? The truth was that he hadn't been thinking since he'd got here, at least not with his head. The truth was, he hadn't been thinking with his head especially since 1998 when certain other parts of his anatomy had taken the decision-making lead.

'Yes,' Lucy said. 'And I've come to thank you.'

'Thank me?' Matt shifted from one foot to the other. Why was she thanking him? Suddenly he felt confused and afraid, very afraid.

'Er . . .'

'You see,' Lucy said, snapping her legs down from his desk in one smooth manoeuvre and twisting his chair round to face him. 'If you hadn't written your column about me, if you hadn't written, for example . . .' She scanned the page. ' "This little vixen was all over me from the moment we sat down, wearing a dress that left nothing to the imagination and let me know just exactly what sort of a good time I was in for. I offered her another drink but she was already good to go and practically dragged me back to my place . . ." If you hadn't written that, for example, then I would never have had the idea for my own piece. And I never would have been pissed off and ballsy enough to take it to my editor and ask her for a chance to write for the magazine. But you did and so I did, *et voilà!*'

Lucy handed him a copy of her own magazine. 'You've given me my very first byline,' she beamed at him, her bright eyes sparkling. Dragging his eyes off her, Matt looked down at the glossy page. The headline shouted 'How to Avoid Terrible Sex!'

Matt's eyes scanned the first line. 'We've all done it, we've all felt a little low, got a little drunk and found ourselves in a compromising situation with a man we barely know. We think this liberates us, sets us free, but invariably the next morning we feel foolish and used and worst of all have usually experienced a night of terrible sex. The last time this happened to me was only a few weeks ago . . .'

Matt looked up. 'You've written about me and you?' he asked her, incredulous.

'Yep,' Lucy nodded, a wicked grin lighting up her face. 'What? Not thrilled for me? Don't want to read on? Don't worry, I've memorised it, let me recite for you. "This guy, let's call him Matt . . ."'

'Hey, that's my real name!' Matt protested.

'Yes, but the readers don't know that. "This guy obviously thought he was the cat's pyjamas in bed. But the truth is from the moment we got into his bedroom I was looking for a reason to leave. Was it his cheesy predictable lines that put me off? After all, how many times have you heard them tell you they've never seen a woman with eyes as beautiful as yours, yeah right like they care about your eyes! Or was it his fumbling amateurish kisses that felt a bit like I was being slobbered all over by a Labrador? Why don't men ever learn that less is so much more when it comes to tongue? No, it was none of that, it was simply that the moment I let him get me into bed I realised I was going to be bored. Bored, bored, bored, and that for the next five minutes I was going to have to try my best to look like I wasn't."' Lucy stood up and strutted towards Matt. She was now standing very close to him, her eyes sparkling with fury and laughter, the heady scent of her perfume in his nostrils. '"And that's what I'm talking about, ladies."' She went on quoting her piece. '"That's why we are all doomed to a terrible sex life unless we take action now. No more pretending that him fumbling at your privates is a turn-on, no more moaning and groaning out loud when really you're wondering if you remembered to record *Grey's Anatomy*. And most of all no more pretending that you've had an orgasm after a couple of minutes of squelching about when we all know that it takes a lot longer and a lot more effort to get one of those. Take a stand now! Say no more to terrible sex just to make some guy feel good about himself. If they're awful at it, tell them so. And if you're reading this, Matt – just so you know – you are shocking in bed."'

As she finished her manifesto she dropped her magazine at his feet and turning on her heel marched out of the office to rapturous applause.

'Hey mate?' Raffa clapped him on the shoulder. 'Have you lost a bit of weight?'

'What?' Matt looked at him.

'It's just I think that bird left with your balls!'

Matt blinked as the office doors swung shut behind Lucy. He had no idea that she was so . . . well, so cool.

'Wow, that's never happened before,' he said, sinking down into his chair. He felt embarrassed, exposed and vulnerable. He closed his eyes. What a prick he was. He'd been doing to women for over a year what Lucy had just done to him. And as clever and as funny as her piece was, it hurt, it stung like a very hard slap. How many people had he hurt that way without a second thought?

'Never been bitch-slapped in public before?' Pete sneered.

'Never been stung by a revenge column. You got to hand it to her, the girl's got balls,' Matt said quietly.

'Yeah, yours.' Raffa repeated his joke, clearly annoyed that it hadn't got a big enough laugh the first time.

'You need to pull it together, son,' Pete went on. 'Where's the dark destroyer, hey? And more importantly, where's your piece on that drive-through brothel?'

'Hang on, I only got the brief yesterday,' Matt said, although last night in the pub did seem like an aeon ago. 'I wasn't entirely sure that Dan was even serious.'

'Dan is always serious. Come on mate, you've got a week to go until the end of your probation and I've got to say it, you look knackered. Please tell me the reason you let that little tramp walk all over you is because you were up all night seeing to your landlady?'

'Lucy isn't a tramp.' Matt felt he had to defend his nemesis. Seeing the look on Pete's face, he added, 'Yeah, I was up with Ellen all night. It's true what they say about older women being at their sexual peak!' His grin was perfectly synchronised with his sense of inner self-loathing. Lucy, Hannah, the idea of writing a piece on a drive-through brothel after what he'd seen last night and this morning – he felt sick to his stomach. Half-naked girls who were no more than breasts and bums, writing about sex week in week out – that wasn't his dream job. It had never been

279

his dream job, and Matt couldn't remember any more why he'd ever thought it was. Lucy, Hannah – especially Ellen. They reminded him that he liked women, he loved them. He found them interesting and funny and beautiful in ways that were more subtle and complex than their cup size or how much they'd had to drink. How on earth had that joy and fascination with the opposite sex turned itself into this? Matt sighed. Now on the cusp of completing his probation, it was not the time to be developing a conscience and a desire for something better. But nevertheless both those impulses were there and he couldn't shake them off. What was happening to him, he wondered miserably. And then a memory of the scent of her hair as she had embraced him this morning came back to him and he realised. Ellen – Ellen was happening to him. He had a crush on his landlady.

'Then there's your next column,' Pete said. 'Get your research on the brothel done and a first draft for your column today, and as for that piece of work that just came in here and stomped all over us . . .'

'Who, Lucy?' Matt said anxiously.

'That's war, mate,' Pete declared. 'That's magazine war. Come up with a plan of attack by the end of play.'

As Pete lurched away, Matt sank down further into his chair and considered the consequences if he just got up, walked out of the office and never came back again. Right now, after everything that had happened recently, after everything that had happened last night, the *Bang It!* office was the very last place that he wanted to be.

Eliza didn't know whether to be thankful for the full moon or dread it. At least its eerily strong silver light would show her the way, but then again it made escape all the more dangerous. She had been praying for a miracle to free her ever since the captain had brought her to Oxford jail. Theirs had been a silent journey, three days of riding during which the captain barely looked at her, let alone touched her. Eliza supposed she should be grateful for that small mercy at least, for it was clear that whatever desire the captain might have felt for her once had drained away completely since he had discovered she was a murderess, and an unrepentant one. But as she journeyed nearer and nearer to what would almost certainly be her doom, she found herself longing for some human touch, even his.

At least he had seen that she had the luxury of a cell to herself, enough to eat, and had given orders that she should not be disturbed or molested by any of the guards on pain on death. Eliza had half expected him to guard her himself, but as soon as he had deposited her within the prison walls, making a generous payment for her board, he disappeared. He didn't even look over his shoulder as he walked away. Day after endless featureless day Eliza waited for news of what was to become of her, each hour edged with a curious mix of dread and boredom, terrified of how her confinement would end yet longing for that moment too.

After two weeks of solitude the captain came at last. He looked at her for a long time as her cell door was closed behind him, making Eliza all too conscious of her tangled hair, dirty and torn clothes. She had fallen a long way since his first lustful encounter with her, and now she could not read the expression in his dark and hooded eyes. She found herself longing to see that light of desire she had so often feared before, but now there was nothing. It seemed that he was truly done with her and, by the set of his jaw and shoulders, so was life.

'They are going to hang you,' the Captain informed her, not moving from the door. 'You have proved yourself both a murderess and a spy – they consider you a very dangerous woman.'

'Me?' Eliza gasped. 'God knows, all I wanted from life before I met you was to attend to my needlework and wait for my uncle to find me a good husband! You, you have brought me to this. You have used me, ruined me, cast me in the path of unscrupulous men and now you are done with me you lead me merrily to the noose.'

'Eliza, that's not true . . .' Eliza's heart leapt as the captain took two steps towards her, but before he could reach her he halted and turned away, going instead to the high and narrow cell window. 'You are to be hanged, Eliza. At dawn on the morrow. If there were anything, anything I could do, you know I . . .'

Eliza felt her knees buckle beneath her but she steadied herself against the wall, determined that the captain would never see her spirit broken.

'So I am to die in the morning, at the age of nineteen, for defending myself against a man who would surely have beaten, raped and murdered me without a second thought. A man I would never have encountered if I had not been running from you. You have put the noose around my neck, Captain.'

'If only you had not run, Eliza.' The captain turned, crossing the tiny room in one stride to clasp her to him. 'If only you had stayed, if only you had let me marry you, let me love you, then you would be my wife now, you would be safe.'

Eliza had remained unmoved as she watched the tears tracking down the captain's face, his broad shoulders shaking. He turned on his heel and left the room, slamming her cell door as he went. Eliza listened for the turn of the lock and the slide of the bolts that would seal her fate for ever. She heard none. And then she noticed the captain had left something, on the floor in the shadows by the door. Gingerly she bent down and picked the bundle up, wondering what it could possibly be. It was a cloth bag, within it a few gold coins and something else wrapped in a silk scarf. Carefully Eliza let the scarf unravel, depositing its treasure on the floor. It was the captain's dagger, *with the jewelled hilt and his initials inscribed on the blade. Her heart thundering in her chest, Eliza searched the bag for something else, a note perhaps, but there was nothing. He could not see her go to the scaffold so easily after all — perhaps he did truly love her as he claimed? Eliza held her hand over her breast, as if to still her heart. She could not dare to hope, to dream that this nightmare might yet end, but still there was now just a glimmer of light in the darkness — the captain had left her with the means of escape.*

Ellen rubbed her eyes and looked at the words on the screen that Allegra had dictated to her. For the first time since she had begun this job, Ellen hadn't really been caught up in what Allegra was saying.

'So what do you think should happen next?' Allegra asked her. Ellen looked over at the older woman. She was immaculately dressed, as ever, but there were violet shadows under her eyes, and there was something else about her that was different too, that Ellen couldn't quite identify.

'I don't know,' Ellen said wearily. 'Is the captain waiting for her outside the gates with a horse? Is he going to rescue her after all?' She glanced at the ceiling, thinking of Hannah, who still slept. After Matt had gone to work Ellen had gone back to her bedroom, and dragging the piles of clothes off the velvet armchair by the window she had sat and watched Hannah closely. She had been sleeping peacefully, especially after she'd taken the pain medication, and relieved as Ellen was to see this, she was fearful of how she would be when she woke, sober. Ellen was afraid of what Hannah would remember.

'That would be what my readers would expect,' Allegra confirmed, as if the idea disappointed her.

'Maybe he could be waiting and then Eliza could murder him with his own dagger, steal his horse and run away to America. Maybe we could make this the first ever postmodern feminist bodice-ripper,' Ellen suggested testily, wondering what state the man who had hurt Hannah had been in when he woke up this morning, if he even had any idea what he had done.

Allegra pressed her lips into a thin smile, and as Ellen focused on her she realised what was out of place. For the first time ever in her presence Allegra wasn't wearing her vintage red lipstick.

'Feeling a little tense today?' Allegra asked her.

Ellen shook her head, unable to talk for the threat of tears.

'I haven't asked because I don't like to pry,' Allegra began deliberately. 'But Ellen, I am an old woman. On a good night I barely sleep more than three or four hours, and what with all the comings and goings last night I didn't sleep a wink. I wasn't going to say anything, but I can see that you've been up all night and that you are very upset. And if you are upset we cannot work efficiently. And besides, I worry about you – I like you. Do you want to tell me what happened?'

Ellen looked out of the open French doors, down the length of the garden. Of course Allegra had been disturbed last night, the poor woman must have heard almost everything. It hadn't occurred to Ellen that her lodgers would be affected. She hadn't seen Sabine at all, not even this morning, so had no idea if she had been woken by all the to-ing and fro-ing. If she had, Sabine had chosen to stay out of the way. But Allegra deserved an explanation. So slowly, deliberately careful because of her own muddled brain and the strange dreamlike quality of the previous night, Ellen began to talk.

'. . . so I don't know,' she concluded. 'I don't know why she lost the job that she loves and why she's gone so utterly off the rails. Nor do I know what really happened to her last night, and worst of all neither does she.'

Allegra nodded. 'And what about Charlie? Does he know?'

Ellen shook her head. 'I don't think so,' she said. 'He was plugged into his iPod all night and he didn't even mention Hannah when he came down this morning.'

Charlie had seemed happier than he had been for months when he arrived in the kitchen in time for breakfast, probably because he'd been worrying for so long about her, unable to feel he could talk to her, shut out by her grief. The idea of him, unhappy and alone with his problems, tormented her; it was only now that he had begun to talk to her that she realised how much he had been bottling up, how much she had missed as tightly closed and as cut off from the world as she had been.

Ellen had just collected Hannah's torn and stained clothes from the bathroom floor and was holding them in her hands, dithering between putting them in the washing machine and saving them as . . . what? Evidence? Then she heard Charlie thundering down the stairs and hastily shoved them into the washing machine. She could always turn it on later.

'Matt gone?' he'd said on entering. Ellen nodded, slotting two pieces of bread in the toaster.

'You sleep OK?' she asked him.

'I think so. So have you had a chance to think a bit more about, you know, what we talked about yesterday?' Charlie's voice was light and high. Ellen felt her heart contract – he was trying his best to appear unconcerned.

'About my agoraphobia?' She smiled, sitting down at the table with him. 'You did make me think, Charlie. I checked the calendar and I realised something pretty shocking. You are right about one thing. I haven't been out, not since Dad's funeral. I haven't been out in nearly a year and the frightening thing is I didn't even realise.' She had shrugged, conscious of Charlie watching her closely. 'But I'm not agoraphobic, Charlie.'

'But Mum . . .'

'No, wait. I haven't been outside for a year and that is strange and wrong and I *have* been hiding in here, but it's not because I just woke up one morning and decided that I was afraid to go out. To me it seems like yesterday that we found out Dad was gone. Somehow the last year has both dragged by and gone in the blink of an eye. I've been caught up in all this grief and I haven't noticed or cared about the outside world. I haven't needed to. I didn't realise I'd been stuck in this house all those months, but I'm not afraid of going out, Charlie. I'm just out of practice.'

Ellen covered his hand with hers and squeezed it. 'I've been lost in sadness, but I think I'm coming out of it a little bit now, and I'm looking around and I'm seeing how things are and how things should be. So don't worry about me, OK? It's not as bad as you think, I promise.'

'You mean you could just grab your bag and walk to school with me now?' Charlie asked.

'I think so, if you really want your mum walking you to school,' Ellen smiled.

Charlie thought for a moment and then reached into his school bag, dumping a selection of printed leaflets and pages and pages of information that he had evidently printed off the Internet on to the tabletop, spreading it out with the palm of his hand. 'I still think you could have a form of agoraphobia, Mum.

It's very common after some traumatic event. Apparently it's not unusual for the sufferer to be in denial about what's really going on. But it's totally treatable, you don't even need drugs, just something called cognitive therapy and a support group.'

'So where do you go to find an agoraphobic support group, surely they don't get out much?' Ellen attempted to joke, but Charlie was not amused.

'Mum, all I'm trying to say is that this year it's been weird and difficult, it's been like you've been on another planet half the time, the house is full of weirdoes and now even Aunt Hannah's gone mental. I miss Dad, I miss him too but I'm ready now for life to be a bit normal again. I'm ready for you to be you again. I'd like it to be OK to feel happy and have a laugh and moan when you drag me round the supermarket and make me push the trolley. I want to bring my friends home for tea so that you can be all embarrassing and offer them Jammy Dodgers like we're all still nine. So please, don't talk to me like I'm a stupid kid who doesn't know anything. I've thought about this a lot. I even went to the doctor's and got those leaflets, on my own, and I think I'm right. So I want you to take me seriously. I want you to find out about getting help. After all . . .' Charlie picked up a leaflet and read from it. ' "There is no shame in admitting that life has dealt you a blow you are finding it hard to recover from. Help is just a phone call or a mouse click away." '

And Ellen had wished with all her heart that she wasn't so tired and confused by everything else that was going on so that she could enjoy this moment, she could enjoy her son really talking to her for the first time in an age. And she had to take notice of what he had said. She put her hand down on the papers and nodded.

'OK, OK – I'll take you seriously, I'll read all of this and if I think I need it I'll speak to someone about more help. OK?'

Charlie's smile would have been reward enough, but his arm around her shoulder and the kiss he planted on her cheek was a bonus that she did not expect. After he had left for school she had still been smiling, until she remembered her sister lying beaten and battered upstairs. Also, Charlie had left his school bag sitting on the kitchen floor, something that Ellen knew she would pretend she hadn't noticed, because the idea of picking it up and running down the road after him filled her with the dread certainty that if she stepped out the front door something really, really terrible would happen to her or the people she loved.

'I think Charlie is fine, actually,' she told Allegra. 'I think he is better than he's been in a long time. I think he feels like he's taking a bit of control about what's going on in his life. That's why I don't want him to see Hannah. Not like this.' She hesitated for a moment before adding, 'Funny thing is, he seems to have cheered up since he diagnosed me as agoraphobic.'

She waited for Allegra to snort with derision or chuckle at her son's eccentricity, but the older woman merely nodded, her expression passive.

'You don't seem that shocked!' Ellen laughed nervously.

'You forget, I saw how frightened you were about the idea of going out for lunch,' Allegra said. 'And I've noticed that you still dry all your laundry in the dryer even though you have a perfectly good washing line at the bottom of your garden and this has been the hottest June on record. I don't know what you did before I arrived, but I know that in the last month you haven't gone anywhere, and as a consequence neither have I. So if

288

anything I think your son might have a point, he's a very astute young man.'

'Well, perhaps he's right about some things but . . . I'm not ill. I'm just grieving. I'm grieving, that's all.'

'I wonder . . .' Allegra said thoughtfully.

'What do you wonder?' Ellen asked her impatiently.

'Ellen, describe your marriage to Nick for me.'

Ellen sighed. 'Why?'

'Please indulge me,' Allegra pressed her.

Ellen thought for a moment. 'Nick was very caring, protective. He made me feel safe, and he ensured that I never had to worry about anything. He let me take care of our home and Charlie while he dealt with all the difficult stuff. I never had to think about anything, Nick took care of it all. He really loved me, he cherished me. I'll never have that again.'

Allegra was silent for a moment. 'Ellen, I'm only saying this because I care about you and because I want better for you than this closed-down half-life you're leading at the moment. When you describe your relationship with Nick I don't get the same picture of it as you do at all. The picture I get whenever you talk about Nick,' she went on carefully, 'is of a man who controlled and imprisoned his wife, who kept her like a bird in a gilded cage. Who told her what to think and what to wear, who slowly and systematically stripped her of her own personality until she wasn't sure of her own thoughts or feelings any more. She became so reliant on him as her jailer that when he was suddenly taken from her she had no idea how to function in the real world, so she simply stopped trying. I think Charlie might be right. I think perhaps you are agoraphobic, and I don't think it started on the day of Nick's funeral. I think it started a long time before

289

that, because that's the way your husband wanted you. Whether it was conscious or not, whether he meant it or not. He wanted you pinned down. He wanted you trapped.'

'What?' Ellen stood up. 'How dare you, how dare you talk about Nick that way?' She was surprised by the force of her fury. 'How dare you, Allegra? Nick loved me, he would have done anything for me, he was the kindest, sweetest, loveliest man and the best father, and you . . . you didn't even know him!'

'All I'm saying is that you're looking at this from one very narrow viewpoint and that as with all things there are other interpretations . . .'

'Oh, this is ridiculous,' Ellen said. 'I don't know what I'm doing even trying to work this morning, anyway, with my sister lying upstairs beaten to a pulp after God only knows what happened. I know you like to think you're some wise old woman, Allegra, who knows everything and sees everything, but you can't be that astute, otherwise you wouldn't have ended up old and alone.'

She finished her rant, her eyes blazing, the meaning of the words she had spat out catching up with her after a second's delay.

'I expect you are right,' Allegra said stiffly, every one of her seventy or so years suddenly apparent on her face. 'After all, here I am living in the former dining room of a woman I barely know. No husband, no children, not a single relative to turn to when I'm made homeless. The only friend I have ever kept is Simon, and the only other person I have met in decades who I am remotely interested in knowing is you. So I expect you are right, I expect I have got it all wrong. Now, if you'll excuse me, I think we should leave it for today. I think I might take myself for a little walk. It's been a long time since I felt the sun on my face.'

'Allegra, I'm so sorry . . .' Ellen began, but before she could say any more the dining-room door opened and Hannah appeared around it. From that moment everything in the room was eclipsed by the sight of her sister, her face swollen and bruised.

'Sorry, am I interrupting anything? Only I can't find the bread knife.' Hannah's voice was thick and still a little slurred.

'God, Hannah, look at you,' Ellen whispered. 'Go and sit down, I'll get you something to eat.'

'Goodness,' Allegra said, what little colour there was in her cheeks draining rapidly.

Gingerly Hannah touched her face. 'Yeah, that was some drinking binge . . .'

'Drinking binge – Hannah, you've been attacked,' Ellen told her, wishing she could retract the brutal words as soon as she had uttered them, but also realising that she needed to hear them out loud just as much as Hannah did.

Hannah's face was so immobilised by swelling it was hard to tell how she reacted, except that she turned her head away, unable to look Ellen in the eye.

'Anyway, I'm ashamed to say that last night is all a bit hazy. What exactly did I say when I got in? Didn't make a fool of myself did I, Ellie?'

'That's it? That's all you're worried about? What you said? Hannah, stop it! Stop trying to pretend this didn't happen!' Ellen took her sister's wrist and led her into the kitchen, where she pulled her dirty clothes out of the washer, holding up Hannah's skirt.

'Look at this, it's ripped, there's blood and . . . and semen. Hannah, whatever happened you don't have to put a brave face on it. You don't have to shrug this off like you've grazed your knee!' Ellen ignored her sister's wince as she took her by the shoulder and propelled her to the hall mirror. 'Look at your face! Someone did that to you, Hannah. Why are you acting like it doesn't matter?'

Ellen stood behind Hannah as she forced her to confront her reflection, watching her. Hannah's good eye stared back at itself for a long time and then slowly a tear fell from her blackened and swollen eye, making its way down her livid cheek.

'It doesn't matter,' she said, her voice tight. 'I got drunk and took something, and got given something and had sex with some man, maybe men, I didn't know, who roughed me up a bit. It's my own fault, Ellen, I deserve it. I went out on my own, wearing next to nothing, got drunk and got fucked. I'm an adult, I knew what I was doing, I deserved it. So anyway, I was pretty far gone by the time I got here, what did I say again?'

Ellen stared at Hannah's reflection, unable to understand what she was saying.

'Hannah, no matter what you were wearing, no matter how drunk you were, you didn't deserve that, no woman deserves that. You're so bright and beautiful and in charge of your life. You should know better than anyone else that whatever happened last night was wrong.' Ellen released her grip on Hannah's shoulders, slipping her arms around them and hugging her from behind. 'Please let me help you. I know I've been . . . stuck, stuck inside my own head and my own life, not just since Nick, but for years possibly. And I know I let you go, pushed you away. But I do love you, Hannah, and I can't bear this. I can't bear to see you of all people like this, as if . . . as if it doesn't matter what happens to you any more.'

'But don't you see, Ellie, I don't care. I don't care what happens to me any more,' Hannah said bleakly as Allegra emerged from the dining room. She stood uncertainly in the hallway, just as appalled by Hannah's appearance as Ellen was.

'Look. I think you may be in shock or something, but even though you've had a bath it's not too late. We've still got evidence, I haven't washed your clothes. I can still call the police . . .'

'Ellen please, please tell me, what did I say last night?' Painfully Hannah removed Ellen's arms from around her and turned to face her. 'Did I . . . did I talk about Nick?'

'What? Ellen struggled to understand. 'Nick? Yes, yes – that's right. You said that one of the men you were with was called Nick too, so that's something to go on. That's something we can tell the police. Please let me call them.'

Hannah shook her head.

'And that's it, that's all? I didn't say anything else about Nick, about your Nick?' she asked urgently.

'Hannah, why is this important, what if you did? What is important now is that you face this and do something about it. What if they attack another woman tonight, you have to . . .'

Hannah shook her head again and with some difficulty made her way back into the kitchen, where she stood at the sink filling the kettle. Ellen looked at Allegra, shrugging in despair.

'Give her some time,' Allegra said. The two women followed Hannah into the kitchen where Ellen stood for some moments, struggling to find the right words. If her sister wanted to know what had happened after she got here last night, she would tell her.

'Matt found you,' she began. 'You'd made your way to the bottom of the street and he found you. He thinks you'd passed out in some neighbour's garden, it was lucky you came round when he was there. He brought you home and woke me up. When I saw you I was horrified, I was trying to get you to tell me what had happened, but you were out of it. You told me that you had had sex with Nick and you kept asking me to forgive you. You kept making me promise that I would always love you. Nothing you said made any sense really . . .'

Ellen stopped in her tracks as she ran the last sentences over again, hearing the words as if for the first time. 'You kept asking me to forgive you . . .'

At last Hannah set the kettle down and turned around. When Ellen looked into her eyes she knew the truth.

'You had sex with Nick,' she said slowly. 'You had sex with my husband.'

'Oh God.' Hannah buried her bruised face in her hands. 'Oh God, I was afraid I'd let it slip, after all this time . . .'

Ellen battled against the words that demanded repetition, and lost. 'You had sex with my husband. My sister had sex with my husband. Oh my God . . .' She lurched forward, steadying herself heavily on the tabletop. 'Oh my God, I'm going to be sick. You threw yourself at him, you threw yourself at the one thing I had that was mine!'

'No.' Hannah took a tentative step towards her. 'No, it wasn't like that. You have to listen, it wasn't just sex . . . and it wasn't because either of us didn't love you. It was . . . It wasn't just sex, Ellen, we . . . Nick and I loved each other, too.'

294

Ellen stared at Hannah, every sinew in her body caught in the moment, every fibre straining against what she was hearing.

'Get out,' she said. 'Get out of my home now.'

'Ellen, please, I've tried. I've tried not to tell you. At least now you know we can talk, we can work things through, we can support each other . . . Please, all I want is for you and me to be OK.'

In that second Ellen snapped. She grabbed her sister by the arm, oblivious to the pain that shot across Hannah's face, and she dragged and pushed her by turn into the hallway and out of the front door, shoving her with one violent push after another up the garden path and on to the street.

'Get out, get out, get out,' she repeated over and over again, deaf to Hannah's protests. Finally, with the midday sun blazing down on their heads, the two of them stood in the road.

'You're right,' Ellen told her sister. 'I hope they hurt you, I hope they used you and hurt you because you were right, you deserved everything that happened to you. You're nothing more than a common whore.'

Turning her back on her, Ellen felt the world tip and tilt, felt herself no longer bound by the rules of gravity, about to slip off the face of the earth. She felt the oxygen rush from her collapsing lungs, her heart fight and pound, about to explode in her chest as she sank on to her knees, the boiling paving stones burning her bare skin. Suddenly the front door seemed a thousand miles away and still the world slipped on its axis, revolving ever upwards as if she were a parasite it was keen to be rid of. Breaking her nails against the stones, Ellen began to claw her way to the shadow and shelter of the house, fighting for each breath as she went. After what seemed like an eternity she was aware of someone at her side, thin fingers supporting her under her armpits, dragging her, guiding her towards the distant country of her home, of what once had been her home, and at last the sun was eclipsed by shadow and she felt the cool ceramic tiles pressed against her cheek.

As Allegra shut the door firmly on Hannah, Ellen lay there, waiting for the world to right itself, and then she realised that was impossible now. Nothing would ever be right again.

Chapter Seventeen

It took Matt a long time to work out why he did and did not want to go home.

Since he had arrived at work that morning to find Lucy locked and loaded and waiting for him, his head had swum with a thousand images, of Hannah beaten and bruised, of the photos of half-naked women tacked, taped, sprawled and spread out all around him, like an obscene collection of butterflies pinned up for his delectation, and most of all, of Ellen in the moments before he had woken her and dragged her into a world of confusion and chaos.

She had looked beautiful, not in an interesting or flawed way. Not because of the usual frailties that so often fascinated him about women, but because to him she simply was beautiful. Her hair had been spread across the pillow, twined between her fingers, her lips were slightly parted as if in preparation for a kiss and her bare throat had shone in the half-light, a glowing pathway that promised to lead to an undiscovered country. For reasons that Matt could not fathom, the sight of her had taken him back twenty years to an English class and to a poem by some dead bloke whose name he would never remember in a million years. And yet just then, one single line that must have slotted its way into his otherwise inattentive brain on that wet and wintry morning all those years ago presented itself to him as if it had been waiting ever since that time to make itself known.

'*O my America, my new found land.*'

In fact, if Matt remembered rightly, that poem had been the reason he became interested in writing in the first place. He'd forgotten that entirely until now. How could he have forgotten something as pivotal as that? And what was it about Ellen that made him remember that moment, that moment all those years ago in a cold dingy classroom where he'd been unexpectedly inspired to write a love poem, to simply write?

And in the middle of the images of Hannah and the parade of topless models that assailed him from all angles, Matt found himself wondering what would have happened if he had walked into Ellen's bedroom to wake her for another reason entirely.

He worked through his exhaustion, labouring away over a fictionalised account of what had not happened between him and Ellen for the column, but every time he tried to make it seem like a funny or racy anecdote he'd realise that it had become romantic and fantastical. As if he was trying to remember that poem and rewrite it in prose for a men's magazine. Still, Pete didn't have to know that, so Matt had gone with it, allowing himself free rein to think about her, to describe her in every detail and to imagine coaxing her to reveal herself to him, layer by layer, a lazy unveiling that when he pictured it got him much hotter under the collar than any of the photos that surrounded him. Which was odd, because Matt always maintained that men were simple creatures with simple desires, yet nothing that he had started to feel for Ellen was simple. 'To His Mistress Going to Bed', that was what that poem was called, the title suddenly popped into his brain. How odd that he'd remembered that now, all these years later. Matt had allowed himself a few more minutes imagining himself reading that poem to Ellen as if he were its author and as if she were the mistress of his heart. Then he caught Pete's eye across the office. He had to resign himself to the fact that there was no place for poetry at *Bang It!*, unless you counted the limerick someone had scrawled on the wall in the Gents.

As soon as the sun was up in Nevada Matt had put a call in to Fifi's Cat House and drive-through brothel, where the self-employed girls chose between renting a room in the house or entertaining their clients in the comfort of their cars in a series of dingy garages. Of course, the sun coming up seemed to mean that the workforce went to bed, but eventually Matt got through to someone and he was not surprised to discover that his was not nearly the first request for information. A very pleasant-sounding woman called Angel Delight had promised to email him a press pack and had lined up some Skype interviews with a selection of the professionals, but he had to wait until eight o'clock that evening for them to begin, which still gave him a couple of hours to kill. Matt wondered about phoning Ellen to find out how Hannah was, and how she was. He wondered if it was appropriate. He thought it should be – after all he had been the one who'd found Hannah, who'd brought her back and stayed up all night with Ellen. He'd been the one whom Ellen had embraced, but somehow he wasn't sure that gave him any special privileges. He remembered telling this girl he'd dated for a week or two in Manchester that one of the reasons he wanted to break up with her was because she was too clingy.

'Too clingy? You call me calling you after nearly a week too clingy?' she had exclaimed. 'You don't mind sleeping with me, seeing me a couple of times a week for sex, but only as long as I know my place and I don't expect that you sharing my bed gives me the right to actually talk to you every once in a while? I don't play those games, Matt, either we're together or we're not. Which is it?'

Matt had responded with a resounding 'not', and gone on his way without giving the girl a second thought. But today he understood how intimacy, even simply emotional intimacy, could lead a person to think it was OK to phone another person and see if they were OK. Only what if the other person thought he was being invasive, nosy or even clingy? Matt realised that Ellen made him feel like a girl, which was a sensation he wasn't entirely thrilled about. This was how he'd been making girls feel for years.

As the clock ticked on towards eight Pete had invited him to sit in on a casting. A couple of girls were in Dan's office, stripping down to their underwear in the hope of making a spread. But as several staff members, including the post-room boy, found spurious reasons why they absolutely had to be there, Matt realised that he didn't want to be part of it. Instead he had to resist the urge to walk in there and tell the girls to cover themselves up, and have a little self-respect. That, of course, would have been career suicide, and even if he was beginning to wonder if this was the career for him, he couldn't afford just to walk away from it. How would he pay Ellen rent then?

Matt decided to kill time in the pub. With a bit of luck the rest of the lads who hadn't found a way into Dan's office would be caught up watching the secret filming of the casting in the conference room for at least an hour and he'd get a chance to think.

Of course, Lucy stepped into the lift when it stopped at her floor. She looked him up and down and then studied the wall with interest.

'I thought that was pretty cool, today,' Matt said.

'What's this, a line?' she asked him, without taking her eyes off the wall. 'Trying to trick me into thinking you're not so bad after all, to prove to all those gormless goons up there that you can get me back into bed?'

Matt smiled. 'That would have been a plan of pure evil genius, but no – actually that thought hadn't occurred to me. Seriously, I . . . I treated you like shit and I used you and I deserved all of that. I really did.' He felt surprised by his confession, perhaps even more surprised than Lucy. She peered at him suspiciously.

'Have you found God or something, because even if you have I'm still not going to have sex with you ever again.'

'Well, I'd hate you to be bored,' Matt said as the lift reached the ground floor and they stepped out into the foyer, pleased to see a tiny smile tugging at the corner of her glossed lips. 'Or to have to fake anything.'

Lucy grinned at him as they walked out into the blaze of the evening.

'Isn't it funny that two people can do something so intimate and so . . . close and not really know each other at all?' she remarked.

'I suppose it is,' Matt said.

'I mean, here I am looking at you and you're cute and everything but it seems like another person who went to bed with you, not me at all. I never ever would have gone to bed with *you* if I'd got to know you.'

'Bloody hell, Luce.' Matt winced. 'You've had your revenge in a national magazine. Can't you lay off now?'

'No, that's not what I mean,' Lucy said. 'What I mean is that you are far too nice to have sex with.'

'Oh God,' Matt groaned.

'You're more like a brother really,' Lucy went on.

'Shut up!' Matt cried.

'Yes, that's it – a little gay brother.'

'Right, fine, fine – I'm your little nice gay brother. Sex is totally off the table. Now we've established the facts, what are the chances you'll come and have a drink with me? We can talk about fashion, and shoes and . . .'

'What?' Lucy grinned at him. 'Interior design?'

'Remember that dragon of a landlady I was telling you about?' Matt said, sensing that even after everything that had happened he could trust her. 'Well, she's got me feeling a bit confused.'

'Oh, so you are gay after all. Tell all to Agony Aunt Lucy, I'll set you straight or bent, one or the other.'

Matt remembered that Lucy liked a white-wine spritzer and sat one down in front of her as she openly flirted with a man in a tight T-shirt at the bar.

'Don't sleep with him,' Matt advised her. 'He's even more of a prick than I am.'

'How do you know?' Lucy asked him. Matt nodded at the man's left hand, a faint white mark visible on his ring finger.

'Oh my God,' she moaned, covering her face with her hands. 'Why am I such a terrible judge of character?'

'Start from the assumption that every man you meet is out to get you, keep them far, far away until you know different and then eventually you'll meet one who will see all the brilliant things about you, apart from your face and your body. They'll go dippy over the way you tell a joke, and how your eyes flash when you're mad and that sweet weird little dimple on your right shoulder. And they won't be able to stop thinking about you, and wondering about you, and you'll have them wrapped around your little finger, I promise.'

Lucy looked at Matt for a long minute and then said, 'You are sure you're not in love with me, aren't you, because you're nice and everything but really . . .'

'No, it's not you. It's my dragon landlady. I've become a bit obsessed with her.'

'In a stalky, weird, want her because you can't have her sort of way?' Lucy asked him. 'Because let me tell you, there is nothing that pisses me off more than a man who's all about the thrill of the chase and then as soon as he's got you, he goes off you.'

'No, no – not in that sort of way. In a wanting to write her a love poem sort of way. In a caring about what she's thinking and feeling and worrying about her sort of way. In a wanting to lie down beside her and hold her and stroke her hair sort of way.' Matt's confession poured out of him – once he'd started to talk about the way he felt about Ellen, he discovered that he didn't want to stop. 'She's got this inner quiet about her, you know. A sort of stillness and silence. I look at her and I get the feeling she'd bring me . . . peace.'

'Fuck me, you are gay,' Lucy said, grinning as Matt blushed. 'Sorry, I didn't mean that. What I meant was, it sounds like you have sort of written her a poem already. And it sounds like you really do like her.'

'I really, really do,' Matt said. 'And I have no idea what to do about it.'

'Tell her?' Lucy suggested.

'I can't do that – it's the anniversary of her husband's death soon, and she's got a kid, and besides she's in the middle of a great big awful mess with her sister. I can't just tip up and tell her how I feel.'

'Maybe you doing that is exactly what she needs,' Lucy mused.

'Plus I'd actually die before I'd have the guts to,' Matt added.

'You know what I don't get,' Lucy scrutinised him, 'is you, Matt Bolton, trashy column writer, coming up with all this poetic shit? Either it doesn't seem like you or you don't seem like someone who should be writing for *Bang It!*.'

'Which is funny, because it's my dream job,' Matt told her grimly.

'What, you set out wanting to fill in the gaps between photos of women's tits, did you? I do admire a man with ambition.'

Matt laughed. 'I thought I did, I thought there couldn't be a better job for me. But no, the first thing I ever tried to write was a poem and then when I was a bit older I wanted to be a journalist, like a war correspondent. Then girls happened, my column happened. I fucked up my life in Manchester by having sex with my best friend's girlfriend and ended up here. I thought I was following a career path, but really I've just been letting stuff happen to me. And now I don't know what to do.'

'Apologise to your best friend,' Lucy told him.

'That will solve all my problems?' Matt sighed. 'Anyway I can't, he's not talking to me. He kicked me out and took custody of the PlayStation.'

'Then try again and keep trying until you get through to him.

Show him you care enough to persist. Best friends are hard to find, and if you're about to fall in love with someone then you're going to need him for when it all goes horribly wrong and you're an emotional wreck. Besides, it's karma. You need to clear up your negative karma and as tracking down all the women you've upset or offended recently would take about a million years, your only hope is to sort things with your friend, take stock of your work and then tell your landlady how you feel about her.'

'What if she runs a mile?' Matt asked.

'Life's not all about dead certs, sunshine,' Lucy informed him. 'It's not all about lining up some tipsy bit of totty in a bar for ten minutes of fun . . .'

'Hang on, it was more like twenty . . .'

'It's about taking risks, it's about putting yourself out there, really *living* your life. And I don't get the feeling that's what you are doing now. You're treading water, and you are too nice, and sweet and clever to let that happen to you.'

'Can you strike the nice and sweet bit from that list?' Matt asked her. 'I'm actually the dark destroyer.'

'No you are not!' Lucy snorted into her drink. 'You are one of the nice guys. Which means two things. Firstly that it's time you admit it, and secondly that I can never, ever fancy you again. There's always a bright side.'

It was gone ten by the time that Matt had finished chatting to the ladies of Fifi's Cat House, and all very pleasant they were too. There were two single mothers who had discovered that working there was one of the very few jobs they could fit in around their children while earning enough to pay the bills. There were a couple of young girls, barely twenty, who just did it for fun, one who was putting herself through college while she studied for a degree in forensic science and one woman who just plain liked the work. It was only when Matt had logged off that he realised he hadn't got any of the sort of stuff that Dan would be expecting. All the notes he had made about the women he talked to were about them, their backgrounds, their motivations, even the names of their pets in one case. He hadn't asked a single one of them what their favourite position was. Maybe Lucy was right, either he was going gay or . . . Lucy had used the term 'falling in love'. Matt preferred to think of it as 'having feelings'. Having feelings seemed a lot less frightening than either of the alternatives.

Still, he'd finished work now, everyone else was in the pub and at last he could go home. He could find out how Hannah was, he could see Ellen again. And yet as much as he wanted to, which was very much indeed, Matt decided to go back to the pub again. Because although he really wanted to see Ellen again, he also didn't want to see her. He wasn't at all sure he was ready to be 'having feelings'.

Ellen stared at herself in the wardrobe mirror. She had been staring at herself for some time now, she wasn't sure how long. It was like reading a familiar word over and over again – the more she looked at it, the less it made sense. Sabine had come home to find her still sprawled on the hall floor, an anxious Allegra trying to talk her to her feet.

'What's this?' Sabine had asked, with some consternation. 'Why is Ellen on the floor?'

'She has just discovered that her sister Hannah, who last night appeared to have been rather savagely attacked, was having some kind of sexual dalliance with her late husband,' Ellen heard Allegra tell Sabine as if from a very great distance.

Sabine must have checked the time, because the next thing Ellen heard her say was, 'This is no good. Charlie will be home soon, Ellen. Do you want him to see you like this? You must get up at once and go and wash your face.'

Ellen had rolled on to her back and begun to laugh, but Sabine was clearly in no mood for joking. She had grabbed Ellen's hand and pulled at her arm until Ellen realised she either had to get up or have it torn out of its socket.

'Ellen, come now – you are not a lunatic, so stop acting like one.'

'Actually I am,' Ellen giggled. 'I am officially mad, it looks like I am agoraphobic after all. I tried to kick my sister out on to the street and ended up nearly giving myself a coronary. Charlie was right, I'm afraid of the outside, I'm afraid of grass and flowers and bumblebees and . . . and noise and people and crowds and buses. No wonder Nick . . . no wonder he . . . you know it all makes sense now. At least now it all makes sense.'

'I've tried talking to her but she's in shock, I think,' Allegra said anxiously. 'I called Simon but he's not in the office. I really didn't know what to do.'

'I tell you what we will do,' Sabine said firmly. 'We will go to your room, Ellen, and wash your face and you will rest. When Charlie comes in I will take him to the pub for tea, tell him you have a headache or something. Allegra will stay with you and you will talk about everything that's happened and you will see that it is not so very bad.'

'Not so very bad?' Ellen laughed. 'My deadbeat sister is in love with my dead husband. How can that not be bad?'

Sabine thought for a second before answering. 'Well, at least he is already dead. That saves you from having to kill him.'

True to her word, she had forcefully escorted Ellen up the stairs and into her bedroom, propelling her into the bathroom where she scrubbed her face all over with a sponge, like a mother cat cleansing a kitten.

'You are very hurt,' she informed Ellen as she guided her back into the shadowy room, curtains still drawn from the night before. 'And you are very shocked. And you are very tired. You should sleep and get drunk and then talk to Hannah – find out exactly what this means.'

'Do you think he had a list of things he couldn't stand about me?' Ellen asked her. 'You know, frumpy, sexless, boring, meek, never goes out. Do you think he had a list like that? I really thought that he was the first, the only person in the world who didn't prefer Hannah to me, but of course he did. I mean, look at her and look at me. Of course he did.'

'Ellen,' Sabine said, sitting Ellen down on the edge of her bed and crouching in front of her. 'I know what it feels like to find out that the man you love is or was in love with another woman. I know it rips you in half. But think about it, you only have Hannah's word. Nick isn't here to defend himself. You only have her version of events and who knows, perhaps over the last year she has made something, nothing maybe, into some grand affair that never was. And as for everyone preferring Hannah to you, I think that's in your head only. If you don't expect very much for yourself you won't get it.'

Ellen looked at Sabine. 'Do you think so?' she asked. 'Do you think that whatever it was that happened wasn't that serious?'

'It's possible.' Sabine shrugged. 'I'm just saying don't fall apart. Not yet. Not until you know something that you have found out for yourself.'

'But if it wasn't true, if it was all in her head then she wouldn't have been doing what she was doing, drinking, messing up at work – putting herself at risk. She wouldn't have allowed whatever happened to her last night if all this was imaginary. You should have seen her, Sabine, she looked like a broken doll. She kept telling me that whatever had happened to her didn't matter, that it was just what she deserved. And I kept saying that she was wrong, but you know, what I kept thinking, even before this, even before she told me about Nick, I kept thinking she was right. I kept thinking she *did* deserve it, that she careers through life expecting everything to fall into place around her and that maybe this time she'd learn that is not how it works. What sort of person does that make me, to think that when she's been so badly hurt?'

'Ellen, sleep. Rest. I'll take Charlie out for tea and later when you have a clear head we will talk. We can make a list, look for evidence. We can find out the truth ourselves. But for now, rest. I promise you, sleep is a welcome refuge from even the worst the waking world can offer.'

Sabine had all but pressed Ellen back on to the bed and left her lying there staring at the ceiling, her head swimming in confusion. Ellen thought she must have slept for a little while at least, her body giving willingly into the physical exhaustion, unlike her mind, and she was dimly aware of the sound of Charlie's feet on the stairs and someone opening the door to look at her. When she woke again the house was silent and she had sat up abruptly, coming face to face with her reflection in the wardrobe mirror.

Her hair, which she hadn't brushed since yesterday, nested around her shoulders in a mass of dark tangles. Her face was creased with sleep, the seam of a pillowcase indented across one cheek, her lids were swollen and red. She looked like a grieving widow, she felt like one. She felt that she had lost Nick all over again, and worse than that, she'd lost every memory, every moment they had shared together which she had treasured so dearly. If what Hannah had told her was true, she would never be able to think about them again.

As Ellen stared at herself she thought of the woman she had believed herself to be, the woman who was a little shy and reserved, who avoided crowds and noise and enjoyed nothing better than getting lost in a good book. A woman who was adored by the husband she had happily devoted herself to, a mother who always put the needs of her son first. A widow who having faced adversity had found the strength to carry on.

But Ellen realised as she stared into her reflected eyes that she was none of those things. She was a woman betrayed by her own sister, deceived and mocked by a husband who, if Allegra was to be believed, thought of her as nothing more than a possession that he could control. A husband who had not loved her, at least not for the last year of his life and very possibly even longer than that. She was a woman who had virtually ignored her son for the past year, so caught up was she in her own sorrow, a woman who hid from the world, who shut it out along with life so that she could live a virtual existence between the pages of a book. She was a coward, and a fool. A misguided, smug and selfish fool who had allowed herself to be led by hand into a prison cell and who, now the door was wide open, still didn't want to leave.

Ellen stood and pressed the tips of her fingers against those of her reflection. This could not be the story of her life, it couldn't end like this. A thought occurred to her and she flung open the wardrobe and rooted around in the back. Somewhere, somewhere . . . She pulled out the dress she had worn on her first date with Nick. It was dark bottle green cotton jersey, figure-hugging with as low a neck as she would ever dare to wear and a hem that sat just above the knee. Ellen laid the dress on her bed and smoothed it out. She had felt so wonderful wearing it, so powerful and sexy. She remembered walking through the restaurant, returning to her and Nick's table after a trip to the Ladies, and feeling heads turning in her wake. For the first time in her life she had felt that she was on the brink of discovering who she really was, the woman she could be, the woman who didn't merely watch the world go by but who took part in all life had to offer.

That night Nick told her that she was the most beautiful thing he had ever seen. This was why she had been surprised when a few weeks later, after she had put the dress on to go to some work function of his, he had asked her to change into something else.

'I thought you liked me in this,' Ellen had said, smoothing her palms over her hips.

'I do, I do like you in it,' Nick told her, glancing up briefly from the newspaper he was reading. 'That doesn't mean I want the rest of the male population to like you too. You're mine now, Ellen, save that for the next time we are alone.'

But although she always kept it as a token of that first date with Nick, Ellen had never worn her green dress again. She racked her brains and thought and thought, and realised that if she wasn't very much mistaken that might have been the last piece of clothing she had ever chosen on her own. Uncertain of exactly what she was doing, she knelt on the bed and rummaged through her drawers. Pair after pair of sensible knickers floated on to the floorboards, along with firm-control bras in shades of white and beige, until she found what she was looking for. A set of underwear that she had bought to surprise Nick with, the first Valentine's Day after Charlie was born.

Things had gone off the boil after Charlie came along, in fact Ellen recalled getting the impression that in those early days Nick was more resentful of Charlie's demands on her time and her body than he was proud of his newborn son. What she was certain of was that Nick thought of her differently after her pregnancy. He didn't look at her or even touch her in the same way, his finger never tracing the stretch marks that ran across her belly and hips, his mouth hardly ever seeking out her larger and newly shaped breasts.

Ellen had been at a loss as to how to get him to come back to her as the lover she had come to depend on until she read an article in a women's magazine about how to incite passion on Valentine's Day. There were several hints and tips, some involving ice cream and melted chocolate or various dressing-up outfits. Inspired by an alluring photograph, Ellen had decided her best bet was sexy underwear. She went on a lengthy quest for exactly the right thing, steering clear of all the bright red nylon and feather-trimmed bras that seemed to line the shops that February. Eventually after enduring the humiliation of a fitting by a very young, very pert girl, she had chosen a black lacy underwired bra and matching panties. Probably tame by most women's standards, for Ellen it was quite risqué. That night as she waited for Nick to come in she made preparations that would give them at least an hour to themselves, feeding Charlie and putting him down in his cot at just the right moment. She had timed it to perfection: the house was silent, Charlie was asleep and as she heard Nick coming up the stairs she slipped off her dressing gown and lay on the bed in her new underwear.

Nick walked in and he chuckled. This hadn't quite been the response that Ellen was expecting, but still she tried her best seductress smile on him.

'Dinner's in the oven, Charlie's fast asleep, I thought perhaps . . .'

Nick had sat on the bed and kissed her on the cheek. 'Bless you,' he said. 'But, Ellen, you don't need to do all this for me. To be honest I'm exhausted and I want a shower before I eat. Why don't you get dressed and talk to me while I clean up, OK?'

He hadn't been cruel or unkind. He hadn't mocked or insulted her, but as Ellen dragged on her clothes she had been awash with the humiliation and rejection.

She felt the humiliation again as she relived the memory. This was not going to be it, she decided. The last ten years, the way she had folded in on herself, losing herself to her house and her husband, were not going to be the sum total of her life. She was adamant about this. True, she didn't really know what had happened between Hannah and Nick, but she knew that something had, because whatever Hannah was she was not a liar. But even if Ellen hadn't found that out, she had been changing, these last few weeks. She had been evolving and now she was determined that a wife, a mother, a flawed sister, a lost widow . . . an agoraphobic . . . would not be all she was. She would not let one more minute of her life slip away unlived to its fullest potential.

Spontaneously she slipped off her clothes and stepped into the underwear that she had bought all those years ago. After hooking up the bra she returned to look at herself in the mirror, avoiding full eye contact with her reflection for some moments. The bra was now a little too small, and her breasts gently swelled over the lace trim, but, Ellen was surprised to see, the effect wasn't too disgusting. In fact, as she ran her fingers down towards her waist and the curve of her hips, although her gently rounded stomach still bore the silvered stretch marks of her pregnancy, and her bottom was dimpled and a little more generously proportioned than it used to be, as she turned first to one side and then the other she found that her body wasn't nearly as old or as repulsive as she had imagined. After a moment she slipped the green dress on. It didn't fit her in the same way as it had all those years ago, it strained across her breasts and clung more to her bottom, but unless Ellen was very much mistaken it didn't look that bad.

Impulsively she sat down at her dressing table and rummaged through her drawer. At the back of her mind thoughts and feelings about Hannah, Nick and everything else clamoured for attention, but she ignored them. She was certain that somewhere in here was some mascara and lipstick.

After several minutes Ellen finally found a long-neglected stick of lipstick. Very slowly and carefully, her hands trembling, she applied the dark red gloss to her mouth. Nick had never liked her in lipstick, he always said it made her mouth look too big. But when she checked her reflection in the mirror she felt that her already generous mouth was improved by more definition and colour.

'Fuck you, Nick,' she said out loud, unaware that she had

spoken at all. Then she unscrewed the mostly dry and caked tube of mascara and batted her lashes at the wand. The result here was less pleasing: there were black clumps that she had to tease out of her lashes with her fingernails and a fine powdery dust on her cheeks, leaving a smudge when she tried to wipe it away. But after several minutes with a damp cotton-wool pad Ellen decided she'd done the best job possible, and what remained of the black mascara did seem to intensify the green of her eyes.

After dragging a brush through her hair, she knelt down and slipped a shoe box out from underneath her bed. Unwrapping the tissue paper they were nestling in, she took out her one pair of smart shoes, black, plain with a low heel. They were her funeral shoes.

Ellen looked at them for a long time, so sedate and sensible, the dull smooth leather emitting a faint shine. She realised for the first time that she hated them, they were ugly, frumpy shoes – the kind that Nick would have picked for her, that she had picked for herself, choosing only that which he would have approved of, unaware that she despised them. Without a second thought she took them to the window and promptly threw them out, hearing them clatter on the path below. Then just as purposefully she marched to Sabine's room, knocking on the door even though she knew that Sabine was still out with Charlie.

Sabine had very many pairs of shoes and Ellen selected the highest, shiniest pair she could find, silver sling-back sandals with stiletto heels. Sitting on the edge of Sabine's bed she fiddled with the minute jewelled buckles for several minutes before she finally managed to secure the shoes to her feet. They were rather tight and the straps pinched her toes, but she didn't care. They were the finishing touch, the final element of a plan that she had barely been aware of formulating until she took her first teetering steps in those shoes. Just as she was about to leave, she spotted a bottle of wine on the dressing table, a Rioja with a screwtop. Next to it was an unwashed glass, and from what she could tell about one glassful worth of wine was missing from the bottle. Pursing her lips and shrugging, Ellen picked up both the bottle and glass and took them with her.

Returning to her room, she heard Charlie and Sabine coming in from the pub. Hastily she climbed into bed, pulling the covers over her as her son's feet thundered up the stairs, hoping that if he did appear he wouldn't notice her make-up.

'Charlie,' she heard Sabine whisper. 'Let Mum sleep, OK? It takes a long time to get over a migraine. We could hook up our DSs if you like and play Mario Cart.'

'You've got a DS?' Ellen heard Charlie outside the door, clearly impressed.

'Of course, and I'm pretty good too. Come on. Let's go downstairs and see if we can't teach Allegra how to race too.'

'OK,' Charlie said after a moment's hesitation. 'Yeah all right then, probably best to let her sleep it off.'

And then it was just a matter of waiting, taking one more sip of the warming numbing wine and waiting. For Charlie, who came in to see her around ten o'clock.

'Mum? You OK?' Ellen, regarding him from over the edge of her quilt, nodded.

'Yes, Charlie, I'm fine. I think I just overheated a bit, that's all.'

'Your headache, it's not because of me, is it? Because of what I said and making you look at the leaflets?'

Ellen held one bare arm out to him, careful not to let him see any of the ensemble that she still wore beneath the covers, complete with the silver sandals. Most of her lipstick had worn off now anyway, and she suspected she'd have to reapply the mascara too, which had flaked all over the pillow while she'd been waiting. 'No, no – not at all. And you know what, Charlie? You were right. You were utterly and totally right. I have got a problem and I do need some help. I finally realised that today, but I don't know if I ever would have, if you hadn't been brave enough to tell me. I've a few other things to sort out but I promise you, I will get better. I will be a good mum again.'

'You are a good mum,' Charlie insisted, taking her hand. 'Anyway, guess what? I had scampi and chips in the pub. It was nice.'

'Charlie, that's great!' Ellen said, sitting up to hug him, forgetting her secret ensemble for a moment. Fortunately a green dress and an old shirt were all the same to an eleven-year-old boy.

'Calm down, Mum,' Charlie mumbled. 'It's no big deal. It's just today I fancied a change, that was all.'

'I know,' Ellen said, 'I know what you mean. Goodnight, love.'

She kissed him on the forehead and waited for what would be Sabine's inevitable follow-up visit. It came less than two minutes later.

'You borrowed my wine, I see?' Sabine said, sitting down in the place that Charlie had just vacated.

'Yes, do you mind?' Ellen asked her.

'Of course not, I think under these circumstances alcohol is really the best remedy. Also it will help you sleep.'

'And Charlie, he doesn't know about anything that's happened?'

'No, he was on good form actually. A little worried about you but not unduly. He seems . . . lighter.'

'I think he is,' Ellen said. 'I think he's been carrying around this worry for months all on his own, and now he's found the courage to talk to me about it he feels better. Which is why he mustn't know about anything that has happened with Hannah.'

Sabine nodded in agreement. 'Allegra has retired. I think Charlie and I wore her out. Would you like me to make you some food before I go to my room? I'm having another Skype conference with Eric, but not for twenty minutes.'

'No,' Ellen mustered a smile. 'I couldn't eat anyway. It all seems so surreal. So artificial. Like I've just read it in the chapter of a book.'

'I know,' Sabine said. 'Well, for tonight at least that is good. Tomorrow when the sun is up and you have rested we will think what to do next. For now drink the wine and sleep and let it all seem unreal.'

'Thank you, Sabine,' Ellen said. 'When I took in lodgers I never expected that I'd be taking in friends too, but you and Allegra and Matt, that's exactly what you are.'

'Well,' Sabine said. 'Most people are good. Most people apart from my stinking, evil, good-for-nothing husband, that is.'

When she had gone Ellen looked at the clock. It was almost eleven. Not much longer to wait before the house would be quiet and asleep. She would be able to go downstairs, find another bottle of wine and implement her plan.

Because tonight, giddy with the kind of reckless abandon that she had never thought herself capable of, Ellen had decided she would not let another minute of her life slip by unlived. Tonight Ellen was going to take charge of what happened to her next. Tonight Ellen was planning her second-ever seduction attempt.

Tonight Ellen had decided that she was going to have sex with Matt Bolton.

Chapter Eighteen

It took Matt several seconds to locate the keyhole with his key. He hadn't considered himself very drunk at all, at least not by *Bang It!* standards. When he left the pub, the others were off to find a legendary and possibly mythical drinking club that was supposed to be open all night under an adult entertainment shop called Venus Videos in Soho. Matt had questioned the point of an illegal drinking den when there were plenty of legitimate places that stayed open all hours these days, but he had been shouted down and pelted with a good many very offensive insults regarding his sexuality and gender assignment. His sleepless night catching up with him at last, he'd bowed out and saved his reputation by telling them that he was off home to sort out his landlady.

Despite the weariness that crowded his head with ill-advised thoughts of Ellen's hair spread out across her pillow, Matt had elected to take half an hour or so to walk home, preferring the enduring heat of the evening to the crowded and noisy night buses.

Living a little dangerously, he'd tipped his head back as he walked, hoping to be able to see some stars, despite the city lights obliterating any chance of communing with the cosmos.

Matt didn't know why he had the urge to do this anyway, it wasn't like he'd spent his childhood in some rural idyll at one with nature. He'd spent it growing up on a Manchester council estate where nature consisted of grass verges and the occasional privet hedge. But something had happened to him, something that made him remember a line of passion from some seventeenth-century poet, that made him dream about curling a tress of glossy dark hair around his fingers, that made him want to search the heavens for some meaning to his life in the random patterns of the universe.

'Fuck,' Matt had mumbled to himself as he tried to find the keyhole again. 'I'll be reading my star sign next.'

He took great care to close the door behind him, and stood for a second in the quiet cool hallway appraising the situation. There was no light in the living room, or under Allegra's bedroom door. But there was a low greenish light coming from the kitchen, which meant that Ellen was in there having a cup of tea because she always switched on the under-unit lights whenever she was in there alone, thinking. Weary and confused, his body numbed by alcohol, Matt felt he probably shouldn't go into the kitchen to talk to Ellen tonight, not tonight and not in this state. Before he knew it he'd be quoting her poetry and telling her he loved her or something equally insane, taking risks, putting himself out there or whatever it was Lucy had said. Yet even as the last tiny rational part of his brain was making these decisions, his body had already propelled him to the last place he knew he ought to be.

He pushed open the kitchen door, but Ellen was not there.

Well, she was not there in any sense that Matt understood, at least not at first. She was not sitting at the table in some oversized shirt, her hair tied up, embracing a mug of tea. She was leaning against the countertop directly opposite the door, more like lounging actually, and she was wearing a dress. And not just a dress, but a *dress*, dark green and so figure-hugging that in one single second all the mysteries that had been Ellen's body were laid almost bare to him, and he was unable to tear his eyes from the curve of her breasts, the deep cleavage that ran between them, nor the delicious rise of her hips undulating from her waist with what seemed like a glorious decadence. Matt had heard the phrase 'all woman' many times before, but he had never really had cause to use it, at least not so accurately.

Ellen tilted her head so that her long glossy hair strayed over one shoulder, and she smiled at him. She had lipstick on, Matt noticed, confused. Why was she wearing lipstick and a dress?

'Glass of wine?' she asked him. A bottle and two glasses stood ready. She poured him a drink.

She'd been expecting someone, Matt realised, wondering who it might be. And then with a sudden cold thrill he realised that she'd been expecting him. Fuck. *Fuck*, what was he going to do? He felt fifteen again for the first time since he was fifteen and Charlotte Mackenzie had told him they could have sex if he liked as long as he was careful. Except he'd fancied Charlotte Mackenzie from the age of eleven, and just the thought of doing anything so intimate with her had meant that it was all over for him before he'd even laid a finger on her. Charlotte Mackenzie hadn't spoken to him after that, and he had hoped not to be so humiliated ever again. Suddenly, exhilarated and terrified all at once, Matt felt just like that fifteen-year-old boy again. This couldn't be happening, not here, not now. Not like this. He wasn't ready, he didn't know how he felt about her and besides he was really, really drunk. He was never any good at sex when he was really, really drunk and . . .

'I wanted to thank you for staying up all night with me last night,' Ellen said. Slowly she walked across the kitchen towards Matt, which was when he noticed her silver high heels, an observation that was inevitably followed by an image of her wearing nothing but these very shoes. He swallowed and backed away, praying that she wouldn't touch him. What had happened in the fifteen or so hours that he had been out of the house? Had some kinky alien life force with a thing for plunge bras come and taken over Ellen's body? Where was the offer of tea and biscuits? Where was the debrief of the day, when he'd tell her what had happened at work and she'd tell him about something Charlie had said or done?

It was going to be much harder to admire her from afar if she actually started throwing herself at him.

Please don't touch me, please don't touch me, please don't touch me, Matt implored silently as Ellen approached him. She handed him the glass of wine, which he took as a defensive tactic, assuming that a receptacle full of liquid would act as some barrier between them. He was wrong.

Ellen took one more step on her silver high heels into his personal space and rested her hand on his shoulder. She looked into his eyes.

'I wondered if there was anything I could do to thank you?' she asked him, batting her smoky lashes.

'Um . . . well, a coffee would be great?' Matt squeaked as Ellen's hand traced its way down his torso over his waistband and . . . He grabbed her wrist before it got any further.

'Ellen,' he said, studying her face at close quarters, noticing the slightly swollen lids and reddened eyes that hid behind the newly applied and dusty mascara. 'Ellen, what's all this about?'

'Oh God, you don't fancy me, do you?' Ellen asked him, stepping away and stumbling. Matt realised she was probably as drunk as him, if not a little more so. 'I knew it, I knew there was no way I could carry this off. Here I am being reckless and spontaneous and it never occurred to me that you just didn't fancy me. I'm delusional, that's what I am.'

Matt took a second to assimilate everything that she had just said.

'What, are you joking? Of course I fancy you, I don't think I've ever fancied anyone more,' he told her, feeling compelled to haemorrhage compliments. 'You look stunning, that dress . . . Your body looks slamming, Ellen. It's impossible to ignore.' Matt swallowed. 'But it's just not like you. Which is why I'm wondering what all this is about?'

'Really?' Ellen perked up, smiling a bit like the old Ellen. The one who wasn't a sex-crazed, alien-possessed siren. Matt was considerably relieved to see her. 'Because, you know, you spend so long not noticing yourself or looking at yourself that you sort of have no idea what you look like any more. I used to be beautiful once, and I mean once. It was a Thursday evening in 1998. I was wearing this dress. That was the last time I was beautiful.'

'That's not true, Ellen,' Matt said. 'You . . . you are one of the most beautiful women I have ever seen. And I know that sounds like a line but it's true. I've never, not since Charlotte Mackenzie, wanted anything as much as to . . . touch your hair.' He winced. 'Which makes me sound a bit weird, doesn't it?'

'You can touch my hair,' Ellen purred at him softly, taking a step back towards him. 'You can touch me anywhere.'

She pressed herself against him so that they stood breast to breast, hip to hip.

'The thing is,' Matt said, finding it difficult to keep his hands away from her beautifully rounded bottom, 'is that I can't. I can't just come in from work and find you, you Ellen Woods, dressed up and a bit drunk and up for it, and take advantage of that. I can't.'

'You mean you don't want to?' Ellen asked him, her hot breath tickling his neck.

'Oh God,' Matt groaned, knowing by the tone of her voice that she could feel for herself exactly how much he wanted to. 'I want to, Ellen, I want to – but not like this. Not with you. I mean when I left the house this morning you were in a full-blown crisis. How is Hannah? And what about Charlie, how is he coping?'

'I don't want to talk about any of that,' Ellen breathed, her hand travelling up his inner thigh. 'Now, I'm a bit out of practice, in fact totally out of practice when it comes to taking charge, so you must tell me if I get it wrong.' She cupped her hand over Matt's erection and pressed it gently. 'How's that working for you?'

'Oh God.' Unable to resist any longer Matt released his glass of wine, uncertain of where it landed, and pulled Ellen to him, a hand cupping her bottom and the other finding its way immediately to one breast, which it squeezed hard as he kissed her deeply. He moaned in his throat as he thrust her back against the kitchen worktop that she had had him pinned against only seconds ago, taking his hand from her backside and entangling it in her hair, pulling her head back and covering her neck with kisses and bites, pulling at the neckline of her dress, tearing the lace of her bra and exposing her breasts to his lips. Suddenly resolute and focused, Matt lifted Ellen by the hips on to the worktop. He pushed up her skirt and with one fluid movement ripped her panties off, dropping them on the floor.

It was when his hand was on his belt buckle that he noticed the expression on her face. There was desire there, yes, a flush of heat rising from her throat. But there was something else too. Fear? Uncertainty? Even sadness? Matt let his hand drift to his side as he looked at her there, the woman who made him think about poetry and gaze at the stars, with her clothes asunder, her underwear ripped. At that moment she looked sexier and more desirable than any woman he had ever known. But this sordid centrefold affair wasn't how it was meant to be, not between him and Ellen.

The two of them looked at each other for one breathless silent minute and then Matt scooped Ellen up in his arms and held her. She wound herself around his body and buried her head in his neck. Matt increased the pressure of his embrace as he felt her frame begin to shake with sobs.

'Ellen,' he whispered, retreating to sit on one of the kitchen chairs and pulling her on to his lap, cradling her in his arms. 'Ellen, tell me. Please, tell me what's happened?'

Ellen pushed her hair back from her face, which was streaked with tears, and looked into his eyes.

'You must think I'm such a fool,' she said. 'What would someone like you want with a past-it old woman like me?'

'I think you can see why someone like me would want someone exactly like you very, very much.' Matt smoothed the tangle of hair off her face. 'But when you are ready and when you are sure that it's what you want. And you're not sure, are you?'

Ellen looked into his eyes for a second and then shook her head, a response which surprised Matt by how much it stung and disappointed him. For the first time in his life he wanted a woman who didn't want him back.

Ellen climbed off his lap and half turned her back on him while she rearranged her clothes to restore her modesty. Sheepishly she scooped her knickers off the kitchen floor, and uncertain what to do with them, eventually put them in the plastic-bag drawer.

'I mean I do, I do want you, but I'm not sure if it's for very sensible reasons,' she sniffed, glancing nervously at Matt. He felt uncomfortable as he sat there, the heat of desire taking some time to subside.

'What happens next?' he asked her. 'I'm not sure what to do after some amazing making out and then a break to reassess the situation. Apart from explode maybe, or bash my head against the tabletop until I've got enough brain damage to stop me from coming over there and getting you.'

The two of them looked at each other, Ellen trying to work out what was going on between them.

'I'll make us a cup of tea?' she offered.

'I'll do it,' he said. 'You sit down. And talk, start talking and explain to me what happened today to make you decide to give me the most difficult night of my life.'

'I'm not really that difficult to resist, am I?' Ellen smiled shyly.

'Woman,' Matt said, turning his back on her and closing his eyes. 'You have no idea.'

*

When Ellen stopped talking and looked up at Matt she wondered just how much he must pity her. He had not looked at her at all while she had been telling him about Hannah, about her sister's claimed love affair with Nick, and how even venturing just beyond her front gate had made her feel like she was going to slip off the face of the planet and die. While she had been wondering out loud how she could explain to Charlie why he was never going to see his aunt again, and if she should feel guilty that she'd thrown Hannah out when she was so badly hurt, he had not lifted his gaze from the tabletop. Ellen knew that for a few seconds back there Matt had looked at her and he hadn't seen Ellen Woods. He'd seen a woman whose clothes he wanted to rip off before having unbridled sex with her, whether she wished it or not, just like Captain Parker, just like whoever it was who'd hurt Hannah. But Matt wasn't like either of those men, imagined or real. He'd seen the expression on her face, he'd recognised the uncertainty and he'd stopped. It was something that Ellen was deeply grateful for, and yet she mourned the passing of only her second beautiful moment. She wasn't sure that another would ever come again, at least not with Matt. Not now he knew everything about her.

Matt said nothing for a while, the muscles in his jaw tightening reflexively as if he were actively trying not to say something. And then he shrugged.

'Well, this is a bit of a mess isn't it?' he said finally.

'Yes.' Ellen nodded. 'I've got a horrible feeling that the last ten years of my life have slipped by while I believed they were one thing, when they were something else entirely. I thought I was one half of a loving committed marriage. That's what Nick made me think, but I wasn't, if anything I was his trophy for a while, his pet and then . . . then I was this burden that he had to care for when all the time he longed to be with someone else.'

'That's not true,' Matt said.

'Isn't it?' Ellen asked him. 'He was having sex with my sister. Why did she have to tell me, Matt? Why couldn't she have just left me alone with my sad little delusion? At least then I had some . . .' Ellen wanted to say pride or dignity, but neither of those words seemed to fit. 'At least then I had *something*. I was his widow. It was my reason for never looking in the mirror, never going out, never trying to live life. Now? Now I have no excuse. Now I am just a pathetic drunk old landlady who throws herself at her lodgers. Now I am a character from a seventies sitcom.'

'Listen.' Matt seemed to be struggling with some emotion that Ellen couldn't pin down. 'If anyone ever had an excuse to be fucked up, it's you, OK? You could dress in rags and never leave the house again and no one would blame you. But you can't let that happen, Ellen, I won't let that happen. Not to you. Some bloody, arrogant, selfish fuckwit didn't have the brains to see what an amazing wonderful wife he had, and I can promise you if he were alive now I would kill him. And I am not letting him, or Hannah, or the road outside stop you from being who you are for one more minute. You're great, Ellen, you're funny and strong and a brilliant mum and a great . . . copy-editor probably. There is so much more waiting for you out there. Starting from tomorrow we're going to get you back on track again.'

'Really?' Ellen looked at Matt, trying to see if he was still drunk. 'Only won't you be a bit busy, with work and bedding girls and all that?'

'I can handle work,' Matt said, grinning a little sheepishly.

'And as for girls, well – you're the only girl I can think about, and even if you need me to be there as a friend for you for now that won't change in a hurry.' Ellen dropped her gaze, not quite able to understand what she was hearing. 'What I'm trying to say is, don't worry, Ellen, you're not alone. You've got me, Sabine and Allegra. And you've got Charlie. We all . . . care about you. Yes, someone's gone and ripped a fucking huge hole in your chest and filled it with despair, but it will get better.'

'I don't know what I did to deserve such nice lodgers,' Ellen said sleepily as Matt pulled her to her feet.

'Well,' he said as he escorted her up the stairs, 'you make a lovely cup of tea.'

For the first few seconds after Matt woke up he was confused, wondering where he was. It was a familiar feeling, opening his eyes on an unfamiliar room, searching around for some kind of marker or clue as to where he had ended up after a drunken night out. The pressure behind his eyes, the ache in his limbs and his bone-dry mouth told him that he had a hangover, and normally that feeling coupled with seeing the window in a different place meant that he had gone home with a woman. With the mix of excitement and dread that always accompanied that first sober look at a woman he'd just spent the night with, he turned his head towards the sound of steady breathing. And that was when it all came back to him.

Matt felt something like a silent rent in his chest when he looked at Ellen sleeping next to him. When he had taken her up to her room sometime early this morning she had asked him to sit and talk to her for a while, explaining that she didn't want to be alone because when she was alone she started thinking, and look what happened the last time she did that, she decided to get drunk and throw herself at her lodger.

Matt didn't tell her that he didn't want to be alone either for almost exactly the same reason, except what he would have been thinking about was what would have happened if he hadn't stopped things when he did. So he had sat on a chair by the bed trying not to look at the strangely erotic array of sensible underwear that was scattered all over the floor, and as she took a shower he told her all about his drive-through brothel assignment. He had to struggle, as he talked to her, with the image of the water running in rivulets down that body that he had experienced all too briefly. When Ellen emerged wrapped in a large towel, her hair dripping wet, Matt had been compelled to cross his legs and remove an embroidered cushion from behind his back so that he could reposition it on his lap.

Ellen had peered into her already open wardrobe. 'I don't know what to wear. For the last twelve months I've been wearing Nick's clothes so that I could feel close to him, and now I don't want to. I don't want to wear anything that I had from then.' She turned to Matt as if she'd just had a very controversial idea. 'Maybe I'll sleep naked, why not?'

'I'll be off then,' Matt said, feeling the heat sweep across his face. Ellen saw his expression of horror and her face fell.

'Oh God, Matt, I'm sorry – that sounded like I was trying to seduce you again, didn't it? I promise I'm not. I know, I'll wear what Mum bought for me last Christmas. I've never worn it.' She stepped back into the bathroom, emerging a few minutes later in a full-length white cotton nightgown with white lace trim. 'I have no idea what she was thinking, I look like a heroine from a Victorian novel. Any minute now I'll catch a chill and die!'

'It suits you actually,' Matt told her, trying not to notice how the damp hair that trailed down her back had made the material of the nightgown slightly translucent.

Ellen climbed into bed and pulled the quilt over her. She looked around her, as if taking in every tiny detail of the room.

'This was our place, mine and Nick's. This was where we were alone. Do you know I never guessed, I had no idea at all that he was seeing another woman, maybe even was in *love* with any other woman, let alone my own sister. There wasn't anything, not any of the signs that you read about. He didn't start changing his underwear more often or going to the gym. He didn't treat me any differently at all. Do you suppose that means that the whole thing was incidental to his life here, irrelevant to it?'

'Maybe it was,' Matt said, thinking of that conversation that Nick had had with Charlie about loving him no matter what. 'But if you weren't expecting anything then perhaps you didn't notice.'

Ellen lay back, her head on the pillow.

'Will you come and sit by me and talk to me until I go to sleep?' she asked him. 'You don't have to, but if you will I promise not to touch you.'

'Of course I will,' Matt answered painfully. Ellen patted the side of the bed and with some trepidation he had got up and gone and sat on the very edge, leaning back awkwardly against the headboard, keeping one foot on the floor like he'd read the censors made the actors do in old films if there was any scene with a bed in it, so as to indicate that no sex was going to take place.

'Tell me about the Nevada hookers again,' Ellen said. 'Tell me about the one who's studying to become a CSI, what's her name?'

'Lola Lagoona, that's her professional name, but her real name is Paige Anthony. She's really clever, aced it all through high school even though her mum was an alcoholic and her dad was never around . . .'

At some point they had both slept. Matt had no idea who drifted off first or when, but here he was stretched out on Ellen's bed with her sleeping next to him. The sight of her made him catch his breath.

> *'Licence my roving hands, and let them go,*
> *Before, behind, above, between, below.'*

As he propped himself up on one elbow to get a better look at her, two more lines from that poem that Matt had had no idea he remembered popped into his head. Quite suddenly he remembered something else that he'd forgotten. In class along with all his mates he'd completely ignored the teacher, talking over her, passing notes, throwing chewed-up bits of paper at the backs of girls he fancied. At the end of class he'd stuffed the photocopied handout into his bag, and later that day when he'd been looking for something else he'd pulled it out and read it, and read it again. And then slowly, very slowly, he'd realised what he was reading. It was a man describing his girlfriend taking off her clothes, and then talking about having sex with her. Matt had been unable to believe that olden-day people even knew about sex, let alone wrote about it so explicitly. And, for that one evening, he'd read and reread it, trying to picture in his head exactly what the poet was describing, and though he would never have admitted it to any of his friends it had been one of the most erotic experiences of his life. The next day he'd screwed the photocopy up and thrown it in the bin and sniggered over the page three girl in the *Sun* that one of his friends had nicked off his dad, and never given the poem a second thought. Not until he met Ellen, Ellen who the poem seemed to have been written for, over four centuries ago.

His head pounding, his mouth dry, Matt found that he was desperate to read it again, to know every line again and most uncharacteristically of all to read it to Ellen. To experience it with Ellen. He fell on to his back and looked at the ceiling. What was happening to him?

Then two things happened at the same time.

Ellen moaned a little in her sleep, and turning on to her side flung her arm across Matt's chest. At that precise moment her bedroom door opened and Charlie walked in.

'Mum, I've made you break—' He halted in his tracks, a tray with some toast, tea and a near-dead rose in a beaker in his hands.

'What?' Ellen sat up, confused.

'Charlie, mate,' Matt said. 'This isn't what you think.'

Ellen sat bolt upright, catching up with the situation vital seconds later than them. Rapidly she clambered out of bed.

'Charlie, Matt and I were just talking, that's all, and we fell asleep.'

Suddenly galvanised into action by the sound of his mother's voice, Charlie flung the tray at the bed and ran out of the room. Ellen raced after him and Matt ran after her, but as he reached the top of the stairs he could see that she was too late. Charlie had slammed the front door behind him, certain that she would not follow.

Chapter Nineteen

By the time Matt reached the bottom of the stairs Ellen was beating her fists against the front door in frustration, tears streaming down her face.

'What the hell is wrong with me?' she sobbed. 'I can't go after him. I want to, I really need to but I can't. I'm stuck . . . stuck behind this bloody door. I'm too scared to go after my own son when he's upset!'

She turned to Matt and he was shocked by the genuine fear on her face. She really was terrified of going out – he didn't think he had fully understood it until that moment.

'I'll go,' he offered. 'Look, he won't have gone far. He'll be at the end of the road or down the shops or something. Give me ten minutes.'

Matt opened the front door and jogged up the garden path and on to the street in bare feet. It was quiet for a Saturday morning, a toddler and her mother ambling down the opposite side of the road, a few kids kicking a ball around on the corner. Matt jogged up the street to where the boys were, hopeful he'd find Charlie amongst them. But he was nowhere to be seen. Where would a boy go who thought he'd just caught his mum in bed with her lodger, Matt wondered.

Well, wherever it was it was further away than he could travel without shoes on. His hands on his hips as he caught his breath in the glare of the morning sun, he went back to the house.

'Where is he?' Ellen asked him desperately the second he got in through the door. 'What did he say?'

'I didn't catch him,' Matt said. 'Maybe he got on a bus or something? What does he normally do on a Saturday? Maybe he's gone into town.'

'He normally stays here with me,' Ellen said miserably.

'What's happened?' Sabine asked coming down the stairs, winding her long hair around and around one hand before tucking it into a knot on the back of her neck.

'Matt and I stayed up talking last night,' Ellen explained, feeling heat flare across her cheeks as she thought of Matt pushing her skirt up and gripping her thighs. 'We both fell asleep in my room and Charlie saw us, put two and two together and made five.'

Sabine looked concerned. 'He got the wrong idea and ran out?'

'Yes and now we don't know where he's gone,' Ellen said in dismay. 'I should have gone after him, but I can't . . . I hate this, I hate myself, I hate my shitty life!'

She slammed her fist against the front door again and again, making it rattle in its frame, her heart accelerating at the thought of being on the other side of it. 'I can't have him out there thinking I've betrayed his father that way. I can't.'

'Have you tried ringing him?' Sabine suggested.

Frantically, Ellen dialled Charlie's mobile. She wasn't surprised that it went straight to voicemail. 'Charlie, it's Mum. I swear to you, that wasn't what you thought it was, OK? Matt and I were just talking and we fell asleep, that was all, I promise. Please come home, darling.'

'What did Charlie see?' Allegra emerged from her room. 'Honestly, if I had known that there would be more comings and goings in this house than Piccadilly Circus I might have taken the insurance company's caravan after all.'

'He found Ellen and Matt in bed together, and ran off,' Sabine explained, eliciting an expression of pure delight from Allegra. 'But apparently no intercourse took place.'

Sabine and Allegra looked the other two up and down as if they were searching for visible traces of indiscretion, which Ellen was sure must be written all over her face.

'How wonderful,' Allegra said. 'Well, let's go and have breakfast and you can tell me all about it. I want all the details, Ellen, it's been far too long since I was in the grasp of a virile young man. It seems to me that Charlie is a very sensible boy, I'm sure he'll be fine . . .'

'Oh no,' Ellen said, a thought suddenly occurring to her. 'I know where he will have gone.'

'Where?' Matt asked.

'To the same person he always goes to when he's angry with me,' Ellen said anxiously. 'To Hannah. Oh my God, what if she tells him about his dad . . . I can't let him find out, especially not from her.'

'Right, well, let's go then,' Matt said. He glanced at his bare feet and Ellen's nightdress. 'Let's get dressed and go.' At the look on her face, he revised his offer. 'I'll get dressed, you tell me where Hannah lives and I'll go. Maybe Sabine could come with me, she knows Hannah better than I do?'

Sabine nodded. 'Of course.'

'No, no,' Ellen said, her body suddenly pumped full of adrenalin, her need to find her son eclipsing everything else. 'No. I am not this person who's terrified of leaving her house. I won't be. I can't be this person and be *me*. I can't be someone who abandons their son because they are afraid of . . . of what? Buses and noise and people and certain death? That's not what a mother does. A mother does not abandon her child because she is afraid of anything. I'm going to Hannah's.' Her determined expression wavered a little as she looked at Matt. 'But you will come with me, won't you?'

'Of course,' Matt told her. 'Give me five minutes.'

Sabine put a hand on her forearm. 'Ellen, are you sure? Agoraphobia is not something you can get over just because you feel like it. You'll need a lot of help, therapy – medication, perhaps. If you force yourself to go out now you might make things worse.'

'I have to go now, I haven't got time for therapy or drugs. I need to get to Charlie before Hannah says anything. I have to go now, before I lose my nerve, and that's that.'

As Ellen and Matt rushed to get dressed Allegra followed Sabine into the kitchen, where Sabine offered to make her breakfast.

'I hope she knows what she is doing,' Sabine said anxiously.

'I think she does,' Allegra reassured her. 'I think she has finally decided to become the heroine in her own story, and she is strong, much stronger than she realises.'

'She will have to be, that's for sure,' Sabine said as she tugged a full bag out of the kitchen bin and dropped it outside the back door.

'So do you think anything else apart from chatting and falling asleep happened last night?' Allegra asked her as she looked for a replacement liner. Sabine paused for a moment as she opened the plastic-bag drawer, and then gingerly picking up a pair of black lace panties turned to Allegra and replied, 'I would say that's a distinct possibility.'

Ellen stood at the threshold of her house. She knew perfectly well that what was actually outside the front door was a street of red-brick Victorian houses with modest and mostly well-kept front gardens nestling behind neatly trimmed privet hedges. She knew the pavement would be a patchwork of different shades of tarmac, depending on which utility company had dug it up most recently, and the traffic would be relatively quiet except for the thunder of buses full of Saturday shoppers, rattling past the end of the road. She knew the air would be warm, scented with summer flowers and petrol fumes, and the most threatening thing out there that she was likely to encounter was an angry wasp. She knew that with her rational mind, but no matter what she might see with her eyes when she opened that door she felt as if she would be confronted with a cliff edge, a precipice so high that you could not see its foot, and that she would be compelled to throw herself off it.

Matt opened the door and held a hand out to her. Ellen took it and stepped on to the path with him. Immediately the air rushed from her lungs and her head spun.

'I can't,' she said, closing her eyes and clutching Matt's arm.

'You can,' Matt said. 'Come on, we'll just get to the gate. Let's get there and see how you feel.'

Screwing her eyes tight as if she were on a roller-coaster ride that would soon be over, Ellen let him lead her to her front gate. He put her hands on the rough wood.

'This needs replacing, really,' he said in a matter-of-fact voice. 'The paint's peeling off and the wood's rotting round the hinges. A few more slams from Charlie and it'll be done for, don't you reckon? Ellen, don't you think so?'

Slowly Ellen opened her eyes and looked down at the garden gate, a waist-height picket affair that she and Nick had painted green not long after they moved in. It had suffered for lack of attention in the last year. Ellen ran her fingers over the rough and cracked surface, and then glanced up at her house. It was the first time she had seen it from the outside in months. The wisteria had grown heavy for lack of pruning, its weight pulling away from the building in some parts, while in others it had begun to stray across the windows, including the one in Ellen's bedroom. At some point the old cast-iron guttering must have become blocked with autumn leaves, because a tidemark of where it had overflowed could still be traced running down the brickwork. The front lawn, now standing a good ten inches high, had yellowed and gone to seed in the unremitting sunshine and was in a sorry state, except for where it had migrated into the cracks in the garden path, where it seemed to be sprouting quite happily.

As Ellen looked at the neglected house that she loved so fiercely, she realised that one of the reasons she felt so safe within its walls was that time seemed to stand still there. As if she were waiting for clocks to start ticking, hearts to start beating and the world to start turning again. Waiting for order to be restored, for Nick to walk in through the door after work and her life to begin again. She looked at Matt. Her heartbeat slowed, the panic and fear subsiding a little.

'We'll go to the end of the road and get a cab,' Matt told her. 'There'll be loads this time of the morning.'

Casually he opened the gate and taking Ellen's hand off the wood, tucked it through his arm and began walking her up the street.

'I'm sorry,' he said. 'All of this is my fault. I didn't mean to crash out in your room.'

'It's not your fault,' Ellen told him, fighting the rise of vomit in her throat as her stomach lurched and contracted painfully. She stopped walking, turning back towards home, but Matt kept a firm grasp of her hand beneath his arm and walked her on.

'And I'm sorry about the other thing, the, you know . . . taking some of your clothes off thing,' he said. He'd normally have never brought it up, but he'd decided that he needed to take Ellen's mind off what they were doing, and he didn't think small talk would be sufficient distraction.

'Oh God.' Ellen stopped for a moment, bending double and retching. 'Oh God, Matt . . . I think I have to go back. I can't breathe . . . Matt, let me go back, this is too much. This is too far. I can't do it, I'm not strong enough.' An overwound clock began unravelling in her chest, time spinning out of control as she fought for breath. Matt would not let her go.

'It's just as far to the end of the road as it is to get back now,' he said calmly, rubbing between her shoulder blades. 'Just take deep breaths in and out, in and out.'

He paused while he waited for her breathing to even out a little. Her eyes were darting fearfully left and right.

'You know, I didn't stop what was happening in the kitchen because I didn't want to. I really wanted to, Ellen, a lot. But it

341

didn't seem like the right time, I mean you were drunk and kind of throwing yourself at me . . .'

Ellen straightened up, dragging the back of her hand across her mouth, and looked at him with watery eyes.

'I'm dying of a heart attack here and you're reminding me of the worst and most humiliating moment of my life,' she gasped on a ragged breath. Matt smiled. His plan of extreme distraction seemed to be working.

He put his arm around her waist and propelled her forward as he talked. 'You feel like you are dying, but you aren't. You're having a panic attack which is pretty scary and very real, but it won't kill you. The trick is to try not to think about it. Which brings me to the next thing I want to say.'

'You don't need to tell me, I know,' Ellen said, looking around anxiously as Matt continued to move her along. 'I behaved ridiculously last night. I'm not exactly sure that's going to help when it comes to having a panic attack.'

'No, look, I've been thinking about you for a couple of weeks now,' Matt said. 'By which I mean I've become very attracted to you. You looked amazing last night, but you didn't need that dress or that underwear to turn me on. I'd been thinking about what it would be like to make love to you since long before that.'

'You . . . what? Are you trying to pull me now, when I'm on the verge of vomiting and there's an aneurysm that I'm fairly sure is about to pop in my head?' Ellen asked him, aghast.

'I'm just telling you the truth,' Matt said, aware that was not entirely accurate. He was telling the truth about how he longed for her physically but the emotional stuff, that seemed to be tied up together with how much he wanted her, he kept to himself. This bonding of emotional and physical passion had never happened to him before. If he thought too much about it he'd give himself a panic attack and then where would they be, two mental wrecks stranded in Shepherds Bush. 'You are a very attractive woman, Ellen. And if . . . when the dust has settled a bit and you're not quite so . . .'

'Insane?' Ellen asked him, wild-eyed as they approached the busy main road. She clutched on to him, winding her arms around his chest and pressing her cheek against his shoulder. 'Oh God, Matt, I need to go back. I need to go back. I can't do it, I can't do it, I can't. I'm going to die . . .'

'You're not going to die,' Matt told her as he hailed a black cab. 'Anyway, what I was trying to say was that if you want to have sex with me then I'm up for it. Whenever you're ready.'

As he had predicted, Ellen was so shocked that he was able to bundle her into the cab and close the door behind them both. 'Ladbroke Grove please, mate,' he said to the cabbie.

Ellen sat wide-eyed on the back seat, looking like a wildcat that had been cornered, her chest rising and falling rapidly. Matt folded down the seat opposite and reaching over pulled her seat belt over her shoulder and clipped it into its catch, so that for a second their faces were only millimetres apart. Matt sat back. He had no idea what or how she felt about him, if last night was just some crazy aberration brought on by everything that had happened, or if it was based on something more, something that could be real. And he couldn't exactly press her on it now, but he found that he wanted to know. He hated not knowing what she was thinking or feeling, especially about him.

'A London black cab is one of the safest places in the world you can be,' he told Ellen, as he looked at her wide, scared eyes. 'No one knows the roads better than one of these guys, and these old things,' he patted the side of the cab, 'are built for safety. You've done the hardest bit, Ellen, we'll get dropped right outside Hannah's front door and after we've dealt with . . . whatever we've got to deal with, we'll get a cab all the way back to your house. You know you can go to the end of your road without anything terrible happening, so now you've really got nothing to worry about.'

'I'm not sure about that,' Ellen said, tucking her hands between her legs. 'You just told me you'd have sex with me whenever I felt like it. Don't you know that I'm an agoraphobic widow who's just found out that her marriage was a lie? I'm the actual definition of a . . . of a fuck-up.' For a second she focused her gaze on him.

'Oh you'd be surprised,' Matt said, ignoring her last comment. 'We like the mad ones, the complicated ones. The ones that are going to give us loads of grief and might very well appear standing over us while we sleep with a carving knife in their hand. Sex tends to be better with the mad ones. Well, you were on the verge of proving that last night. What happened in the kitchen – that was the best it's been for me in a long time.'

'Ha!' Ellen gasped, but this time with incredulity rather than for air. As she watched west London slip past, transforming gradually from grubby red-brick Victorian shopfronts into the graceful shabby chic of Georgian villas, punctuated every now and then with an exclamation mark of 1960s modernist archi-tecture, she realised that her heartbeat had slowed and she wasn't gasping for air. She felt almost normal, and much, much less afraid of dropping dead any second. She did feel safe in the cab, sitting opposite Matt. And there was something else, she felt exhilarated. God only knew what mess awaited her at Hannah's place, but she had made it this far. With Matt's help she had made it this far . . . and then it dawned on her.

'You've been distracting me,' she said. 'All this talk of wanting sex with me, it's been to distract me, take my mind off what I'm doing.'

Matt hesitated, unsure of what to let her believe. But he saw the relief in her eyes, and realised that him wanting her so much that every square inch of skin ached for her was the very last thing she needed. So instead he grinned like a kid caught out planting a practical joke.

'It worked though, didn't it?' he said, flinching as Ellen punched him on the thigh.

'You bastard!' she exclaimed, but she was laughing, high on adrenalin.

'Whereabouts, mate?' the cabbie asked as they turned on to the top of Ladbroke Grove. Matt looked back at Ellen, and raised his eyebrows.

'About halfway down, just past the tube station on the left,' Ellen told him. As the cab pulled up to the kerb she looked into Matt's eyes and smiled, resting her hand on his knee.

'You are not the man you pretend to be,' she told him.

'What you saying? I'm a rubbish kisser?' Matt made himself joke, although her touch made him want to grab her and kiss her right there.

'No, in my admittedly limited experience you are an excellent kisser. But you are not this man who doesn't care, who goes from girl to girl without a second thought. You are a very kind and generous and clever man and I'm very lucky that it was you who answered that ad, because I don't know how I would have managed if it had been anyone else.'

'That's fifteen eighty then,' the cabbie said a touch impatiently.

'Ready?' Matt asked her as he stuffed a twenty through the slot in the Perspex screen that separated them from the driver.

'As I'll ever be.'

Matt got out first and held out his hand to her. Inhaling deeply, Ellen took it and the pair of them ran to Hannah's red-painted front door like children running through a rainstorm. When they reached the door and Ellen threw herself against it, pressing her palms against its hot glossy surface, her shoulders heaving as she fought to get her breath back, she remembered why she had come. The light in her eyes faded as rapidly as the colour in her cheeks.

'I've got this far,' she said, more to herself than Matt. 'I can do this.'

Matt nodded. 'I'll wait here for a minute, give you two a chance to talk.'

Ellen pushed Hannah's doorbell and waited.

It was Charlie who opened the door.

'Oh thank God you're OK,' Ellen said, flinging her arms around him and hugging his rigid body. 'How long have you been here, what's Hannah said? Did you get my message?'

She released him, but he was immobile.

'Charlie, Charlie – look at me? I've come. I've come to find you. I came all the way here to find you and tell you that there is nothing going on between me and Matt. Nothing at all! Aren't you pleased?'

Charlie looked at her and shook his head.

'Mum, it's Aunt Hannah, I can't wake her,' he said, his voice tearful and tight. 'I'm so glad you're here, I don't know what to do.'

Ellen swallowed, finding her throat painfully tight, fear flooding through her veins.

'Where is she, Charlie?' she asked.

'In there.' Charlie nodded at the bedroom door. 'When I got here there wasn't any answer, and I didn't want to go home so I took the key out of the window box and let myself in. I thought she was out so I had a look around and she's . . .' He paused. 'She's in bed. She's not moving. I can't get her to wake up. Mum, I think she might be dead.'

When Ellen was confronted with her sister lying in her bed two emotions tore through her in quick succession. The first was relief. Hannah was not dead; she stirred as Ellen came into the room, turning over on to her back. By her bed, though, was a packet of sleeping pills with two empty blisters and half a bottle of vodka that was a quarter empty. Hannah might have been seeking oblivion, but she had not been trying to kill herself. The second emotion was shame. Since the moment Hannah had made her confession everything else had seemed insignificant to Ellen: nothing mattered any more except that Hannah had betrayed her and her life had fallen to pieces. She'd forgotten that Hannah had been attacked and hurt. As she looked at her lying on her back, her face swollen and misshapen, a livid rainbow of bruises tracking their way down her face and throat, ranging in colour from shocking pink to a sickly yellow, Ellen felt her stomach heave. She had abandoned Hannah at the worst moment in her life, and nothing, not anything that had happened between them, could justify that.

Yesterday she'd been furious with Hannah for putting herself

347

in this situation, for getting herself attacked, blaming her for searching out the ultimate distraction technique to avoid getting into trouble for sleeping with her sister's husband. Ellen had been determined not to let Hannah off the hook so easily – so *easily*? No one would choose to put themselves through this to get off the hook. It was something that might be impossible to recover from, Ellen feared.

Belatedly she sensed Charlie standing in the doorway, twisting his fingers in the hem of his T-shirt.

'She's not dead, Charlie. She's just very deeply asleep.' Ellen pondered her sister for a moment, and then turning ushered Charlie outside into the hall.

'You must have been very frightened,' she said, putting her hands on his shoulders and looking into his eyes. It was something of a shock to realise that he was almost as tall as her now and that it wouldn't be long before he towered over her, as his father had.

'I thought she was dead, her face is so . . . hurt,' Charlie whispered. 'And I didn't know what I should do, I was going to phone you – but then you came. *You* came here for me. That's brilliant, Mum.'

'I didn't want you to get the wrong impression about me and Matt,' Ellen told him, dropping her gaze. 'You're right about me, Charlie, I have got a problem. I wouldn't have been able to come after you if it hadn't been for Matt. He got me here, he more or less dragged me, and I'm just as terrified of leaving here and going home as I was of coming. The world scares me to death, I think it always has in a way, but when your dad died, when one of the things that I always told myself wouldn't happen happened, that's when this fear of going out started. I lied to myself, and I lied to everyone else. You were the only one who was brave enough to face up to what was happening.'

As Ellen talked, she glanced back up at Charlie and saw his eyes fill with unshed tears, and she realised how much pressure her son had been under, how much pressure she had unwittingly put him under.

'I'm ill and I need to get some help to put me back on my feet, but the good news is I can get the help and it will work, and I will get better and be dragging you round the shops in no time. So we don't have to worry about me any more.' Ellen nodded at Hannah's bedroom door. 'For now we have to look after Hannah.'

Matt pushed open the front door and hazarded a smile at Charlie.

'Tell you what, why don't you and Matt make a pot of coffee and I'll see if I can wake up Hannah and see how's she feeling.'

Charlie scowled at Matt. 'Can't I come with you and see how she is?'

'I think she'll want a bit of time to get herself together, Charlie. Give her a bit of space, OK?' Ellen watched her son eye Matt. 'I did tell you, nothing happened between me and Matt. We're just friends.'

'OK, I s'pose,' Charlie muttered. 'Mum . . . she will be all right, won't she, Aunt Hannah?'

Ellen stopped herself from responding reflexively. How could she reassure him that everything was going to be OK? If there was ever any boy who knew things weren't always all right in the end, it was Charlie.

'I hope so,' she said. 'The main thing is to be here and look after her and help her as much as we can. Go and put some coffee on and make some toast too. If I know Hannah she won't have eaten.'

Matt put his hand on Charlie's shoulder and guided him down the hallway towards the kitchen. Taking a deep breath, Ellen went back into Hannah's room.

'So how the bloody hell does this work?' Matt said, staring at an orange Gaggia espresso machine. It looked like it had never been used in its life and had been bought more to go with the other orange-accent features in the smart kitchen than to provide a daily shot of caffeine.

'I don't know why you're here,' Charlie shot at him, reaching up and taking an orange cafetière out of a cupboard. 'You've got nothing to do with this. And Aunt Hannah never uses that. She uses this, I can do it.'

'Good one,' Matt said, wondering why, as he went to the fridge to look for milk, he felt as if he were being interviewed by a stern father, which was ironic because he'd spent most of his adult life avoiding fathers of any description. The fridge was empty except for three bottles of wine, half a bottle of gin, two bottles of tonic water and half a lime. Matt slammed the door shut and turned around to find Charlie carefully pouring boiling water into the cafetière.

'I'm here to help your mum, Charlie. She needed a hand to get over here, but I swear nothing would have stopped her from coming after you. She didn't want you to get the wrong idea.'

'And what about you?' Charlie asked him. 'Did you want me to get the wrong idea?'

'Not sure I follow,' Matt said, perplexed.

'Well, first of all you're all matey with me, following me

350

around being a laugh, and then you make the moves on my mum. On my mum? Why?' Charlie's blue gaze narrowed dangerously.

'I would never . . . that's not what it's about. Charlie, I made friends with you because you're a laugh and I like you, even if you are a gooner. And as for your mum, well . . . I like her a lot too.' Matt gestured at the cafetière. 'Look, fancy walking down to the shop to get some milk while that's brewing?'

'I can go on my own,' Charlie said bullishly, and then after a moment's hesitation held out his hand. 'Give us a couple of quid.'

'Look, mate – I get why you're pissed off,' Matt said. 'You think I've been trying it on with your mum. You're bound to be riled about that. Any bloke would be, it's natural – you want to protect her . . .'

'Well yeah, I do – but that's not the only reason I'm pissed off,' Charlie said, retracting his hand and crossing his arms across his chest.

'What then? Cos you and me are mates, and you know what, you're right, the first rule of mates is that you never go after a mate's woman, especially not if that woman is also his mother.'

Charlie shook his head. 'Arsehole,' he said, deliberately failing to keep the utterance under his breath.

'Arsehole?' Matt laughed, noticing a twitch of a smile around the boy's mouth in response. 'Fuck, say it like it is.'

'Well, you are,' Charlie told him. 'You are a proper arsehole. Look, my mum likes you a lot. I'm not a kid, I know she goes all stupid around you and I don't think I mind if she wants a boyfriend. I want her to be happy and laugh and go out places and dress up again. I think Dad would want her to be happy too.

351

But not with you because you won't even love her, because you are an arsehole.'

'Wouldn't I?' Matt asked him, even though he sensed that was the wrong question. 'Why not?'

Charlie went over to his rucksack that he had thrown in the corner, and unzipping it brought out last week's issue of *Bang It!*.

'I read your column,' he said. 'You have sex with girls and then write about it. If you do that to my mum I'll kill you, I swear it.' Matt fully believed the glare that Charlie shot at him with deadly accuracy. He watched as the boy flicked through to the centre pages where Kelly from Doncaster lolled, legs akimbo, squeezing together bits of her anatomy that were designed to make a grown man do a little more than blush. '*And* you spend all your time around young naked girls. My mum is pretty but she doesn't look like *that*.' He nodded at Kelly, who was pouting sulkily from the pages, her mouth slightly open and a strapline running beneath her photo that read 'I deserve to be spanked, I'm a very naughty girl'.

'So don't go pretending to be my mate and my mum's mate when all you're doing is making fun of her.'

'*O my America . . .*' The words sprang into Matt's head again and he thought of the incredible thrill that had raced through him when he pulled Ellen's dress away from her breasts, the excitement of discovering the unknown. He picked up the magazine and looked at the image of Kelly. Airbrushed and manipulated into impossible perfection, she seemed about one step away from a blow-up doll.

Matt sat down at Hannah's shiny white table, clear of any sign of use except for an orange set of condiments.

'Men are simple things,' he said. 'Mainly we think about sex.

And when we think about sex mostly we think about breasts and bottoms, and somehow at some point it all started to be about girls that looked like this.' He gestured at Kelly. 'In the olden days it was big pale flabby birds that were where it was at.'

'What?' Charlie asked, sceptically.

'Yeah, I saw a programme about it once, when the Sky box was broken in the flat and we could only get BBC2. This artist called Reuben used to paint like seriously big women and everyone thought that was the bee's knees. Naked paintings of fat birds was the olden-day *Bang It!*.'

'Gross,' Charlie said, wrinkling his nose.

'And then when I was growing up it was all about skinny. No breasts or hips or bottoms. All the fit girls were the skinny ones. At the moment it's all about this.' He tapped Kelly on the face, which seemed the only appropriate place to touch her. 'But this isn't real. Big round breasts aren't what make a girl beautiful or make you love her.'

'What about the girl you had sex with and wrote about? You said she was blonde and had big tits.'

'Did I?' Matt said uncomfortably, thinking about Lucy and how she'd listened to him bleat on about Ellen, how funny and bright she had been once he'd stopped looking down her cleavage and started looking into her eyes.

'She had more than a handful, you wrote,' Charlie told him. 'Enough in her bra to sprain your tongue, you said.' He wrestled briefly with some internal dilemma and then asked, 'How do you sprain your tongue on a girl's . . . bosom?'

'. . . *my new found land*.' Matt replayed the line over again. He'd wanted to write a novel once, or poetry. How did he ever end up writing about tongue sprain and Nevada cat houses?

'You can't, not really. I was trying to be funny. I was making it up. Most of that I made up, just like most of this photo is made up. Kelly's waist isn't that slim, and her breasts aren't that big and her legs aren't that long. She's got a little bit of acne on her chin and on the day of the shoot she had shadows under her eyes because she'd been up all night. And I'll tell you something else. She looked a million times prettier in real life than she does in this photo.'

'Did she have her top off?' Charlie asked him, wide-eyed.

'No,' Matt lied. 'She had all her clothes on.' Charlie looked disappointed. 'And that girl I wrote about, I lied about her too. In real life she's funny and smart and kind and I didn't write about any of that, any of the stuff that makes her a great person. I just made up a load of stuff to make me look big and clever. I feel pretty shit about it actually.'

Matt sighed; he was starting to wonder exactly who he was. This identity that he'd been nurturing for so long was slipping like a mask, and he wasn't sure that there was anything behind it.

'One day you'll realise, wanting someone, falling in . . . you know . . . like sort of love, isn't just about bits of bodies. It's about attraction, yeah, but not the obvious sort. Like your mum. When she thinks you're talking rubbish she sucks in the left corner of her bottom lip, just a fraction. She doesn't even know that she does it and it makes you think . . .' It makes you think about kissing her until she laughs, Matt wanted to say, but he refrained. 'It makes you think about how nice her mouth is, and how she expresses what she's thinking even when she thinks she's not.'

'Like Emily's hair,' Charlie said thoughtfully.

'Whose hair?' Matt wondered if he was talking about another *Bang It!* model.

'This girl at school, Emily. She's got long hair that reaches all the way down her back, it's sort of a dark yellow colour, but when the sun shines on it it looks amber, like honey running down her back. And she plays the electric guitar in a band and when she's on stage she looks like . . .' Charlie trailed off. 'Like the whole world can go and jump in a lake, because she doesn't care about anything but the music. She's the coolest girl I've ever met.'

'Sounds to me like you like this Emily bird,' Matt said seriously, without a hint of mockery or condescension.

'I really, really do,' Charlie confessed earnestly. 'But every time I try to talk to her I go all stupid and say crap and she looks at me like she thinks I'm mental and pathetic.'

'Maybe you should write her a poem,' Matt suggested.

'What, so then she'd think I was gay too?' Charlie exclaimed in horror.

'No, trust me, poetry can be one of the best ways of pulling a girl ever. Look at Shakespeare, or this bloke who wrote this poem I can't get out of my head recently. They knew exactly how to woo a lady with the power of words.'

'To what a lady? Is wooing a lady how you sprain your tongue?'

Matt shook his head. 'That stuff you said about Emily's hair, about it looking like honey and shit. That's romantic. You should write that down and give it to her and I bet you she wouldn't think you were gay. She'd think you were sensitive and romantic and not because you're acting sensitive and romantic to get her to snog you, but because you are that way, Charlie.'

'Am I?' Charlie looked sceptical.

'You are if you are anything like your mother.'

'I don't know,' Charlie said thoughtfully. 'All I can think about is what it would be like to touch a girl's . . . bosom.'

'Yeah,' Matt nodded. 'And that probably won't change until the day you die. Even after you've touched a girl's bosom, you'll be wondering what it would be like to touch another girl's bosom and another. That's just being a bloke. It's just this thing we're lumbered with. But it doesn't mean you can't care about a girl or you know, like love her and shit.'

Charlie fixed him with his level blue eyes and Matt shifted uncomfortably on his chair.

'So are you saying that you could fall in love with my mother then, even though she's old and a bit fat?'

'She's neither of those things,' Matt chuckled. 'She's . . . she's lovely, and brave and strong in ways she doesn't know, and she's beautiful. And yeah, I could fall in love with your mum, I reckon. If things were different.'

'If what things were different?' Charlie challenged him.

'Well, you know, it wasn't long ago that your dad died and then there's all this stuff with her sister and the going out of the house business and . . . other stuff.'

'You helped her today,' Charlie stated.

'I got her here, I don't know if that actually counts as helping. There's a small possibility that I've permanently traumatised her.'

'She likes talking to you,' Charlie said. 'You make her smile. I hadn't seen her smile or laugh, not a real smile that she means, not until you came.'

'That's not exactly surprising. You've both had a shit year.'

'Yes, but I don't want next year to be shit too. I miss Dad, and

I still love him but I want to be happy again. I want Mum to be happy and you make her laugh. So if you promise not to write about her and not to be mean to her, then I don't mind if you ask her out on a date. But I don't think you should have sex right away.'

Matt pushed the plunger through the coffee, watching the dark liquid swirl and surge through the filter.

'I don't reckon she'd say yes,' he said. 'I don't reckon she'd think it would be a very good idea. I mean like you say, I'm not exactly boyfriend material.'

'You could write her a poem,' Charlie suggested. 'Show her you're sensitive and romantic.'

Matt snorted a derisory laugh. 'I don't know, I've been writing bollocks for so long now that I'm not sure I could.'

'Tell you what,' Charlie said. 'You write her a poem and I'll write Emily a poem and we can read each other's and see if they are bad or not, and if they aren't too bad we'll give them to them on the same day and ask them out. Like a pact.'

'A suicide pact?' Matt joked, but he saw that the boy was deadly serious and he remembered for a moment what it was like to be Charlie's age, when anything was possible and the future was place waiting to be filled with dreams come true. 'You know what?' he said, holding out his hand. 'Let's do it.'

Charlie spat in his palm, took Matt's hand and shook it.

'Deal,' he said.

'Cool,' Matt replied. 'But the spitting was a bit over the top, mate.'

'Hannah?' Ellen knelt down beside the bed so that her face was level with her sister's. 'Hannah? Wake up, sis, you need to eat.'

Hannah stirred, mumbling something unintelligible, moaning as she rolled over, turning her back on Ellen, reminding her of the days when it had been her job to drag her teenage sister out of bed and coax her to go to school.

'Hans, Hannah – wake up, come on now.' Gingerly Ellen shook Hannah's shoulder, the bruises left by someone's fingers still visible, scared of hurting her again.

Slowly, stiffly, Hannah rolled on to her back and opened her eyes, although only one was able to open completely. She turned her head and looked at Ellen.

'Ellen?' she whispered through dry cracked lips. 'Are you here?'

'Yes,' Ellen said awkwardly. She had no idea how reconcile her feelings, the fury that she still felt every time she looked at Hannah because of what her sister had done to her, and the pity and horror at what she had been through. Ellen felt she needed to be two people, or have two sisters, to be able to slip through a hole in time and exist in two parallel universes simultaneously. She had no idea how to handle this. There was no choice but to take it second by second. 'Charlie ran off this morning; we had a bit of a disagreement and he came round here. I wasn't sure what you would say to him.'

Ellen thought Hannah might have frowned, but her features were immobilised by swelling. 'You thought I'd tell him about me and Nick?'

Ellen felt as if Hannah had slapped her in the face. She hadn't been making it up then; Ellen hadn't imagined it. It really was true.

'You didn't tell me before exactly what happened between you and Nick,' Ellen said steadily. 'And I need to know before I drive myself mad, was it a one-off thing? Were you drunk – where did it happen?'

With some difficulty Hannah turned to look at her.

'It wasn't a one-off thing . . . it was a relationship. We were together for about a year.'

Ellen pressed the back of her hand to her mouth to stifle the wave of nausea that swept over her. She nodded, gesturing to Hannah to go on.

'You know that I never really liked Nick, not when I first met him. I thought he was pompous and overbearing and that he was changing you. I always thought you were so cool, so together and then Nick came along and . . . you weren't my big sis any more, you were Mrs Ellen Woods, his wife. Your whole life was about being his wife.'

Ellen didn't say anything, she couldn't.

'Then we were at a family thing, a Christmas thing and I'd been feeling a bit down. You know, another new year coming up and still no Mr Right. I was in Mum and Dad's kitchen knocking back the Baileys and he came in. He asked me what was up. I can't remember what I said, something rude probably, telling him where to go and he just leaned over and kissed me. Not a massive snog or anything, just a kiss on the lips and he said that no woman like me should be alone. That's when it started, although I tried I tried to stay away, that's when I started to see him, when I started to fall for him.'

Hannah paused and reached for the glass of stale water by her bed. Her voice was paper-dry.

'I tried to stay away from him, I swear. I suddenly got it. I suddenly got how much you loved him and what he saw in me. He saw the good in me and I knew that's why you loved him so much. And I never, never wanted to . . . but then one night he just turned up at the flat. It was dark and raining and he just turned up here. He stood there on the doorstep in the rain just looking at me and then we . . . we kissed. He said he'd tried to stay away too, he'd tried but he couldn't. He said he needed me. It started then and I . . . I loved him, Ellen, I loved him and he loved me too. We were going to tell you. We were going to face up to it all and be together until . . . The last year, it's been hell because I've had to grieve for him in secret, knowing how I've betrayed you. Torn between wanting to be near you, with you and Charlie, and running away so that you two never found out what I'd done.'

'But If Nick hadn't died, if you two had run off together, Charlie would have found out then. You can't have cared about that.'

Ellen watched for a second as Hannah struggled to sit up and then she hooked her arms under Hannah's and helped her to rise, plumping pillows behind her to support her back.

'I did, I thought about it all the time and so did Nick. We worried and worried about it. Nick never wanted to hurt Charlie or you. If it had been up to him he would have left it as it was. Living at home with you, coming round to me two or three times a week. If I hadn't been so selfish I would have been able to live with that, but I'm not like you, Ellen. I'm not the sort of person who can live on the sidelines. I wanted to be everything to him, so I forced his hand. I gave him an ultimatum. I told him he had to choose, either me or you. Just before he died he promised that it was going to be me, that he just wanted to wait a few more weeks and then we'd be together. We decided we'd talk to you together and then he'd talk to Charlie. I made him promise that he'd look after you, financially. That you'd be able to keep the house and he'd make sure you were comfortable.'

'How big of you,' Ellen said, coolly. Hannah burst into a splutter of painful-sounding coughs, clasping her ribs with each spasm.

'I know what it sounds like,' she said. 'I know that I sound like a heartless bitch, but, Ellen, nobody ever loved me the way he did. No one ever looked at me the way he did. He made me feel so special, so beautiful.'

'Yes, he was good at that,' Ellen said bitterly. Hannah had recited almost word for word what she had told Allegra about her husband only a few days ago.

'I know you loved him,' Hannah went on. 'And I know he loved you too once. But people change and grow apart.'

'I know that he changed me,' Ellen said. 'I know that he stopped me in my tracks at a point in my life when I could have been anything or anyone, and he made me into someone who was just his wife. He would have changed you too, Hannah, in the end.'

'Well, perhaps I needed changing,' Hannah told her. 'I mean, look at my life without him. Look at what happens to me when I'm left alone.'

Ellen straightened and stood up. 'This, this is not your fault. This has nothing to do with Nick.'

Hannah nodded, silent for a moment. 'What do we do now? Is this the last time I see you and Charlie?'

Ellen looked at her sister. 'Charlie can't ever know about this,' she said. 'Whatever Nick was, he was a good father and Charlie adored him. We can never let him have a reason to think differently about his father.'

'And what about you?' Hannah asked her.

'I loved Nick, I loved being his wife and if I hadn't found out about you then I suppose I always would have. You've taken that away from me, Hannah, I can never get that back.'

Hannah turned her face away. 'I know. I never meant to tell you, I wouldn't have if—'

'But I'm glad I know,' Ellen interrupted her. 'I think I needed to see the life I had with Nick the way it actually was, not the way I thought it was. I don't think he was a bad man, I think he was just a man who wanted it all, and all his way, and I let him get away with that. Maybe you wouldn't have, but then again maybe you would. There's no way of knowing now. But at least now I can go forward again, knowing that the best part of my life isn't over, that it's yet to come . . . And one day, so can you.'

Hannah turned back to look Ellen in the eye.

'Can you ever forgive me, Ellen, will it ever be like it used to be between us again? When we were girls and you used to hold my hand till I went to sleep.'

'I love you, Hannah, that's all I can tell you right now. And I won't let you deal with this on your own.'

As Hannah began to sob, Ellen put her arms around her and pulled her into her embrace.

'I keep trying not to . . . not to think about it but every time I close my eyes it comes back in flashbacks, a little bit more each time and . . . Ellen, what if I've caught something, what if I'm pregnant? I'm so scared.'

Ellen held her sister for a long time, rocking her back and forth, letting her tears soak through her clothes. Then she gently pushed Hannah away a little so that she could look into her eyes.

'We have to face this. We have to get you the help you need, get you emergency contraception and tested and . . . Hannah, you were beaten and raped,' she said with deliberate blunt force. 'You can't think that it doesn't matter, or that you deserve what's happened to you, because of Nick – because it does matter and you don't deserve it. You need to go to hospital and get properly checked out, get proper care, and you need to report it to the police. Because if they've done it once, they'll do it again. You are the only person who might be able to stop that happening. I know it will be horrible and hard but I think you need to do this for your own sake, and I promise you I will be there every step of the way. Because I love you and I can't stand that this has happened to you and you think that it's just something you'll get over, like a bad cold, or . . .'

'Someone dying?' A tear rolled down Hannah's damaged cheek.

'Will you go to hospital?' Ellen asked her. After a moment Hannah nodded once.

'Right. Now, we're getting some coffee into you and some food, and then we're going to casualty to get you checked over and we're going to report this to the police. We have to, Hannah, there is no other choice.'

'But there's no evidence,' Hannah said. 'I got changed, I had a bath.'

Ellen thought of the bundle of clothes that remained unwashed at her house.

'There is evidence.'

'They'll think I deserved it, that I'm a drunk and a slut,' Hannah sobbed with such feeling that Ellen almost reached out and touched her. Instead she sat down on the bed, trying to calm her with quiet words.

'Maybe, maybe that's the way you think too. But whatever happened, Hannah, you *don't* deserve to feel that way. Maybe it is impossible to catch the people that did this to you but if you don't do something, tell someone, get some help, then you will always feel that way. And I don't want that for you.'

'Saint Ellen,' Hannah whispered, a tiny smile pulling at the corners of her mouth.

'No,' Ellen said. 'Just Ellen – Ellie. Just me again. For the first time in a long time, I'm just being me.'

Chapter Twenty

'I will never surrender!' Eliza cried as the Royalist soldier knocked her off her horse and sent her sprawling to the ground.

'You'll do a lot more than that before I've finished with you, my pretty,' he sneered, sliding off his horse and standing over her in the mud. Eliza glared at him.

'Do your worst,' she challenged him. Licking his lips he glanced around, and seeing no other gate guard was nearby, he shrugged and decided to give himself a treat with the Puritan vixen.

Holding her breath Eliza waited, her hand clenched around the hilt of Captain Parker's dagger, hidden in the folds of her torn and dirty skirt. The soldier knelt astride her, assuming that she was powerless to resist, and looked down at her in the moonlight.

'Pretty little thing, ain't—' But before he could finish his sentence Eliza thrust the dagger upwards between his legs into a man's most vulnerable spot. He howled with pain, sending the horses bolting for cover. In the distance she could hear his fellow guards shouting, evidently having heard his cries. Twisting the blade before she pulled it out, Eliza toppled his weight off her and scrambled to her feet, taking a moment to look at him curled up, sobbing in pain.

'Never mind, you might not ever bed a woman again, but I hear the King is very fond of falsetto,' she told him, kicking him in the ribs for good

measure as the noise of the oncoming soldiers drew near. Her stolen mount abandoned, she ran for the cover of the shadows under the trees, the bright moonlight now seeming more of a curse than a boon.

Eliza gasped when she found out what awaited her in the dense dark shadows. She felt a hand close gently over her mouth, and when she breathed in she knew who stood beside her. It was Captain Parker.

'Madame, I was just on the verge of rescuing you,' he breathed into her ear. 'But it seems you are perfectly capable of rescuing yourself.'

Eliza made to reply, but the captain kept his hand firmly clamped. She saw the soldiers were upon them, only a few feet away, having come to the aid of their injured colleague. She felt the captain's other arm encircle her waist and pull her body close to his. Eliza fought the urge to lean back against his muscular torso – how could she long for a man that she hated so? Even now, even after he had enabled her escape from the noose, she could not forget his lustful behaviour, and how it had ruined her quiet and peaceful life. They stood in silence, body to body, until the guards hauled the screaming man over a horse and led him away, and they remained there for several minutes after all was quiet again. It was the captain who spoke first.

'Milady, it seems that you have made good your escape,' he whispered, nuzzling against her neck. Eliza stepped away from him.

'Only for now. I need a mount and a change of clothes, for I cannot travel to London dressed as a woman.'

'London?' The captain looked startled. 'You will not make it there, Eliza. No, I have a plan. I have a small house a little north of Cambridge. I will disguise you and take you there and you will live out the rest of the war posing as my maidservant. When the war is won, I shall return and marry you.'

'I will not and you shall not,' Eliza told him hotly. 'If I was once the marrying kind I am not now, Captain. And if I was once the maidservant kind I am not now – and both of these things I owe to you. Besides, when the war is won I think you will most likely find your head on a spike over Traitors' Gate.'

'Well, we cannot stand here and argue,' the captain said, taking her hand. 'Come with me, I know a place where we can rest the night and find fresh horses.' He hauled her up behind him on to his mount, forcing Eliza to wind her arms around him so as not to become unseated.

She must have been more exhausted than she realised, because it wasn't long before the rhythm of the horse and the heat of the captain's body lulled her to sleep. She wasn't sure how long she had been sleeping when she awoke in his arms as he gently laid her on a pile of hay.

'No!' she said, scrambling away from him. 'No, no man shall ever touch me without my consent again. You've seen what I do to those who try – you would be no exception.'

'I don't doubt it,' the captain said, lighting an oil lamp and setting it carefully away from the tinder of dry hay. 'Eliza, I helped you escape because you are right, I brought you to this. But also for another reason, because I love you. You are the fiercest, bravest, most wonderful woman I have ever had the pleasure to meet. I don't expect you ever to love me back – how could you after our dark beginning? – but I knew I had to find a way to let you live, and a way to tell you that you have changed me. You have made me into a man who can love, even if it is only one woman who will ever claim that prize, and even if it is the very woman who will never love me back. I did not suppose you would let me take you away and hide you in my house, let alone marry you. But I had dared to hope.'

Suddenly Eliza pulled out the dagger and quick as a flash held it at the captain's throat.

'Breathe without my permission and I'll kill you,' she told him.

'I believe you,' the captain said, holding her gaze.

'Lie down,' Eliza instructed him, pushing him back into the hay. She looked him up and down, a slight smile playing around her lips as she

grabbed a handful of his shirt. Inserting the blade of the dagger between its
fastenings, she ripped it open, baring his chest to her gaze.

'You will do exactly what I tell you,' Eliza informed him.

'I believe I will,' the captain said.

'Well, it certainly is different,' Allegra said thoughtfully once Ellen had stopped reading. 'It's not at all the sort of ending that my readers will be expecting . . .'

'I know,' Ellen said. 'And of course I only did it for fun. After we got back from the hospital that night, it had been such a difficult day, my mind was racing and I couldn't make my heart slow down. I needed to take my mind off everything that had happened, because I could feel the panic there in the corner, just waiting for me to fixate on something and fall apart.'

She thought of the journey that she and Hannah had made to St Mary's Hospital in Paddington a couple of days before. Charlie and Matt had wanted to come too. Despite wishing to have them with her, Ellen was determined to protect Charlie from finding out anything more, at least yet. She had persuaded Matt to take Charlie home, but only after he had installed both women in a black taxi, whispering in Ellen's ear, 'Remember you are in the safest place in the world,' as he secured her seat belt.

Ellen had clutched on to the bright yellow handlebar as the cab pulled away, struggling to control her breathing, but she looked at her sister and she forced herself to be calm, reaching out and covering the clenched hand that Hannah rested on the seat with her own. Once they had arrived at A&E Hannah had hung back, while Ellen bypassed the queue at reception to stop a nurse and tell her why she had brought her sister in. Within minutes she and Hannah found themselves in a private room with a female doctor, who gently asked Hannah several questions and then asked permission to examine her. Ellen held her hand as the examination took place, keeping her eyes on her sister's face as the tears streamed silently down Hannah's battered cheeks. They had stayed there for hours, until two women police officers arrived and took Hannah's statement. Ellen told them about the clothes that she still had at home and they told her they'd check the CCTV footage of the places that Hannah could remember visiting on that ill-starred day.

After the ordeal was finally over Ellen and Hannah had stood at the hospital exit for a long time clinging on to each other, wanting neither to step back inside or go outside. 'Matt said he'd come to collect us,' Ellen reassured herself as much as her sister. 'He'll be here in a minute.'

'This is hard for you, isn't it? All these people, all this noise and the smell. Especially here. I know how much you hate hospitals.'

'This is living hell,' Ellen told her candidly. 'I don't want to be here a single second more, but I wouldn't leave you here either.'

'I never told you how sorry I was, after you lost the baby and everything else that happened. I never told you that I cried for you – I knew how much you wanted more children. I wish I'd told you that I cried for you.'

Ellen smiled wanly at Hannah. 'I wish you'd told me that too, it would have helped.' She took a deep breath of hot exhaust-heavy air. 'I had to come here to identify Nick, you know. They brought me that afternoon to come and look at him. All the way here I was praying, praying that they'd got it wrong because I just couldn't imagine him not being alive . . . it was impossible. I was so certain that they'd got it wrong, I don't think I took it seriously until I saw him. I remember there was someone outside laughing in the corridor. I remember wondering why they didn't shut up. Of thinking how is it possible that life can go on for anyone when it's stopped for me. Maybe that's when I decided that I didn't ever want to go out again. Maybe it was then.'

'You went through all of that alone,' Hannah said, linking her arm through Ellen's.

'I don't think there is really any other way to do it.'

'If it helps you, even though everything that just happened was so awful and so horrifying, I feel better. I feel like I've done something about it. I mean I hurt like fuck and it's no fun having three broken ribs, but . . . thank you. I must be the worst sister in the world.'

Ellen did not look at her. Instead, as she saw Matt's face in the window of a nearing cab, she simply said, 'But I love you, I'll keep on loving you. How can I do anything else?'

'Will you drop me off at my place?' Hannah had asked.

'Don't be an idiot,' Ellen told her. 'You are coming home with me. Where else would you go?'

When they got back Sabine had helped Ellen get Hannah into her bed. Allegra prepared soup while Charlie fussed over his aunt, even offering to lend her his DS. After encouraging Charlie to go to a friend's, Ellen had sat with her sister and spoon-fed her until the new pain medication she had been given kicked in, and for the first time in a long time Hannah looked almost relaxed.

'You know,' she murmured sleepily, 'I think I knew that Nick would never choose me, I knew that he would drag me down and hurt me, but it didn't matter, nothing mattered. I just wanted to be loved and he loved me. Maybe it was all a game to him, and maybe he never meant it, but he made me believe that he loved me and I thought I needed that more than anything else. That's all I've been clinging to ever since.'

'I felt the same as you, once,' Ellen said as her sister drifted off into a mercilessly painless sleep. 'Now I'm not so sure.'

A succession of dark images and shadows paraded through her mind after she had gone to bed, threatening to engulf her at any minute. Unable to sleep in the unfamiliar box room, Ellen had got up and gone downstairs to the kitchen, half hoping, half expecting Matt would be there, but it was empty. She had taken her writing pad out of the drawer it had languished in for the last year, sat down and wrote. She wrote to keep the tigers at bay. For the whole of Sunday she had concentrated on making Hannah as comfortable as possible and readjusting her mind once again to change. But she'd been aware of the notepad, sitting in that drawer, her words waiting to be read. Now Monday morning had come she felt a little embarrassed that she had ever thought her amateur offering was fit even for Allegra's scrap-paper pile, but still her new life was not about sitting on fences, it was about grabbing thistles – and Allegra could be a particularly thorny one.

'So anyway,' Ellen continued her explanation. 'Normally when I felt so frazzled I would read one of your books, but I was so desperate to know what happened to Eliza that I thought I'd write my own version. I mean why should Eliza have to get rescued, why should she always be the helpless victim? After everything she'd been through she'd be a stronger, worldlier woman, wouldn't she? I think she would, anyway, and it worked, writing did make the panic go away. It all seems a bit foolish now. I only read it to you because I thought you'd think it was funny. So, let's start work on the real ending. I know that Simon is anxiously awaiting the next Allegra Howard.'

'Yes he is, he always is,' Allegra said. 'And I think I might have found her.'

'Huh?' Ellen asked her.

'Ellen, haven't you noticed that it's not really me who's written this book at all, it's you? You had a vision for how it should be, it was your thoughts and ideas that shaped the characters and the plot. In truth this book really belongs to you.'

'To me?' Ellen laughed. 'Allegra, that's so silly. All I've done is a lot of typing and had a few thoughts. I've been here listening to you telling the tale, weaving the words together to make a story. I can't possibly do that!'

'But you've just proved that you can,' Allegra said, nodding at the sheets of lined paper filled with Ellen's scrawl. 'That ending was as well written as anything I could have done. It's not the right ending for my book, my readers would have massive heart attacks, but it could be the right ending for *a* book – for your book.' Allegra tapped a long finger against her thigh.

'No, I'm not a writer, I'm just me, Ellen Woods. I read books, I don't write them. I can't do that, Allegra, it's too hard and too late now. You are very sweet to be so nice about my efforts, but I know my limitations.'

'Do you want to know my real name?' Allegra asked her.

'Um, I do, don't I?' Ellen was confused.

'Joan Fisher,' Allegra stated. 'My real name is Joan Fisher. I wasn't born Allegra Howard. I was born Joan Fisher, daughter of a dentist, who grew up in Hull. I am Joan Fisher who just about scraped through secretarial college and got a job in a bank, who got married at the age of twenty-three in 1960 to Graham

Howard, who gave up work and moved into a semi in Surbiton and spent the next ten years keeping house, cooking, wearing an apron, letting all the fun and frolics of the sixties pass me by while I read and daydreamed and waited for children. But children never came and in 1972 Graham Howard told me he was in love with another man. Another man, Ellen. He said he couldn't hide his true feelings from me any more, that he loved me but he would never love me in that way. We agreed that we would stay married, and perhaps adopt a baby. That he would have his life and I would have mine and we wouldn't ask questions.' Allegra smiled faintly. 'Graham was a lovely, kind man. He never wanted to hurt me, and at first I thought I would be happy with that. I'd lived one way for so long that I thought I would be . . . content. And then one morning I woke up alone and I realised that I was never going to be happy stuck in my semi in Surbiton married to a man who felt more passionate about my Biba knee-high boots than he did about me. So I changed my life. It's a long story, there were many ups and downs, mistakes and triumphs, but at the end of it all I had become Allegra Howard, romantic novelist. Simon's father gave me my first book deal at Cherished Desires and I divorced Graham in 1978. By 1980 I was published in nineteen different languages. I changed my life, Ellen, I changed who I was, from the inside out. But the most important thing is that I didn't change *from* the real me into someone false and made up. I changed *into* the real me, the person I was always supposed to be. It's a cliché, but I found myself, and rather wonderful I turned out to be too.'

'Wow,' Ellen said. 'I had no idea, I just thought that you were always you.'

'No one arrives in this world, like Aphrodite, born from the sea, the image of perfection. It's a struggle to become yourself, to find the path in life that is going to afford you the greatest satisfaction and joy. Many people never try, they simply let their lives dwindle away down whichever path they start from, and for some that is enough. But it wasn't for me and it shouldn't be for you, Ellen. There is so much more to you than you realise. I see a lot of me in you, and you are like a butterfly who's been trapped in a jam jar. Now is your time to be free, to spread your wings and find yourself. And besides, you'd be doing me a huge favour. I've been trying to retire for years, but each year Simon persuades me to write just a few more books while he's looking for the "next Allegra Howard". I keep telling him I'll be dead soon. I'm tired of writing about beautiful half-naked nineteen-year-olds. I want the chance to write something for myself, something about a woman my age – something for my own vanity and pleasure.'

'So you want me to take over as Allegra Howard?' Ellen asked, her head spinning with thoughts and feelings that hadn't quite connected yet. 'To become you?'

'Good God, no, darling. Let's not try running before we can walk.' Allegra shook her head. 'Firstly you should get all the credit – or otherwise – for whatever you write in your own right. And I don't see you as writing carbon copies of my books, I think you have many more modern and forward-thinking ideas than I do. And secondly I've earned this name, it belongs to me, I would never simply give it away. Even to someone I am as fond of as you. It took me a long time to become myself, Ellen, and I intend to hold on to that until I'm ashes in the ground.'

'Yes, but – Ellen Woods, romantic novelist. Somehow it doesn't sound quite right, does it?'

'Of course not, it's not nearly grand enough. You'll need to make something up. Try a porn-star-name formula. Your first pet's name combined with the street name where you were born, that's a good one.'

'Well, we had this long-eared rabbit called Velvet and we lived on Waters Crescent, so that would make me . . . Velvet Waters,' Ellen said uncertainly. 'It does sound more like a porn-star name than a writer's name,'

'It might be a little tacky,' Allegra mused. 'You need a name that sums you up as the kind of woman who writes powerful, sexy women in charge, historical romantic fiction.'

'Then what about my name?'

'I thought we agreed . . .'

'No, not Ellen – Ellie. I always used to be Ellie. I still am Ellie. Ellie Woods, that's the name of the person who goes places, has sexual adventures and who laughs. Ellie Woods, that's who I am.'

'Perfect.' Allegra smiled at her. 'Now all you need to do is have an idea, write a proposal and we'll show it to Simon and get you started on your first book. You'll have to write it in between helping me put together my magnum opus, of course, but that shouldn't be a problem – you seem to have a fondness for staying up all night anyway.' She smiled knowingly.

'*That's* all I need to do? That's *all* I need to do!' Ellen exclaimed. 'Allegra, life is not that simple. I can't just have an idea . . .'

'You can if you try. Oh, I don't know, start thinking of one.'

'I have no clue how to write a proposal . . .'

'I'll help you,' Allegra told her.

'And I wouldn't have the first idea how to start writing a book.'

'Why not? You've read thousands of them, you've had plenty of ideas for *The Sword Erect*. Why couldn't you put all of that insight and imagination into your own project?'

Ellen hesitated. She couldn't think of a reason why not right then, except that it seemed so . . . outlandish, as if Allegra were suggesting she take up time travel or flying to the moon.

'Well, Simon will never take me seriously, not as a writer – why would he?'

'Because he knows you, he knows how good you are at your job and how much you bring to a book, how much creativity and vision you've brought to my book. And he is no fool, he wouldn't let a talent like yours pass him by.'

'A talent like mine?' Ellen blinked.

'You heard me correctly,' Allegra told her. 'Now we have to think about getting Ellie into print and me off the hook.'

Ellen sat perfectly still behind Allegra's desk, attempting to pull together in her mind the pieces of information that Allegra had thrown at her. Could she really do this? Could she really have an idea and write a book? She felt a giddying sense of excitement at the idea, a childhood dream that she had always assumed would be impossible to realise, but could she have been wrong? After all, if the great Allegra Howard believed she was capable, then . . . well, she might be, mightn't she?

'I suppose I have always been fascinated with the early settlers in America, you know, the pilgrims on the *Mayflower*,' Ellen mused. 'I wrote my dissertation on it.'

'Perfect,' Allegra told her. 'Then you'd have the American market in your sights too.'

'I suppose I could try and think of something, a, you know – a plot or something to weave around the history.'

'I suppose you could, you could take a chance, do something a little different, take a risk and see if it just might change your life for ever.' Allegra's smile was warm but brief. 'Now, as for my book – I have my ending ready and I think you'll agree it is rather splendid. Let's get it typed into the computer and finally deliver *The Sword Erect* to Simon. The poor man will die of shock when he realises that I've actually finished at last. Although hopefully not before he's paid me.'

'You first,' Matt said, as he and Charlie sat on a bench in the park behind the house.

'Well, I thought you should go first, because you are an actual writer,' Charlie said, fingering a grubby piece of folded paper that looked like it had been ripped out of an exercise book.

'Which is why you should go first,' Matt told him, tapping the closed lid of his laptop. 'I don't want you to feel intimidated by my skill.'

'Ha.' Charlie rolled his eyes. 'Coward.'

'Look, just read me what you've got and let's get on with this. Neither of us want anyone to see us sitting in a park talking about poetry, right?'

'Right,' Charlie said, glancing over at a group of his mates who were kicking a ball around nearby. Sighing, he unfolded his piece of paper and flattened it on his thigh.

'In the sunshine your hair looks like honey,

Running down the handle of a spoon.

And your skin as smooth and soft as the petal of a rose.

I like the way you laugh, like you don't care what anybody
   thinks.

And I wish that I could be more like you.'

Hastily Charlie folded up his paper and stuffed it in his pocket.

'It doesn't rhyme and I'm not sure about the last line, because maybe she might think that I want to be a girl and that makes me look a bit gay.'

Matt said nothing for a moment and then he clapped his hand firmly on his laptop lid.

'That's it, I'm not reading you mine,' he said. 'Yours is a million times better.'

'Really?' Charlie seemed appalled at the idea.

'Yeah, yours is simple and heartfelt with imagery and shit. Mine is bollocks. I'm not reading it to you.'

'You have to, that's the deal!' Charlie protested, eyeing Matt's laptop as if he were considering snatching it.

Sighing, Matt flipped open the top of his laptop, angling the screen away from Charlie so he would not be able to read over his shoulder. He looked at it for a second, opened his mouth as if he were about to speak and then slammed it shut.

'No, sorry, Charlie. I know it was the deal. But the thing is, your mum, she makes me feel all weird and a bit soppy. This poem sucks, I can't ever show it to anyone. Not you and especially not your mother. She'd laugh me out of town.'

'But are you still going to ask her out?'

'Are you still going to ask Emily out?' Matt hedged.

'I am if you are,' Charlie said. 'But now you've chickened out of the poem thing you have to do it first. You have to do it tonight.'

'Tonight?' Matt shook his head. 'You don't impose a deadline on a man about to make a romantic declaration, mate. It's an organic thing, you have to bide your time, wait for the right moment.'

'Tonight,' Charlie insisted. 'When we get back. Like how hard is it to go up to my mum and say, "Ellen, would you like to go out with me?" How hard is that?'

Matt shifted uncomfortably on the bench. Never before had he hesitated about asking a woman out, in fact he'd asked a good many women out without giving it a second, or on some occasions, a first thought. But this time it was different, it was very different. It mattered if Ellen turned him down. If Ellen turned him down then he'd… Matt didn't want to think about it.

'You do it tonight, I'll do it tomorrow. After music. Deal?' Charlie held out his hand and fixed Matt with his steady blue gaze.

'It's great being nearly twelve,' Matt said as he shook on the deal. 'Everything's black or white, right or wrong, deal or no deal. Life is so simple.'

Charlie sighed. 'All I can say is that you must have a very bad memory.'

Chapter Twenty-One

Ellen and Hannah stood in the kitchen doorway, each with a cup of coffee in their hand.

'So you don't even want to go down there?' Hannah asked, nodding at the untidy rear of the garden, ablaze with colour.

'I didn't, I didn't have the impulse to go anywhere, but now – I want to go. I just . . . can't.'

'We could hold hands,' Hannah offered. 'Like you did with Matt when you came to rescue me. Or wouldn't that be quite the same thing?'

Ellen gave her sister a warning sideways glance, but it was accompanied by a small smile. It was good that Hannah was here, it was good that they were talking again, that Hannah was able to tease her ever so gently. Ellen only wished she could remember why they had stopped talking like this in the first place.

'When I came over to yours I was pumped up full of adrenalin and still half drunk, most likely. Matt more or less dragged me there, talking all sorts of nonsense on the way to keep my mind off things. Now I don't feel like that, I feel . . . OK.'

'So feeling OK means you can't get to the bottom of the garden?' Hannah said. 'Freaky.'

'Yeah, thanks, sis, freaky – that sums up my condition perfectly,' Ellen said mildly. 'If I tried now the world would turn inside out, I'd have a panic attack and you'd have to scrape a gasping, gibbering wreck up off the patio. It's quite something that I'm standing here with the door open, and that I'm thinking what fun it would be to take a strimmer to that grass and sort my plants from the weeds. That's progress – after all, I've haven't got my hands dirty in quite a while.'

'That's not what I heard,' Hannah muttered into her coffee.

'I beg your pardon?' Ellen asked her.

'Nothing.' Hannah paused and then shrugged. 'It's just Sabine happened to mention in a bid to cheer me up that she'd found a pair of panties in the plastic-bag drawer, that didn't belong to her or Allegra.'

'Oh, I forgot about those!' Ellen exclaimed before she could clap her hand over her mouth. 'How embarrassing.'

'So?' Hannah asked. 'Come on, it's your duty to spill. Take *my* mind off things. What happened between you and Matt that meant your undies ended up . . . off?'

Ellen hesitated. The truth was, she was desperate to talk to somebody about what had happened, so she could make sense of it herself – but she wasn't sure it should be Hannah, not when why it had happened in the first place was mostly because of her. And yet . . . yet maybe Hannah was exactly the right person.

'I'd just found out about you and my husband,' Ellen told her. 'I was angry and drunk and I just wanted to be seen again. The way that Nick used to see me, the way that Matt sometimes looked at me. So I waited for him to come in and I threw myself at him in the most unseemly way. And for about a minute or two it, we . . . well, it was pretty exciting, and then I realised what was about to happen, and Matt sensed I wasn't sure and he developed the most annoying conscience about it all and was so gentlemanly and sweet. So my knickers came off but that was about it, really.'

'Wow,' Hannah said. 'Matt's gorgeous. I would.'

'Well, we all know *you* would,' Ellen said before she could stop herself.

There was an awkward silence between the two women. Since arriving back from the hospital neither of them had mentioned what had happened with Nick, in some unspoken pact or truce. But Ellen supposed they couldn't go on like that, not if they were ever to be really close again. There was no point in shying away from it. Hannah and Nick had had an affair, Nick might have even loved Hannah – there was no way of knowing now. And somehow Ellen had to live with that, she had to accept it, just as Hannah had to accept that the man she had fallen for would never ever belong to her.

'I've hurt you so badly,' Hannah said, turning away from the garden and retreating inside to sit at the table, as if she were the one who was suddenly afraid. 'I don't know how you can even stand to look at me, Ellie, let alone have me here.'

Ellen followed her inside and sat down too. 'The only reason I find it hard to look at you is because of the state of your face. When I think about what happened to you . . .' She paused as Hannah turned her face away, aware that her sister was not ready to think about that yet, perhaps not ever. 'The odd thing is, Hannah, now I'm over the shock and the anger I don't hate you, in fact I'm sort of grateful to you.'

'Grateful?' Hannah looked up at her, perplexed.

'You've given me the key to moving on. I was stuck with this

382

memory of my marriage, a perfect, happy, loving marriage – but it wasn't like that. It wasn't bad, it wasn't awful – as far as I knew. But it wasn't perfect either. Whether he meant to or not Nick diluted me, he watered me down. He made me dependent on him and he spent so much time caring for me that when he'd gone I could barely care for myself, let alone Charlie. I loved him, I loved him with all my heart and he was the best dad that Charlie could have ever had and I miss him and I'll still grieve for Charlie, for the family life that he had and he lost. But I can move on now, I can be myself again, once I've worked out exactly who I am. And I think if it hadn't been for you telling me what you did, it would have taken a lot longer. So yes, I am sort of grateful to you.'

Hannah nodded, chewing the tip of her thumb, waiting for a wave of emotion to pass before she could speak.

'I miss Nick,' she whispered, tears streaming over her bruises. 'I've missed him so much for every second of the last year. I'd watch you getting all the flowers and the sympathy and I'd want to shout, "What about me? He loved me, you know. I lost him too!" But I couldn't, so I just tried to be close to the nearest thing I had to him, to you and Charlie. But the more time I spent with you the more I realised that what I had with him . . . it was nothing compared to the life he had with you and his son. And the more I came round the more annoyed you seemed to get with me for being there. I used to think that you knew, that you'd found out somehow but hadn't told anyone. Do you think you sensed it, sensed something was wrong?'

'I doubt it,' Ellen said. 'I don't think I could sense anything very much for most of the last year. I think I was just caught up in all the pain. I don't suppose I wanted to share it.'

'I was jealous of your pain, jealous of you,' Hannah said thoughtfully. 'Just like I always have been since we were little girls.'

'Jealous of me?' Ellen exclaimed. 'Don't be so ridiculous.'

'Why on earth wouldn't I be jealous of my beautiful, clever, kind big sister who everybody always admired, always said was so lovely, such a wonderful mother with such a wonderful family. And then there's me, going from one bad relationship to the next, always single, living alone, working all hours because I had no one to go home to. Of course I was jealous of you.'

Ellen laughed. 'Well, that's just crazy – because I was always jealous of you. Younger, thinner, prettier, with your life all sorted – direction, a career – your independence. I felt old and frumpy and useless next to you.'

The two sisters regarded each other across the kitchen table, and after a moment Hannah extended her hand tentatively. Ellen looked at it for a second, and then covered it with her own.

'Hey,' Hannah said. 'Do you remember that time when Charlie was about five and he lost his favourite bear down the park . . . what was it called?'

'Midnight,' Ellen recalled. 'Black fluffy thing. He couldn't eat, sleep or even go to the loo without it. I told Nick not to let him take it out of the house, but he was insistent. Said it would be fine. Typical Nick, he always thought everything would be fine.'

'And they came back an hour later, with Charlie howling his head off because Midnight was lost and they couldn't find him anywhere. I was here, why was I here?'

'Because Mum and Dad were coming up for the weekend,' Ellen reminded her.

'I just remember Charlie sitting at this table asking you if

384

Midnight was dead and you said don't be so silly, he's just gone on a little trip to visit Father Christmas. You said he'd be back on Christmas Day. And suddenly Charlie stopped crying and he was all smiles again, laughing about what fun Midnight would be having with the elves. You made everything all right.'

'Until I found out that they didn't make Midnights any more and he was obsolete,' Ellen said.

'We searched high and low for another of those blasted bears, didn't we?' Hannah laughed. 'And Christmas was getting closer and Charlie was getting more and more excited, and we couldn't find one anywhere and then . . .'

'And then you paid about ten times what it was worth for one on eBay,' Ellen remembered. 'You were so pleased with yourself, and I was so relieved.'

'So we spent ages writing a letter from Santa, explaining why Midnight looked so new and had his bow back again and that missing eye replaced with a new one . . .'

'And on Christmas Eve I crept into his room and laid Midnight on the pillow beside his head,' Ellen recalled. 'I don't think I'd ever been more excited about giving him a present.'

'And the next day . . . Charlie hardly noticed he was back. He didn't even play with him once. Because that was the Christmas he went off bears and on to train sets.'

The two sisters laughed.

'I can't keep up with how fast he's growing up,' Ellen said. 'It makes my head spin. It seems like five minutes since he was a tiny baby in my arms, or howling his head off over Midnight. And now here he is interested in girls, giving me advice, sorting *me* out.'

'He's a brilliant kid,' Hannah said.

'Yes he is,' Ellen agreed.

'So you're going to do what he wants, get some help – some treatment so that you can go down the bottom of the garden and weed again? Maybe even have al fresco sex with Matt?'

'Hannah! Poor Matt must be scared to death of me by now. I shouldn't think that will be on the cards again. And yes, yes – I am going to get help. I am going to get down to the bottom of the garden and out of the house again. I am.'

'Good,' Hannah said. 'Because then I'll be able to take you out and buy you some decent clothes at last.'

When the doorbell sounded Ellen assumed that it was Matt and Charlie come back from the park, even though both of them had a key. She was a little surprised to find a stranger standing there, a fair, shortish, stocky man in a pair of Bermuda shorts and flip-flops.

'Hello?' she said, eyeing him up and down.

'Hello, is Sabine here please?' he asked her. Ellen guessed his accent was German.

'She's not back from work yet, can I take a message?'

The man looked very disappointed. 'I'm Eric, Sabine's husband,' he explained.

'Oh, you!' Ellen was surprised. 'Aren't you supposed to be in Austria declaring your love to a married Catholic woman?'

'Oh, she told you about that then.' Eric's neck flushed bright red.

'Yes, she did.' Ellen nodded, crossing her arms. 'And can I just say that I think you are very lucky to have a woman like Sabine in your life and if I were you, I'd pick up your socks, cut back on the lap dancers, forget this Austrian and try your best to hang on to a really wonderful woman.'

'She showed you the list?' Eric looked supremely uncomfortable.

'All three categories,' Ellen confirmed.

'You're right,' Eric said. 'I know you are. Sabine told me to go to the woman I loved. So I did. I came to Sabine.' Just at that second the gate swung open and Sabine stood at the top of the path, staring at her husband. 'Sabine is the woman that I love, and I don't deserve her but I hope she might reconsider leaving me.'

'Ask her yourself?' Ellen suggested, nodding over his shoulder.

Eric turned and saw Sabine. His face lit up. 'Sabine! I came to tell you that you are the woman I love, and that I've been a fool. I want you back, Sabine.'

'You treacherous, stinking, hideous pig,' Sabine said as she marched down the path. And then she kissed him.

'Blimey,' Matt said as he and Charlie arrived a few seconds later. 'It's all go here.'

'Love is in the air, that's why,' Charlie said pointedly, winking at his mother as he walked past the embracing couple as if it were a sight he saw every day.

'Random bloke?' Matt asked Ellen.

'Returning husband,' Ellen explained, before calling to the couple. 'Do come in if you fancy a cup of tea?'

They did not break their embrace to reply.

When Ellen made her way back into the kitchen she found that Hannah had been joined by Allegra, Charlie and Matt. Allegra was making herself a pot of Earl Grey tea.

'I do believe I have finished my book,' Allegra stated, smiling at Ellen. 'Normally I like to celebrate with a bottle of vintage champagne, but we are in Shepherds Bush and needs must, so Earl Grey it is. I telephoned Simon to tell him, and all about our plans for you, my dear. He was very excited.'

'What plans?' Charlie and Matt asked simultaneously.

'Oh it's nothing,' Ellen muttered.

'It's *everything*. I have discovered that your mother has a rare gift for writing that if nurtured correctly might one day almost rival mine. So I intend to turn Ellie Woods here into the next big publishing sensation!' Allegra declared. 'I do so love a challenge.'

'Cool!' Charlie exclaimed.

'Brilliant,' Matt said, smiling steadily at Ellen. He wondered how it was possible that she could seem even more beautiful every time he looked at her. She was like a flower blossoming before his eyes, which was what he had tried and failed to write a poem about.

'So go on then.' Charlie elbowed Matt in the ribs.

'What?' Matt looked at him.

'Ask Mum that thing you wanted to ask her,' Charlie growled out of the corner of his mouth.

'What thing?' Ellen asked.

'Oh . . . um it was about . . . um – the loo. I've run out of toilet cleaner.' Matt winced.

'That's not it!' Charlie laughed. 'You are *so* gay.'

'Charlie, how many times!' Ellen exclaimed. 'Don't use the word gay in that context, please.'

'Well, he is,' Charlie muttered.

'There are about a million people here,' Matt said. 'I'm not doing it in front of an audience.'

'Doing what?' Ellen asked, confused.

'Ohhh.' Hannah caught Charlie's eye. 'Oh, I see – I've got it. Allegra, would you like to join me for a turn around the garden? And you too, Charles.'

'Well, we might need a machete to get through some of the undergrowth, but I should be delighted.' Allegra nodded, gesturing at Charlie to follow. 'Come along, young man. I will teach you the Georgian art of flirting. It's all about the angle of the fan, you know.'

'What? What's going on?' Ellen looked anxiously at Matt. 'Have you got bad news or something?'

'Depends what you call bad news.' Hannah winked at Allegra. 'Come along, Charles.'

'I always get to miss all the good bits,' Charlie moaned, following the others reluctantly.

Matt suddenly found himself standing alone in the kitchen with the woman who had somehow come to embody every single one of his dreams. Funny how love is so unpredictable, he thought. The evening sun was dusting Ellen's skin with gold, lighting her green eyes from within. He'd never thought the woman who'd capture his heart would be an older, widowed, agoraphobic. But she was.

'What are you grinning at and what is going on?' Ellen asked him. 'Have you done something, have you burnt a hole in my carpet because you iron your shirts on the floor? I know you do it, you know.'

'No,' Matt said. 'I . . . look, there's this poem. I didn't write it. I tried to write you one but it came out wrong and there was this poem that made me think of you. I couldn't quite remember it all so I googled it. It's by this bloke called John Donne.'

'And?' Ellen looked at him, the intensity of his gaze causing her to catch her breath. Matt took a step towards her.

> *'Come, madam, come, all rest my powers defy;*
> *Until I labour, I in labour lie.*
> *The foe ofttimes, having the foe in sight,*
> *Is tired with standing, though he never fight,'*

he recited as he came nearer.

'I beg your pardon?' Ellen seemed confused. Matt stood in front of her and traced a finger along the line of her jaw, down to the hollow at the base of her neck.

> *'Licence my roving hands, and let them go*
> *Before, behind, above, between, below.*
> *O, my America, my new found land,*
> *My kingdom, safest when with one man mann'd,*
> *My mine of precious stones, my empery;*
> *How am I blest in thus discovering thee!'*

He whispered the words , leaning in to kiss Ellen gently on the cheek.

She looked up at him, his face a hair's breadth from hers.

'Did you just tell me that you fancy me?' she asked him.

'Yes, but in seventeenth-century poetry it sounds better, doesn't it?' Matt replied. 'You are my discovery, Ellen. You are my new found land, and it's through you that I've found me again. The bloke I used to want to be before I somehow ended up the one I am. Charlie wants me to ask you out. I want to ask you out. But I have to warn you, I'll be asking you for more than just a date, because I've . . . I've fallen for you, Ellen, hook line and sinker.' Carefully Matt placed his hand over Ellen's heart. *'To enter in these bonds is to be free, then, where my hand is set, my soul shall be.* Ellen Woods – will you go out to dinner with me?'

'You know that I'm the best part of ten years older than you, don't you?' Ellen said. Matt shrugged.

'And that I'm recently widowed with a demanding son and a very complicated past, not to mention a panic disorder that means going out to dinner would be a *bit* of an issue, at least initially.'

'I had noticed that.' Matt nodded.

'And none of that bothers you?' Ellen asked him.

'None of that is you,' Matt told her. 'You are beautiful, bold, brave, brilliant Ellie Woods. That's you.'

Ellen smiled and placed her hand against his cheek.

'And what about the fact that I haven't had a second to stop and think, to find out what I really feel, or even if I could ever feel anything serious for another man again? Doesn't that bother you?'

Matt hesitated for a moment, feeling his heart tremble as he placed it on a knife-edge. 'A friend of mine told me that life isn't all about dead certs. It's about making a gamble and taking a risk. I'm prepared to take a risk on you, because if you do find out you feel the same way about me, it will be more than worth it. And if you don't, then – well, I won't be lying awake at night wondering, will I?'

'Well, going out to dinner is out of the question,' Ellen said softly, moving her lips against his as she spoke. 'But I suppose we could always stay in and see how that works out.'

Acknowledgements

Thank you so much Kate Elton and Georgina Hawtrey-Woore and all of the team at Arrow who continue to show me unfailing support and loyalty and whose hard work on my behalf makes me work all the harder for them.

To dearest Lizzy Kremer, my marvellous agent, thank you for always being there and for standing by me through thick and thin!

Thanks also to my friends Jenny Matthews, Rosie Woolly, Cathy Carter, Clare Winter, Sarah Darby, Margi Harris, Kirstie Robertson, Catherine Ashley, Natalie Jerome and Katy Regan. You have made tough times seem much less difficult than they would have without you.

Thank you to my mum, who has been brilliant over the last year, always there to turn to. Thank you to Adam, for listening to my ideas and always having something interesting and inspiring to say in return. And finally thank you to my delightful children, to baby Fred who makes me smile even at three a.m. and my beautiful Lily who really is my best friend.

If you liked *A Home for Broken Hearts*, then why not try

WE ARE ALL MADE OF STARS

Turn the page for a sneak peek . . .

Dear Len,

Well, if you are reading this, it's happened. And I suppose that I ought to be glad, and so should you. We've both spent such a long time waiting, and I could see how much it was wearing you down, as much as you tried to hide it.

Now, the life insurance policy is in the shoebox in the bedroom, on top of the wardrobe, under that hat I wore to our Dominic's wedding – remember? The one with the veil you said made me look like a femme fatale? You might not; you drank too much beer, and four of Dominic's friends had to carry you upstairs, you great oaf. It's not much of a payout, I don't think, but it will be enough for the funeral at least. I don't have any wishes concerning that matter. You know me better than anyone else will. I trust you to get it right.

The washing machine. It's easy, really: you turn the round knob clockwise to the temperature you want to wash at, but don't worry about that. Just wash everything at forty degrees. It mostly works out all right. And you put the liquid in the plastic thing in the drum, not in the drawer. I don't even really know why they have those drawers any more.

You need to eat – and not stuff you can microwave. You need to at least shake hands with a vegetable once a week, promise me. You always made the Sunday night tea – cheese on toast and baked beans on the side – so I'm sure you'll be able to keep body and soul together if you put some effort in. I expect at first lots of people will feed you, but you'll need to get a cookbook. I think there's a Delia under the bed. I got it for Christmas last year from Susan, and I thought, what a cheek!

Len, do you remember the night we met? Do you remember how you led me on to the dance floor? You didn't talk, didn't ask me or anything, you rogue. Just took my hand and led me out there. And how we twirled and laughed – the room became a blur. And when the song stopped, you kissed me. Still hadn't said a word to me, mind you, and you kissed me right off my feet. The first thing you said to me was, 'You'd better tell me your name, as you're the girl I'm going to marry.' Cheeky beggar, I thought, but you were right.

It's been a good life, Len, full of love and happiness. Just as much — more than — the sadness and the bad times, if you think about it, and I have had a lot of time to think about it, lately. A person can't really ask for more. Don't stop because I've stopped; keep going, Len. Keep dancing, dancing with our grandchildren, for me. Make them laugh, and spoil them rotten.

And when you think of me, don't think of me in these last few days: think of me twirling and laughing and dancing in your arms.

Remember me this way.

Your loving wife,

Dorothy

Prologue

STELLA

He was a runner. That was the first thing I knew about Vincent.

One hot July, four years ago, I saw him early each morning, running past me as I walked to work, for almost three weeks in a row.

That summer I'd decided to get up before seven, to enjoy the relative quiet of an early north London morning on my way to start a shift at the hospital. I was a trauma nurse back then, and there was something about the near stillness of the streets, the quiet of the roads, that gave me just a little space to exhale before a full eight hours of holding my breath. So I walked to work, sauntered more like, kicking empty coffee cups out of my way, flirting with street sweepers, dropping a strong cup of tea off to the homeless guy who was always crammed up against the railings by the park, working on his never-ending novel. It was my rest time, my respite.

At almost exactly the same time every morning, Vincent ran past me at full pelt, like he was racing some unseen opponent. I'd catch a glimpse of a water bottle, closely cropped dark hair, a tan, nice legs – long and muscular. Every day, at almost exactly the same time, for nearly three weeks. He'd whip by, and I'd think, there's the runner guy, another moment ticked off on my journey. I liked the predictability. The flirty street sweeper, the cup of tea drop, the runner. Sort of like having your favourite song stuck in your head.

Then one morning he slowed down, just a hair's breadth, and turned his head. For the briefest moment I looked into his eyes – such a bright blue, like mirrors reflecting the sky. And then he was gone again, but it was already too late: my routine was disturbed, along with my peace of mind. All day that day, in the middle of some life-and-death drama or in the quiet of the locker room, I found the image of those eyes returning to me again and again. And each time it gave me butterflies.

The next morning, I waited for him to run past me again, and for normality to be restored. Except he stopped, so abruptly, a few feet in front of me and then bent over for a moment, his hands on his knees, catching his breath. I hesitated, sidestepped and decided to keep walking.

'Wait . . . please.' He took a breath between words, holding up a hand that halted me. 'I thought I wasn't going to stop, and then I thought, sod it, so I did.'

'OK,' I said.

'I thought you might like to come for a coffee with me?' He smiled – it was full of charm; it was a smile that was used to winning.

'Did you?' I asked him. 'Why?'

'Well, hoped, more like,' he said, the smile faltering a little. 'My name is Vincent. Vincent Carey. I'm a squaddie, Coldstream Guards. I'm on leave, going back to the desert soon. And you never know, do you? So I thought . . . well, you've got lovely hair – all curls, all down your back. And eyes like amber.'

He had noticed my eyes – perhaps in that same second that I noticed his.

'I'm a very lazy person,' I told him. 'I never go anywhere fast.'

'Is that a weird way of saying no to coffee?' I liked his frown as much as his smile.

'It's a warning,' I said. 'A warning that I might not be your kind of person.'

'Sometimes,' he said, 'you just know when someone is your sort of person.'

'From their hair?' I laughed.

'From their eyes.'

I couldn't argue with that.

'Mind if I walk part of the way with you?' he'd asked.

'OK.' I smiled to myself as he fell in step next to me, and we walked in silence for a while.

'You weren't kidding about being slow,' he said, eventually.

The second thing I knew about Vincent was that one day I was going to marry him. But the first thing I knew was that he was a runner.

Which makes it so hard to look at him now: his damaged face turned to the wall as he sleeps, and the space where his leg used to be.

Chapter One

HOPE

I can't sleep. I can never sleep these days – not in here, anyway, where they don't let it be truly dark, not ever. But it's not only that; it's because I can't stop thinking about how I came to be here. I know, of course: I caught something – a bug, bacterial, which is dangerous news when you live with cystic fibrosis. I almost died, and now I'm here, in this place where they never really turn the lights out on the long and painful road to recuperation. I know that, but I what I don't know, what I want to know, is *how*. I want to know precisely the second that little cluster of bacteria drifted like falling blossom into my bloodstream. I can't know, of course, but that doesn't mean I don't want to or that I can stop thinking about it. The frustrating thing about my condition is that I have a lot of time on my hands to think, but not a lot of time on the clock to live. Time moves slowly and quickly at the very same time – racing and stretching, boring and terrifying. And you can live your whole life with the idea of mortality – that one day it will be the last day – and still never really know or care what that means. Not until the last day arrives, that is.

I was at a party, when Death came to find me.

I hate parties, but my best friend Ben made me go.

'You can't stay in all your life,' he said, dragging me out of my room and down the stairs. 'You are twenty-one years old, nearly twenty-two. You should be out every night, enjoying the prime of your life!'

'*You* are in your prime of your life; I'm most likely middle aged,' I told him, even though I knew he hated me referring to my short life expectancy this way. 'And anyway, I could. I could stay in all my life and listen to Joni Mitchell and read books, and design book covers, try and work out the solo of "Beat It" on my guitar, and I'd be perfectly fine.'

'Mrs K.?' Ben dragged me into the living room, where my parents were watching the same old same old on TV – some police detective, who drinks too much and lost his wife in a bitter divorce, chasing down some psycho-killer. 'Tell your daughter: she's a twenty-one-year-old woman. She needs to go out and have fun! Remind her that life is for living, and not for sitting alone in her room reading about how other people do it! Plus it's all the old crew from school, back from uni now. We haven't been together in ages, and they are all dying to see her.'

Mum turned in her chair, and I could see the worry in her eyes, despite her smile. But there was nothing new there: she'd been worried for every moment of my twenty-one years, constantly. Sometimes I wonder if she'd wished she could change my name, after I was diagnosed as a baby and the situation was officially hope-less, but it was too late by then; it was a name that already belonged to me – a cruel irony that we both have to live with now. My poor darling mum, she had enough on her plate. It wasn't fair to make her decide if I went out or not, because she'd spend the rest of the evening worrying either way, and later she would have torn herself to pieces with blame. So, making my own decision, that was one of the things I did right that night. It was just the choice that was wrong.

'Oh, fine, I'm coming out, I'll get changed.'

Ben grinned at me and sat down on the bottom stair, and I thought of him there, in his skinny jeans, an outsize jumper sloping off one shoulder, jet black hair and eyes lined with smudges of Kohl, as I rifled through my wardrobe, looking for something, anything, that might even nearly equal his effortless cool. It wasn't fair, really – that little odd duckling, the boy that the other kids left out or pushed around, had suddenly grown into a sexy, hip swan. We had used to be lame kids together. That was how we came to be best friends; it was part of the natural process of banding together, like circling our wagons – greater safety, even in our meagre number of two, than being alone. Him: the skinny, shy kid with the grey collars and worn-down shoes; and me: the sick girl.

I don't think it was then that Death entered, when Ben came into the house, though it could have been. He could have left a trace of a germ on the bannister or the damp towel in the downstairs loo. It could have been then, but I don't think it was, because near-death by hand towel isn't even nearly fitting enough.

I dressed all in black, trying to hide my skinny frame with a skater skirt and a long top, and wondered how many other girls my age longed to put weight on. I rimmed my eyes with dark eye shadow and hoped that would do the trick.

The moment we walked in through the door, and the wave of heat and sweat and molecules of saliva, which I know are in every breath I take, hit us, I wanted to go home. I almost turned around right then, but Ben had his hand on the small of my back. There was something protective about it, something comforting. And these were my friends, after all. The people I grew up with, who were always nice to me and did fun runs in my name. Who I could sit and have a coffee and a laugh with; who would always find something for us to talk about, while carefully avoiding those potentially awkward questions like, 'How's it going? Still think you'll be dead soon?'

'Hopey!' Sally Morse, my sort-of best female friend from school, ran the length of the hallway to engulf me in a hug. 'Oh shit, it's so good to see you. You look great! How's it going? What's new? You're like an entrepreneur or something, aren't you?' She hooked her arm through mine, briefly resting her head on my shoulder as she led me into the kitchen, and I noticed the slight pinkness around her nostrils: the remnants of a cold.

'I'm OK,' I told her, accepting a beer. 'I started designing book covers for people, and it's going quite well.'

'That's so cool,' she said happily. 'That's so totally cool because, you know, really university is a huge waste of time; there are no jobs out there, and you end up in loads of debt – it's a very expensive way to get laid and drunk. I emailed you loads, but you're shit at replying. Too busy, I suppose, being a businesswoman.'

She paused for a moment, scanning my face, and then dragged me into a hug, filling my face with a curious combination of lemon- and smoke-scented hair, and I hugged her back. I'd thought I didn't miss any of that: the people I once saw almost every day for most of life. I'd told myself that, anyway, but it turned out that I did. I was happy to see her in that moment, happy I had come. Perhaps it was then, perhaps in that little moment of optimism and nostalgia, in the midst of that hug, I'd inhaled my own assassin. I hope not. Although it would be just like the universe to try and undo you when you are happy, because in my experience the universe is an arse.

But the good thing about being amongst my old friends was that there was no need to explain – no need to have the eternal prologue of a conversation when I tell them about the CF, and they look sad and awkward in turn. It was a relief to be amongst the people who have been preparing for my exit, almost since the very first moment I made my entrance into their lives.

It wasn't long before Sally was tonsils-deep in some guy who I thought she'd most likely brought with her, because I didn't know him, so I made my way through the mass of people, looking for Ben.

'Hope!' Clara Clayton shrieked, planting a glossy kiss on my cheek. 'It's so good to see you! If you're here, that means Ben is here, and I want to see him. Bloody hell, he's grown up hot . . . Hey, are you two . . .?'

'Hello, Hope,' said Tom Green, the school heartthrob for so many years, and now no less sweet, blonde, or strappingly broad-chested. 'How are things? How are you doing?' He was still awkward, polite, kind, tall – all of the things about him that used to make me swoon when I was thirteen years old, though not anymore, I was interested to notice; now I thought he was lovely but sort of dull.

'I like your look,' he said, with some effort. 'Really . . . cool.'

As I made my way through the party, cigarettes being hastily put out as I approached, I relaxed. I felt at home here, amongst friends. I felt like a twenty-one-year-old woman at a party. I relaxed, and that was probably my mistake.

It could have been in any one of those miniature reunions that Death made its move, during that long hour of leaning in too close to people while they told me what degree they got, and what they were going to do next. It might have been then, or it could have been when the taxi driver coughed all over the change he gave me on the way over. But I don't think it was.

I think it happened when Ben kissed me.

Because, let's get this straight, I spend most of time in my bedroom in my parents' house pretending that designing a few book covers is a proper grown-up career, and reading books, lots of books. And a man kissing me would definitely be the cause of my demise in a Victorian novel.

I'm prone to dwelling. I'm a dweller.

Ben was drunk, in the way that only he gets drunk, which is not at all, then all at once. And he'd gone from being ubercool to dancing and laughing and spinning, and hugging, and playing air guitar, and chatting up girls, who lapped up his nonsense, while I stood in the corner of the room, watching him, smiling despite myself. He loves to think he's cool – the guy in the rock band, the 'I don't give a toss about you' rock star – but it doesn't take very much for him to be his great big dorky self: the boy I used to know. The one who'd fill his pockets with worms to save them from other boys stomping on them; the guy who might look like he could snack on bats' heads by night but who is an assistant manager in Carphone Warehouse by day.

Suddenly, he careered into me, grabbing hold of my shoulders, and we both fell back onto the sofa laughing – him a little too hard, and me a little too politely.

'You are such a dick,' I told him, reasonably fondly, though.

'Then why am I your best mate?' he asked me, winding his arm around my shoulder and pulling me even closer to him, fluttering his ridiculously long brown lashes.

'Oh, shut up,' I said, screwing my face up as he rubbed his cheek against mine, like an over-friendly dog. I made my move to protect him from himself, which was to make him think he was protecting me, which meant he'd stop drinking quite so much, so fast. 'You know what? This party, it's not really doing it for me. I think I'm going to go home. Will you take me home?'

'No, don't go!' Ben grabbed my face in his hands and made me look into his eyes, squeezing my mouth into a frankly ridiculous pout. 'You're always leaving places early. Stop leaving me, Hope. When are you going to get that I hate you leaving me behind? I want you around all the time.'

'Don't be a twat,' I'd said, although hesitantly, because the way he was looking at me just then was angry and hurt all at once. It was hard to read, and I am not a fan of ambiguity. Just for a moment, for the briefest of seconds, I glimpsed that perhaps something about the way he was acting tonight had to do with me.

'Just don't go,' he said.

'But Ben, I . . .'

Which was when he kissed me.

I mean really kissed me. Ben, who I had known since I was five years old. Ben, who once waded into a patch of nettles to carry me out. Ben, who'd held my hair and made small talk while I hawked up globules of mucus, during my nightly coughing rituals. Ben kissed me, and it was a real kiss, urgent and hard, and with his tongue. It was physical, and awkward, and it took me by surprise, because I'd never been kissed like that before, with this kind of force or, well, *need*. As he pressed me back hard into the sofa, suddenly I felt like I couldn't breathe. I panicked and I pushed him away.

'Shit,' he said. 'I'm really drunk. Sorry. Sorry, shit.'

I got up and went to the bathroom. Flounced is probably a better word – I flounced off to cover my confusion, feigned fury and offence. I spent a long time looking at myself in the mirror, looking at my kiss-stained mouth. Somehow I knew that everything had changed, and that it wasn't going to be for the better.

When I came back, Ben had passed out on the sofa, his head lolling back in the cushions, his mouth wide open.

I got a taxi home alone and was in bed before midnight.

When I saw Ben the next day, he said he hardly remembered anything and told me to never let him drink again. He didn't mention the kiss, and I still have no idea if he has forgotten, or if he'd rather just not talk about it.

A week after that, I was admitted to hospital with a bacterial lung infection.

The pain, the pain, and the gasping for air, and the desperate need all the time for there to be more of it, took up most of my energy, but not all of it. There was a moment, just one, of perfect clarity, when I heard the doctor say to my mother, 'It's touch and go, I'm afraid.'

And I thought, I am not ready. I am not ready yet.

I made it, I'm still here, still alive, almost ready to go back to life. I won this round. But I can't sleep, you see, because even though I can't know, I want to know. I need to know the exact moment that I let Death in, and I can't sleep – because what if I'm not ready the next time it finds me?

Dear Maeve,

Kip and me, we always promised we'd write to the other's wife if it came to it. And well, Maeve, it came to it, didn't it? I am only sorry that it's taken me this long to write the letter I never wanted you to have to read. I wish, I wish I was good with words, that I knew how to say what I have to say. I wish I'd never made this promise to Kip, but I did. And he was the closest thing to a brother I ever had.

We did it all together. We were green new recruits together. Trained together. Kip was the worst recruit the sergeant had ever seen. But we all loved him. He knew how to make us laugh on days when everything could have been so dark. By the time we went on our first tour in Afghanistan, Kip was the best soldier.

He talked about you and little Casey all the time. You were the lights of his life. We used to hear what Casey had been up to, how she is more beautiful, funny, clever than any other kids, all day long. Kip was a soldier, but he was a family man first. I know he tried to be the best husband and dad he could be.

The day it happened started out like any other day. Routine patrol, defending the province against the Taliban. No intel or chatter to suggest we had anything more to worry about than normal. Not that normal wasn't enough to worry about. We all knew it wouldn't be long before we were allowed home on leave, but command told us: ears and eyes, stay alert, right up until the last second of our tour, and we knew that.

When the missile hit, it was . . .

Chapter Two

STELLA

Whenever there is a moment of quiet, of stillness, I stop and I listen, and I wait for it to pass. It's hardly ever silent at Marie Francis Hospice and Rehabilitation Centre, even at night. Quiet chat, murmurs in the half-dark, laughter sometimes, sometimes singing. Sometimes a dream lived out loud. But it's hardly ever quiet. So I listen in those moments, and I wait for the noise again. And then I breathe out.

I feel a warm body wind itself around my legs and look down to see that Shadow, the very unofficial hospice cat, has emerged out of nowhere again. Pitch black with no markings and huge emerald-green eyes. No one knows where he comes from, or when he will come; he just appears when he pleases, knowing that when he does, he will be made a huge fuss of by everyone who meets him. He's large, clearly looked after by someone – someone who probably has no idea of the humanitarian mission he goes on through the day. He's young, I think, and kittenish still, despite his size. He sees a shadow from a flickering light and pounces on it, twisting and turning 180 degrees with every lunge in a bid to catch his prey. I reach out to him, and he bats at my hand playfully until I catch behind his ears with my nails and scratch. Suddenly mesmerised, and softly lambent, he lets me lift him onto my lap and hold him for a moment. I feel his small heart rapidly beating against my skin, and the rise and fall of his chest. This is the reason that the administration turns a blind eye to Shadow, and lets us keep a pack of Dreamies in the nurse's station drawer for him, because it's well known that contact with animals is therapeutic, soothing, comforting. And Shadow can do what most of our doctors, and us nurses and Albie, our chaplain's daft Labrador, can't, which is take himself from room to room, always seeming to know which patient needs his attention the most. Smiling, I smooth down his black silky fur in the long firm strokes that he likes, listening to the satisfying rattle of his purr. Lucky me, to have a few moments of his attention tonight.

'Tea, Stella?' Thea nods at my empty mug. 'You're due a break, surely – Shadow seems to think so. He was sitting with Issy till she dropped off.'

'No, I'm full to the brim,' I tell her. 'I've got my obs to do, and I've promised to sit with Maggie for a bit. She likes a chat and I said I'd write her a letter.'

'She could chat for England, that one,' Thea says, but without malice. There's a sort of inevitable closeness amongst the patients and their families here, a solidarity. It eases the journey, I think, for them just to know they aren't in this alone.

'How are you doing?' I ask her. Thea's answering smile is small and almost worn through, but steady. It's an expression I've become familiar with, a kind of all-defying hope in the face of certain disappointment. I've known Thea for eighteen months now. A single mother, she's been bringing her fourteen-year-old daughter Issy to the hospice since she was first diagnosed with a

412

final stage case of a rare bone cancer, Ewing's sarcoma. At first it was for a brief burst of respite care, to allow Thea to have a little more time for her younger daughter, and for herself, but now after years of treatment, it's because it is almost time.

We aren't supposed to form bonds, or relationships, with the families that we care for, but sometimes it's impossible not to. Not when they are here every day, when they are living out the defining moments of their lives right in front of you, looking to you for reassurance and certainty where there is none. So she and I have become not friends exactly but companions in the midst of an endless succession of sleepless nights. And Thea keeps smiling, keeps hoping. If there's one thing I've learned while I've been working the night shift at Marie Francis it's that this is the one thing that sets us apart from other animals, the one thing that makes us human. Hope.

'I'm OK,' Thea says. 'Issy is smiling in her sleep. I like to try and guess what she's dreaming about. There was this holiday a couple of years back – we went to a water park with a huge great big slide. She shrieked like a banshee all the way down and then went back for more. Maybe she's dreaming about that.'

'I'll be in after I've seen Maggie,' I promise her.

On an average night here, there are maybe fourteen patients at any one time, plus two nurses, three health-care assistants and one doctor sleeping in the on-call room – all of us engaged in this kind of ballet, this dance that is something like a rain dance. Except, if we get it right, we're not calling down the rain but keeping pain at bay. This world, this night world, is the one we small crew inhabit alone, in between the busy, sunny days of outpatients, and counselling, therapy groups, music, dances and fundraisers. Family time, healing time, breathing time. Here during the night, no more than twenty of us are negotiating the path that at some point each of us will have to travel. But never alone if we can help it, that's the promise we make on the night watch. Although we can't come with you, you will never be alone when you take that final step.

And I always work the night shift. I asked if I could when I was offered the job. After some hesitation they let me, as long as I take enough days off in between, because no board ever wants their nurses only to work the difficult night-shift slots, even someone as experienced as me. No one ever asks me why I only do the night shift – because it's not like I have childcare to worry about. But, anyway, I only half understand the reason myself. I think it was a gradual thing. I think so, although it may have happened all at once. In the months since Vincent left the army, it's been hard to get a clear sense of anything very much, except that somehow the strands of our lives that were so closely woven together began unravelling into two separate threads – quickly enough for it to feel like I have no control over it. Perhaps taking the night shifts has been about holding up a white flag and declaring surrender, because if our house is the battlefield, then it's easier, less painful, less dangerous, if only one of us is in it at a time. It's my house during the day, and at night it belongs to Vincent.

Thea hesitates still, and I sense there is something she wants to ask me.

'How's Vincent doing?' she asks, and Shadow, suddenly tired of my affection, leaps onto the desk and nudges her hand up from where it is resting and onto his head. He has trained us all very well.

'Great.' I smile, nodding. 'He's doing really great. Never still since he got the new prosthetic fitted. State of the art it is, apparently. He got back from the sponsored bicycle ride last week, and he's already talking about training for the Marathon . . . He's doing great. He's barely ever still.'

'OK, good.' She stands there for a moment, and takes a breath. 'So you're writing a letter for Maggie?'

I nod.

I began it one night for a patient who could no longer hold a pen, and who wanted to make sure her husband would know how to work the washing machine after she'd gone. That's when the letter writing started, and it grew from there – each letter another story, another life, another legacy. Not every patient wants to put their final thoughts on paper, not every patient has to, but there is something comforting about leaving a physical relic of your mind in this world, something reassuring.

'Do they ask you, just before, you know . . . Is it like they know? They know it's time for a letter?'

And suddenly I know what it is that is terrifying her, what it is that she can't quite bring herself to articulate.

'Issy hasn't asked me to write a letter,' I say.

'Well.' She nods, dropping her gaze from mine as she holds up her empty mug. 'OK, I'd better get back to her.'

It seems like Shadow agrees: he drops down from the high desk with easy grace and trots off towards Issy's room, his tail high and purposeful.

'I'll be in soon,' I reassure Thea, with a smile. And I watch her go back to Issy's room, thoughts of a cup of tea forgotten as she quietly shuts the door behind her.

I take my pad of plain writing paper out of the desk drawer, and root around in my bag for my favourite pen: blue ink, ball-point, smooth flow, looks like it could be a fountain pen, but doesn't smudge. I love the feel of it, gliding over the slight texture of the paper, filling it with swirls and loops that always, no matter what words they go towards forming, mean so much more than simply what they say.

Dear Franco,

I don't suppose you remember me. Why would you? It's sixty years since we met, and we didn't know each other for long. I have no idea if you still live in Monte Bernardi or if you are even still alive, though those spread adverts on the telly seem to say that Italians lives for ever, so I hope so.

It was 1954. I was twenty years old, and me and Margaret Harris from the bank where I worked had a day trip to Brighton. Down on the train, best dresses and hats. Mine was primrose yellow and had flowers embroidered on the pockets.

We were walking along the front when we saw you, although you didn't notice us. We thought you had to be a movie star or something: the way you stood there, with your sunglasses on – hair all slicked back, black T-shirt, white trousers. We went round the corner to peep at you, and then we put on some lipstick and walked past you again, swinging our skirts and giggling like we were ever so fascinating. You said hello in Italian. We ran away, screaming with laughter; what a pair we were.

I didn't see you for the rest of the day, not until the dance at the end of the pier. And there you were, in a pale blue suit. When you came over to talk to me I thought I might die, maybe from the excitement. Your English wasn't very good; my Italian was non-existent. But, oh, your accent.

We kissed all night, never stopped for a breather, or a drink. You whispered strange words in my ear, might have been a shopping list, for all I knew. I didn't care, because it sounded like music.

That's when I found out that Margaret had got the last train home without me – in a pique, I expect, because it was me you had eyes for. You walked me back to your bedsit and snuck me up the stairs without the landlady noticing. I'd never been with a boy before – I thought something dreadful would happen, that I'd get pregnant or catch some disease, but I was stupid and young and it didn't seem to matter more than that moment.

The next morning, you wrote your address in pencil in my address book and kissed me goodbye. I never heard from you again. I didn't catch anything or get pregnant. I wasn't brave enough to write. I married a good man a few years later, and I've been happy. It's been a good life. But every time I've changed address books, I've copied your address into the new one, once again. Monte Bernardi; a reminder of one night when I risked it all for a little excitement. So it would seem an awful shame not to use it just once.

Thank you for the dance,
Susan Wilks

WE ARE ALL MADE OF STARS

Rowan Coleman

Stella Carey exists in a world of night. Married to a soldier who has returned from Afghanistan injured in body and mind, she leaves the house every evening as Vincent locks himself away, along with the secrets he brought home from the war.

During her nursing shifts, Stella writes letters for her patients to their loved ones – some full of humour, love and practical advice, others steeped in regret or pain – and promises to post these messages after their deaths.

Until one night Stella writes the letter that could give her patient one last chance at redemption, if she delivers it in time . . .

We Are all Made of Stars **is an uplifting and heartfelt novel about life, loss and what happens in between from the** *Sunday Times* **bestselling author of** *The Memory Book.*

ALSO BY ROWAN COLEMAN:

THE MEMORY BOOK

When time is running out, every moment is precious . . .

When Claire starts to write her Memory Book, she already knows that this scrapbook of mementoes will soon be all her daughters and husband have of her. But how can she hold onto the past when her future is slipping through her fingers . . .?

A *Sunday Times* bestseller and Richard & Judy Autumn Book Club pick, *The Memory Book* is a critically acclaimed, beautiful novel of mothers and daughters, and what we will do for love.